Rising Storm

Bundle One

Tempest Rising, Episode 1
White Lightning, Episode 2
Crosswinds, Episode 3
Dance in the Wind, Episode 4

Copyright 2015 Julie Kenner and Dee Davis Oberwetter

ISBN: 978-1-942299-69-1

Published by Evil Eye Concepts, Incorporated

Rising Storm

Bundle One

Episodes 1 through 4
Season 1

By
Julie Kenner
Lexi Blake
Elisabeth Naughton
Jennifer Probst

Story created by Julie Kenner and Dee Davis

EVIL EYE
CONCEPTS

Sign up for the Rising Storm/1001 Dark Nights Newsletter
and be entered to win an exclusive lightning bolt necklace
specially designed for Rising Storm by
Janet Cadsawan of Cadsawan.com.

Go to http://risingstormbooks.com to subscribe.

As a bonus, all subscribers will receive a free
Rising Storm story
Storm Season: Ginny & Jacob – the Prequel
by Dee Davis

Table of Contents

Foreword

Dear reader –

We have wanted to do a project together for over a decade, but nothing really jelled until we started to toy with a kernel of an idea that sprouted way back in 2012 ... and ultimately grew into Rising Storm.

We are both excited about and proud of this project—not only of the story itself, but also the incredible authors who have helped bring the world and characters we created to life.

We hope you enjoy visiting Storm, Texas. Settle in and stay a while!

Happy reading!

Julie Kenner & Dee Davis

Tempest Rising, Episode 1

By Julie Kenner

About Julie Kenner

Julie Kenner (aka J. Kenner) is the *New York Times, USA Today, Publishers Weekly, Wall Street Journal* and #1 international bestselling author of over seventy novels, novellas, and short stories in a variety of genres.

Praised by Publishers Weekly as an author with a "flair for dialogue and eccentric characterizations," JK writes a range of stories including super sexy romances, paranormal romance, chick lit suspense, paranormal mommy lit, and, with *Rising Storm*, small town drama. Her trilogy of erotic romances, The Stark Trilogy (as J. Kenner), reached as high as #2 on the *New York Times* list and is published in over twenty countries, and her Demon-Hunting Soccer Mom series (written as Julie Kenner) has been optioned by Warner Brothers Television for the CW Network.

A former attorney, JK lives in Central Texas with her husband, two daughters, and several cats. One of her favorite weekend activities is visiting small towns in the Texas Hill Country. Visit her website at www.juliekenner.com and connect with JK through social media at
http://www.facebook.com/juliekennerbooks,
http://www.facebook.com/jkennerbooks,
http://www.twitter.com/juliekenner,
and as @juliekenner on Instagram.

Also from Julie Kenner

Dark Pleasures
Caress of Darkness
Find Me in Darkness
Find Me in Pleasure
Find Me in Passion
Caress of Pleasure

Demon-Hunting Soccer Mom Series
Carpe Demon
California Demon
Demons Are Forever
The Demon You Know
Deja Demon
Demon Ex Machina
Pax Demonica

Blood Lily Chronicles (urban fantasy romance)
Tainted
Torn
Turned
The Blood Lily Chronicles (boxed set)

Protector Superhero Series
The Cat's Fancy (prequel)
Aphrodite's Kiss
Aphrodite's Passion
Aphrodite's Secret
Aphrodite's Flame
Aphrodite's Embrace
Aphrodite's Delight
Aphrodite's Charms (boxed set)
Dead Friends and Other Dating Dilemmas

Writing as J. Kenner

Stark Series
Release Me
Claim Me
Complete Me

Stark Ever After novellas
Take Me
Have Me
Play My Game

Stark International novellas
Tame Me

Stark International Trilogy
Say My Name
On My Knees
Under My Skin

Most Wanted
Wanted
Heated
Ignited

Devil May Care Series
(with Dee Davis)
Raising Hell (Julie Kenner)
Hell Fire (Dee Davis)
Sure As Hell (Julie Kenner)
Hell's Fury (Dee Davis)

Acknowledgments from the Author

For Dee. Who rode the storm with me.

And for Liz and MJ, for helping the storm to brew!

Chapter One

Pounding rain battered the roof of Ginny Moreno's twenty-year-old Toyota Camry, and she tightened her grip on the steering wheel even as she leaned forward, as if that would somehow help her see through the impenetrable sheets of rain. A flash of lightning illuminated the dense trees that lined this section of the country road, turning them temporarily into grasping skeletons. A crack of thunder shook the car and Ginny jumped, then cursed herself for being so on edge.

Beside her, Jacob took his feet off the dashboard. "Want me to drive?" he asked gently.

"I can drive my own damn car," she snapped.

He held up his hands as if in supplication. "Sorry. I just thought..."

He trailed off with a shrug, but Ginny knew exactly what he'd been thinking. Jacob Salt had been her best friend since forever, and he knew how much she hated thunderstorms—and why. He'd been at her house the morning that Dillon Murphy, then just a deputy, had come to the door and delivered the news. An eighteen-wheeler had lost control on the rain-slicked surface of Interstate 10 in San Antonio. Her parents had been coming home from a concert.

They'd died instantly.

So, yeah, Jacob got it. And even though Ginny might be pissed at him right now, she knew that he was only trying to help.

"I'm fine," she lied. "I just want to get past Bryson's Creek before it floods, okay?" That was the trouble with the Texas Hill Country. It might be absolutely beautiful, but with the latticework of creeks and rivers, flash flooding was a common thing, especially in the summer when rain clouds tended to roll through on a daily basis.

Bryson's Creek intersected the country road just past the Storm city limits, and right then, all Ginny wanted was to be home. She wanted to see her little brother Luis. And, yeah, she even wanted to see her older sister Marisol, who was half parent and half pain-in-the-butt.

For the first time since she'd started at the University of Texas, Ginny was excited about coming back home for the summer. The year had been weird for a lot of reasons, mostly because of men she had slept with even though she probably shouldn't have. And, yeah, "men" included the guy sitting next to her, otherwise known as her best friend and The Guy Who Should Have Been Off Limits.

So, yeah. She needed a breather. She needed Storm.

And, yes, she knew she was being bitchy. But that was only because he'd been such an ass lately.

"We probably should have left earlier. Avoided the storm and gotten home before dark." He spoke casually, as if he had no clue that anything other than the storm was bothering her. Then again, wasn't that the problem? Ever since that night, he'd acted like there was absolutely nothing filling the space between them.

"I had to work," Ginny said. "Some of us have jobs at school. And you didn't have to drive with me. You have a car, too, you know."

He popped a CD into the player. "Max wanted to borrow it," he said, referring to his roommate. "It's not like I need it in Storm," he added, his voice rising a bit to be heard over George Strait, whose soothing, sexy voice now filled the car, competing with the timpani of the rain on the roof.

It was *The Chair*, the same song that had been playing the night they'd sat on the roof drinking tequila. The night they'd done so much more than just talk.

What the hell was the matter with him? Was he intentionally rubbing it in?

"Can you turn that down? It's already loud enough in the car with the rain pelting us."

"We should have stopped in Fredericksburg," he said, referring to the popular Hill Country tourist destination about an hour east of Storm. He leaned over and turned down George. "We could have crashed at one of the motels on the outskirts and then finished the drive in the morning."

She took her eyes off the road long enough to gape at him. "Come on, Jacob. Really? I mean, *really?*"

In a flash of motion, he slammed one Converse-clad foot against the dashboard, making her jump. "Dammit, Ginny, what is going on with you? You've been a total bitch for a while now."

"Gee, I wonder why? Maybe because you've been a total prick for the same amount of time?"

He stared at her, that perfect boy-next-door face reflecting total confusion. Then he tilted his head back and exhaled loudly, looking suddenly sixteen instead of twenty-two. "Oh, hell, Gin." He sounded tired. "I thought we were cool. I mean, we talked about it." His voice was low. Gentle. "I thought we were okay, you know?"

She blinked frantically, willing herself not to cry. "It's been weird," she said. "You've been weird. You've bailed on me twice when we'd planned to go see movies, and then when we were supposed to have brunch at Magnolia last week, you canceled again. You're avoiding me, and I don't like it, and you've always been my best friend, and I'm really, really afraid that we screwed something up when we—"

"Oh, shit, Gin." He bent forward and dragged his hands through his hair. "No. *No.* You are my best friend. I wasn't avoiding you. I was studying—organic chemistry's been kicking my ass, and I needed to ace it. I can't screw up my chances of getting into a top-tier med school."

"But you never have to study." She knew the second she said the words that they were idiotic.

"Believe me, I know. I'm not used to getting papers back with C's and D's." He sucked in air. "It wasn't you. I was just a complete head case." He reached for her hand, and she let him take it. Because that's what best friends did.

"You should have told me."

He shrugged. "I've got my brilliant valedictorian persona to guard."

"You don't have to put on an act around me. You know that."

He cocked his head. "Do I? You've been a little off lately, too."

She pressed her lips together and nodded, feeling like a complete loser. God, she'd been so unfair. He hadn't been weird. *She'd* been the one who'd gotten freaky after they'd gotten naked.

The night had started out okay. Jacob had been all sad and lonely because he'd broken up with Whiny Wendy. And Ginny had been a basket case because she'd been sleeping with the wrong guy—and even Jacob didn't know about *that* massive secret. It had started out all hot and exciting, but it didn't stay that way. And Ginny hated the fact that it wasn't real and that he was married and that she'd been so stupid, stupid, *stupid* to get involved with someone that far up the food chain.

So she'd gone to Maggie Mae's with Jacob and Max and Brittany in part to console him about Wendy, but also because she'd needed to cut loose, too. And when she'd talked to Jacob, everything had felt better. They'd known each other forever. They'd loved each other forever. And they'd drunk too much, and even though they'd shared a bed dozens of times since middle school, this time when they'd returned to the house he and Max rented, one thing led to another and to another.

She should have stopped it. She knew that.

She should have told him that he was just feeling sad about Wendy.

She should have said that they'd regret it. That if they slept together, then everything would change, because didn't sex change everything?

But she hadn't said a word. Because, dammit, maybe she'd secretly wanted things to change. She'd been best friends with Jacob Salt since he gave her his peanut butter and banana sandwich in grade school. And maybe, just maybe, she'd wanted more.

So when George Strait had seduced them into bed, she'd gone with it. It had felt good. It had felt right. Like maybe they were going to get a fairy tale ending.

And how stupid was that? Because Ginny Moreno knew better than anyone that fairy tales never really ended well. The witch ate Hansel and Gretel. The wolf devoured Little Red Riding Hood. And all Rapunzel got was one hell of a headache from all that damned hair-pulling.

"So are we okay?" he asked now, his voice underscored by the battering rain. "I don't want everything to change because we got drunk and stupid one night."

"Of course we're okay," she said as they finally passed the sign she'd been waiting for: *Welcome to Storm, Texas. A Hill Country gem.* "And nothing's going to change." Except that was a lie, too. Because things had already changed. And Ginny knew that sooner or later she was going to have to own up to the fact that she didn't want that night to have been drunk and stupid. She wanted it to have been earth-shattering and magical.

But if she couldn't have that, at least she could have her best friend back.

"Good," he said. "Great. Except..."

He trailed off, and she shifted in her seat to look at him. "What?"

"Nothing," he said, but now there was a definite teasing tone in his voice.

"Oh, God. What is it now?"

"It's just that it really was pretty awesome. There's still time to cut back to Fredericksburg and get a room at that—"

She reached over and punched his arm. And just like that they were past the weirdness. "Jacob Salt, you are a complete ass," she said happily as lightning illuminated the sky.

"Hell, yeah, I am. That's why you lov—*shit! Ginny!*"

He lunged for the steering wheel, then tugged it sideways even as she slammed on the brakes, her mind whirling in confusion as she registered a deer that had leaped in front of the car.

She felt the thud of impact, then the wash of nausea as the car began to spin.

And when her head exploded and she tasted blood, all she could think was that they were never going to be okay again.

Chapter Two

She hurt, and the pain was black and red and spiraling all around her.

And she was cold, so cold that her body shook constantly, shivering in a futile search for warmth. Needing heat. Needing comfort.

So cold. So lost.

So tired.

Dark fingers seemed to pull her back, away from the red-hot knives that cut through her. The shards of glass and metal that sliced her.

But she couldn't go—she couldn't leave. She needed to open her eyes. She needed to help Jacob.

Jacob!

Jacob!

She needed to find him.

She needed to save him.

But all she could do was fade.

All she could do was sleep.

* * * *

"Vitals...good...lacerations..."

"Next of kin...authorization..."

"Nine weeks?"

"No parents...her sister...find Marisol..."

"Fetal heart rate...one-fifty..."

"No signs...placental abruption...monitor..."

"Lucky girl..."

"Doctor, her eyes..."

"Ginny? Ginny, it's Doctor Rush. You're safe. You're in the hospital. Can

you open your eyes for me? Can you come on back to us now?"

"*Her pulse...*"

"*She's scared. It's okay, baby. Your sister is here—go get Marisol—everyone's worried about you, but you're doing fine. You're doing just fine. All you need to do is wake up. All you need to do is come back.*"

The words floated around her, and Ginny tried to grab onto them. She wanted to come back, but she was scared. Too scared.

Because memories were coming with the voices, and as the black faded to gray and the gray gave way to images, she saw what had happened. Right there in her head like a movie. She saw the deer. She saw the car slide in a full circle, then go off the road.

She remembered the sensation of flying. Of being upside down. The expression on Jacob's face. Shock. Fear.

And then the bright, liquid red that bloomed across his chest.

Her throat had burned, and she realized now it was from screaming.

And she didn't want to wake up. She didn't, she didn't, she didn't.

Because she knew what she would find when she did.

She knew that Jacob was dead.

Chapter Three

Most days, Sheriff Dillon Murphy loved his job.

Today wasn't one of those days, and yesterday had been a crapload of shit, too.

He'd been the first on scene last night after a passing motorist had seen the old Toyota upside down in the ditch. He'd been an hour away from going off shift, and he'd been walking around the square, chatting with the local business owners as he did every night before he wrapped up for the day. He'd been just about to pop into his dad's bar to grab a cup of coffee—the stuff at the station ran toward swill—when the call had come in.

He'd beaten his brother, Patrick, and the rest of the fire and EMT crew there by barely three minutes, and while he'd managed to get Ginny Moreno out of the car, there'd been nothing he could do for Jacob Salt. The poor kid was DOA, and that was a goddamn shame.

As soon as Patrick and the rest had arrived, Dillon took over the duty of determining the cause of the wreck. Not hard to figure out.

A deer and the storm and some bald tires that didn't surprise him, considering Ginny and Jacob were both college kids.

Christ, he'd known them since they were in diapers, and it had been just over ten years ago on another stormy night that he'd gone to the Moreno house and told Marisol that her parents were dead. Ginny had only been about ten and Luis even younger. They'd sat like little statues at the Formica table. Marisol had looked like someone had ripped her guts out.

He guessed he had.

She'd been barely twenty, and in the space of a heartbeat she'd become a parent to her siblings. And he could remember seeing the spark of youth and innocence fade in her eyes as the news sunk in.

Yeah, that had been a truly bad day.

At least last night he'd been able to tell her that Ginny was alive. With the girl still unconscious, though, that was only a small blessing. She'd suffered severe head trauma, and although Dr. Rush had told him that Ginny had miraculously avoided any serious breaks or internal injuries, until the girl woke up, she wasn't out of the woods.

But at least with Ginny, there was hope. With Travis and Celeste Salt, the conversation had been much more painful. He'd knocked on their door just after ten and his gut had twisted when Celeste had flung the door open, laughing and saying that it was about time. Her face had turned wary immediately, with that kind of prescient awareness that he'd seen all too often in parents. She'd said nothing, and it had killed him to keep his expression pallid. To ask if Travis was home because he wanted to speak to both of them. And then to deliver that horrible, crushing blow.

It was bad enough for a cop in a big city like Austin to deliver the news of a child's death. In a town like Storm, where most folks knew each other, it was gut-wrenching.

They'd wanted to see Jacob right away, of course, but Dillon had put them off. Told them there were procedural things that needed to happen, when really he just wanted to give the medical examiner time to make the body presentable.

They'd agreed reluctantly to wait, and had arrived at the hospital just a few hours ago. It was already well past noon, and Dillon couldn't even imagine the kind of hell they'd been suffering as the hours ticked by.

Right now, he was standing by the admitting desk. Storm boasted an excellent, but small, hospital, and the desk served as a center point for pretty much everything that went on within the sturdy limestone and granite building. The north hall lead to the ER, ICU, and Ginny. The east to the labs and morgue. Rooms for patients not needing critical care lined the west hall. And the southernmost part of the building boasted the vending machines, a small coffee and sandwich cart, and a half-dozen tables where visitors could grab a bite, gather, and catch their breath before going back in to check on their loved ones.

From his vantage point, Dillon could see Marisol sitting at one of the tables. He knew she was a tall woman, but today she seemed small, like a child, as she kept her hands curved around a Styrofoam cup filled with bad coffee.

During the entire time he'd been standing there, she hadn't taken a single sip. It wasn't about the caffeine, but the warmth. Marisol, he imagined, was cold to the bone.

His shoulders sagged, and he walked over to her, then took a seat. "Need me to refresh that coffee for you? That stuff you're drinking looks like crude oil. Hope you didn't pay too much for it."

It was a bad joke—the coffee was free, with the pot perched next to a jar labeled *donations*. The fact that the jar usually had less than five dollars in it was some explanation for the wretched coffee.

She looked up at him, and despite everything, she smiled. That was Marisol—always keeping it together. "It's fine, thanks. I just wanted something to hold on to."

"Any news on Ginny yet?"

Marisol shook her head. "Dr. Rush says all her vitals are good. But she hasn't woken up, and I can't help but be afraid that—" Her voice broke. "I just hate seeing her in that bed. All small and fragile."

"She's a strong girl, Marisol. A real strong girl. How's Luis doing?"

"He doesn't know yet." She licked her lips. "I—I didn't want to tell him. If the worst happens... I mean, we've already lost our parents and—" She sucked in a deep breath. "He'd gone to the movies with Jeffry. I called and asked Payton if he could sleep over. She'd already heard about it from Layla," she added, referring to Dr. Rush, "but she promised she wouldn't say anything, and she kept him there today telling him that it was good to give me some time alone." She made a self-deprecating noise. "Honestly, alone is the last thing I'm needing right now."

Dillon nodded, wishing there was something tangible he could do for her, but glad at least that she didn't have to worry about her younger brother. The Rush family was Storm royalty, and Payton Rush was the current queen, being that she was married to Texas State Senator Sebastian Rush, who also happened to be Dr. Rush's older brother. Jeffry was Payton's son, and Dillon recalled that he often saw Luis Moreno and Jeffry Rush hanging out on the square or in front of the local movie theater.

"It's good he has a place to go," he said. "And soon enough you'll be able to call him to come see his sister, and you'll be able to tell him that everything is just fine."

"Thanks, Dillon." She took a sip of the coffee and made a face.

"Now I really am gonna get you a fresh cup."

As he stepped over to start a new pot brewing, he saw Travis and Celeste approaching from down the east hall. Travis had his arm around his wife's shoulder, and even from that distance, Dillon could see the shock and grief on their faces. They moved past him, holding each other, and he was about to call out to them when Celeste saw Marisol and hurried that direction. Marisol rose, and Dillon's gut twisted as the dam that had been holding back her tears burst. She clung to Celeste, who held on just as tight, as Travis stood behind them, his face ashen and his eyes rimmed in red.

Finally, they all three sat in their silently shared grief, and as soon as the coffee was streaming into the pot, Dillon snagged three cups. He put them on a tray and headed to the table. He didn't want Travis driving just yet, and he knew the man was too damn proud to leave his car there and accept a lift.

"Thank you, Dillon." Celeste took his hand. "Thank you for letting us see our little boy."

"Celeste." He felt his own eyes sting. "I'm just so damn sorry."

"He was like a brother." Marisol's voice was thick with tears. "I can't imagine him not being around. Not playing those horrible video games with Ginny or—or—" She closed her eyes, visibly gathering herself. "I'm just so sorry."

"How's Ginny?" Celeste licked her lips, and Dillon realized that he'd never before seen her without her lipstick. The woman was always put together, just like her sister, Payton. Not so, today.

"Still unconscious," Marisol said. "She hit her head pretty bad and has all sorts of abrasions. But she's alive and the ba—" She pressed her lips together, then took a deep breath. "She's alive."

"Thank God." Celeste released Dillon's hand to reach out to her. "Can we see her?"

"She's not awake yet."

"I don't care. I need to see her. I need to be able to tell Jacob that she's okay. She was his best friend. They were so close. Do you remember when she had chicken pox and he snuck over so that he'd get them, too?"

"And it worked." Marisol actually smiled. "God, they were both pink with Calamine lotion."

Celeste tugged her hand free and pressed it to her mouth even as Travis slid an arm around her shoulder and pulled her close, then gently stroked her hair.

Dillon hadn't grown up with either of the Salts. Celeste was a Storm native, but she was almost ten years older. Dillon had been in high school when she'd come back with Travis after college. Even so, Dillon knew enough to know that Travis was always good in a crisis. And he was relieved to see that trait was holding fast today, which was surely one of the worst days of each of their lives.

When they'd first arrived at the hospital and he'd escorted them to the morgue, Dillon had been worried that Travis might pull away. Might close off into himself and not be there for Celeste, who'd always struck him as sweetly fragile in that porcelain doll way that so many wealthy Southern women seemed to project. Some were steel magnolias. But others were brittle twigs, and if bent too far, they really would snap.

His fears about Travis weren't entirely unfounded. There were two people in every small town who always got wind of the local gossip—the sheriff and the bartender. Dillon had the first locked up. And considering his family owned the local pub, he got a peek at the Storm underbelly from that side too.

So while he knew nothing specific, he'd seen enough to know that Celeste and Travis's marriage wasn't the pillar of strength that many in the community thought it was. Travis didn't talk about himself much, but he did come to the bar just a little too frequently, staying away from home until prudence required him to leave.

Maybe there was trouble between them, and maybe there wasn't. If he had to guess, he'd come down on the side of financial issues. But he'd never tried to make that guess. At the end of the day that really wasn't Dillon's business. But part of his job was comforting victims, and he was glad to see that whatever relationship woes the Salts might be suffering, Travis was still there for his wife.

He looked up to see Francine Hoffman, the attending nurse, hurrying toward them from the north hall. "Marisol," she said. "Sweetie, Ginny's awake."

The relief that swept over Marisol's face was enough to make Dillon's chest tighten, and she pushed back from the table, almost knocking over her coffee as she did. Travis grabbed it, then stood up and steadied her. "You're okay, honey. Go see your sister."

Celeste rose as well, then turned pleading eyes on Francine. "Can we come, too? I need—I need to see that Ginny's still here. Jacob needs to know that—"

Francine took her hand. "Of course you can. You may need to go in one at a time, but we'll talk to Dr. Rush. We'll make it okay."

She caught Dillon's eyes, and he nodded. He'd dealt with Francine more times than he'd like to remember, bringing in accident victims, drunks, kids with playground injuries. She was always steady. Always calm. And Dillon had been relieved when she'd come on duty earlier in the day.

She started to lead Marisol and the Salts away, and he followed, hoping for his own update on Ginny's status. They were a few yards down the hall when the metal doors that separated the hall from the ER opened behind them.

There was no real reason for Dillon to turn back and glance that direction, but he did. And his breath caught and his heart squeezed just a little.

Joanne.

Her head was bent, her usually gleaming blonde hair hanging limp around her face. She had her right arm clutched to her chest and was holding a tightly wrapped wrist with her left. He couldn't see her face, but everything about her stooped posture and hunched shoulders suggested that she was in pain.

Her asshole husband Hector had one arm around her waist. In his other hand, he held tight to her discharge papers. They crossed the hall, heading to the small window that served as the service counter for the in-hospital pharmacy.

Dillon froze, his attention entirely on Joanne. His focus on not exploding right then and there.

He didn't have proof. He didn't have evidence. But he was goddamn certain that Hector had done this to Joanne. That he'd done it before.

And that the bastard would do it again.

"Sheriff?"

Nurse Francine's voice drifted over him, and he forced his attention back to the group.

"Are you coming?"

He hesitated, knowing that he should catch up. Instead, he shook his head. "You all go on. I'll be along in a minute."

And then, without waiting for Francine's reply, he turned and started off after Joanne.

Chapter Four

Ginny's head didn't hurt, but she felt like it *should* hurt. Like there was pain hidden underneath all the cotton and fuzz that seemed to have replaced her skin and her blood, turning her into this floating, numb creature with wires taped to her and tubes inserted in her.

But at least you're alive.

She winced. Because rather than being a comfort, the voice in her head sounded like an accusation.

She was alive, yeah. But Jacob—

God, she hated even thinking it.

She blinked up at Dr. Rush, who was standing beside her looking at a clipboard.

"He's really dead?"

She knew what the answer would be. She'd asked the question at least a dozen times so far—sobbed hysterically at least as many times—and the answer never changed.

"He died on scene, sweetheart. He didn't feel a thing."

Ginny nodded, grateful at least for that small blessing. "I was driving." Her lips and throat were so dry the words were barely a rasp. "I killed him." The words hurt—her throat, her head, her heart. "Oh, God. I killed him."

Dr. Rush hurried to put her clipboard on the bed and take Ginny's hand. "No, honey, no. I've talked with the EMT guys and with the sheriff. It was an accident. A horrible accident. You hit a deer, and with the rain and the slick road it was—well, it was all over very, very quickly. It wasn't your fault, honey. It wasn't anybody's fault. Do you understand?"

Ginny nodded, but only because she knew Dr. Rush expected it.

No matter what anyone said, Ginny knew the truth. And the truth was that Jacob was dead.

After that, no other truth much mattered.

"Where's my sister?" Ginny asked.

"Coming."

"Coming? When? And Luis?" Panic was rising inside her, and her voice was climbing. And she knew it—she could hear it—but she couldn't stop it. And her heart was pounding so hard in her chest that all the machines around started beeping louder and faster and—

Dr. Rush took her hand. "I'm right here, Ginny. Marisol's coming. Luis is coming. You're safe, and we're going to get you better. Okay?"

Ginny just lay there, trying to breathe.

"Can you look at me? I want to see that you're okay."

She moved her head to the side, saw Dr. Rush, and managed to nod.

"I need to tell you something before they come in. Your sister knows. We had to tell her in order to take care of you."

A riff of fear seemed to skitter over Ginny's skin. "Tell me what?"

Dr. Rush shifted so that she was holding Ginny's hand in both of hers. "Honey, did you know that you're pregnant?"

Pregnant.

The word hung meaningless in the air as Ginny tried to wrap her head around it. *Pregnant?*

"Wait. Pregnant? You mean, like, with a baby?"

To her credit, Dr. Rush didn't even crack the slightest of smiles. "Yes. With a baby. About nine weeks. You didn't know?"

"I—no."

A baby.

"But that can't be right. I can't be pregnant." She was in college. She was a good girl. She never got in trouble—had never gone in the bleachers with boys in high school. And yes, sure, she had maybe done some things she shouldn't once she moved to Austin and was away from home and in college, but *a baby?* No. That just wasn't possible.

"Have you ever had sex, Ginny?"

"I, yes. I mean, I'm twenty-one, so—"

"If you've had sex, sweetie, you can be pregnant. And although I can see that this is a shock, I assure you that you are. Trust me. I'm a doctor."

Ginny swallowed. "I heard—earlier—stuff about fetal heart rates and placentas." She turned her head and saw the second line showing a heartbeat faster than her own. And when she pushed down her blanket she saw the wire hooked up to her belly. "I'm really pregnant."

"You really are. And the trauma put the baby at risk. But we've run tests and everything looks okay. You didn't wonder when you missed your period?"

"I—I've never been regular."

"Are you on the pill?"

She shook her head.

"When you had intercourse, did you use birth control?"

"Condoms," she said, but it was a lie. When she'd slept with the senator in Austin, he'd said he didn't wear condoms and hadn't since high school. And Ginny had told him she was on the pill the first time, then after that, she'd used a diaphragm. Mostly. Sometimes he'd grab her the moment she stepped inside the hotel room and insist that he had to have her. Like right then, and he was so hot for her there wasn't time to go do the whole mess with the diaphragm.

With Jacob, they'd been so drunk—on alcohol and on each other—that they hadn't even thought of using a condom.

"As I said, your sister knows because I had to tell her out of medical necessity. But what you do now is up to you."

"You mean I could—" She closed her eyes. She couldn't even think the word.

"You're a healthy, young woman. There's no reason to think this pregnancy won't go smoothly."

But Ginny understood what the doctor wasn't saying. If she wanted an abortion, now was the time.

"Do you know who the father is?"

Ginny nodded, because nice girls always knew who the father was.

But did she? Did she really?

It had to be the senator's. They'd been fucking like bunnies until she'd broken it off, her shame finally getting the best of her. And fortunately he'd let her walk away without question. Over. Final.

Except now maybe it wasn't.

There'd only been the one time with Jacob. And, yeah, it had been just a little over two months ago. But still—it had only been once. And the odds were really *not* in his favor.

But, oh, if only the baby was Jacob's. It would be almost like having him back. Almost like maybe she hadn't destroyed everything.

"I'm keeping the baby," she said firmly, suddenly realizing that at some point she'd placed her hands protectively over her belly.

"Then we need to make sure you get the proper care. But we can talk about that later." Dr. Rush nodded toward the glass walls that identified this room as part of the ICU wing. "Looks like you have some visitors."

Beyond the glass, Ginny saw Marisol standing with Jacob's parents, Celeste and Travis. Suddenly, her throat filled with tears again, and then—as if there were just too many to hold inside—the tears spilled over her lashes and down her cheeks. "Please," she said. "Can they all come in?"

Dr. Rush pressed her lips together, and Ginny understood why. She'd never been a patient in a hospital before, but she'd seen movies and she knew that she was in intensive care, and she knew that visitors were limited. But she had to see them. Had to know that they didn't hate her because she was alive and their son was dead.

"Please? For just a minute?"

"All right. But not for very long."

The nurse—Ginny thought her name was Francine—had stepped just inside the doorway. Now Dr. Rush motioned to her, and Francine held the door open as the three visitors filed in.

Marisol was first and fastest, and she swooped down on Ginny like an attacking bird, then pulled back at the last minute before throwing her arms around her sister. "Oh God, I don't want to hurt you."

"I'm okay." Ginny held out her arms to receive a gingerly hug, then watched as Marisol stepped back, her hand over her mouth.

"Luis?"

"He's with Jeffry. But I called just a minute ago, and he's on his way."

She nodded, wanting her brother there. Needing to hold on to him just the same way she was now reaching out to cling to Marisol's hand.

At the foot of the bed, Celeste stood with Travis. She'd known Jacob's parents for almost her whole life. The Salts had been the perfect family. Everything she'd lost when her parents were killed. A mom and a dad. Regular dinners on the table. Dollars that didn't have to be squeezed so tight they screamed.

She'd always been welcome there, and although she loved her

brother and sister so, so much, she'd craved what Jacob had and what she'd so violently lost.

Jacob. Oh dear God, he was really gone.

"I'm sorry," she whispered, and the tears just started pouring out again.

"Oh, baby, oh, Ginny." Celeste hurried to her, then held her hand tight and stroked her hair as Ginny drowned herself in her tears and a stream of *I'm sorry, I'm sorry, I'm so, so sorry*. "It was an accident, honey, we know that. We know. And we are so grateful that you're safe. Jacob adored you, and he'd be so glad to know that you weren't badly hurt. If there's anything you need, you just ask us."

"That's very kind, Celeste," Marisol said. "But you don't need to do that."

Ginny glanced between the two of them, and as she did, she saw Luis and Jeffry standing outside the glass—and Sebastian Rush was standing there with them.

Senator Sebastian Rush.

The senator she'd slept with.

The senator whose baby she was probably carrying.

Was he there now to see her? To tell her how worried he'd been? To squeeze her hand in a silent, secret moment of compassion?

"For Jacob's best friend?" Celeste was saying. "For Ginny? Of course we'll do whatever we can."

Ginny barely heard the woman. Instead, she was focused beyond the glass, on where Senator Rush pressed his hand on Luis's shoulder. Ginny's breath hitched and she stiffened, preparing for the moment he walked through her door.

But he didn't.

He just took one more quick glance at her through the glass, then turned away and disappeared down the hall, not even bothering to ask if he could come in and say hello.

Bastard.

Jeffry hung back, then said something to Luis before the two guys hugged and Jeffry went off after his father.

Finally, Luis poked his head in. "Can I—can I come in?"

Marisol urged him over, and he hurried to Ginny's side, looking way, way younger than his sixteen years. He hugged her then stood up, his lips pressed together before he put his arm around Marisol. He was the man of the family, after all.

"I was just thinking about the garden you two planted in the backyard." Celeste's voice was thick with emotion. "We sodded over it after y'all left for college, but just last month, some cucumber plants started peeking through the grass. I think I'm going to let them grow," she added, her voice breaking at the end.

"Does Lacey—I mean, have you told Lacey yet? About Jacob?" Lacey was Jacob's younger sister and about a year older than Luis.

Celeste shook her head. "She's spending the weekend at a friend's house in Fredericksburg. We—we don't see any point in telling her just yet. Better to get ourselves together first, I think." Tears fell again, and she wiped them roughly away. "Damn it," she said, and Travis stepped up and put a hand on her shoulder.

"It's okay, Cee," he said, his voice gentle and soothing. "You just go ahead and cry."

She nodded, then turned and pressed her head against her husband's chest.

Ginny sighed, letting herself be soothed as well. That's how the Salts always were. She could remember Travis helping Jacob with everything from learning to ride a bike to learning how to drive, and being so easy and encouraging. For so much of her life, Ginny'd had no one to help her. And the way Celeste had always been so motherly with Lacey. There'd always been cookies and milk when she came home from elementary school. Ginny and Jacob used to steal them, then race back upstairs to do their own homework.

The first few times, Ginny was afraid they'd get in trouble because, according to Celeste, cookies and milk were for the little kids. But then Jacob pointed out that Celeste always made too many cookies. She knew what they were doing, and the cookies were like her secret gift.

Their house had always felt warm and comfortable and perfect. And although Marisol had tried, everything at the Moreno house was always slightly off. Like it was running without a full set of wheels.

And now so was the Salt's house. Ginny had made it horrible for them. And she'd never be able to fix it. Not ever.

Not really.

Except maybe—

"You're looking tired, sweetie," Celeste said, finally getting herself back under control. "We should go." She looked at Marisol. "You'll let us know when she's out of ICU?"

"Of course. Dr. Rush said it would probably be tonight," she added, and Ginny realized that the doctor had slipped out of the room at some point.

Celeste and Travis started to do the same.

"I—I'm pregnant!" Ginny blurted out the words without thinking, then gasped, almost as surprised as Celeste and Travis looked when they turned back to face her. Beside her, Marisol was biting her lower lip, and Luis was staring at her, his big, brown eyes huge.

"I didn't know. I just found out. I never thought that—at any rate," she continued in a rush, "it's Jacob's."

"Oh!" The word slipped from Celeste, and Ginny saw a glint in the older woman's eyes that she thought was pleasure.

"Are you sure?" Marisol asked.

Ginny didn't look at her sister. She kept her eyes on Celeste. On the glow that was starting to fill her eyes. "I'm sure. I haven't—you know. There hasn't been anyone else."

It was a lie. A horrible lie. And for just a moment she thought that she should take it all back.

But then Celeste reached for Travis's hand and held it tight. And she was so happy. And Senator Rush didn't even care, so why shouldn't Ginny let Jacob be the father?

"It's a miracle," Celeste said.

And as Celeste thanked God for sending them this miracle even in the middle of their pain, Ginny told herself that it couldn't possibly be a bad lie if it made two people so very, very happy.

Chapter Five

Dillon leaned against the wall in the north hallway and watched as Joanne stood behind her husband at the pharmacy window. Hector was arguing with the clerk about whether or not their insurance covered the cost of Joanne's pain meds. No surprise there; Hector was always riled about something.

"It's a crock of shit is what it is," Hector said. "All you damn bureaucrats in bed with the insurance companies, and all I want to do is get some fucking meds for my wife. Take a look at her." He stepped aside so the clerk had a full view of Joanne. She immediately stepped back, shoulders hunching even more in her pale yellow dress as she looked down at her scuffed espadrilles.

Dillon realized his hands had clenched into fists, and he did his damnedest to unclench them. It wasn't easy.

"She's in pain, dammit. I'm trying to help. And you and your co-pay crap aren't doing shit."

"I—I'm sorry, sir. I'm just the cashier. I could call the admin office. Or maybe—"

"Fuck it. You're costing me an extra fifty bucks so I can take care of my wife."

He slapped a credit card onto the counter, and as Dillon watched, the clerk swiped the card at pretty much the speed of light. He dropped the bottle of pills into a bag, stapled the receipt to it, then handed the purchase to Hector.

"Are you an idiot? Didn't I just tell you she was in pain? Christ almighty."

He turned his back on the clerk, who looked about ready to cry, then ripped open the bag and the bottle before tapping a single pill out into his hand and giving it to Joanne.

She looked up at him with a small smile. And as she did, Dillon saw the faint bruise rising on her jaw.

Goddamn Hector all to hell.

Fury pushed him forward, and as Hector put his hand on her back and started to lead her toward the exit, Dillon couldn't resist calling out, "Joanne."

She turned, her eyes going wide with surprise.

"Dillon! I—Oh—" She swallowed, then tilted her head up to look at Hector, whose expression was nothing short of thunderous.

"Sheriff." Hector smiled, but it didn't quite reach his eyes. The truth was, Hector was the kind of asshole who had the looks to make even smart women swoon. Hell, even in high school he'd been more good-looking than he'd deserved, and though all the teachers had adored him, Dillon had always seen through the sheen to what he was. A selfish, narcissistic prick who'd put stars in Joanne's eyes and now held her trapped.

Even right now, standing there in his grease-stained coveralls, the guy looked like he'd just walked off a movie set, and it made Dillon's stomach curl to see the way Joanne clung to him.

Dillon reached up and tapped the edge of his Stetson in greeting. Honestly, he'd rather have flipped the man the bird. "Everything okay, I hope?"

He asked the question to Joanne. It was Hector who answered.

"Took a spill off the back porch stairs. Landed hard on her wrist and banged up her face on the sidewalk."

Dillon studied Joanne for a moment, though she didn't once look up at him. "That's a shame. What made you trip?"

Again, it was Hector who answered. "Clumsiness."

"Funny. I could have sworn I asked Joanne."

She lifted her head then, and it seemed to Dillon that her green eyes were pleading. But whether the plea was for help or for him to drop the subject, he really didn't know.

Goddamn her. Didn't she see what she'd done? Didn't she understand what she could have had? What she'd destroyed when she'd run off with Hector?

Hector put his arm protectively around Joanne's shoulders, and she leaned against him, the movement making Dillon's skin crawl. "Come on, baby. We need to get you home."

She nodded, and her eyes met Dillon's briefly before she looked away.

Christ, it took every ounce of strength in his body not to follow them down the hall and arrest the son-of-a-bitch right now, but he didn't have one damned iota of proof that Hector had laid a hand to his wife. All Dillon had was instinct and the past and what he saw in Joanne. And what he saw was that the light he'd seen throughout their childhood was fading fast. She'd always been so vibrant. A woman so bright and alive that she drew people to her like a flower.

A woman he had wanted desperately for years, and had never worked up the courage to ask. Would things be different if he had? Would she be safe now, if only he'd managed to find his courage back then?

She'd gone and run off with Hector right after high school— eloped all the way to Vegas. They'd come back to settle in Storm, though, and suddenly Joanne Grossman had become Joanne Alvarez. Dillon could remember the scandal like it was yesterday, especially the brouhaha when Robert Grossman—Joanne's father and one of the local attorneys—publicly and loudly disowned her.

Her name wasn't the only thing that changed in Joanne, either. At first, she'd seemed fine. Happy even. But then slowly her light began to dim. She turned clumsier, or so she said. And she spent all her time at home or at the florist shop where she worked.

Dillon knew that money was tight, especially with three kids. He tried to tell himself that it was just stress that had stolen the light from Joanne. The pressure of being a working mom. Of having a husband who drank most of the paycheck he earned as a mechanic/attendant at the gas station on the edge of town.

He told himself that, but he didn't believe it.

And, goddammit, he was going to do something about it.

* * * *

Dakota Alvarez frowned at the handwritten sign on *Cuppa Joe's* front door that announced that the bakery and coffee shop was closed due to a family emergency. What the hell? Marisol really needed to hire someone other than Lacey if she was going to have to close up the shop anytime someone got a case of the sniffles.

And Dakota had really, really wanted one of Marisol's fabulous gingerbread cupcakes. She'd just done serious damage to her credit card at Pink, the cute little dress shop that had finally moved onto the square and actually sold decent clothes. Not that Dakota wasn't always looking for an excuse to go into Austin, but it was still nice to have a place that was local.

One day, though...

One day she would be completely done with Storm and she wouldn't care about the stores on the square. She'd get out, and she'd get out in style, on the arm of a man who could take care of her. A doctor, she thought with a little smile, picturing a certain future doctor's deep brown eyes. Jacob Salt might not know it yet, but he and Dakota were going to be very, very happy.

She swung her shopping bags as she strolled down Cedar toward Second Street, pausing only briefly in front of the Hill Country Savings & Loan. She looked through the windows at the long wooden counter behind which she sat every goddamn day taking deposits and handing over other people's money when they didn't even pay her well enough for her to have a decent account herself.

She gave her shopping bags a little shake. Her mother was always telling her that she needed to save, but honestly, what was the point? She barely made enough every two weeks to buy a few nice outfits. It's not like the couple of hundred she just spent would make a dent in a savings account. It wasn't going to get her a high-rise apartment in Austin or a big sprawling house in Westlake.

Might as well enjoy it while she could.

She made a right onto Second Street, following the perimeter of Storm's town square, and headed to the entrance of the Bluebonnet Cafe. As much as she wanted to shake free of Storm, she couldn't deny that her hometown had charm. And, thankfully, at least a few good places to eat.

Right now, Dakota was positively starving.

Through the glass, she saw Jeffry Rush sitting by himself at a booth. At eighteen, Jeffry was two years younger than her and still in high school. But with his dark blond hair and athlete's body, he was definitely worth looking at.

Truth be told, he looked a lot like his dad, Senator Sebastian Rush, which really wasn't a bad thing. Not that Dakota had had a piece of that yet. Senator Rush had made it clear that he was very, very interested, but Dakota was looking for a permanent fix for her Stormseclusion, and a married man didn't seem like the smartest ticket out.

Still, even though she'd called him an old pervert, she'd been flattered. He was a senator, after all. And, to be honest, a really hot senator at that.

Now, she hesitated before entering the cafe, taking the time to use the window as a mirror. Despite the summer humidity, her blonde hair still hung in soft waves around her face, with no signs of frizz. She wore a black T-shirt that dipped to a V to show off not only the cleavage that she inherited from her mother—thank God she only got the boobs and not the milk toast personality—but also a hint of lace from her bright red bra. She'd ended the outfit with shorts that made the most of her legs and her ass, and she'd paired it all with heels that gave her a needed three more inches in height.

For the most part, Dakota liked the way she looked—no body issues for her like so many of her friends had. But she really wished she were just a few inches taller.

Then again, men liked to feel big and strong, and being petite only helped that illusion.

She headed to the door, added a bit of swing to her step, and swept into the cafe like she owned it.

From behind the counter, Rita Mae Prager, one of the actual owners, waved at her, her elderly face breaking into a smile. "Dakota Alvarez, as I live and breathe. How's your brother, sugar?"

"Just fine, ma'am." Marcus used to work for Rita Mae and her sister, Anna Mae. He helped at the cafe and at their bed and breakfast—Flower Hill—on the outskirts of town. He'd left town without even saying good-bye right after high school. Dakota had been pissed and hurt, and even though he'd later called to tell her that he'd left because of their dad, that didn't make it better. She loved Marcus, sure. And she missed him desperately. But she never did understand the bullshit between him and their father. Daddy was the best, after all. There wasn't a thing he wouldn't do for Dakota, and it just pissed the hell out of her when her mom and brother and little sister got all weird around him.

But whatever. Other people's problems were just that—other people's.

Right now, she wanted a slice of chocolate pie and company, and so she slid into the booth across from Jeffry and aimed her best smile at him. "I was going to just settle for a cupcake at Marisol's bakery, but this is better. I get Rita Mae's pie and your company."

"Hey, Dakota."

She frowned. He sounded positively morose.

She tried again, making her smile brighter. "Of course, it's hard to beat those gingerbread cupcakes. Have you had them? I wonder why Marisol closed up on a Saturday. That's one of her busiest days."

Jeffry stared at her like she was wearing bright purple eye shadow or something.

"What?" she demanded.

"You haven't heard."

"I—" She licked her lips, suddenly not sure that she wanted to hear. Jeffry wasn't the kind of guy who walked around with a cloud over him. "What haven't I heard?"

"There was an accident last night. During the storm. Ginny and Jacob—they were coming home from Austin for the summer, and—"

Dakota grabbed Jeffry's wrist. "What? What happened? Is Jacob okay?"

"Ginny's in the hospital. She's messed up, but my aunt says she's gonna be fine."

"What about Jacob?" Dakota couldn't keep the panic out of her voice, and the longer she looked at Jeffry, the more afraid she became.

"He's dead, Dakota. Jacob's dead."

Dead.

She let go of Jeffry, yanking her hand back as if she'd been burned.

Dead.

He couldn't be dead. He was hers, goddammit. *Hers.* Not fucking Ginny Moreno's.

He was hers.

He was her way out.

And now he was dead and fucking Ginny was alive and Dakota would be trapped in Storm forever.

* * * *

Celeste had to keep moving.

She had a rag in her hand and the Murphy Oil Soap in the other, and she was going over every piece of wooden furniture in the living room and den. Because she couldn't let things slide. Not now, when they could so easily get out of control.

And she couldn't let her daughters, Lacey and Sara Jane, think that she wasn't handling it. This horrible thing that she couldn't even think about because it just hurt too much. Too damn much.

Goddamn this stupid china cabinet! Why had she let her mother talk her into buying it? The curving woodwork was like a magnet for dust, and no matter how much she tried she couldn't get it clean even if she scrubbed and scrubbed and—

No.

She hurled the spray bottle of cleaner across the room, accidentally upsetting the little box of coasters on the coffee table. They tumbled off, clattering on the hardwood floor.

As if the noise was a stage cue, Celeste collapsed to the floor as well, her knees just giving out.

She buried her face in her hands and cringed as she heard Travis's footsteps, then felt his hands on her shoulders.

She jerked away. "I'm okay. I'm okay."

"Celeste, sweetheart, you're not." His voice was gentle—more gentle than she'd heard it in a very long time—and she squeezed her eyes tightly shut, certain that she would start crying again. But no tears came. How could they when there were no tears left inside her?

"How are we going to tell them?" she asked as he pulled her up, then helped her to the couch. "Veronica's mom is driving Lacey home right now—I told her we've had a family emergency. But she's so young, Travis. Seventeen is just far too young to lose somebody so dear, and she loved Jacob so much. She—"

She had to swallow because her throat was thick with the grief.

"She'll get through it," he said. "It will be hard and it will be horrible, but you're here for her."

Celeste nodded. "And there's the baby. Travis, it's such a miracle."

She still couldn't wrap her head around it. She knew that Jacob was gone—that pain stabbed her in the heart each and every minute—but to know that there was another little life out there. Another little piece of him that she could hold and love and watch grow. A grandchild that she'd never expected, and certainly not like this.

She hoped it would be a boy. She hoped—

"She'll let us see him, won't she? Ginny?"

"Of course," Travis said gently. "That's why she told us."

"But what if—" She cut herself off, not even sure of what scared her. Just knowing that she needed Ginny near. She needed the baby near.

A baby. Jacob's baby.

Another thought slammed through her, and she frowned. "What about Lacey and Sara Jane? What if they don't understand? What if they think that having Jacob's baby around is too painful? What if—"

"Sweetheart, calm down. You're overwrought."

"Of course I'm overwrought," she snapped. "My son is dead. *Dammit*." She squeezed her eyes shut and forced herself to breathe in, breathe out. When she opened them and looked at Travis, he was looking back at her with concern, his posture strong, his eyes firm and loving. He was her strength right now, and she let that new, strange reality settle over her.

"I'm sorry," she said. "I'm just—I just don't want to have to tell the girls."

"I know. Believe me, I know. But they have you to help them. And Celeste, you're so good with the kids."

She managed a wry smile. "Am I?" He used to tell her she focused too much on the kids. But how could she not? Family was what mattered after all, and wasn't that what she'd been trying to do her whole life? Build a family?

She'd never understood his protests that she spent too much time working on the kids' school projects with them, or being the room mother for each of their grades, or heading up the PTA. She always managed to get dinner on the table, didn't she? Always made sure his clothes were washed and pressed and the house was clean and the kids' lunches were packed every morning.

He used to complain that she did too much and they should spend more time going out. Taking walks. Driving the Hill Country. And sure those would be lovely things, but they'd started a family and had responsibilities. And how much more would he complain if he had to go run their pharmacy in a wrinkled shirt? Or if he got a call from one of the kids begging for lunch money because she'd slept in and not bothered making it?

Then he stopped complaining and she'd been relieved because that meant he understood. At least she'd hoped that he understood.

And now here he was telling her right out loud that she was good with the kids, and wasn't that exactly what she'd been wanting to hear practically since Sara Jane was born? And it took a tragedy—it took

Jacob dying—to make him say it. To make him sit beside her the way he was now, just holding her.

"I don't want to have to tell them," she repeated as he pulled her close and she leaned against him.

"You don't have to do it alone. I'll be right there with you."

She tilted her head up, seeing a side of her husband that she'd missed. She'd thought he'd lost the strength that had attracted her to him so many years ago. Now that she was seeing it again, she couldn't help but wonder if it had been there all along and she'd just been too blind or too busy to see it.

"Sara Jane will seem to take it better than Lacey," she said softly. "She always appears so level—she's like you, Travis. She can hold it all in. But inside, she's going to be all ripped up."

"You called her?"

She nodded. "She's in San Antonio. Went with that new music teacher for a drive in the country and then dinner on the river." Sara Jane had just finished her first year as a special ed teacher at the elementary school, and Celeste was so proud of her daughter. "He's bringing her right back. I didn't tell her, either. Just that she had to come home. She's disappointed—I think she likes him. What's his name? Roger? Ryan? I'm not sure."

"Hush, sweetheart. We'll tell them when they get here. We'll both tell them. Right now, you just rest. Are you cold?"

"No. Yes. I don't know."

He got up, then tucked a blanket around her. With a sigh, she tilted her head up to look at him. "You're taking care of me."

"Of course I am."

He said it as if it was the most normal thing in the world, but it wasn't normal at all.

"I tried," she said. "You know that I tried, right?"

"Tried what, sweetheart?"

"To keep us all together. To keep our family together."

"Of course you did. You did a wonderful job."

"I did everything I could." Tears streamed down her face because she really had. And in one little twist of fate, the family she'd built had been broken forever.

Chapter Six

Mallory Alvarez heard the front door open and immediately pushed the button on the remote to mute the television. Her dad hated to have the television on when he came home from work. And as much as Mallory liked to go a little crazy sometimes, it was *really* crazy to piss off her dad.

"Mom? Mal?" Dakota's voice filled the house—not surprising because Dakota was about as loud as it got. She'd moved into a tiny garage apartment just off the square two years ago when Mallory was fourteen, and the place had been *way* more quiet ever since.

That was just one of the reasons that Mallory had been happy to see her go. Another was the fact that Dakota was a spoiled princess who was always ragging on their mom and sucking up to their dad. And Mallory hated that shit. Of course, her older brother Marcus had gone first, and Mallory had truly been sad when he'd left. And now she was left alone in the house with her parents, and most of the time that really blew.

She shot Luis, her boyfriend, a defiant look, then pushed the button to unmute. After that, she slowly cranked the volume all the way up. As she'd hoped, Luis smiled—although only just a little. He'd had a horrible day, what with his sister being in the hospital and Jacob being dead.

Mallory hadn't known Jacob very well, but she'd known Luis forever and had been in love with him for at least that long. He had the long, lean body of an athlete and curly dark hair that she used to imagine twirling around her fingers. Now she could do that whenever she wanted, because as of the spring dance—when she'd finally gotten up the nerve to ask him—they were officially a couple.

Today, his angular face looked tired and his hair hung just a little limp. She wasn't surprised. Luis's sister Ginny had been Jacob's best friend, so of course Luis was shaken. He'd come over in a funk after going to the hospital, and they'd been self-medicating with really bad reality television and beer. Her mother, Joanne, would give her shit for the beer since they were both only sixteen, but the day called for it, so there you go.

"God, what the fuck?" Dakota shouted as she came into the living room. "I've been screaming at you to turn that down."

Mallory cupped her hand to her ear. Dakota snarled, then grabbed the remote and turned the whole system off.

"Hey! We were watching that. Luis needs to de-stress. It's been a shitty day."

To Mallory's surprise, Dakota actually teared up. Then Mallory felt pretty shitty herself because she'd been thinking about Luis, and not about Dakota. Because, honestly, when did she bother thinking about Dakota?

But today, she should have. Because even though Dakota never did much about it or said much about it, Mallory knew she'd had a crush on Jacob since, like, forever. And even though her sister was a huge bitch, Mallory would never wish this on her.

"You heard?" she asked gently.

Dakota opened her mouth, but no words came out. Instead, she swiped at her eyes and nodded.

"Oh, man." Mallory leaped to her feet and threw her arms around her sister, who hugged her back tight, something she did less than never.

After a minute, Dakota pulled back then looked at Luis. "Ginny's okay?"

He nodded. "Yeah. She's—" He shook his head. "Doesn't matter. But she scared the shit out of us. She's okay, though." He pulled Mallory over for a kiss on the cheek. "I'm gonna go. Marisol's been sitting with her, but I should spell her, you know?"

"You okay to drive?" Mallory asked. "Want me to go with you?"

He shook his head. "Thanks. I'm good. Only drank half of one. Nothing much tastes good?"

He gave her another quick kiss, then headed out, leaving Mallory alone with her sister. "So what's up? You hardly ever come by anymore."

Dakota lifted a shoulder. "I wanted to see Daddy."

"He's at work."

"Really? It's almost six."

"He took Mom to the hospital this morning. She hurt her wrist."

Dakota rolled her eyes. "Thank God we didn't inherit her clumsiness, right?"

Mallory just stared at her, wondering if her older sister could really be that stupid. "She's not clumsy. He's a drunk."

"Pot calling the kettle," Dakota said, pointing at the beers.

"He's a mean drunk."

Dakota lifted a hand. "We're not even talking about this shit. Daddy works his ass off to take care of her, and we both know it. I figure if he wants to chill with a beer or two, what's wrong with that?"

Mallory shrugged. It wasn't the beer so much as what came with it. But she wasn't going to get into that with her sister. God forbid you said anything bad about King Hector in front of Princess Dakota. And it wasn't like Mallory knew what to say anyway. Every time she'd even hinted at it with her mother, Joanne just changed the subject. And surely if Hector was really being horrible, she'd do something to stop him, right?

But still...

That's what it seemed like, and she didn't know what to do, and she hated thinking that way. And the truth was that she'd been thinking that way for a while, but just hadn't wanted to say it out loud. Mostly, she spent her time out of the house because it was easier to be gone. She could hang out behind the feed store and drink beer and be with her friends and it was easy. But she was starting to really worry about her mom.

At the end of the day, Mallory had learned only one good lesson from her parents—marriage was for suckers.

For about the millionth time, she wished Marcus was around. He'd know what she should do. Dakota wasn't any help at all.

"So where's Mom, then?" Dakota asked.

"Grocery store. Dad told her he'd be starving when he got home, what with putting in later hours." Her mom *should* be asleep with all those pain meds in her. And Mallory had offered to go to the store for her. But Joanne Alvarez was proud, that much was for sure.

The purr of the ancient Oldsmobile's engine caught both their attention, and they hurried to the screen door that opened off the kitchen. The floor sloped just a bit there—the house was old and Hector never seemed to get around to fixing it—and so Mallory felt even more off-kilter as she waited for Joanne to come inside.

She had a bag in her left hand, and Mallory saw her struggling to carry everything with her injured wrist. "Oh, shit," Mallory said, then trotted outside to help her mom.

"Thanks, baby," Joanne said. "Help me get dinner on?"

"Sure. You can sit at the table and I'll do it."

"No. Your dad likes the way I do it."

"What are we having?"

"Tacos. Quick and easy." Soon enough, she was in the kitchen and working on the meal. She dumped the ground beef into the cast iron skillet and started adding spices from the rack on the back of the stove. "Can you girls put away the rest? He'll be home soon, and it took longer at the store than I'd thought."

She didn't meet Mallory's eyes, and Mallory knew that the reason for the delay had been her wrist and not a flood of people at the local H-E-B.

Dakota looked up from where she was seated at the round Formica table. "Mom, I need some extra cash."

Joanne frowned at her, and Dakota stood, suddenly interested in helping to put away the groceries. Mallory almost rolled her eyes at her sister's transparency.

"You're a bank teller, sweetheart. You make a decent wage."

"Decent? I make a crappy hourly rate. And I have to cover my rent."

Joanne tilted her head. "I've seen your paychecks, Dakota Alvarez. What are you doing with that money if it's not going for rent?"

"Jesus, Mom, am I a naked, starving monk? I have to eat. I have to wear clothes. And, guess what, I like to go out and have some fun sometimes."

Joanne pursed her lips together. Mallory turned away in case she laughed out loud.

"I don't have any money. You know your father fills up the household account only on the first of the month."

"Yeah, but you could lend me just a little bit of your money, right?"

"Dakota. I don't have it."

Dakota rolled her eyes. "You work at the florist. And, hey, you're a Grossman, Mom. Give me a break. I mean, Grandma's practically rolling in money."

Mallory had been putting away the vegetables, but now she turned back to gape at her sister. Mentioning their grandparents really wasn't done, especially around Hector.

For a second, Mallory almost wished Hector was home so he could see that his little princess was really Princess Bitch.

At the sink, Joanne froze while rinsing a head of lettuce, then said very slowly, "You know my father doesn't speak to me since I married your dad."

"He shouldn't punish you for who you married."

"I couldn't agree more."

"Grandma still comes by."

Joanne drew a deep breath. "But she's not going to give me any money."

"Then I'll ask Daddy. He'll give it to me."

Joanne spun around, the head of lettuce still in her hands. "Dakota, don't you ask that. Your father needs every—oh!"

The back door slammed open and Mallory jumped as Hector strode in, stinking so much of beer she could smell it from all the way at the table.

"Just now getting dinner on the table? Christ, Jo. Can't you do anything right?"

Mallory cringed, but the princess seemed oblivious that Hector was being such an ass.

"Daddy, I need money for rent. Just an extra hundred. I'm just a little short."

"'Course baby. Can't let you fall behind."

She eased up against him and kissed his cheek, making Mallory want to gag. "Thanks, Daddy."

"Hector...I don't think..."

"Is it my job to provide for this family?" he snapped at Joanne, who seemed to be shrinking right in front of Mallory.

Joanne kept her eyes down, focusing on the ground beef. "Yes."

"Is it your job to serve up the food that my earnings buy?"

"Yes."

"Then until you get your job handled, don't be telling me my job. Okay?"

Joanne nodded. "Okay."

And suddenly Hector was all smiles. He crossed to Joanne, kissed her cheek, then smacked her lightly on the bottom. "That's my girl." He took a deep breath. "Well, it may be late, but it smells damn good."

And then her mom turned to him and actually smiled. And it was warm and genuine and happy.

Mallory didn't get it.

Not any of it.

Not her parents. Not marriage. Not one little bit.

* * * *

From the outside, the Salt house looked the same as it always did. A Victorian charmer a few blocks off the square that had been ramshackle back in the day, but that Celeste and Travis had lovingly restored. Mostly with Celeste's elbow grease and Travis's checkbook. Celeste had spent countless hours sanding floors, stripping wallpaper, priming and painting. She'd spent a year with grout under her nails and callouses on her knees. But it had been worth it.

The house had been a battered mess when they'd purchased it before Sara Jane was born. But they'd transformed it from an eyesore into a home that was always featured in the Christmas Tour of Lights.

The lawn was tidy, the flowers bright. Even the picket fence had been recently repainted.

So there wasn't a thing about the house to suggest that anything was wrong inside.

Celeste was grateful for that small favor. At least her daughters had enjoyed a few extra minutes of blissful ignorance before the truth fell into their laps.

And fall it had.

They'd arrived within minutes of each other, and now they were seated at the round dining table with Celeste and Travis, both of them in the chairs they'd claimed when they were just toddlers. With one chair disturbingly empty.

Both girls had a tall glass of homemade lemonade with a slice of strawberry, a shared favorite from childhood, but neither had touched it once Travis had delivered the blow.

Thank God it had been Travis who'd told them. Celeste was seeing a side of him she hadn't seen in a long time. A strength and a purpose. A sense of being with the family. And though she was grateful, it saddened her to know that it took tragedy to restore that closeness she'd been missing lately.

She reached over and squeezed Lacey's hand. Her sweet baby girl looked like she'd just been through a war. "Honey?"

Lacey just lifted her shoulders. "I can't believe it. I just can't believe he's gone."

"I just talked to him on Wednesday," Sara Jane said, her voice raw from crying.

"And Ginny's really pregnant?"

Travis nodded, then reached for and took Celeste's hand. "Your mom and I think it's a miracle. A gift from God. We never thought—" He bowed his head, his words echoing what was in Celeste's heart. "We never dreamed."

"I didn't even know they'd started dating," Lacey said. "I mean, Ginny's been like a sister."

"I can't believe he didn't say anything."

"Ginny says they were going to tell us when they got here—that they were dating," Celeste clarified. "Ginny just learned about the baby, too."

"Still, it's weird, right?" Lacey said. "I mean, they've always just been buds."

"That's the best kind of relationship." Celeste took Travis's hand in her own. "Friends first, then lovers. It makes for strength in a relationship, and in a family. Isn't that right?"

"That's right." Travis squeezed her hand, then looked at the three of them in turn. "We're going to get through this, ladies. We're going to be strong together. As a family."

Chapter Seven

Pushing Up Daisies had been a Storm establishment for close to fifty years and had occupied the limestone and brick building on the corner of Main Street and Pecan since Hedda Garten had opened the store after her husband was killed in Vietnam.

Despite the name, the store did weddings and parties at least as much as they did funerals.

Today, however, it was the latter that was on everybody's mind.

The store opened at one on Sundays, as did most of the Storm establishments on the square. The hours allowed for family and church time, while still playing to the economic realities of Hill Country tourism. In other words, most folks driving the Texas Hill Country did so on the weekends. Storm was a bit farther from both San Antonio and Austin than the more common Hill Country destinations like Fredericksburg, but it still got its share of weekend shoppers. And in the economy of small-town tourism, keeping stores open when customers were present was a big part of the game.

Travis had asked Celeste if she could go alone to talk to Kristin Douglas, who not only planned parties but helped the bereaved choose the proper arrangements. And she'd said yes, because this was something that had to be done, and she couldn't keep clinging to him. He could keep the pharmacy closed for a while, but the bottom line was that he had to be there to fill prescriptions. People needed him, not just her. And Celeste tried very hard not to be a selfish woman.

But then they'd arrived downtown and had parked in front of Prost Pharmacy, just as they had so many times when she joined Travis at work.

It was an easy walk. She'd made it a hundred times.

Up Pecan and then across the street to the florist, sometimes just because she wanted to pop in and see Travis, and then get some fresh flowers to take home.

But today, her feet wouldn't move. At least not until he took her hand and fell in step beside her. "Why don't I go with you after all?" he'd said quietly. "You shouldn't have to do this alone."

And now she still clutched his hand, even though they'd been chatting with Kristin about the flowers for at least ten minutes.

Or, rather, Celeste had been chatting. Because Travis was uncharacteristically quiet as Kristin told them how sorry she was for their loss and that she would be happy to take care of the flowers for them, coordinating with the church and funeral parlor.

"Lilies, please," Celeste said, and realized it felt good to be making a decision. "And baby's breath. And something with a hint of yellow. I know it's not original, but he was so young and so innocent. And he was like a little bit of sunshine whenever he entered a room."

"I think that's a beautiful sentiment," Kristin said. "I'll put it together and call you to get your okay. You don't need to worry about a thing."

"Thank you," Celeste said, releasing Travis's hand to shake Kristin's. Beside her, Travis wiped his hands on his pants, not even noticing that Kristin had held out hers to shake.

Celeste cleared her throat, and Travis glanced up, looking confused, and then settling into calm.

He took Kristin's hand. "Forgive me. I'm a little off-kilter. I—I thought I was doing okay. But being in here has—well, it's affected me."

"I completely understand." She looked at him with so much compassion it made Celeste's heart twist, then Kristin smiled sadly at Celeste as she released Travis's hand. "He was an exceptional boy. I'm so sorry for your loss."

"Thank you," Celeste murmured. Travis said nothing. But he looked a little shell-shocked as they turned toward the door.

"Are you okay?" she asked once they were back on the street. They walked the short distance to the corner and paused for the light to change so they could cross Pecan.

"I think it's just sinking in." He frowned. "Everything's going to change."

Celeste drew in a long breath. The light turned green and the little box started flashing the image of a pedestrian in motion. But she didn't move, and she tugged her husband's sleeve when he started to walk because she'd caught a glimpse of familiar reddish blond hair.

"Pastor Douglas!"

The young Lutheran minister turned toward the sound of his name, his expression shifting to sympathetic when he saw who had hailed him.

"Celeste. Travis. I've been praying for you." They'd seen Pastor Douglas—Bryce—late Friday. Sheriff Murphy had been kind enough to ask the pastor to pay a visit a few minutes after he'd gone. And, yes, it had helped.

"Thank you. Are we keeping you?"

The pastor shook his head. "I like to walk the square after the second service. It's relaxing, especially on a pleasant day like today. I usually grab a muffin then pop in and see my sister at the florist."

"Kristin," Travis said.

Pastor Douglas nodded. "But no muffins. Today, I'm trying to lay off the carbs." He patted his stomach. "How can I help you?"

"Do you believe God still performs miracles?" Celeste asked.

She saw the flicker of emotion pass over his face. Surprise. Uncertainty. She wanted to reassure him that she wasn't expecting her son to rise from the dead. But before she had to do that, he answered.

"I do."

"And if you witnessed a miracle, then it would be foolish to look away. To not acknowledge it. Maybe even try to help facilitate it?"

Both his and Travis's brows furrowed. "Celeste, forgive me, but what's on your mind?"

But she wasn't ready to talk to him about it. Not yet. "Nothing. Just silliness. Just the kind of big thoughts that enter your mind in a crisis." She smiled. "Thank you for indulging my curiosity."

"Of course," he said.

"But would you?" she asked.

"Would I what?"

"Ignore a miracle."

An unfair question, she supposed. Because a man of God could hardly say he would look the other way. And yet without knowing her motivation, he couldn't possibly know whether he should encourage her or not.

But he *was* a man of God, and that meant he would answer

honestly. And that meant he would give her the answer she wanted.

And *that* meant she would have ammunition.

"No," he finally said. "It is not in my nature to ignore a miracle. But Celeste, you should take care not to confuse good fortune with the miraculous."

"Of course, Pastor." She tried not to smile too triumphantly. "Thank you so much. We shouldn't keep you from your sister."

He hesitated, looking between the two of them as if unsure whether he should go on. But then he nodded and wished them a pleasant day before continuing on his way.

"What was that about?" Travis asked.

The light to cross Main Street changed, and she tugged him that direction—heading for the courthouse and the famous Storm Oak tree instead of to Pecan Street and the pharmacy. "Five minutes," she said. "Just sit with me. Please."

He eyed her warily, but he sat.

"The baby's a miracle," she began. "We both know that." She paused to let him comment, and when he didn't, she continued on. "And we need to make sure it's healthy and safe and well taken care of."

Again, he stayed quiet.

"I want Ginny to move in with us."

"What?"

"I want our grandson's mother to be in our care. To have a room in our house. I want to help her with medical bills and with decorating a nursery."

"Celeste, sweetheart, I don't know—"

"But you do, Travis." She could hear the plea rising in her voice. "We both know what a miracle this is. To have a child of Jacob's, that's miracle enough. But to be blessed with it even as we've lost him—neither one of us would ever have believed that could happen, but it did. And I think it's our responsibility and our pleasure to help that sweet girl out."

"She has a family."

"She does, of course. And I don't want to take her away from her brother or her sister in spirit. But she's going to need help and care. Marisol's done right by that child, but she's not Ginny's mother. She won't be the baby's grandmother. I think she would welcome the help. Welcome knowing that someone is home with her pregnant little sister—with her sister and her nephew after the baby is born. She works such long hours just making ends meet. It can't be easy. You remember all the talk—their parents had no life insurance and everything fell on that poor girl's head. I want to help her with that burden."

Travis was smiling.

"What?"

"Nephew? Not niece?"

Celeste felt her cheeks heat. "The baby's a miracle, Travis."

"But the baby's not Jacob and never will be."

She licked her lips and looked down at the well-tended grass that surrounded the courthouse. "I know that. I do. But I still want him near me. Don't you?"

He sighed, then looked across the street, his attention on the florist shop where they'd just picked out the flowers for their son's funeral. Where the pastor who'd told them that miracles do happen had just stepped inside. "You need this, Celeste? This will make you happy?"

She took his hand and clung tight. "Yes. Oh, yes."

Another moment passed. "All right. We'll leave it up to Ginny. You ask her, and if that's what she wants, then she's welcome in our home."

Celeste felt the tears welling in her eyes. "And that's what you want, too?"

Travis's shoulders rose and fell. "I want Jacob back. But if that's not possible, then I want to do everything I can for his child. And," he added as he lifted his hand and gently stroked her cheek, "for you."

* * * *

Joanne perched on the stool behind the counter at Pushing Up Daisies and watched as her friend Kristin leaned against the table that formed the centerpiece for the store. Today it was topped with an extravagant arrangement of tropical flowers—an arrangement that Hedda had put together before bidding the younger women a happy Sunday and taking off to putter in her own garden.

"Are you okay?"

As she watched, Kristin's shoulders rose and fell as if she was breathing hard. "Yeah." She drew herself up, then turned to Joanne.

She looked put together as always, in a light blue sheath dress that highlighted her blue eyes and contrasted her russet hair. But right now, those eyes looked cloudy. And her usually shining face seemed dim.

Joanne frowned. "Are you sure?"

Kristin held up a hand as she visibly pulled herself together. "I do funerals—it's part of what I do. But in a town this size, there just aren't that many. And when it's the death of someone so young..." She trailed off, wiping a finger carefully under her eye.

Joanne was about to reply, but the little bell above the door jingled and Bryce—or, rather, Pastor Douglas—came in and walked straight to his sister at the center table.

From her vantage point behind the counter, Joanne watched Kristin with her brother. She had become close to Kristin since they'd both worked at the florist shop for several years now, and she couldn't help but think of him by his name, especially since Joanne had never been one to go to church.

Together, they looked like a set of dolls, both with blue eyes and reddish hair and all-American good looks.

Folks had never called Joanne all-American. She was too built. Too blond. And she'd always thought that her green eyes made her look just a little bit devilish. She'd never acted that way, though. She'd always been a little too shy, and she'd hated that about herself. Then Hector had swept her off her feet during senior year, making her feel like she was the queen of the world.

He'd wanted her to be better—he still wanted her to be better. And she knew that she frustrated him sometimes when she messed up. And so she tried very hard not to mess up, because he worked relentlessly to keep a roof over their head, and she knew that if she just did better he'd be less stressed and things would be the way they used to be.

So she tried—she really did. But it was just so hard.

"—you don't mind?"

Joanne blinked, realizing she'd been lost in thought. "I'm sorry. What?"

Kristin cocked her head toward the metal swinging door that led to the back area. "I'm going to show Bryce something in the back. You'll watch the front?"

"Of course." She slipped off the stool and was about to walk out onto the main floor when the bell jingled again, and Hannah walked in looking more or less like she'd just rolled around in a haystack. Knowing Hannah, she probably had. Her sister was a vet, after all, and like so many small-town vets, her practice included domestic and farm animals.

To be fair, though, today she looked much tidier than usual, with her jeans and button-down shirt open over a tank top. Her long blond hair was pulled back in the single braid that she was in the habit of wearing, and she wore one of her many pairs of cowboy boots.

Not for the first time, Joanne wondered how they were sisters because Joanne owned exactly one pair of cowboy boots, and they'd been a Christmas present from Hannah.

"I was hoping you were working today," Hannah said. "Isn't it horrible? I wanted to get some flowers for the service on Thursday."

"It's a tragedy," Joanne agreed. "Mallory spent some time yesterday with Luis. He and Marisol are so relieved that Ginny's okay, but it's so horrible about Jacob." She turned to the refrigerated case behind her. "Do you have something in mind, or would you like me to just put together an arrangement for you?"

"Would you? You know I suck at that kind of thing."

Joanne nodded because her younger sister did suck at that kind of thing. If it didn't involve animals, Hannah was pretty much clueless.

"Thanks. Just send a bill to the office, okay? Or you can bring it to lunch tomorrow."

"Are we doing lunch tomorrow?" Joanne frowned, afraid she'd forgotten something.

"You have Mondays off, right? Mom thought you could come by. Visit for a little bit."

Joanne's stomach twisted at the thought. "I don't know. What if Daddy comes home?" Her father had told her that if she married Hector, she was no longer his daughter. At the time, she'd thought that he was just spewing invectives. Her father had always adored her—had adored both her and Hannah, really, but with Joanne there was a special bond.

But he'd meant it. And ever since she came back from Vegas married, her father didn't even acknowledge that she was alive.

She told herself it no longer hurt, but that was a lie.

"That's the thing," Hannah said. "He's out of town tomorrow. So we can catch up."

"I—I can't," Joanne said. "I'm working. My hours changed." That part was true. What she didn't say was that she could easily change her hours if she wanted to. Kristin would cover, or Hedda would come in for a bit—she liked to pretend that she was retired and had "her girls" to run the store, but Joanne knew how much she loved to still be a part of the daily life at Pushing Up Daisies.

But she didn't say any of that, because the truth was that it just wasn't worth it. Her mom was awesome, true. And she'd kept in touch despite Joanne's father's stern instructions not to. Debbie Grossman had helped care for Joanne's kids, snuck money to her when the grocery budget ran tight, and just generally been there.

And Hector hated that almost as much as Robert Grossman did.

So maybe Robert was out of town, but Hector wasn't. And Joanne really didn't see the point in getting on her husband's bad side. Not when his bad side was so bad. Of course, his good side could also be so very good.

"Maybe some other time," she said. "Maybe we can go to a restaurant." That wouldn't bother Hector as much. He knew that Joanne saw her mother. But going to the house—doing anything that put her in Robert's circle—pissed him off royally.

Hannah looked at her, frowning. "What happened to your wrist?"

Joanne turned back to the refrigerated case and pulled out a rose. "Tripped. Stupid, really."

"You've gotten to be such a klutz," Hannah said, her voice deceptively level. "You never were clumsy when you were growing up."

Joanne turned back around with a shrug, then bent down to pull out a sheet of tissue paper, the action hiding her face. "Well, I've had kids. Maybe they threw me off-kilter."

"Is that a metaphor?"

Joanne looked at her sister, then shook her head fondly. "Yeah. Your nieces and nephew are enough to throw anyone out of whack."

As she'd hoped, Hannah grinned. "True that."

"Here." Joanne passed Hannah the single rose wrapped in tissue. "Put it in your office. You need some color in there—not just stainless steel and leather. And I'll call you later about the arrangement, okay?"

Hannah took the rose and bent her nose to sniff it. Then she looked up at Joanne. "Jo—" She shook her head. "Never mind. We'll talk later. Okay?"

Joanne nodded, more relieved than she should be, then she came around the counter and walked her sister to the door. As Hannah left, Joanne looked out across the street to the square and the lovely old courthouse. Her eyes were on the view at first, and then she noticed the man on the sidewalk, just standing there looking at the store.

Dillon Murphy.

The sheriff stood in his jeans and uniform shirt, his Stetson pushed back a bit so that she could see his face and a hint of his thick black hair. She couldn't see his eyes, but she knew them. Deep and blue and as bright as the sky, and just thinking about them looking at her made her shiver despite herself.

As she watched, he reached up and brushed the rim of his hat in greeting, and all the while his eyes stayed firmly on her.

She felt the blush touch her cheeks even as her stomach did a few funny little jumps, and before she could talk herself out of it, she lifted a hand and waved.

Oh, man. She shouldn't have done that.

But why not? He was the sheriff after all, and she was just being polite.

"Who's there?" Kristin asked as she and Bryce returned from the back. Bryce kissed his sister's cheek, then left the store as Joanne hurriedly turned away from the window, barely even responding to Bryce's parting words.

"Joanne?" Kristin pressed.

"Nobody." She cleared her throat and forced herself to stay level. "Just the sheriff." But even as she spoke the words, Joanne knew that Dillon wasn't "just" anything. Not to her. And she wasn't just any girl to him.

It was a nice feeling. A sweet, secret little feeling.

But also a very, very dangerous one.

"Hey, listen," Kristin said, her words bringing Joanne back to reality. "I couldn't help but overhear you and your sister."

Joanne looked at her, then walked deliberately away toward the counter.

Kristin was not deterred. "If you really did trip, that's one thing. But I have to be honest, Jo. I'm worried about you."

"Don't be."

"A lot of bruises. A lot of falls."

"Kristin—"

"Joanne, dammit, you should talk to someone."

"Really?" Joanne didn't mean to snap, but it was all just building up, and God knew she couldn't snap at home. "Really? *I* need to talk? Maybe *you* need to talk. I'm not the one having an affair with a married man."

She knew the arrow had struck home when Kristin's face turned dead white. "What are you talking about?"

"You know exactly what I'm talking about."

"How do you— Who—"

"Don't worry. It's not gossip around town, and to be fair, I don't even know who he is. But I know it's true—and if I didn't before, I do now. So dammit, Kristin, leave me alone. People in glass houses, and all that, right?"

Kristin licked her lips, then nodded. "We should both probably talk about it," she said softly.

Joanne sighed. "Maybe," she admitted. "But we're not going to."

Chapter Eight

Ginny hated when everybody left and she was all alone in the room with nothing but the television, a book, and all the beeping machines.

But she was out of the woods now, so that was something. And they'd moved her from ICU to this regular room last night. Dr. Rush said that everything looked great and that normally they'd go ahead and release her, but because of the baby, they were being cautious.

The baby.

She still hadn't quite gotten her head around it. She was going to have a baby. She was going to be a mother.

She barely even remembered her mother, so how on earth was she supposed to manage that?

Maybe she'd hit her head harder than they all thought because what had she been thinking when she said she'd keep the baby? Of course, she wouldn't have an abortion—she didn't think she could do that—but she could give it up for adoption. Probably should. Because she'd been on the five-year plan at UT, what with her work-study schedule, and with a baby she'd be pretty much on the twenty-year plan.

How the hell was she going to make a living without a college degree?

And how was she going to get a degree if she had to take care of a baby?

Why, oh why, weren't Marisol or Luis here? Someone to talk to. To take her mind off all of this? The baby. Jacob.

She squeezed her eyes tight and told herself not to cry again. But she missed him so damn much. And if it was his baby—and she was going to just keep saying that it was over and over in her head until she really believed it—then it broke her heart that he'd never get to see it.

That was the part that made her sad.

The part that made her scared was that if Jacob were here and the baby was his, he'd marry her. He loved her—and even if he didn't really love her like that, the sex had been awesome and they were best friends, and that was better than most marriages, right?

So he'd marry her and they'd raise Little Bit together. He'd get student loans for med school and they'd live in cheap housing, and she'd do some sort of work-at-home job so that she could raise the baby, and then he'd be a doctor and everything would get easier, and when they were old they'd look back and laugh about how they had to scrimp and save when they were young and had a baby.

Except Jacob was never going to get old.

She pressed her hands over her belly and closed her eyes, hating the way it just kept sneaking up on her. So far, she hadn't had nightmares. The counselor who'd come in to talk to her had told her to be prepared for them, but if she talked about it and didn't try to hold in her grief, she might not suffer in the night. Either way, she was better off just letting herself feel bad, and not trying to push it away.

Well, no problem there. She felt bad. Bad that she'd survived and Jacob hadn't. Bad that she'd been driving the car. Bad that she was having a baby that might—okay, it was a very small might—be his and that he'd never see it.

And bad that she'd lied to his parents by telling them that the baby was Jacob's. But the look on his mother's face had broken her heart, and when she'd learned about the baby, she'd lit up.

She grimaced. Somehow that thought had circled her all the way back to the brutal reality. She was about to be a single mom with only a high school diploma.

"We can do it, Little Bit." She rubbed her belly and whispered to the baby. She didn't know that she believed the words, but she wanted the baby to believe them.

And maybe it all *would* work out. Marisol kept telling her over and over that everything would turn out okay. Hadn't they survived after their parents had died? If they'd held together as a family through that, then they would all pull together through this new addition.

And that was all well and good and Ginny knew that Marisol loved her and meant every word, but Marisol wasn't exactly the Chef

Ramsay of small-town bakeries, and the baby was going to be one more mouth to feed. Ginny so wanted her baby to have a whole family. To have everything she'd missed out on. A mom and a dad. Grandparents. The whole Norman Rockwell small-town American dream.

She'd missed out on it, and now her baby was going to miss out on it, too.

Enough.

She was reaching for the remote so that she could watch something mind-numbing on television when Celeste walked in, her face an odd mixture of sadness and hope. "I'm so glad you're out of ICU. And the baby is doing well?" She stood by Ginny's bed, her hand poised over the blanket on Ginny's tummy. "May I?"

"Sure," Ginny said because she could see how happy the thought of a baby made Celeste. "But I think it's too early to feel anything."

"But we know," Celeste said, cupping her hand over Ginny's stomach. "You and me and the baby. We know that he's in there and that he's safe and that he's a little part of Jacob, too."

Ginny stiffened at the words and hoped that Celeste didn't notice. She liked Celeste. Loved her, really. The Salts had always treated her like one of their own, and it was because Ginny loved them—because she'd felt so horrible about Jacob being dead and her being alive—that she'd told them the baby was Jacob's.

It was like she was giving them Jacob back.

But now, it felt less like a gift and more like a lie, and the guilt of that lie was weighing heavy on her.

"Celeste—"

"Wait one second," Celeste said, interrupting Ginny. But that was okay because in the end she wasn't entirely sure what she wanted to say. She knew what she *should* say, but she wanted to hold on to the fantasy a little bit longer, too. "There's something I want to talk to you about."

"Oh." Fear swirled inside her. Surely Celeste didn't know about the senator?

"You must be very excited to go home tomorrow."

Ginny nodded, unsure where this was headed, and Celeste pressed on.

"And the truth is that I'm sure Marisol and Luis are going to be so happy to have you back. But sweetheart—" Now she leaned forward, grasping Ginny's hands and holding tight. "—they aren't going to be able to give you the attention you need and deserve. Luis is a teenage boy, and he needs to be out with his friends. And Marisol—bless her heart—can't take time away from her own business, no matter how much she might want to."

"I know," Ginny said. "I don't expect them to. I'm—we're—used to being on our own a lot."

Celeste nodded sagely. "Of course you are. And that's a sad thing for a child—for you. For your brother. And for your sister who—like you—got responsibility handed to her far earlier than she deserved."

Ginny frowned. Everything Celeste was saying was true, but she wasn't really in the mood to hear how much tomorrow was going to suck and how alone she was going to be.

"I realize this may sound a little strange, but Travis and I have talked about it, and—well, the truth is that we want you to move in with us."

Ginny sat up so fast she upset the cup of ice she had tucked in by the bed rail. "Leave it, leave it," she said, when Celeste bent down. "What did you say?"

"We've worked it all out. You can have Jacob's old room and we'll turn Sara Jane's into the nursery. And once the baby's born if you feel like you need more room for yourself, you two can move into the apartment," she added, referring to a small two-bedroom cottage that had once been a stable but that the Salts had converted into a small rental property that they offered to tourists for a week at a time.

"I don't—" It was coming at her so fast. "Are you sure?"

"Sweetheart, you need family near you. We're family now, too."

Family.

A home. A real house with real parents and supper on the table every night and the kind of security that she'd never known, but for which she'd so envied Jacob.

It was like a gift.

"And we want our grandchild nearby, even before he's born. It—it will make it seem like a little bit of Jacob is there with us."

And there it was. The guilt.

She had to tell them. They had to know.

But oh, dear God, how she wanted that life. That cocoon. That safety net as this baby grew inside her.

She didn't know what to say, and so she didn't say anything, and

Celeste's smile was so gently maternal that Ginny almost cried.

"Don't answer just yet," Celeste said, then reached forward to press her soft hands to either side of Ginny's face. "You just think about it, okay? And talk to Marisol. And I'll talk to Marisol, too, if that's okay with you."

Ginny nodded, a little awed, a little amazed. And still a whole lot guilty.

"Whatever you decide, you know we'll be there for you. You're family now, sweetheart." Celeste stood, then bent down and kissed Ginny on her cheek, just like her mother might have done once upon a time.

And though it was hard, she managed to hold it together until Celeste left the room. But once the door clicked closed behind her, the tears began to flow.

* * * *

"You on a stakeout, son? Because I wouldn't have pulled that Guinness for you if I'd known you were still on duty."

Dillon took another sip of the stout in question, then turned away from the window and faced his father across the bustling bar. "Just keeping an eye out for someone. I was hoping to have a word."

Aiden Murphy, Dillon's father, narrowed his eyes as he pulled a pint for Zeke Johnson, a local rancher who also happened to be the mayor of this fine town—and a regular at the bar. Him and a lot of other folk. There was no disputing that Murphy's Pub was the most popular watering hole in town, with its fine mix of Ireland and the Lone Star State. And that wasn't just family prejudice talking.

The main room had the look of an Irish pub but boasted a selection of beers to make any Texas cowboy happy. Not to mention a wine list filled with offerings from local Texas wineries—and the less interesting California and French selections, just to round things out. And, of course, all the various hard liquors were well represented. High-end liquors that also included local offerings like Tito's Vodka, Balcones Single Malt Whisky, Dulce Vida Añejo tequila, and Deep Eddy Ruby Red vodka, to name just a few.

There were peanut shells on the floor of the back room and enough space for two-stepping on a Friday night. The back room boasted its own entrance, too. And on unfortunately rare occasions, someone like Lyle Lovett or Willie Nelson might drop in and be persuaded to sing a song or two.

"A word," Aiden repeated thoughtfully. "Would this be with a suspect in one of your many cases or with a person of the female persuasion?"

"You stick to pouring drinks. I'll stick to what I do."

Aiden chuckled but didn't argue. He passed Zeke the pint, then went back to stacking the tray of freshly washed glasses.

Dillon watched his father fondly for a moment—the old man was in his element, that was for sure. Then he let his gaze track over this bar that had been practically a third living room for him growing up. Right now, early on a Monday evening, nothing that interesting was going on inside the bar. And that was fine with Dillon. He was all about what was going on out there on the street. He kicked his booted feet out, tilted back his hat, and continued to look out the window.

Half a pint later, he saw her.

It hadn't taken him any time at all to realize that Joanne was a creature of routine. The Sheriff's Department was housed in the courthouse that sat smack-dab in the middle of the town square. The annex—which the Sheriff's Department shared with the local police—was on Pecan, right across from Pushing Up Daisies. All of which meant that Dillon spent a lot of time near Joanne's workplace.

Joanne parked in one of the city lots just off the square, and she daily made the walk north on Main Street, then left on Cedar—and that path put her in view of the annex, and sent her right past both the courthouse and Murphy's Pub.

Dillon hadn't needed to stalk her. All he'd needed in order to know her routine was to not be blind or stupid.

Since he was neither, he'd known that she'd be coming along soon enough.

And now that she was here, he intended to have a word.

He waited until she passed the doors of the bar, then said his good-byes to Aiden and Zeke before stepping onto the sidewalk himself and falling into a rhythm behind her.

She wore a cotton blouse and a pale green skirt that moved around her lovely legs and clung enticingly to her rear. He wanted to hold her—hell, he wanted to protect her.

And it pissed him off that not only did he not have that right, but that the man who did didn't deserve her. Didn't even come close.

Hell, the only thing Hector Alvarez deserved was a long stint in a cold cell.

She reached her car—an Oldsmobile so old he knew it didn't have airbags—and shoved her key in the lock. She was pulling open the door when he said, slowly and gently, "Joanne."

She jumped, spinning toward him, her hand going to her throat, as she cringed back against the frame of the car.

Dillon forced himself not to clench his hands into fists—but goddammit, he wanted to. Yeah, she should have been paying more attention to her surroundings, but this was a woman who was too jumpy by half.

"Dillon! You about scared the life out of me." The sweetest red blush started to creep up her neck, and although Dillon longed to believe that was a result of her proximity to him, he had to admit that it could be plain, old-fashioned embarrassment.

"I'm sorry—I am. But a woman alone should pay more attention to her surroundings."

Her smile flickered like the sun peeking out from the clouds. "It's Storm, Sheriff. And it's hours before the sun goes down. If I'm not safe right now, then you must not be doing your job right."

He had to laugh. "Well, you've got a point there."

"Besides, I promise you that I'm very aware of my surroundings."

"Are you?"

The bloom in her cheeks deepened. "For instance, just yesterday I was aware of you standing across the street from the shop, just looking at the windows. Or were you looking at me?"

Was she flirting? Or was she pissed? It was probably a testament to how long it had been since he'd been on a date that he couldn't tell the difference. But why date when there was only one woman he was interested in, and she was standing right in front of him?

He took a step toward her, wanting her to understand how he felt even though he couldn't tell her. Couldn't cross that line. And yet she needed to know that she had a safety net. People who cared about her. Who loved her.

And that if she would just walk away from Hector once and for all, she *would* survive.

"You," he answered simply. "I was looking at you."

"Oh." She licked her lips. "Why?"

Oh Christ. He felt his skin heat. His hands go clammy. He took another step toward her and saw the way that she nervously bit her lower lip. "You know why." A beat, then another, but he couldn't say it. Not so boldly. Not yet. Instead he said, "I worry about you."

Her smile was tremulous, and she didn't meet his eyes.

He wanted to yell. He wanted to curse. Instead he spoke softly and gently, just the way he would with any victim. "Joanne, sugar, I need to know. Does he hit you?"

She looked at her hands. And she picked at her cuticles.

"Joanne."

When she looked up, her eyes were defiant, and her lips were pressed tight together. She angrily held his gaze for a moment, then shifted to look at something over his shoulder.

"Joanne. Does he hit you?"

"Why are you doing this?"

Her voice was so soft he almost couldn't hear her.

Tenderly, he took her chin in his hands and turned her head so that she had no choice but to look at him. "Because it kills me to think that he's hurting you."

"He's my husband," she said, the word seeming vile on her lips.

"That's not what I asked."

She shook her head, and the single tear that trickled down her cheek was answer enough for Dillon.

"He's my husband," she repeated, and her next words cut him to the core. "And I love him."

Chapter Nine

The Morenos lived only a few blocks off of Main Street in a small, blue-trimmed bungalow. The house had a tin roof and a wooden porch that boasted two rocking chairs that Ginny and Marisol had refinished together the summer before Ginny left for college.

Honestly, Ginny couldn't wait to see it. The porch, the tiny kitchen, and the bedroom she'd painted pink in a fit of middle school insanity, and then never bothered to repaint.

Soon, she thought as Nurse Francine pushed her in the wheelchair to the small receiving area for the hospital, where Marisol waited by the car, ready to take her home.

"I can walk, you know."

"Two things about that," Francine said. "Rules, and I'm a stickler for rules. And even more, there are only so many times in life when people pamper you. Being rolled out of a hospital is one of them. Sit back and enjoy it."

Ginny grinned. She liked Francine. The nurse was probably in her fifties, but she had a youth to her that made her seem younger. More than that, she really cared about her patients, and Ginny had been so appreciative of the times Francine would come into her room just to chat and check on her, even after Ginny had left the ICU and Francine wasn't officially assigned to her anymore. "Thanks for everything."

"You're going to be just fine, honey," Francine said as they moved out through the automatic doors to where Marisol stood, practically vibrating with emotion.

"Oh, sweetheart!" She helped Ginny out of the wheelchair, then hugged her so tightly that Ginny had to hold her breath. "Let's get you home."

"Good-bye, sugar. Don't be coming back until that baby's ready, okay?"

Ginny grinned. "Deal."

Marisol bustled her into the car, then actually leaned over and checked Ginny's seatbelt. Normally, Ginny would have rolled her eyes and slapped her hand away. Today, she put up with it. She knew that Marisol was a little freaked.

And the truth was that Ginny was about to freak her out a little bit more.

Once they were in the car, Marisol headed down Main Street toward her bakery, Cuppa Joe, and the square. "Can we stop?"

"At the shop? I just came from there, and although I need to get back pretty soon, I'd rather not make folks think we're open right now."

"You're closed? What about Lacey?"

Marisol turned sad eyes to her. "I gave her the week off, honey. If she's at work, everyone's going to just come in to give her condolences. She'll have to think about it—remember it—all the more."

Ginny nodded, feeling stupid, because of course Lacey would be beat up, too. Jacob was her brother, and she was probably feeling as numb as Ginny was.

"I wasn't actually talking about the shop. I wanted to go to the square."

Marisol's brows lifted.

"Just for a minute. We used to—you know—hang out there." Now that she was saying it out loud, she felt stupid. But she and Jacob used to bring blankets and homework and spread out under Storm Oak, the massive five-hundred-year-old oak tree. Or they'd hang out on the gazebo and watch the tourists and locals go in and out of the shops. They'd had all their best conversations there, and maybe it was sentimental and strange, but Ginny was sure that if she went, she'd feel Jacob.

And then maybe she could decide what she should do. If she should keep her secret. If she should move in with Celeste. If it made her a horrible person because she so desperately wanted to just hold the baby—hold Jacob—tight and pretend like Senator Rush never even existed.

More than that, she wanted to talk to Marisol on neutral territory.

For a second, she thought that Marisol would argue. She'd say she needed to get to work. That she wished she didn't have to, but that they needed the money and she couldn't afford to keep the shop closed over the lunch hour, which meant she had to be back and behind the counter in just over ninety minutes.

But her sister surprised her. She gave a quick nod, then pulled into one of the fifteen-minute slots. "We can't stay long," she said, and Ginny could hear the apology in her voice.

"That's okay. Come with me to the gazebo?"

From where they'd parked, they couldn't see the structure, hidden as it was on the other side of the courthouse. But as they walked toward the ancient oak, past the courthouse on their left, it came into view. They turned to the left, then strolled over the well-tended lawn. The sun shone down on them, making the gazebo's white paint gleam and the courthouse sparkle just a bit from the granite that made up most of its facade.

"Celeste came to see me," Ginny said as they walked.

"Of course she did. She misses Jacob, but she's always adored you, and I know she's happy that you're safe. And there's the baby, of course."

"That's mostly why she came." She chewed on her lower lip as they climbed up the gazebo steps, then sat in the shade that did little to fight the Texas heat that would only get worse as summer progressed. "She asked if I wanted to move in with her."

"Oh."

Ginny tried to read Marisol's tone and face, but couldn't quite manage it.

"She said I'd have a room and the baby'd have a nursery, and they wanted to be close to their grandson. She said that we're family now." Ginny didn't look straight at her sister. She was simmering in a stew of guilt, and not just about claiming the baby was Jacob's, but now making it seem like poor Marisol hadn't been family enough.

"Marisol—"

Her sister turned to her with a big smile that looked a little too forced. "Honey, no. It's okay. She's right. We *are* all family now. I think it's sweet of them to suggest it." She rubbed her palms down her jeans, a sure sign that she was uncomfortable. "What are you going to do?"

"I don't know. I—I wanted to know what you thought."

For a second, she thought Marisol would really talk to her. That she'd give her the kind of advice that their mother might have shared. But then Marisol just smiled again and hugged her tight and said, "Baby, whatever you decide, you know that I'm there for you."

Ginny looked down at the whitewashed planks under her feet. "You don't think I should?" Was that good? Did that lessen the lie if she didn't move in with them?

Marisol stood up. "I'm sorry, but I have to get back to the shop."

Ginny grabbed her sister's hand and held her in place. "Marisol— come on. Talk to me."

Her sister tugged her hand away, then shoved both into the back pockets of her jeans as she studied one of the gazebo's posts. "I'll just miss you if you go," she said.

And while Ginny knew that was true—and that she'd miss Marisol, too—she still didn't know what to do.

* * * *

Marisol squirted some Windex on the glass case inside Cuppa Joe and started to shine the glass. As she did, she caught Mallory's reflection, hovering somewhere over the pumpkin spice cupcakes. "There's still a little coffee in the pot, Mallory, if you want it. But drink up because once I'm finished doing this and tomorrow's prep work, I'm out of here."

"Thanks for letting me hang, Ms. Moreno."

"Marisol, and you're welcome." She glanced at the case, saw that an even dozen assorted cupcakes were left over to end the day. And she knew just how tight money was at the Alvarez house. "You want to do me a favor and take eight of these home with you? If I take them all, we'll just eat them, and trust me when I say that my family gets more than enough in the way of cupcakes and muffins."

"Really?"

"Come pick your flavors." She put together a pastry box, lined it with tissue, and gestured for Mallory to go behind the counter and help herself.

"Okay. That's really awesome of you. Thanks."

"You're very welcome." She'd already locked the door, and was surprised to hear a tap on the glass. Cuppa Joe was popular, but people rarely demanded entrance.

She headed that way and opened the blinds, then hurried to

unlock the door when she saw who it was—Celeste Salt.

"Celeste. Come in." She ushered her inside, and the two women hugged, and Marisol was struck by how easy it was to bond over shared grief. She'd known Celeste forever, of course, but it had been Ginny and Jacob who were tight. The rest of the family members had drifted along casually.

Until now.

"Is something wrong?"

"No, no. Am I interrupting?"

Marisol shook her head. "I'm just cleaning. I close the shop at five on Tuesdays. The crowds thin out during the evenings until the weekend."

"Of course," said Celeste, though it was clear she couldn't care less. "I was just—well, I wanted to talk to you about something."

Marisol froze because she knew what was coming. But she pretended she didn't. "Sure," she said brightly. "Of course. Do you want coffee?"

"No, no." She pointed to a table. "Can we sit?"

"Oh. Sure. Yeah." They each took a chair at a small round table, and Celeste clasped her hands together.

"Well." She cleared her throat. "I suppose I should just dive right in," she said with a small laugh. "You see, Travis and I would like Ginny to move into our home."

"Oh. I see." Marisol licked her lips, not sure why she was pretending like Ginny hadn't already told her. Maybe she wanted to hear it from Celeste. The what and the why of it. Maybe if Celeste wanted to take away Marisol's little sister, then Marisol wanted to hear all of it straight from Celeste.

She wasn't sure, but she said nothing else as Celeste continued, talking about having someone at home to take care of Ginny during the pregnancy, about Jacob and wanting to feel close to him, about being part of the family now and the baby having a nursery and how Celeste had already talked to Ginny but feared that Ginny didn't want to hurt Marisol. And on and on and on until Marisol was just sitting there feeling numb.

"I've overwhelmed you."

"No. No."

"I've angered you."

"No! Really. I'm just—" What? What was she?

She blinked, then grappled for something to say. "What about Lacey? Won't it be strange having Jacob's best friend in the house?"

Celeste sat back. "Well, this has all been hard on her, of course. But she's my steady one. And the truth is that she's always felt like she was part of your family—you've always been so sweet to her that I know she thinks of you as a big sister."

"Really? She's a great kid."

"She is," Celeste agreed. "And she adores Ginny."

"She wouldn't resent her? Or the baby? Lacey is going to need you and Travis and Sara Jane now more than ever."

"I promise you there's no resentment. And Travis and I have enough love to go around. Lacey's always been such an adult. You know. Responsible. Smart." She nodded firmly, almost as if she was sealing a bargain—or maybe convincing herself. "This is a good decision, for the entire family. And you, Marisol, are part of our family too now."

Marisol drew in a long, slow breath, trying to process it all. Everything Celeste said about Lacey was true. Goodness knew Marisol had known the girl for years, both through Jacob and from the part-time work she did at Cuppa Joe. And although Marisol had always feared that Lacey Salt was the kind of girl who might go a little wild when given the chance—like when she finally went away for college—Marisol knew that maybe she was just projecting her own life onto the seventeen-year-old. Because Marisol had never had the chance to go wild, and there were times when, in her fantasies, she pretended that she hadn't shouldered the world. That she'd shrugged instead and let the responsibilities roll off her.

But she hadn't. She'd survived—hell, she'd thrived. And Lacey would too.

Still, as hard as Marisol had worked, it had never been enough for her shattered family. Wasn't the fact that Celeste was sitting there now proof of that? She felt her throat thicken and cursed, because she'd done enough crying over the last few days to last a lifetime. "I've tried so hard to give Ginny and Luis everything, but I can't give them what you're offering." She felt the tears sting her eyes. "And I know I should be grateful to you and Travis—I do. But at the same time, I just can't help but feel like I failed."

She blinked hard, determined not to cry.

"Oh, Marisol, no." Celeste was on her feet and pulling Marisol up from her chair in an instant, her arms going tight around Marisol. "I told you—we're family now, too. And as family, I think I'm allowed to say that you've done an amazing job with both the kids. Carried a terrible burden. And now it's time to let someone else help shoulder the load."

And that was all it took. The tears flowed like a faucet. And for the first time in a long time, Marisol felt like a child again, being held in the arms of her mother.

"I'll talk to her," Marisol said when the tears slowed enough that she could speak. "It's up to Ginny, but I'll tell her that I don't mind. And that I think it's probably even a good idea."

"Do you?" Celeste pulled away, her brow furrowing as she looked Marisol over.

"I'll miss having her at home, but now it's not just about Ginny. It's about the baby, too. So yeah. I do." She reached out and took Celeste's hand and squeezed hard. "Jacob adored you and Travis, you know. I guess—well, I guess now I see why."

It wasn't until after Celeste left that Marisol remembered Mallory. She flipped the lock on the door and turned back to the counter to see the girl sheepishly rising.

"I didn't know what to do. It was all so serious, and I didn't want to interrupt. I'm sorry I heard everything." She licked her lips. "I didn't know Ginny was pregnant. Luis didn't say."

"Don't blame him. I asked him not to. Not until Ginny was ready."

Mallory nodded. "I get that." She hooked a thumb toward the door. "I should go," she said.

"Probably should."

She came out from around the counter, the box of cupcakes in her hand. "Um, Marisol? Are you okay?"

"Sure. I'm fine." Marisol forced a smile and tried again. "I'm just fine," she repeated, and wondered if she said it often enough if it would somehow, someway, turn out to be true.

* * * *

"Mom!"

Joanne jumped, startled out of her thoughts. Which, frankly, was a good thing, as she'd been thinking about Dillon since he'd approached her yesterday. And thinking about Dillon was a dangerous thing.

She put the iron down and leaned sideways so that she could see Dakota as she burst through the front door. "In here!" she called from where she had the portable ironing board set up on top of the kitchen table. She'd told Hector she would be done with all the laundry by the time he got home. He hated it when the kitchen wasn't tidy and her housework was scattered everywhere.

But today was hard, as she'd ended up staying at work past closing just to help get all the orders organized and ready for the funeral in two days. She'd been happy to help, but now she was running behind.

"Look!" Dakota demanded, indicating a nasty brown blob on a white linen shirt.

"Oh, sweetie. What happened?"

Her oldest daughter frowned, even as Mallory trotted in from the living area where she'd been playing some very loud video game on the system that Jeffry Rush had lent her. Joanne hated that they couldn't afford to get Mallory a system of her own, but at least she had a good circle of friends.

"What's going on?" Mallory asked.

"You, take over this," Joanne said, handing Mallory the iron. She pointed to Dakota. "You, take off the shirt."

It would be close, she knew. Mallory wasn't nearly as fast or as good at ironing, but Joanne wasn't going to turn Dakota away, especially when the girl so rarely came to her for help, preferring to curl up at Hector's feet. She'd always been a Daddy's girl, and that was fine. But sometimes Joanne felt invisible around her daughter.

Dakota stripped, not the least bit self-conscious. Not that she should be. As a mother, Joanne was proud of how lovely her daughter had turned out. And, as a mother, she often wished that Dakota would keep some of that loveliness hidden beneath more modest clothes.

Today she was reasonably modest, having obviously come straight from the bank.

"So why'd you spill?" Mallory asked as Joanne went to the small laundry closet to find some stain remover. "Just clumsy or did you freak when you heard the news?"

"What news?" Dakota pulled out one of the chairs and sprawled at the kitchen table. Joanne pushed aside a pile of clothes waiting to be ironed and went to work on the shirt.

"Ginny Moreno is pregnant. And it's Jacob's baby."

If Joanne hadn't been looking, she might have missed the quick, horrified expression that crossed Dakota's face. It was gone in an instant as the girl gathered herself, and Joanne supposed that she really shouldn't be surprised. Dakota and Jacob had gone out a few times in high school, and though her daughter never talked about boys with Joanne, it had been easy to see that Dakota had been head-over-heels for the boy. So much so that Joanne couldn't help but wonder if his move to Austin and UT hadn't been the driving force behind Dakota's semi-regular diatribes about how she was going to get out of Storm and find a better job in the capital city.

But whenever Joanne had seen them together, Jacob had always seemed polite and sweet to Dakota, but he'd never given Joanne the impression of a man desperately in love.

"That's bullshit," Dakota said. "They're buddies. Ginny Moreno is like Jacob's best guy friend."

"Yeah? Well, you're an idiot, then, because she's knocked up."

"*Mallory*," Joanne snapped. "Don't speak that way to your sister."

Mallory grimaced. "Sorry. But Dakota's being a twit. They were always together. I mean, it's not hard to do the math."

"No fucking way," Dakota said, grabbing one of Hector's shirts from the pile of ironed laundry and shoving her arms through the sleeves. "I'm never going to believe those two screwed."

"Were you raised in a barn? Watch your language, Dakota Alvarez."

"Believe what you want. It's all true. Ginny's even going to move into the Salts' house."

Dakota opened her mouth, then closed it again. And though Joanne may have been mistaken, she thought she saw her daughter's eyes glisten with tears before she leapt to her feet and turned away, ostensibly to stare into the refrigerator.

"If you're not getting something out, shut the door," Joanne said automatically.

A few moments passed, and then Dakota pulled out a Diet Coke and one of the cupcakes Mallory had brought home.

She popped the top, then sat back down. "It's not true," she said defiantly.

Mallory shrugged. "Whatever. But I was in Cuppa Joe when Marisol was talking about it to Celeste, and I think Celeste would know."

"God, Mal. You can be such a little bitch. Why don't you just take your—*Daddy!*"

Dakota jumped up and Joanne flinched as Hector burst through the screen door behind Joanne. He hugged his daughter, then shot his wife an irritated look even as Mallory put down the iron and slid quietly back into the living room to turn off Assassins Gone Wild or Bloody Zombie Mania or whatever game she'd been playing in there.

"Christ, Jo." He held one arm around Dakota's shoulders, and Joanne was suddenly remarkably, fully, completely happy that her daughter had come by. Right then, she needed the buffer. "I work a long day and have to come home to this shit?"

He was standing a few feet away, but she could smell the oil and gasoline on his coverall. Along with the beer.

"Sorry. I was helping Dakota."

"Honest, Daddy. I got her all off schedule."

"Well, then I guess we'll have to let this one slide." He bent to kiss Dakota's upraised cheek, looking entirely like the loving father and strong, sexy husband that she wanted...and worked so hard to have.

But he's not. And people are starting to see that.

Flustered, she untied her apron, then started to refold the already folded laundry.

People like Dillon.

"Mallory!" She forced herself to focus on the house. On getting tidy. On getting dinner.

Dinner.

It was her ticket out of this house. This moment.

"Yes, Mom?"

"Clear the table and start cutting up some potatoes to boil."

"What's for dinner?" Hector said.

"A surprise." She kissed him on the cheek. "But I forgot one thing. I need to run to H-E-B, and then I'll be right back."

She took advantage of the fact that he wouldn't lose his temper now, not with Dakota clinging to him. She grabbed her purse and her keys and ran the opposite direction out the front door, just so she wouldn't have to squeeze past her husband to get out the back.

That meant she had to walk all the way around to get to her car in the driveway, but that was okay. And even though she saw him standing in the doorway looking curious and a little steamed, she didn't stop. She just got in the car, backed it out, and drove and drove and drove until she was all the way to the outskirts of town.

Christ, she wasn't even sure where she was going or what she was doing.

She had to hit H-E-B on the way home, that was for sure. But other than that...other than that she was a mess.

She tasted salt and realized that she was crying.

And then she realized that she was just a few blocks from Dillon's house.

No, no, no.

What was she thinking? What was she doing?

She slammed on the brakes, then just sat in the road, her hands tight on the steering wheel.

And then she breathed in and out and told herself she was a fool and that she needed to get to the grocery store.

Somehow, though, instead of ending up at H-E-B, her car ended up outside the big Grossman house. One of the larger mansions on the outskirts of town, it had been bought and paid for back when her dad had raked in some serious money doing contingency work as one of Central Texas's leading plaintiff's attorneys.

Finances had gotten tighter, sure, but the Grossmans were still among the town's elite.

Joanne, however, was no longer part of the clan.

She sat on the road in her shabby Oldsmobile and thought about everything she'd given up and the man she'd given it up for. He loved her. She knew it. He just had a temper. And she just always seemed to be triggering it. But if she could just do better...

She needed to be more understanding. More helpful. More calming.

With a sigh, she started to put the car back into gear. But the door opened, and she saw her mother, Debbie, hurrying down the sidewalk toward her, looking perfectly coiffed despite probably spending the entire day inside.

"Sweetheart," she said once she'd hurried across the street and Joanne had rolled down the window. "What are you doing here?" She kept her voice a whisper. As if Robert Grossman could hear every little thing said in his corner of the world. "Is everything okay?"

"Sure, Mom. Everything's great. I was just—I don't know. Melancholy, I guess."

"Do you want me to meet you somewhere?"

Joanne pressed her lips together and shook her head. She wanted to go in and sit at the table she'd sat at so often as a child. But she wasn't welcome inside anymore.

"So, can I ask—I mean, Daddy did some bad stuff, right? I mean, he hurt you. A lot. When he walked away from me, I mean. And with him ignoring my kids. Pretending like none of us exist."

Deborah nodded slowly, a little hesitantly. "He did. He hurt me a lot. He hurt both of us."

Joanne licked her lips. "But you're still with him."

"Well, I love him. I love you, too, baby. That's why I still see you, even though I know it would make your father angry."

"But he was wrong. He just shut me out, and that was horrible."

Her mother sighed, her eyes full of torment. "What he did was wrong, but I understand why he did it. Joanne, if this is about Hector..." She trailed off with a shake of her head. "We both know he drinks too much. And you can say what you want, baby, but you were never a clumsy girl."

"He loves me, Mom. And he's never hurt me. Not really."

But her protests were no use. She could see in her eyes that Deborah didn't believe her.

Worse, Joanne was starting to wonder if she even believed it herself.

Chapter Ten

Ginny stood by the brass plaque that designated the magnificent Rush Mansion as a National Historic Registry home and wondered what the hell she'd been thinking.

At the time, it had seemed perfectly reasonable to tell Marisol that she'd go pick up Luis from Jeffry's house. Even though Jeffry's house also happened to be Senator Rush's house. In Ginny's apparently pregnancy-addled brain, she'd thought that because she was so totally over him that it wouldn't be completely insane to be in his house. To possibly bump into him.

Stupid, stupid, stupid, and she blamed her raging idiocy on her hormones. She didn't want to see him. She didn't want to talk to him.

And what the hell would she say if he asked about the baby?

She told herself to calm down. He wouldn't say anything. For that matter, no one was saying anything.

If people knew she was pregnant—which they must, because this was Storm and it was like gossip central—they were keeping quiet. At least around her.

Frankly, she was glad. And she figured that was about the only perk of being in the accident, too. So long as she still had the bandage on her cheek and forearm, she was probably safe from the gossip mill.

And goodness knew the senator would keep quiet, too.

"Miss Ginny!" Carmen, the Rush's housekeeper, opened the door and ushered her inside. "I am so glad to see you looking so well." Carmen had moved to Storm from Laredo when Jeffry was a baby, and so Ginny had known her almost her whole life, as she'd been in the park with Jeffry whenever Ginny was there with Luis.

"Thanks, Carmen," she said, stepping inside and accepting the matronly woman's bone-crushing hug. "I'm supposed to fetch Luis home. Marisol went all out with the cooking."

"Well, good for her. She's got a knack for pastries, I must say."

"She's good with a steak, too. And she splurged on ribeyes."

"Well, then we do need to get you home. Come on. Come on."

Ginny knew the house well. Brittany Rush was one of her closest friends, and she'd been in the Rush house hundreds of times. Being here now gave her a little pang because usually Jacob was with them. She wished that Brit were back from Austin, but her parents had made her stay at school to finish out finals. Brit had been pissed as hell, and they'd cried on the phone together, but in the end, Sebastian and Payton had won out.

Ginny understood that Brit couldn't toss aside a full year of college—really she did—but she longed to have her friend by her side. Especially now. In this house. *His* house.

With a sigh, she followed Carmen through the foyer with its vaulted ceiling and dark colors, past the living room, and then into the massive game room filled with everything from old-fashioned freestanding video games to an electronic descending screen for the massive projection entertainment center now displaying a wild car chase.

Jeffry looked up from the game controls, then nudged Luis. On screen, Luis's Ferrari spun out of control and crashed into a concrete barrier. "Hey! Oh—Ginny. We gotta go?"

"Sorry."

Luis stood up and shrugged. "It's okay."

Ginny almost smiled. Despite everything, it amused her how conciliatory her little brother was to her lately. And all she'd had to do was lose her best friend and have her life turned upside down.

Stop it.

They followed Jeffry back toward the front door, and as they were walking, Senator Rush stepped out of his office, calling for Carmen. "Oh—Jeffry. I didn't realize you had company."

"Ginny just came to pick up Luis."

The senator inclined his head. "Ginny. I'm so glad to see you're looking well after your accident. Horrible tragedy. Horrible."

"Yes, sir," she said, managing to unclench her jaw. The man wasn't even looking her in the eye. He was looking at a spot just over her ear. And he had that fake politician expression of concern.

Asshole.

"My wife will be sorry she missed you." Was it her imagination, or had he overemphasized the word *wife*? "She was asking your brother earlier how you were doing."

"Please tell Mrs. Rush I'm doing pretty good, all things considered." She forced a pleasant smile. "Luis, we really should get home. Marisol's waiting."

Senator Rush didn't even say good-bye. He just turned back the way he'd come and disappeared into his office.

Only when they were in the car did Ginny breathe regularly.

"You okay?"

"He just makes me nervous. Senator Fancy Pants."

"Yeah," Luis said. "You and Jeffry both."

"Really? Jeffry's scared of his dad?"

"Scared? I dunno. Intimidated, I guess. Not much of a dad, you know." He dragged his fingers through his curly black hair. "I think about Mom and Dad sometimes when I'm over there with the senator and Mrs. Rush. I mean, I miss them so much. And I think they would have been awesome parents. Not intimidating like your Senator Fancy Pants."

"He's not my senator," Ginny said firmly as she started the car.

And he wasn't going to be her baby's either.

* * * *

Dillon approached it like a case.

Joanne was a victim.

He was the investigating officer.

And goddammit, he was going to investigate, which he did with gusto.

He went first to talk to Joanne's sister, and he stood like a true Texan in the barn while Hannah performed a well-check on a pregnant cow out at Zeke's ranch. That, frankly, was a first for him.

"Look, Sheriff, I know the score and so do you. But neither one of us has proof, and Joanne's not going to be any help there. And I get that. I've read the articles about women in abusive relationships. But I don't know what to do. How to help her. I mean, I thank God she's never had a broken bone—but I'm certain he slaps her around, and I know he treats her like his little wife-bitch. Sorry. It just pisses me off."

"It pisses me off, too."

She stepped away from the cow, her boots making a sucking noise as she moved through the muck. She wiped her palms on her jeans. "Honestly, I feel as useless as I do when I've got an animal I have to put down. I want to help, but I don't know how."

Dillon nodded. "Be there for her. Pay attention. And keep a record of what you see. And you tell me. If you see him raise a hand to her, you tell me."

He was certain she would. Hannah Grossman loved her sister, but like so many family members of abuse victims, she didn't want to believe it was really happening, and if she did believe, she wasn't sure what to do about it.

Dillon believed.

Dillon knew.

And whether she wanted him to or not, Dillon was going to help Joanne.

He got back in his cruiser and left the ranch, speeding down the winding county road with the oaks and barbed wire lining the path, and cows and goats and horses grazing on the green summer grass that would turn brown in the Texas heat soon enough.

He told himself he was doing the right thing. That he had an obligation to help. He wasn't sticking his nose in where it didn't belong. He was the law, goddamn it. And just because he didn't have the kind of evidence to take to court didn't mean he didn't know that the evidence was out there. Know that he had to somehow, someway, convince Joanne to talk to him.

As soon as he hit the town proper, he slowed down, maneuvering through the streets lined with houses accented by lovely, shaded lawns. He headed farther north until he reached the area just outside of old town. Here, the houses had just as much potential as those within the tourist circle, but most of the owners had neither the time nor the money to fulfill the hidden potential.

He ended up on Houston Street, then slowed as he approached the Alvarez house. Tidy, but rundown. A lot of the fading beauty of that house could easily be fixed if Hector Alvarez got off his ass and did some work instead of guzzling beer at Murphy's Pub and then heading home to guzzle some more.

He parked the cruiser, then got out and started walking up the sidewalk toward the front door, but the sound of voices from the back caused him to shift direction. He cut across the lawn, then started up the crepe myrtle-lined driveway.

"I'm sorry, Hector. I guess I opened my door too fast. I didn't mean to—"

"Dammit, Jo!" They were standing between Joanne's piece of shit Oldsmobile and Hector's polished and babied—and now scratched—Buick. As Dillon approached, Hector lashed out, slapping Joanne hard across her cheek even as Dillon shouted for him to stop.

"It's all good, Sheriff," Hector said, stepping back and raising his hands in supplication as Dillon pulled his weapon and kept it on Hector.

Joanne had buried her face in her hands. She was looking at the ground. Not at him. Not at Hector.

Her shoulders were shaking, and right then Dillon wanted two things. To comfort her. And to blow the head off the fuckwad standing in front of him.

Right then, he couldn't do either.

"Hands behind your head, asshole."

"Sure thing, Sheriff." Hector moved slowly, all polite sugar now. "This here's just a misunderstanding."

"Misunderstanding? I don't think so. I think it's assault. And I'm pretty sure that hospital records are going to show a pattern. You're a good-looking man, Hector. I think you'll be very popular in prison."

Hector didn't say a word, but Dillon saw both fear and hate in the other man's eyes.

"Please." That one soft word came from Joanne. "Please, Sheriff. Just leave it be. Please."

Shit.

"Joanne. This has to stop."

She lifted her head, finally looking at him. "It's not what you think. And it's not your business. It's not."

"The hell it's not. I'm the sheriff here," he said, even though what he wanted to say was that he loved her. That when Hector hit her, he'd felt it as violently as a blow to his gut. But that wasn't the point. Or maybe it was, but he knew enough not to tell her that. Not yet.

"You can't arrest him, Sheriff. You just can't." Her pretty face was flustered. Maybe a little bit scared. But because of him or Hector, Dillon wasn't sure.

Dillon shifted his weight from one foot to the other as he

considered his options. He ought to cuff Hector. Take him to the courthouse and toss him in jail. But Joanne was so fragile he feared she'd shrivel up when the gossip started to flow.

That option was risky, too. He'd seen Hector hit her, and hospital records should prove a pattern of abuse. But in truth he wasn't as confident of the outcome as he'd pretended just now. Dillon had no control over the jury, the sentence, or the term of incarceration. Hector could end up on probation, and wouldn't that be a pisser?

If Dillon walked away right now with a warning, Hector would rein himself in for a day or two, but after that the gloves would come off again. That's the way it was with serial abusers. And next time it would be more than a slap on the face or a sprained wrist.

That meant Dillon needed to go with door number three. Joanne wouldn't like it, but she didn't have to know. And the truth was, it was Dillon's job to protect the people in his jurisdiction. Even if they didn't want protecting.

And even if his methods crossed over into the gray side of the law.

Chapter Eleven

It rained on the day of Jacob Salt's funeral. The kind of wild Texas thunderstorm where the clouds roll in like gray balls of cotton pushed across the sky by an angry wind. The trees swayed. Old newspapers blew across streets. The sky turned eerily green, and once the rain began to fall, a curtain of steam rose from the sunbaked asphalt.

Inside the Lutheran Church, there was a different kind of storm. An emotional battering as Pastor Douglas spoke to the packed pews about the destruction of youth and the shattering of dreams. "Jacob Salt lived a full life in the time that he had. He had family and friends who he loved. He was a calming presence in the center of a town that has seen its share of storms. And while we mourn his passing, we are grateful for the time that he had, and our lives are enriched in having known him. We go forth knowing that he is with us, a piece of Jacob goes on in memories, in family, in love."

Pastor Douglas looked at Ginny as he spoke the last, and she met his eyes, calmly accepting the truth of his words. She and Marisol had decided that they would remain quiet about the pregnancy for at least a few more weeks, but that didn't change the fact that most everyone in Storm already knew. By the time they were willing to talk about it openly, they probably wouldn't have to tell anyone.

As the pastor wrapped up the service, telling the mourners that Jacob's parents would be going across the street to the square to scatter Jacob's ashes under the Storm Oak that he loved so much, Ginny glanced around the standing-room-only crowd. Everyone from town was there. Some she'd known her whole life, and some she just recognized in passing. Surely they all had secrets, too. Lies they'd told. Quiet guilt that they held close, because to reveal it would cause an even bigger hurt.

Because it would. She was certain of it.

And, yes, she'd finally made up her mind.

Across the aisle, Ginny saw Dakota Alvarez standing near Senator Rush, and she hugged herself tight. She was so over Senator Rush it wasn't even funny. Ginny didn't care who the biological father might be; in her heart, her baby's daddy was Jacob. And that's just the way it was going to be.

Marisol and Luis were on either side of Ginny, keeping her steady. And even though Ginny wasn't even interested in looking the senator's way, she appreciated the small smile of solidarity from Jeffry Rush and his mother, Payton. Ginny's best friend, Brit, was there, too, having arrived back home in Storm less than an hour before the service began. Her eyes shone with tears, but she held Ginny's gaze for a moment, giving her silent strength.

Travis and Celeste were in the pew in front of her, clutching each other's hands in support. They were flanked by Lacey and Sara Jane, and although they'd invited Ginny to sit with them, she'd turned them down. She would be part of their family soon enough. Today she was content to look at them. At this gift of family that Jacob had left her. One more small miracle carved out of the most horrible tragedy.

The Salts started to file out of the pew and down the aisle, but Celeste paused beside Ginny, then held out her hand so Ginny could join them. They walked together out into the storm, which was miraculously letting up and had actually stopped by the time they reached Storm Oak.

Travis kept his arm around Celeste's waist, giving her his support until the rest who were joining them beneath the tree arrived. As it turned out, that was everyone.

And then, with the crowd gathered around, Travis released his wife. She kept her hand pressed against his back as he opened the bronze urn and scattered their son's ashes beneath the ancient oak tree.

"We love you, son," Travis said. "And we miss you."

It wasn't profound. It wasn't religious. It was simple and heartfelt, and not one person who'd heard those words had a dry eye.

Slowly, the crowd broke up. Some remained, huddled together to chat. Others headed on to Murphy's Pub, where the local restaurants were offering up a potluck for mourners and where Aiden Murphy was supplying free beer.

Ginny went to Celeste and Travis. "I wanted to say thank you. And—if you still want me—then I do want to move in. This is Jacob's baby as much as mine," she added, determined to make the words as true as they could be. "And we want to be with family."

"Oh, sweetheart!"

Celeste pulled her into an enthusiastic hug. And Travis's, though more subdued, was no less genuine.

"We need to get you settled." She frowned. "But we need to go to Murphy's. After?"

Ginny nodded, content to follow Celeste's lead. Travis held up his phone. "Just got a text. I need to pop into the pharmacy for about half an hour." He pulled them each close, then kissed each of their foreheads.

Then as he walked one way and they walked the other, Ginny paused and looked back at the tree. As she did, the sun peeked out from behind the remaining clouds and wide beams of sunlight burst down through the tree's thick canopy, illuminating Jacob's ashes and lighting the way to a new beginning.

Chapter Twelve

Travis Salt walked as fast as seemed prudent across Pecan Street to his store, Prost Pharmacy. The *closed* sign was still in the window, the shade on the front door pulled down. Everything was just as he'd left it when he'd closed up that morning and then made the short walk to the church to meet Celeste and the girls.

He knew Celeste had been frustrated that he'd gone to work that morning, but as the town's only pharmacist with the exception of Thom, who worked full time at the hospital, there were things he had to do.

Which was true, but also a crock of shit. He'd needed to be alone. He'd needed time to breathe.

Now, though, alone wasn't what he wanted at all.

His hand shook as he put his key in the lock. Such a simple task and he could hardly manage it. Could hardly manage his own goddamn life anymore.

Jacob was dead. His son was dead.

He felt numb. He felt lost.

Once inside, he closed the door behind him, saw that the alarm had already been disengaged, and reset it. If anyone came through that door, he damn sure wanted to know about it.

The lights were off except for the row of fluorescents he kept illuminated, so that everything was in full view through the big display window that fronted the square. Passersby could see the merchandise in the front of the store, as well as the old-fashioned soda fountain that ran parallel with the left wall.

He knew the shelves were tidy, full of everything from over-the-counter meds to basic office supplies to candy and cards.

He knew the soda fountain's red Formica bar top gleamed and the chrome trim on the bar and stools sparkled.

Today, he didn't care about any of that. Instead, he hurried to the back. To the pharmacy proper.

He lifted that hinged section of counter, walked past the cash register, then the shelves of pharmaceuticals, then past his workstation, which was hidden from customers' view.

Finally, he reached his private office, a small room with a tiny window that overlooked the pharmacy and the shop beyond. The window had blinds, and right now they were shut tight.

As a rule, he left the office locked. He tried the door, then smiled when the knob turned easily.

He pushed open the door, stepped inside, and felt the weight of the world slip away when he saw her sitting on his small sofa. Kristin Douglas stood, then walked to him, her red hair practically crackling with the force of the emotion he saw on her face and in her sad blue eyes.

"I've missed you," she whispered as she slid into his arms, and that was all it took to break him.

The sobs he'd been holding in burst free and he clung to her, his body wracked with grief. "I haven't—I couldn't—" He sputtered the words, wanting her to understand. Knowing that she already did. "I've had to be so strong. But I'm not strong. Oh, God, Kristin. How can he be gone?"

"Shh. It's okay, sweetheart. And you are strong, and the death of a child would destroy anyone. But you stayed steady. You helped them, and that's good, but let me help you now."

He nodded, clinging to her, letting the sobs fade, knowing that she was there for him. His secret strength.

Finally he pulled back, then searched her eyes. "God, but I've missed you. I need you, Kristin. You know that I need you. What would I do if I didn't have you to come to?"

He saw pleasure flicker in her eyes, shining past the grief. "You'll never have to find out," she said.

And then, because they both needed it, he drew her close, then kissed her hard, letting himself forget everything but this woman, this moment. Letting the passion between them grow wilder and more frenzied until clothes were coming off and skin was touching skin. Until he couldn't wait any longer to have her, and they both lost themselves in each other, and they left the horror and pain of the last few days far, far behind.

* * * *

Dillon wasn't surprised that Hector wasn't at Jacob Salt's funeral. More than that, he considered it a perk.

It let Dillon enjoy the luxury of watching Joanne, her eyes misty as she listened to Pastor Douglas and then, by the tree, to Travis.

But he didn't talk to her. Not today. Not when he was about to do what he was about to do.

When the crowd on the square scattered—most heading to Murphy's Pub for shared grief and beer—Dillon got back in his cruiser. No one would question his absence. As sheriff, he often missed out on town gatherings. That was part of the job, after all. Being out there in the world protecting and serving.

Right now, he intended to do a little of both.

He got in his cruiser and headed to the Alvarez house, hoping that Hector was still there. If he'd decided to come back to the square for the drinking part of the afternoon, this was going to be a very short trip.

But no, his car was still there. And he saw as he walked down the driveway to the backyard that the paint scratch that had bent Hector so out of shape had already been buffed out and polished.

And just that one small thing—that Hector obviously cared more about his Buick than his wife—added extra fire to Dillon's determination.

He moved quietly up the back steps, then entered the house, not surprised to find it unlocked. Hector wasn't the kind of man who worried. Today, he should have.

Dillon found him in the living room, and after staring at him for a second, Hector leapt to his feet.

"Get the hell out of my house, Sheriff."

"No, Hector. You're the one getting out of your house. So go pack whatever shit you can't live without, get in that car you love so much, and get the fuck out of Storm."

Hector barked out a laugh. He took a step toward Dillon. "Fuck. You."

"Fair enough," Dillon said, then hauled back and punched the asshole right in the face.

As he'd expected, Hector cried out, recovered quickly, and then delivered a return punch that rattled Dillon's skull and had him stumbling backward.

Perfect.

Dillon drew his weapon and held it on the other man. Hector had been moving forward for another blow, but now he stopped cold, his hands in the air.

"Whoa, whoa, man."

"You're leaving, Hector. You're leaving now."

Hector shook his head, then took another step toward him. Dillon cocked the revolver. He'd brought the revolver specifically because cocking the hammer had a definite psychological impact on the person at the other end of the gun's barrel. A nice little benefit you didn't get with a Glock.

"You can't shoot me. You fire your weapon, it has to be examined. Anybody who's seen a crime show knows that."

"You're more clever than I thought. But you missed two points. First, I'm the sheriff. If anyone can manage to circumvent those rules, it's me. And two, that applies to service weapons. This is from my own personal collection. My service pistol's in the gun safe at home."

Hector shook his head, and Dillon was gratified to see he looked a little nervous. He lifted a hand and rubbed his aching cheek and jaw, already swollen from Hector's bashing. "Now go," he said. "Go pack."

"You can't make me leave. Not like that."

"No? Then how about like this: I came by to ask you a few questions about some vandalism at the square." Apparently some middle school kids had gotten their hands on some spray paint. Not exactly the crime of the century, but it served Dillon's purpose well enough. "You invited me in. Following me so far, Hector?"

Hector said nothing.

"Once I was inside, you jumped me. I defended myself. You came at me again. I shot you in self-defense. You fell to the ground, then died. I tried to stop the bleeding, but it was too late. As I was helping you, I discovered a bag of heroin in your jacket pocket, which explained why you'd jumped me, as a vandalism charge didn't seem worth it. The internal investigation goes away because not only is the situation squeaky clean, but because no one bothers to look too hard. After all, you're not a popular guy, Hector. Not anymore. And what's one less asshole drug dealer in the world? We don't put up with that kind of shit in Storm."

Hector's face had turned a sickly gray. "You motherfucker."

Dillon just smiled, thin and determined. "Leave, Hector. Pack a bag. Toss it in your car. And leave. Do it in the next five minutes, and that story is just that—a story. Don't, and it becomes an unpleasant reality."

Hector left. He bitched and swore and said he loved his wife and his kids, but in the end, he loved being alive more.

He packed light, but pulled what looked to be several thousand dollars out of the very back of his bedside drawer. Dillon watched him pack—watched him like a goddamn hawk—just in case Hector had his own gun stowed away. Just in case Hector intended to use it.

But no. After five minutes, Hector was tossing his duffel in his back seat, then pulling out of the driveway.

Just to make sure, Dillon followed him out of town. And then, just to be even more sure, he followed him for another hour, all the way to San Antonio.

Dillon took his time coming home, and the sun was setting as he got back to Storm, the sky vibrant and alive with the wild colors that always illuminated the sunset after a day of storms.

He went back to the square, then sat in the gazebo. Just sat there as the sky shifted from blue to orange to a deep, deep purple.

And as night fell, Dillon stood up and walked to the courthouse and his office.

Soon it would be a new day. He damn sure hoped it would be a good one.

White Lightning

By Lexi Blake

About Lexi Blake

Lexi Blake lives in North Texas with her husband, three kids, and the laziest rescue dog in the world. She began writing at a young age, concentrating on plays and journalism. It wasn't until she started writing romance that she found success. She likes to find humor in the strangest places. Lexi believes in happy endings no matter how odd the couple, threesome or foursome may seem. She also writes contemporary Western ménage as Sophie Oak.

Connect with Lexi online:

Facebook: https://www.facebook.com/lexi.blake.39
Twitter: https://twitter.com/authorlexiblake
Website: www.LexiBlake.net

Sign up for Lexi's free newsletter at www.LexiBlake.net.

Also from Lexi Blake

Masters And Mercenaries
The Dom Who Loved Me
The Men With The Golden Cuffs
A Dom Is Forever
On Her Master's Secret Service
Sanctum: A Masters and Mercenaries Novella
Love and Let Die
Unconditional: A Masters and Mercenaries Novella
Dungeon Royale
Dungeon Games: A Masters and Mercenaries Novella
A View to a Thrill
Cherished: A Masters and Mercenaries Novella
You Only Love Twice
Luscious: Masters and Mercenaries~Topped
Adored: A Masters and Mercenaries Novella
Master No
Just One Taste: Masters and Mercenaries~Topped 2
From Sanctum with Love
Devoted: A Masters and Mercenaries Novella, Coming April 12, 2016
Dominance Never Dies, Coming June 14, 2016

Masters Of Ménage (by Shayla Black and Lexi Blake)
Their Virgin Captive
Their Virgin's Secret
Their Virgin Concubine
Their Virgin Princess
Their Virgin Hostage
Their Virgin Secretary
Their Virgin Mistress

The Perfect Gentlemen (by Shayla Black and Lexi Blake
Scandal Never Sleeps
Seduction in Session
Big Easy Temptation, Coming May 3, 2016

URBAN FANTASY

Acknowledgments from the Author

Thanks to Julie and Dee for creating this amazing world and letting me play in it. Thanks to Liz and MJ and the team at Evil Eye. As always I couldn't do anything without the support of my husband, Rich, kids and my sister from another mister, Kim.

Chapter One

Senator Sebastian Rush sighed as he shrugged out of his Charvet dress shirt and hung it neatly on the valet rack where Carmen, the very efficient maid, would pick it up and ready it for cleaning. Certainly the dry cleaner could press the shirt, but it was a thing of beauty so Sebastian respected it. JFK had worn Charvet. It was a symbol of wealth and understated power. A man who could afford a $425 dress shirt was certainly a man who could be trusted with the country's well-being. No one wanted a failure in power, after all.

The door to the bedroom opened and another symbol of power and wealth walked in. Payton. His wife. She was lovely and well spoken, able to handle fundraisers and reporters with equal ease. She was also aging well. Unfortunately, all the Botox in the world couldn't completely stop the press of time. Women didn't age like men. Men became more powerful, more confident as they moved into their prime. Women simply got old. Some people would call Payton a handsome woman, but he was more concerned with how her breasts had lost their fullness. Still, he was fairly certain his advisors would tell him divorcing the respected wife in favor of some young tail would likely damage his image. There was only one thing Sebastian loved more than his wealth, and that was his image.

"Hello, dear. How was Celeste?" The last thing he wanted to do was open that particular can of worms, but when one had so recently lost a loved one, concern must be expressed. He was nothing if not polite. Dead kid equaled sympathy. He was certain he'd read that somewhere. Possibly Emily Post.

Payton sighed and slipped the Cartier bracelet off her slender wrist. It had been a twentieth anniversary gift purchased by one of his interns. He'd made sure the girl got a little something of her own as well. A necklace or something. He couldn't remember her name, but the girl had been flexible. Very flexible. He'd been able to bend her legs completely over her head when he fucked her. That had been a nice day. Ashley. Ashton. Something Ash. It was hard to remember. Interns were a dime a dozen.

"My sister is as well as can be expected," Payton replied. "The service was beautiful and the Murphys did a wonderful job with the reception. We need to send them and the florist a thank you note. She did an amazing job in a short period of time. I wish you'd been able to come to the reception with me."

And sit in the same bar with Ginny Moreno? Now there was a name he rather wished he could forget. He'd been attempting to avoid her ever since he realized she was back in town. He'd been a little shocked when she'd shown up at his home a few days before. She'd been picking up her brother who was friends with Sebastian's son, Jeffry. He'd managed to push through that encounter. He wasn't going to walk willingly into another one. The church had been one thing. They'd been sitting far from the girl, but he hadn't been able to make himself go to the bar with its potluck and endless rounds of small talk.

He was usually so smart. He usually didn't fuck where he lived, but the Moreno girl had grown up nicely. Slim, with lovely tits and shapely legs. All that dark hair and those innocent eyes. She'd practically been a virgin. His body tightened at the thought of all that young flesh.

Young flesh. Unborn flesh. Fucking hell. Ginny Moreno was pregnant and that could be bad for him.

"Sorry, dear. I had a conference call with Austin. Very important vote coming up." He'd been locked in his office with a bottle of fifty-year-old Scotch wondering how he was going to deal with Ginny Moreno's unexpectedly fertile womb.

Payton shook her head, waving him off. "It's fine, Sebastian. We all know the job comes first."

She really meant that. For other women it would come off as passive aggressive. Payton truly believed that his job, his ambition was more important than her feelings. She really was the perfect wife. Would she still be at his side once Ginny's spawn was out in the open?

Something had to be done. Surely the girl didn't want to be a mother. Maybe a little cash would grease the wheels. He could talk to her, explain that he could pay for the rest of her degree. UT wasn't expensive for residents, but even a few thousand each semester would be tough on the Moreno family. She was likely working a job on the side. Her family was probably scraping by. Those poor bootstrap types were all about helping their families, right? He could explain to her how much extra cash would help her sister. All she had to do was take a quick trip to a quiet clinic and their problems would be solved.

It wouldn't be the first time he'd had to deal with the issue. He was sure he'd paid for the discreet doctor's new boat.

"Well, I hope your sister understands. I'll send her my regrets." As far as he was concerned, he'd done his duty by attending the service. Those types of affairs gave him a headache. If it wasn't politically required, he skipped the overwrought family functions. Political gain was the only way to get him to a funeral or a wedding, or God help him, a baptism. He hadn't wanted to go to his own children's baptisms.

He opened his closet door and selected a sedate golf shirt. He didn't need to dress up to go downstairs and mull over his problems.

"I think she's got enough of our family for now. Brittany is staying over for a few days," Payton said, referring to their daughter, who'd just come home from UT. "She wants to be with Ginny."

He rolled his eyes, happy his wife couldn't see him. Sometimes he wished they lived in a bigger town, one where everyone didn't know everyone else. It was incestuous the way his problems popped up in the form of his children's friends. He'd had to be very careful when he was fucking Ginny, although even he was self-aware enough to admit that had been part of the attraction. He enjoyed the intrigue of forbidden fruit.

He wondered if Brittany was close to the Alvarez girl. Dakota. Blonde and gorgeous and a little nasty when she turned a man down. He'd still love to get that girl under him. Even knowing how dangerous it was. Perhaps that was part of her charm.

He needed to get laid. That would solve some of his tension. He buttoned up the shirt and looked in the mirror. Yes, he was still a powerful-looking man. Fit. Trim.

His wife was still talking when he walked back from the closet.

"I think it's a good idea to let her stay with Ginny for a while. She was mad enough at me for making her finish out her finals. I know she wanted to be here, but it wouldn't do anyone a bit of good for her to have to repeat the semester. Now she can concentrate on helping out.

It's just funny how these things work. Celeste and Travis lose Jacob only to discover Ginny's pregnant with his child." Payton sat down at her elegant vanity, carefully divesting herself of her jewelry as she watched him through the mirror.

He stilled at the very sound of Ginny's name. It was the second time she'd mentioned her. A chill went through him because that was one name that shouldn't be on his wife's mind. She'd just lost her nephew. Jacob Salt had been on his way to a brilliant career as a doctor, and he'd lost it all on a wet road. Perhaps if Jacob had been driving. Men were always better drivers than women. No, he'd been in the passenger seat when his best friend Ginny had hit a deer. The impact killed Jacob.

Why couldn't it have killed Ginny, too?

What had she said? His wife's words started to penetrate. "Did you say Jacob's child?"

She turned and smiled brilliantly, and just for a second he saw the young woman she'd been before life had tempered her. If he'd been a better man, she would have been enough for him.

"Yes." Tears shone in her eyes as she stood up and turned to face him. "It's such a miracle. Celeste didn't even know Jacob and Ginny were a couple. They've been best friends for years, but apparently it turned into something more this year. Poor Ginny didn't even know she was pregnant until the doctors told her. She was shocked. I don't think she's very experienced, if you know what I mean. I would bet Jacob was her first lover."

He would do anything he could to bolster that particular rumor. "I've always heard she's a good girl. Brittany's always spoken so highly of her."

"Well, I'm glad she followed her heart in this case. I think Celeste would have broken down if it weren't for the baby. I know Jacob is lost, but a piece of him is still with us."

"Yes. It's a miracle." It was a miracle if that wasn't his kid. He remembered all the times he'd taken Ginny Moreno's young body under his. She'd promised she was on birth control. He was far too trusting. He was the victim in all of this.

But maybe he wasn't. If Ginny was acknowledging that Jacob Salt was the father of her baby, then maybe he was off the hook.

"She's moving in with Celeste and Travis. Celeste wants to take care of her during the pregnancy. I think this baby might keep my sister sane. Ginny's going to take some time off college so she can focus on a healthy pregnancy. I think Jacob would be so proud of her." Tears filled her eyes again.

He wished she would stop crying. It was becoming tiresome, but this was likely one of those times his advisors would tell him he was being less than compassionate. He put on his best "I feel your pain" face. It worked on everyone from cancer patients to idiots who'd just lost their jobs to automation. He practiced it in the mirror. It was important to ooze empathy without frowning too much. No one wanted an unattractive politician. He reached for her hand. "I'm glad to hear there's some good news."

She didn't try to move into his arms. He'd noticed a few years into their marriage that Payton wasn't the most affectionate of wives. Quite frankly, it was another point in her favor. When he wanted sex he would find a whore. His children had been properly bred with a woman who squeezed her eyes shut and shuddered through the act.

He was sure a shrink would tell him he had mommy issues. He really didn't care. They'd served him well. He had everything he wanted in life. Money. Power. Respect.

"Isn't it going to be lovely to have a baby in the family?"

As long as it wasn't his, he didn't care. Actually, now that he thought about it, the Moreno girl was smart. She'd figured out things very quickly. She could only really get cash out of him once. She could milk the Salts for years. He wondered how he could use this new knowledge to his advantage. "Of course, dear. I think I'll sleep downstairs tonight. I've got some work to do and I don't want to disturb you. I might need to go out for a bit."

She nodded and he could almost feel her relief. "Of course."

He closed the door behind him. He could really use a drink.

* * * *

Dakota Alvarez stormed into her parents' bedroom, her heart dropping. She hadn't been surprised her dad had skipped the funeral. He was very likely working, but she'd expected him to show up at Murphy's Pub afterward. She'd tried to call but he hadn't answered his phone. After the reception was over, she'd come over to talk to him. Only to find this. "I don't understand."

Her mother frowned. "He's gone."

The words didn't even compute. They didn't make a lick of sense. "What do you mean he's gone? Is he still at work?"

She glanced around the house she'd grown up in. It was neat and clean and utterly devoid of the one thing she loved most about it. Her father.

Her mother brushed back a wisp of blonde hair, her eyes hollow as she glanced around the bedroom she'd shared with Dakota's father. "I came home from the reception and it was like this. I don't know anything. Mallory and I have only been home for a few minutes. I tried to call him but he isn't answering."

Half the closet was empty, nothing but unused hangers on the racks where her dad's clothes used to be. His shoes were gone and the good suitcase.

It didn't make sense. Why would he leave? Unless....

She turned on her mother. "What did you do to him?"

Her mother was always on her dad's back. Hector Alvarez was the best husband and father in the world and Dakota had often wondered why he'd picked Joanne as a wife. Her mother was notoriously clumsy and was always running behind with things like dinner and housekeeping. Was it any wonder her dad got a little annoyed? He worked harder than any man she knew and her mother was a pathetic doormat. It wasn't surprising the man would get bored with her, but he would never leave his kids. Not her dad.

Her younger sister, Mallory, showed up, leaning against the doorjamb. She was still wearing the skirt and blouse she'd worn to the funeral. "She didn't do anything, Dakota. She was at the reception with the rest of us and then we came home. We found the place like this. Dad's gone. He didn't even bother to lock the door when he left. I guess he's done with us."

"I don't understand what's happened," her mother said.

Like her mom really cared.

"Maybe he's just gone on a trip." Tears threatened. She hated to cry. It was a sign of ultimate weakness and she wasn't going to do it. She had to believe there was something else going on. Her father loved her. She was Daddy's girl. Her father was the only man she could count on. He wouldn't walk away. Maybe she could believe he would walk away from Mom, but never from her.

"I don't think so. He didn't have any trips scheduled." Her mom stepped out of the room. "I'm going to make a few phone calls. I'll call some of his friends from work."

"Call the police first." Maybe her dad had been kidnapped. It was the only reason he would leave her. He wouldn't pack his things and leave this shit town. Not without her. "Someone took him. Someone hurt him. Oh, God, do you think we'll get a ransom note? We should call the FBI. Don't they handle kidnappings? We need someone who knows what they're doing."

She was about to run after her mother. Her mom would never get it right. She was useless when it came to anything but cooking dinner and taking orders at the florist shop she worked at. Dakota would get the police out and searching. They would find her dad and bring him back, and he would know that Dakota never gave up on him.

She'd lost Jacob. God, her heart still ached with it. No, they hadn't been more than friends, but he was going to wake up and see her for who she really was. Jacob was going to be a great doctor and Dakota was going to be his wife. They would leave this Podunk town and move to Dallas or Houston and have a fabulous life.

Jacob was dead and buried. A sob caught in her throat. He was dead and Ginny Moreno was currently being moved into the Salts' fabulous house. Into her place.

Jacob was dead. Sweet, funny, kind Jacob was dead and he wouldn't get a chance to wake up and see how good they could be together because he wouldn't wake up. Not ever.

"Dakota? Are you all right?" It had been a long time since she'd heard something like concern come from Mallory's mouth.

She shook her head and looked around. How had she ended up on the floor? Her knees hurt. She must have banged them when she'd fallen. Tears streaked down her cheeks and Mallory looked down at her like she gave a shit.

"I'm really sorry about Jacob. I know you liked him," her sister whispered.

Liked? She'd loved him. He'd been her ticket out of this town, out of the nothingness her life had become. She was a cog in a boring, soul-killing wheel and not a particularly necessary one at that. She wasn't smart enough to go to college, wasn't brave enough to walk away without money. She was stuck and Ginny Moreno had taken her place and all because the dumb bitch wasn't smart enough to know how to use a freaking condom.

She forced herself to stand back up, to wipe away the ridiculous tears. They wouldn't do her any good. Action. She needed to take action. "I want to know where Dad is. I want to know what Mom did to drive him away. Do you think I don't hear those foolish rumors she spreads? She's trying to get sympathy by lying about Dad hitting her."

"They aren't lies." Mallory always took their mom's side.

"Of course they are. He wouldn't hit her. She's responsible for this." She'd heard that crap about her father all her life and she ignored it. It was one more thing her poor dad had to put up with.

Mallory shook her head. "You're blind. And he's gone. I don't know why, but I know he's gone and he left on his own."

"How do you know that?" She hated crying in front of Mallory. She really despised the fact that her sister was looking at her like she was something to pity.

"He took the baseball."

No. She strode out to the living room. He wouldn't. It was still there. She could still remember the first time he'd taken it down and shown her. He'd treated that thing like a religious relic.

This was signed by Nolan Ryan, baby girl. Your granddad was a hard man, but he did right by me. He didn't have much, but he saved everything he had and he took me with him up to Dallas when I was just a little kid, not long before he died. I'll never forget that day. I'll never forget sitting in old Arlington Stadium with him and catching this ball. Your grandmother never understood him, but I did. He sacrificed for me. He would have loved you, Dakota.

She stared at the place where the baseball had sat for the entirety of her life. No one touched that baseball. It had its own glass case. It had been the symbol of everything her dad had lost and all the reasons she should leave this town.

Daddy was gone and he hadn't even said good-bye. Her whole world had imploded in the course of a few days. Jacob was gone. Daddy was, too.

"Believe it or not, I'm counting this as a good thing," her sister said.

"Why? So you can play those damn video games all day and no one will stop you? So you and your friends can be as loud and obnoxious as you want?" Her sister was so selfish.

"You've always been blind to him, Dakota," Mallory said softly from behind her. "He was a horrible father. He's a drunk and he hurts Mom. You've never seen the real Hector Alvarez."

She whirled around and before she really knew what she was

doing, her hand was out, smacking Mallory's cheek. The sound cracked through the air and Dakota realized with dawning horror that she'd struck her little sister. She pulled her hand back, shocked at her action.

Mallory's chin came up, her shoulders squaring. "Or maybe you know exactly who he is. Maybe you're just like him."

A little cry came from the back of her throat. "Mallory…"

"What have you done?" Their mother stormed in, her eyes going straight to the red mark on Mallory's cheek. "How could you?"

"I'm sorry. God, Mallory, I'm so sorry." She could barely see for the tears in her eyes. They welled up from some deep place inside her and she wondered if she would ever stop crying again. She'd hit her sister. Her little sister. What was she thinking? "I'm so sorry."

She stumbled out of the house, into the heat of the evening. She had to get out of here, had to find a way to forget.

Even if it was only for a night.

Chapter Two

Brittany Rush fluffed the pillow and helped Ginny ease down into bed, despite the fact it was barely eight o'clock. Ginny winced a little as she sat back. The doctors might have said she was healing nicely, but it was so obvious her friend was still in pain, and the stress of the funeral that day had done a number on her.

"Are you all right? Do you need an aspirin?"

Ginny shook her head. "Can't have one and I'm fine. My back is just a little sore. I think I stood too long at the reception. Could you get another pillow?"

She settled the second pillow behind her so it cradled her lower back. Brittany worried that even after the soreness from the accident went away, the ache in Ginny's soul would last forever. "Better?"

Ginny turned dark eyes her way. Her friend seemed infinitely older than she'd been when they'd seen each other on the last day of Ginny's classes. She'd smiled and laughed and snuck a bottle of tequila into their room. The next morning Ginny had gotten up and left for home. Brittany had still had two more finals, so she was stuck in Austin until they were finished and she too could head home.

"Yes, thank you so much," Ginny said. "I'm feeling better. It was just a really long day. I need to sleep. I swear I can feel the baby zapping my strength. You certainly don't have to stay."

She'd already gotten permission from her Aunt Celeste to stay for a few days. Her aunt had gotten teary and hugged her just a bit too long when she'd told Brittany she should stay as long as she liked. It was a little like Celeste thought if she filled the house with people who loved Jacob, maybe he wouldn't feel so far away. Luckily her mom had been amenable.

It wasn't like she was eager to head home. She loved her mom, but it was an election cycle. She really hated election cycles. It was like the world became an oppressive cloud that constantly told her to smile. Her grandmother wouldn't get off her back about what to say and wear and how important Brittany's father was. Nope, it was better to be here where she was really needed.

"Try getting me to leave." She sat on the side of the bed and reached for Ginny's hand. "I'm just sorry I couldn't get here before today. I understand why Mom did it, but I don't agree."

It was hard to get too mad at her mother. Payton Rush was a paragon of a wife and a mother. More like a martyr, but she would never say that out loud. It was blatantly obvious there was no passion between her parents but her mother was devoted to the family. She'd always been there for her and her brother, so Brit gave her a pass most of the time. She didn't understand the relationship between her mom and dad. She didn't even try.

Ginny shook her head. "Don't even worry about it. I understood. You had finals. If you hadn't taken your last finals, you would have been forced to repeat the classes next year. You could have lost a whole semester of work. You couldn't just walk away. Certainly not when there wasn't anything you could do. You couldn't... I don't know. Celeste kept it from Lacey, too. In some ways it was a mercy to give you another day or hour or even a few minutes when you didn't know Jacob was gone."

She couldn't have stopped the accident and she couldn't fix what had happened. Brittany knew that, but it felt wrong not to be there when her best friends were... dying. Somehow her final in history seemed meaningless when her own history was being written with such a brutal pen. She'd hugged Ginny good-bye that day. She'd waved as Ginny had driven off to pick up Jacob. She hadn't thought twice about it, knowing she'd see them at home in a few days. "I just wished I'd gotten to Storm sooner. I still can't believe he's gone."

Jacob. Her cousin. Her friend. He'd been smart and funny. They'd all looked up to him. Jacob was the model son, the perfect student. How could he be dead?

Ginny's eyes closed and there was no way to miss the tears that squeezed out. Ginny must have cried a river since that moment when she realized Jacob was gone.

Brittany's heart sank. "I'm so sorry. I wasn't thinking."

Ginny squeezed her hand. She looked so frail under the pink and white quilt that it was hard to believe she was carrying a baby. She'd lost so much weight and there were hollows under her eyes. "No. You can't say anything right now that's not going to make me cry. I'm serious. If you were to joke with me, it would make me cry. It's what I do now."

There was so much Brittany wanted to ask. She'd held her tongue because it hadn't been the right time, but now it was quiet and it seemed all right to find out what had been happening under her nose. Ginny had conducted an entire love affair and Brittany hadn't noticed. What had she been doing? How had she missed it? "When did you and Jacob…" *have crazy monkey sex, look at each other and the heat between you formed another whole human being, knew you were silly, stupid insanely in love?* How could that have happened and she hadn't noticed? She settled for "… become involved?"

She was still trying to wrap her mind around it. It was a total change in how she viewed the world. All of her life Ginny and Jacob had been friends. They'd gone to prom together—with different dates. She'd been sure they would stand up as best man and maid of honor at each other's weddings. The idea of them together in bed was a little shocking.

Ginny hesitated and Brittany wished she could call back her words. She should just accept it, but it was so hard. Everything she knew seemed to change overnight. Of course if it was hard for her, it must be agony for Ginny. The relationship had been new. Ginny had just found her love. Her whole life seemed marred by tragedy. She'd lost so much and now she'd lost Jacob.

"It was a crazy night. The first night, I mean." Ginny spoke in halting sentences. She stared straight ahead as though she couldn't look Brittany in the eye. "I was at his place. He'd just broken up with Wendy. You know how sad he was."

At least she was talking. Talking was good. Talking could help heal. "What about you?" Brittany asked. "You didn't date all year. I thought you had a crush on someone. I even thought maybe it was a professor. You started dressing so much more maturely."

Ginny had bought some skirts and low-cut blouses, paid more attention to her makeup for a while. Brittany had teased her about taking a lover. Now she had to wonder.

"No. Not at all." Ginny flushed a nice shade of pink. "I'd…well,

I'd had a long dry spell. I'd been alone for a while. Obviously I was dressing up for Jacob. Who else would it be? Deep down, I suppose it was always Jacob. Sometime during the year my feelings changed for him. I looked at him in a different light."

"You started to love him?" Brittany was still trying to grasp the concept. She remembered them fighting over crayons and sharing bags of Cheetos. Jacob had pulled Ginny's pigtails on the playground and Ginny had spread a terrible rumor that he had a horrible case of cooties.

"I always loved him." There was no doubt that was true. It was there in the ache in Ginny's voice. "I loved him from the moment I met him. It was just different. A couple of months ago we had this one night where we saw each other differently."

"Only one night? And why didn't you tell me?"

"Well, it was obviously more than just one night. It started with one night, but we moved on from there. It was a love affair. We found each other that night. We knew it was right. We were coming back here this summer and we were going to tell his parents and my sister and brother. We knew we were eventually going to get married, though we were going to finish college first. I know I should have told you, but it seemed so new. I thought I should tell my family first. I promise I was going to tell you, too." Ginny sniffled, her eyes on her hands in front of her. She was struggling, but Brittany understood.

She definitely understood looking at a friend in a different way. After all, she'd grown up with Marcus Alvarez. She'd thought he was an icky older boy at one point. They'd been kids and she'd thrown mud pies at him. And now she dreamed about him at night. She wished he was here with her, holding her hand, making her feel safe.

If her parents ever found out... She let that thought go. Marcus wasn't here right now. It wasn't an issue. She needed to focus on helping her friend. Her heart just longed for her beautiful boy. She'd sat in the pews today and wanted his hand in hers so badly. But even if he'd been here he might not have acknowledged her.

"Are you sure you're good with living here for now? Is Marisol okay with it?" Ginny had left her family home in favor of moving in with the Salts. Celeste and Travis had offered her a place to live and support for her and the baby they would all adore. But Brittany worried. Ginny was so young. It seemed like she was making a lot of decisions that could affect the rest of her life. "Are you going to stay here for the summer and then go back to Austin?"

She shook her head. "I can't. I need to be here. I have to think about the baby."

Brittany leaned in. "Sweetie, are you dropping out of school? After all your hard work?"

Not to mention everything her sister Marisol had given up. Ginny had lost her parents when she was young and her sister, Marisol, had sacrificed to raise her and their brother. Marisol had become their parent in that horrible instant they'd lost theirs.

Now Ginny's baby was down a dad.

"I have to think about the baby," Ginny said, sounding resolute for the first time. Her chin came up, a stubborn look clouding her eyes. "Nothing is more important than Jacob's baby. I have to put all my effort into having a good pregnancy. Everyone's counting on me."

It had to be a hard place to be in. "You know you have to think about yourself, too. I know you're going to be a mom, but you're a person, too. You have rights. If you want to go back to school, you should. I know it would be hard, but everyone here will help you. Maybe it would be hard to go back to UT, but online schools are everywhere these days. You can still have a career."

"I don't want to think about it right now, Brit. I'm just trying to put one foot in front of the other and keep moving because if I don't, if I fall, I'm pretty sure I won't get up again."

What kind of friend was she? Her heart sank and she hugged Ginny. Sometimes she thought too far ahead. It was easy to forget how hard the present was when your head was always in the future. "I'm sorry. I'm a planner. I know there's no way to plan for this. Forget everything I've said and just know that I'm going to support you and I'm going to be here for you as much as I can."

Ginny leaned against her and Brittany remembered how she would do the same thing when they were little and Ginny would hurt herself. She would fall while they were playing and scrape a knee and when her mom would clean the wound, Ginny would lean against Brittany and hold her hand. Brittany would try to give her friend strength.

God, they weren't kids anymore and this wasn't something she could put a bandage on and fix with a Popsicle.

It struck her in that moment that their childhood was over. It had died on that rain-slick road and she could never get it back. It would remain in her memory, but she was an adult now. She had to acknowledge that some wounds couldn't be healed. They could scar over and the wounded would move on, but the injured would never be whole again. That was the real world.

"Hey, I'm sorry. I didn't mean to make you cry." Ginny was crying, too.

Brittany didn't try to stop the tears that flowed freely. She wept for more than Jacob. She cried for Ginny and the baby who would never know its dad. She cried for Marcus and she sobbed for herself and her lost youth. She didn't hold back. She didn't have to. This was her best friend, her person. They never lied or held back. Not around each other. "I think it's okay to cry. I think something like this deserves a few tears, don't you? You don't have to be strong. You're with me. We tell each other everything. We'll get through this."

Ginny seemed to still, and for a second Brittany worried she'd said something wrong. Then Ginny nodded. "Yes, we'll get through it together. Just like we always do."

Brittany held her best friend's hand and prayed that she was right.

* * * *

Dillon tipped back a beer and thought about the fact that he should really be feeling guilty. It wasn't like he was a man with no conscience. He was from an Irish family. A deep sense of guilt had been bred into him, but he couldn't seem to dredge it up now. He'd run a man out of town. It had been a little like something out of a Western. Hector Alvarez might not wear a black hat, but there was no question the son of a bitch was a bad guy.

His hand curled around the mug as he thought about the moment he'd seen Hector's meaty hand strike Joanne's delicate body. It was sure to leave bruises, but then she was awfully good at covering those up. She'd had plenty of practice.

"Careful there, son. You're going to break the glass if you squeeze any harder." Aiden Murphy stared at Dillon. His father's eyes were narrowed in that way that let him know he better put on his poker face. His father knew him far too well not to poke around if he thought something was really wrong.

What he'd done to Hector was going to his grave with him. He sighed and sat back. "Sorry. I'm a little tense, Pops. Rough day."

His father stared at him just long enough to make Dillon worry before going back to cleaning glasses. It was a habit with his dad. When things were slow, he wiped down the barware. "It was a rough day for the whole town. It's not right to have a funeral for a kid. It's just not right. It goes against the way the world should be. Parents shouldn't have to bury their children."

Dillon reached out and pressed his palm over his father's arm. He knew what his old man was worried about. Jacob Salt's death had brought up all kinds of anxieties for his parents. His mom was probably feeling the same thing. "Logan is fine, Pops. Don't worry. He's going to come home and we're going to throw the biggest party this town has ever seen."

His younger brother was serving his country in Afghanistan and had been for years. Since the day he'd joined up, they'd all been waiting for the moment when he would come home. After several tours, he'd finally written he was ready to head home. There was a picture of Logan looking resplendent and young in his dress uniform sitting in a place of honor over the bar along with all the other Storm sons and daughters who served. More than one of those pictures was the last taken of the young person it represented.

Jacob Salt had just been on his way home from college and he'd died. Logan was on active duty in one of the most dangerous places on earth. His dad was probably scared out of his mind.

"Keep telling me that, son. I already have the menu planned for his homecoming. All his favorite foods and definitely more beer than this town has seen." His father patted his arm and went back to work. "I just wish one of you had decided to do something safe with your life. But oh no, not the Murphy boys. They have to go and save the world. I worry about the lot of you every single day."

There was a little smile on his dad's face that let Dillon know he wouldn't have it any other way. Despite his parents' worries, both he and Logan knew they were proud. "I will. When Logan gets home, the beer will be flowing. By then, this town will need something good."

"That it will." His dad took an order and filled another glass, sending it down the bar before coming back to Dillon. "On that note, I talked to Marylee Rush today. She came up to me during the reception."

It was quiet in Murphy's now with only a few people still sitting in booths and drinking beer or wine, but only an hour before the place had been packed with people. The back room had been turned into a buffet, and for several hours after the funeral everyone had commiserated over Jell-O molds and brisket and coffee cakes.

"Really? What did she have to say?" The Rush matriarch was actually quite friendly with the Murphys. Dillon had always suspected it was odd for her to be so affectionate toward the riffraff, but Marylee was good at playing the kind lady of the manor. Of course, she was also the senator's mother and she ran things with a tight fist. Marylee could smile all day, but Dillon knew there were sharp teeth hidden somewhere.

"She just wants to get together next week. The Founders' Day celebration is coming up. She doesn't want to let good planning time get away. We're going to get together at the Bluebonnet for breakfast on Monday and start preparing. She's inviting a bunch of people to form the committee. She's already got a list started. You know that woman loves her lists."

Dillon raised an eyebrow. "Should we still have that? Considering what's happened?"

His dad waved a hand. "It's what we need. The Founders' Day celebration has been a town staple for generations. Normalcy is needed at times like this. Trust me. I know. This town needs to come together. Marylee knows that. She wants to make it the biggest one yet. It will give us all something to focus on."

Somehow he thought Marylee was likely more interested in supporting her son's reelection bid than she was in bringing the town together after a tragedy. Oh, she would do that, too, but that woman was laser focused on her son. She always had been. Sebastian Rush was Marylee's grand work in life and she never let anyone forget it. Still, his father had a point. "Let me know how I can help. You're right. We do need something to focus on."

The Murphys had always done the legwork for the celebration. They brought the beer and ran the picnic grounds. It was a tradition. No one knew how to throw a party like his pops. His grandfather claimed it was the Irish in them. The knowledge was in their DNA, he would tell Dillon.

His dad frowned and turned. "Oh, there's trouble. I thought she'd gone home. Poor girl."

Dillon followed his father's line of sight and then he couldn't breathe. Joanne Grossman Alvarez walked into the bar, her fair skin picking up the light from the neon signs. She always seemed so delicate to him. Even back when they'd been in school, she'd seemed fragile. He knew it wasn't true. Joanne could take a beating. She'd been forced to more times than he liked to think, but that was over now.

What was she doing here?

His heart skipped a beat and not just because she was so lovely. She knew. She knew Hector was gone. It was stamped on her face. There was a worried look to her brow and she glanced around the bar as though looking for someone.

She was looking for her husband.

How many times did he have to get kicked? How many times did he have to see the proof of her love for that jackass? She'd chosen Hector before. She'd chosen him when it cost her everything. She'd given up her family for that man.

He stubbornly sat in place, watching her as she moved through the bar. He'd done the right thing. He wouldn't take it back. Not for anything in the world. If he'd let Hector stay, Joanne was going to end up in a pine box. One day Hector was going to hit her just a little too hard or send her falling down in just the right way and there would be no more of her gentle soul in this world.

No. Let her cry over her lost love. It was better than her being dead.

"Hi," she said as she finally approached him. "You haven't happened to see Dakota, have you?"

Her daughter. Relief swept through him. She was looking for her daughter. "No. I haven't seen her all day."

His father leaned forward. "She left here about an hour ago. She seemed very distraught, but who can blame her? Can I get you something, sweetheart? On the house. You look like you could use a drink."

She sniffled a little and then hopped up on the barstool. "I would love a cup of coffee. It looks like I might need it."

"Coming right up." His dad walked back to the coffee maker.

"What's up with Dakota? Why do you think she would come back here after the reception? She's not twenty-one. Pops keeps a list of Storm's kids and their birthdays. No one is getting past him."

"Well, my daughter isn't known for following the rules."

"What happened?" He had a suspicion. Dakota was Daddy's Little Girl. She had been since the moment she'd been born. Dillon had never been able to figure out why Hector would treat his daughter like a princess and his wife like a punching bag.

She took a moment, as though she had to brace herself. Dillon thought she might lie, might give him that half smile of hers and tell him nothing was wrong, but there were tears in her eyes as she turned to him. "Hector left."

There it was again—that punched in the gut feeling. He'd done the right thing, he told himself. "What do you mean?"

"I went home after the reception and all his things were gone. He cleaned out his closet," she said, her voice shaky.

He ached for her, but he was resolute that he was doing the right thing. "I saw his car earlier today. He looked like he was headed out of town."

It wasn't a lie. Dillon had followed him all the way to San Antonio before he'd been satisfied the man was going to mind his manners. It was that or get thrown in jail. Or worse. He wasn't proud of the fact that he'd threatened the man's life, but he'd had no choice. He'd learned long ago that a man did what he had to do to protect those he loved.

Even when they didn't love him back.

"You saw him? Well, I guess that was to be expected. I mean that someone saw him. He was alone?" Her jaw was tense as she asked the question, as though she was bracing for a blow.

It occurred to Dillon that a nice lie would help ease the way for Joanne. If she thought her husband had left with another woman, maybe she would let go more easily. "As far as I could tell. I didn't see anyone in the car with him."

He'd lied to her enough. She didn't need the added humiliation.

"I don't understand it."

"Here you go." His father slid a mug of coffee in front of her along with two sugar packets and a little creamer. "I think that's how you like it."

She beamed at him, her smile dazzling. "Yes. It's so sweet of you to remember, Mr. Murphy."

His father winked and then stepped back, going to greet a new customer.

"I've always liked your father," she said as she fixed the coffee just the way she liked it.

"He's always had a soft spot for you, too." As did nearly everyone in Storm, with the exception of the two men who should have protected her. Her husband and her own father. Robert Grossman had doted on his daughter until she'd made the mistake of running off with Hector.

She'd needed her father's support and he'd disowned her. Yeah, Dillon didn't like Robert any more than he did Hector.

"Dakota didn't take her father's leaving very well. I'm afraid she's going to do something self-destructive. She's not answering her cell phone and she's not at her place. Her car isn't parked in the lot or I would assume she's just not answering. She does that from time to time." She wrapped her hands around the mug as though she needed the warmth. "Only to me. Never to her father. I don't know what to tell her. I don't even understand what's happening. I walked into the house from Jacob's funeral and all his stuff was gone."

That must have been a major shock. "He wouldn't be the first man to walk out without an explanation."

She shook her head. "I understand that. It just doesn't make sense. His job seemed to be going well. He was angry a lot, but he had his reasons. I guess I always knew he could get sick of me, but I thought he loved the children."

His heart ached for her. He wanted nothing more than to put his hand over hers and tell her everything he felt, but now wasn't the time. "You never know what's going through another person's head. He might have just had a mid-life crisis. I've known a couple of men who left their families just because they thought there was something better out there."

She winced. "Well, I'm sure he thought that from time to time."

He was not handling this well. He finally had her alone and he was fumbling badly. "I'm not saying there actually is something better. I'm just saying some men can't be pleased. They don't know a good thing when it's right in their hands. How can I help you?"

She took a long drink of the coffee and shook her head. "You can't. I suppose if you see my daughter, you might give me a call. She did something stupid tonight. She's very emotional. Dakota's never had to deal with real tragedy and she's been hit with two in the course of a week."

"She was close to Jacob?" It seemed like the entire town was feeling his loss.

"Not as close as she wanted to be. I think she had a crush on him.

He was handsome and smart. More than that, he was going to leave this town and I think that's what Dakota wants more than anything in the world. I love my daughter, but I also know her. I know what she's capable of. She's got a good heart, but her father made her believe she was entitled to anything she wants. I happen to know what happens when the rug gets pulled out from under you. You fall and hard. I wasn't ready for it when my father turned me away. Dakota is even less ready than I was."

"I could drive you around. We could look for her together." He hadn't had more than a few sips of his beer. He would feel better if he could help her in some small way.

She shook her head. "No, I need to get home. I suppose she needs some time to herself. I'm fairly certain I'm the last person she wants to see. Besides, I need to call my son. Marcus should know his father's gone."

Marcus, Joanne's only son, had left town the minute he could. One more man who should have watched out for her—gone.

He reached and put his hand over hers, the touch almost electric. The connection he felt to this woman sizzled along his skin.

She gasped a little, but didn't pull back. She looked up, her eyes catching on his.

"Let me know if there's anything I can do to help you, Joanne. You're not alone. Not even close. All you need to do is pick up a phone or knock on my door and I'll be there. I'll get you through this." After all, he was the reason Hector had left in the first place. And he wasn't a man who ran out on his responsibilities.

She nodded, her hand sliding away from his. "I should go. If you see my daughter, just try to take care of her. She's hurting."

Dakota wasn't the only one. Joanne slid off of her barstool and started for the door.

God, he wanted to chase after her, but he had to give her time.

But one day soon he would be the one she could count on. And he would never let her down.

He pushed back his mug.

"You don't want the rest of that, son?" his father asked.

He shook his head. "No, I've got one last thing to do before I call it a night."

He headed out to find Joanne's brat of a daughter so Jo could sleep tonight.

Chapter Three

Sebastian looked around the bar. It was a dank hole-in-the-wall in an unincorporated part of the county, but it wasn't like he could go to Murphy's Pub to find a little tail. That was the problem with being back in Storm for the summer. It was so much easier in Austin. The bars and the clubs were numerous and the hookups they offered were anonymous. It was perfect for a man like him.

Here he had to wonder who was watching.

He took a swig of the bar's prime offering. White Lightning. It tasted a little like hell, but it offered an almost immediate buzz. Most moonshine did. He was a man of elegant tastes but sometimes the cheap stuff did the job.

His phone buzzed and he looked down, sighing as he did. His mother. It was the one call he couldn't avoid. She would just keep up. He flicked his hand over the *accept call* button. "Hello, Mother."

"Sebastian, you're not at home. Payton thought you might be in your office, but I checked there."

She lived in the guesthouse. It was not his optimal living situation. Again, he longed for his bachelor pad in Austin. He had a glorious view of the river and city at night. In Storm, his mother seemed to be three steps away at any given moment. "I worked all day. I decided to grab a bite."

"Yes, I'm sure you're out getting a nutritious meal. Try to remember that there are eyes on you everywhere in this town, Sebastian."

Which was precisely why he'd left town. He wasn't far, but he figured after the funeral and reception most Storm citizens wouldn't be hanging around a dive bar. "I'll be fine, Mother. Is there a reason you called except to harangue me?"

She sighed, a long-suffering sound. "I wanted to make sure you knew I'm putting together a little welcome for the Founders' Day celebration committee and I want you to make an appearance."

He bit back a groan. "I'm actually quite busy this week."

"Make time, Sebastian. You didn't show up at the reception today."

Because he didn't want a run-in with his last mistress, who also happened to be his daughter's roomie and who happened to be knocked up with a baby who might or might not be his. "I had some very important calls to make. Something came up at the last minute."

"I understand. I'm sure it was very important, dear. You have a big job with lots to do, but I want to make sure you remember your future. I know you can get so caught up in doing what's right that you forget you're important, too. You have to take these people seriously. This is a small town. They don't understand how complex your job is. When you don't show up, they believe you think you're too good to pitch in. You have to make yourself available, especially this summer, or have you forgotten what happens in November?"

Of course he hadn't forgotten. He was up for reelection. He really didn't see the problem. "At this point, my only opposition is a politically inexperienced grocer from a town so small you miss it if you blink, and with a budget smaller than Brittany's allowance when she was seven."

"I agree Mr. Dawson is nothing but window dressing at this point, but that can change in a heartbeat, Sebastian. All we need is one do-gooder who decides you're not doing enough for this district. They back Dawson and suddenly you're out of a job. I told you, dear. Just one more term in Austin and then we'll look to bigger things. I've already planted the idea of a run for governor in the party chairman's ear. When the current governor steps down, you'll be in place for an easy run. Oh, your family is going to be the perfect first family of Texas. Won't Payton make a lovely First Lady?"

She would be impeccable and after a term in the governor's mansion, it would be time for the White House. His mother did have a way of refocusing him. "She certainly will. Of course I'll come to the committee meeting."

He raised his hand for another drink and the barkeep immediately poured it for him. He might need to buy a bottle. It would be wickedly perverse to put a mason jar of homemade hooch next to his thousand-dollar Scotch.

"Excellent. I'll make sure you have all the details. I need this Founders' Day to go off without a hitch. We're going to use it as a platform for you to gather more support for your bid for reelection and raise your profile with an eye to the future. I'm going to make sure there are plenty of reporters."

"Why would anyone but local papers want to cover our town festival?" It was a dreadfully dull affair, but a necessary one. He would spend the day glad-handing the locals and pretending he liked things like three-legged races. That wasn't the sort of three-way he was into.

"Besides the fact that you're a very important person? They'll cover it because they won't just be covering a picnic. They'll be covering a town triumphing over tragic loss. I'm already talking to some people at the *Dallas Morning News* and the *Austin American-Statesman*. I have a call in to a friend who works for the *Chronicle* in Houston. Imagine the human-interest story. Town loses favorite son and manages to rise from their grief to rally around their beloved senator. This could get you very good press."

And he could use it. His mother really was a political animal. "I'll follow your lead as always."

He heard the door swing open and someone started talking. He covered his ear to hear his mother.

"Get home soon. Do whatever it is you need to do. Scratch whatever itch you have and get home. I don't want rumors being spread about you. Good night." The line disconnected.

He was quite good at keeping rumors from being spread. Hell, he'd managed to bone his daughter's roommate without Brittany figuring it out. And he'd managed to dodge the bullet of Ginny's womb. He was actually feeling a little lucky. A weaker man might take it all as a sign to slow down, but not Sebastian.

And damn, but his itch suddenly needed scratching. Right across the bar from him a blonde in a short skirt and a tight blouse leaned over, saying something to the bartender. He could barely hear her.

"...my dad? His name is Hector. I have a picture of him here." She turned her phone toward the barkeep.

He studied it for a moment and then slowly shook his head. "I'm sorry, sweetheart. I have seen Hector before. He's in here a lot, but not in the last couple of days."

She sank back on her stilettos. Sebastian appreciated those toned legs of hers. They led right up to a nice and juicy ass. He could already feel those plump cheeks in his hands. Yes, she was exactly what he needed to take his mind off all the crap he had to deal with.

She turned and he caught his breath.

Dakota Alvarez. The one who got away. Well, the one who'd told him he was an old pervert, but he hadn't taken that too poorly. At her age, anyone over twenty-three was ancient.

He wondered if time had given her a new perspective.

She frowned at the bartender and then seemed to sag. "All right then. Can I get a beer?"

The bartender snorted. "If you can show some ID. You look a little young to me."

Her right hand fisted at her side and she started to turn.

Sebastian fished a hundred out of his pocket. If the girl needed a drink, he intended to provide. "Does she look a little older now?"

He passed the hundred over and sure enough, the bartender took it. "Why, yes. I think she definitely looks of age. Sorry. It's hard to tell in this lighting. What can I get you, miss?"

She glanced over at him and bit that full bottom lip of hers. He felt an immediate tightening in his groin. He waited for her to make her decision. She wasn't a foolish girl. He imagined she knew what she was accepting when he offered to buy her a few very expensive drinks.

She would be accepting a quick ride in the back of his Mercedes too.

"I guess just a beer."

And just like that she was caught in his net. "Oh, that won't do. You look like an adventurous girl. Why not try something more exotic? How about a round of White Lightning for me and my friend? And we'll take it in the booth in the back."

He hopped off his barstool and steering Dakota, headed that way.

* * * *

Dakota knew she was likely making a massive mistake, but she couldn't force herself to get back in her car. She'd gone everywhere she could looking for her father. Everyone said the same thing. *Hector, of course I know him. No. Haven't seen him tonight. Sorry.*

It was like he'd dropped off the face of the earth.

"I certainly didn't expect to see you here," Senator Rush said, sliding into the corner booth. The bench was round like the one at the Bluebonnet Cafe where she and her friends used to all squish in together and dip French fries in their shakes. Salty and sweet. She missed those times.

Now it seemed she would miss her father, too.

"I was looking for my father. He's left town, it seems." She hated the pathetic whine to her voice. She slid in opposite the senator.

What was she doing here with this creep? He'd hit on her shortly after her eighteenth birthday and she'd turned him down flat. Now she was willingly drinking with him? Not that he was all that bad looking. He was kind of hot for an old dude. For a dude with money and power.

"Hmm, I'm sure he'll be back." Sebastian stared at her over his drink. Actually, the guy was kind of sexy. No one had ever looked at her like that before, like he could eat her up. Like she was beautiful.

"Maybe. I think something happened between him and my mom."

The bartender put a glass of something in front of her and then took another tip from the senator. Had that been a hundred dollar bill? Jeez. How much cash did the man carry? She picked up the drink and sniffed it. It smelled a little like rubbing alcohol. She wrinkled her nose. Maybe she should start with something fruity. "Do you think I could get a piña colada instead?"

The senator chuckled. "Only if you want to go to Murphy's. This isn't the type of bar that serves fruity concoctions. I would bet if I asked for a wine selection I would be told red or white. This is the house special. It's called White Lightning. It's grain alcohol. If the myth is true, it's almost two hundred proof. It's also illegal. It's only for people with a taste for the wild side. I suppose I can get you a light beer."

At the very sound of the word "Murphy's," she frowned. She'd spent the entire afternoon there watching as everyone in town fawned all over Ginny Moreno. She'd been excellent at playing the frail flower. Ginny had stood in line with the Salts, shaking hands as though she was one of the family.

That should have been her place. Hers. But no, she'd been relegated to walking the line and shaking hands and murmuring how sorry she was and then she'd been utterly ignored. She'd watched as the other young people banded together. Her sister had immediately defected for a group that included Luis Moreno and Jeffry Rush. Once Lacey Salt had gotten away from the receiving line, she'd joined them.

All her friends had left. They were in Dallas or Houston or Austin. They were gone, finding their own lives. And she was stuck here alone.

She took a quick swallow of the drink and came up choking. It tasted horrible. "Why would anyone drink that?"

"Give it a minute," the senator said with a chuckle.

He was suddenly closer than he'd been before. She hadn't seen him move, but now he was on her side of the booth. He patted her back as she coughed.

That was the single worst thing she'd ever put in her mouth and she'd dated high school football players. They didn't always shower. Ick.

Then a warmth hit her belly. It was like when she was a kid and her mom would pull towels out of the dryer and Dakota and Marcus and Mallory would all wrap themselves up. That warmth had a softness to it.

"Oh, that's nice." She lifted the glass again.

The senator's hand came down, covering hers and keeping her from raising the glass. "Not too fast. You're not used to drinking and this is serious stuff. Give it a couple of minutes and you can have another sip."

"You're drinking it fast."

He winked and took another drink. "I'm well acquainted with liquor, honey. I come here for a couple of reasons, the ambience not being one of them. This is some of the finest moonshine in the world. I tend to prefer more elegant establishments. If I go to a restaurant, I would prefer one with a Michelin star or two. But the gentleman who makes this fine liquor will only sell to this bar. I believe the gentleman goes by the name of Cooder. Cooder has a more blue-collar attitude about the world, so I'm forced to come here when I want this particular indulgence. A man has to follow his bliss, you know."

She didn't really get half of what he was saying, but she liked how he said it. His voice had taken on a soothing but elegant tone. He was closer again. Now he was close enough that their thighs touched. Her skirt was so short she could feel the fabric of his pants against her skin. It had been a shitty day, but now she was feeling warm and a fancy man was talking about restaurants. "What's the nicest place you've been to?"

He leaned over and she could smell his aftershave. He smelled clean and fresh, so unlike the sweaty boys who used to grope her under the bleachers. "I've been all over the world, honey."

"I've never really been out of Storm. At least I've never been farther than Galveston."

Her dad had taken them for a beach vacation. They'd rented a condo. Her mom had ruined everything by tripping and falling down the stairs when she was trying to bring the laundry up.

Where was her dad now?

"A pretty girl like you should see the world. You would love New York and London. I'm sure you'd do well in Paris. Where are you going to college?" He took his hand off the glass and nodded. "Just a sip."

It was actually kind of nice that he was looking out for her. No one ever did that. Most boys would be encouraging her to drink as much as she could. She took another sip, managing not to choke this time. After a second the warmth settled in again. She was glad she'd come in here.

"I would love to see all those places. But I'm not in college." She'd scored well on her SATs, but not well enough to get a scholarship. "I have a job. I'm working at your savings and loan."

"Ah." His arm slid around the back of the booth, just brushing her shoulders. "And do you like this job? Or are you looking for something else? Something more challenging?"

She found herself cuddled up against him. He was actually pretty muscular. And he had a handsome face. Yes, he was a little older, but maybe that was a good thing. She thought briefly about the fact that this man had a wife, but let it go. If Sebastian was out instead of at home with his wife, it was likely her fault. She probably didn't keep the man interested. "Definitely something more challenging. It's just there aren't a lot of jobs in Storm."

"No, you're certainly right about that." His words were whispered against her ear, and she could feel the warmth of his lips there. "You should think about going to Austin. A smart girl would make friends who can get her places."

Her heart rate skittered. His hand found her thigh and her mind was whirling. She was allowed another sip, a heartier one this time. She might not be used to the powerful liquor, but she thought she could learn pretty fast.

A smart girl knew how to work the system. Senator Sebastian Rush was the most powerful man in Storm. Could he get her out of this town? Could he find her a job with prospects?

She didn't protest when he brushed his lips against her ear. She sighed because between the liquor and the little spark of hope she'd found in his words, she was feeling nice and warm.

"You are a beautiful young lady," he whispered as his hand crept up her thigh. "You're certainly the most beautiful thing in Storm."

"Thank you." She leaned back and looked up at him. Why had she thought he was old? He was mature, but still hot, still sexy. What did she want with a boy anyway? "Are you going to be staying here in town for a while?"

She wasn't going to be some cheap one-night stand. If he was headed back to Austin in the morning, then she would have to rethink her position.

His lips curled up in a decadent smile. "I'm here all summer, baby girl. How would you like to spend some time with me?"

"Maybe that could be arranged." It wasn't like she had anything else to do.

"Hey, maybe when the summer is over, I can find you a job that's more worthy of you." One finger teased between her thighs. He was being aggressive, but somehow she found it sexy. "I'll just have to study you and find out what your strengths and weakness are."

She giggled and covered her mouth because she hadn't meant to do that. The liquor was really going to her head.

He chuckled. "First though, we'll get you some food. I don't want you sick in the morning. I'll go see if they have any kind of a kitchen. If not, maybe we can find a place that's still open somewhere around here."

"Why?"

"What do you mean?"

"Why would you care if I get sick tomorrow?"

He ran a single finger along her jaw and then brushed his thumb over her lips. He was staring at her like she was truly beautiful. "Because I like to collect the stunning things of this world. I'm a man of taste, Dakota. You're simply the finest thing in this town. Someone should take care of you."

She let her head fall back against his arm and then he was kissing her. He didn't overwhelm her the way the other boys she'd dated had. He didn't jump in and immediately stick his tongue down her throat. No, he caressed her lips with his, a soft brush that left her off kilter and wanting more.

She felt something skim across her breast and when she looked down, Sebastian's hand was covering her.

He immediately pulled away. "Sorry. You're so sexy I'm afraid my hand had a mind of its own. I'll go get that food."

She reached down and grabbed his hand, bringing it back to her chest. She didn't want to let go of how he made her feel. It was there in the back of her head that this was wrong, but she didn't care. She just wanted another couple of moments where she felt good about herself.

He was smiling as his lips descended on hers again and he took her mouth. His hand moved over her, her nipples sparking to life under the material of her blouse. His tongue traced the edge of her lips and when she opened for him, he delved inside. She gave over to him, tasting the liquor on his tongue. That liquor and this man had washed away some of the humiliation of the day.

After a long moment, he lifted his head and stared down at her. "We could have fun this summer, you and I."

She nodded.

He winked down at her. "All right then. Let's get you some food and then we can find a place to be alone for a while."

He moved out of the bench with the elegance of a predator.

He was going to want sex. She wasn't foolish enough to think he wanted to be alone to talk. He would want to take her to a motel and have his way.

She took another shaky drink, longer this time because he wasn't around to slow her down.

"Are you kidding me?"

She looked up in abject horror. Sheriff Dillon Murphy was standing over her, his eyes staring down at her like she was a murder suspect or something. What was he doing here? She was underage. She could get arrested and Daddy wasn't around to fix things. Her mother would likely let her rot.

And the alcohol was really making things fuzzy. Sebastian was right. She needed some food.

"Dakota, I'm talking to you. What are you doing here? Tell me that isn't what I think it is." The sheriff reached out and grabbed her glass before she could pull it away.

"I'm having a drink, that's all."

"Of moonshine?"

"Go away. You're not my father."

He seemed to pale at her words and he softened a little. God, there was the pity again. "I know. I know why you're doing this. That's why I'm taking you home. Now."

She looked behind him. Sebastian was in the hallway that led to the men's room. He was standing in the shadows. Even in her fuzzy brain, she knew what he was doing. He didn't want the sheriff to know he was here. Luckily, he'd taken his glass with him or she would have had questions to answer. He wasn't going to save her.

He looked at her from the shadows. That was where she would be if she chose him. She would be in the shadows, not someone's beloved wife, but the dirty little secret of a powerful man.

She had the power now. She could see it on his face. He was practically begging her not to tell the sheriff. If the sheriff found him here, it would be a scandal.

"Did my mother send you? She hates me. She's so jealous. You can screw yourself, Sheriff, because I'm not going anywhere with you. You can tell the whole town that sweet Joanne Alvarez has a tramp for a daughter. I'm sure she'll love that." She knew how to avoid a scandal with the sheriff. He'd been friends with her mom in high school. Just one little suggestion that her mother could be hurt and he was all about getting the hell out of Dodge.

He sighed and hauled her out of the booth. "You're lucky I don't want your momma to have to bail you out of jail."

She gasped as he ducked down and had her in a fireman's hold over his shoulder. He started for the door, stopping in front of the bar.

"And Cooder's lucky, too. You tell him he better hide that still well. And you, I find out you're serving minors again and I won't care that this is unincorporated territory. I'll send someone out to get her car in the morning."

As he hauled her off she managed to look up. Sebastian was smiling her way.

At least one person in the world liked her.

Chapter Four

Payton Rush looked at Celeste and wished she could take some of the pain away. It was etched there in the fine lines of her eyes and the downturn of her mouth. Her vibrant sister had aged in the days since her son's death.

"Do you think I should go upstairs? It's been a long time," she said nervously, her eyes trailing toward the stairs that led to the bedrooms.

She reached out and put a hand over Celeste's. "It's barely been fifteen minutes. Let Francine do her job. You dragged her over here on her day off. The least you can do is let the woman work in peace."

It was said with a teasing slant. She would do just about anything to get her sister to smile again.

Sure enough, a hint of a grin lifted Celeste's lips. "You think I'm being paranoid."

"I think that baby is your miracle and he or she is going to be fine."

Tears shone in Celeste's eyes. "Is it wrong to hope for a boy?"

She shook her head. "No. It's not wrong as long as you can still love that baby if she's a girl."

A smile of pure pleasure spread over Celeste's face. "Oh, you know I would. A little girl. I miss little girl clothes. Lacey never wears pink anymore. Not that she's let me pick clothes for her in a long time. It would be fun to dress up a baby girl in ribbons and frills."

There was no doubt in Payton's mind that whatever gender the baby turned out to be, he or she would be loved. So loved. "It will be fun. That baby is going to have the best grandmother in the world."

Travis walked in, dressed for work in his neatly pressed shirt and slacks. No doubt Celeste had made certain everything was laid out for him. Tragedy wouldn't stop the Allen girls from taking care of their duties. Responsibility, duty, family. Those things had been bred into their bones.

"Good morning, Payton." Travis nodded her way and then turned to his wife. "Are you all right? You know you can take the day off. I can bring in help."

Celeste dried her eyes with a tissue. "No. I'm fine. I have a ton of things to get done today."

Payton understood the need. When everything was falling apart, she could count on her own two hands to work. Celeste would need to work, to make things as normal as possible.

Still, Travis frowned. "All right then. I'll see you this evening."

"Of course. And I put your lunch by your briefcase. Have a nice day," Celeste said politely.

Sometimes Payton worried that her sister's marriage was as empty as her own. Travis thanked her and walked out, the door closing quietly behind him.

"If having Brittany here is causing trouble, she can always come home."

Celeste shook her head. "Not at all. We love having her here and she's helping Ginny so much. I think Lacey likes having her around, too. They stayed up last night and watched some old movies. They even laughed a few times. It was so good to hear them laugh. We need family around us at times like this."

"Yes, and I'm glad she's helping. I just want you to think about yourself, too." They hadn't been taught to think that way, but lately Payton had been pondering that very idea. Maybe she could be more than just a wife and mother. Maybe she could have something for herself.

Whatever Celeste might have said was forgotten as Francine Hoffman walked in. Celeste stood and walked to meet the nurse. "How is she?"

Francine smiled. She had one of those glowing smiles that lit up a room. Francine was petite, with raven black curls and dark eyes. Payton didn't let the nurse's slight stature fool her, though. She'd seen her easily handle a room full of puffed up doctors when she thought a patient wasn't being treated properly. There was no one in the world

Payton would trust more with Ginny's health than Francine.

"She's doing fine, Celeste," Francine said with a gentle smile. "Her back pain is left over from the accident. I'll leave you with the name of a very good massage therapist. A couple of sessions should really help her."

"And it won't hurt the baby?" Celeste asked.

"Not at all. Prenatal massage can be very beneficial," Francine reassured her.

"Thank you. I'll go see if she needs anything." Celeste patted Francine's shoulder before jogging up the stairs.

Francine set her bag down on the countertop and took a long breath.

Payton sent Francine an apologetic smile. Her sister had been frantic when Ginny said her lower back was hurting. She'd called Payton, certain Ginny was losing the baby. Payton hadn't known what else to do. She'd called the most competent person she'd known and asked if they should take Ginny to the hospital. "I'm sorry she was so stubborn about getting you out here on your day off. We could have gone to the emergency room. She's just really worried about the baby."

"Don't take her to the ER unless you have to. She'll end up waiting forever. I'm happy to help, Payton. More than happy." She glanced at the coffeepot. "But I did have to leave my place without my morning caffeine. Do you mind?"

Payton turned and grabbed a mug, happy to be able to offer her something. "Not at all. Do you need cream, sugar?"

While Payton poured the coffee, Francine sat down at the kitchen table. "No, thanks. I'm a coffee purist."

Payton handed her the mug and shook her head. "I will never understand that. I like coffee but I will admit it's more like I have a little coffee with my cream and sugar."

Francine's eyes lit with mirth. "That's because you're so sweet."

Something about the way she said it made Payton blush. She sat down across from Francine. "I don't know about that."

"Everyone knows Payton Rush is the sweetest lady in town," Francine said with a wink.

"I think that's a rumor my mother-in-law started."

Francine laughed. "Well, you are a definite plus to your husband's campaign. I got a call from the always chipper Marylee yesterday."

She wasn't aware her mother-in-law was close with Francine. For some reason, she didn't like the idea. She rather liked having her friend all to herself. Her friendship with Francine might be the only thing she had that didn't serve any purpose other than her own pleasure. She blushed again at the thought of the word pleasure. What was wrong with her? "What did she want?"

Francine took a long drink from her coffee mug, her eyes closing in obvious satisfaction. "Celeste has great coffee. Seriously. As for Marylee, she wanted to talk about the Founders' Day celebration."

"Really? But that's set for the end of summer." Why would they be talking about it now? She needed to focus on her sister. She couldn't think about a festival at this time.

"I don't know, but she seemed very insistent. She's having some kind of a meeting at the Bluebonnet Cafe on Monday. She wants me to run a first aid clinic in case there are any injuries. It's nothing I haven't done before."

She really didn't like that Marylee was asking Francine. Marylee was a woman of habit. She went to the same people again and again when she needed something. If she was changing things up it meant something had gone wrong. "Doesn't Nurse Taylor usually do that?"

"She's out of town that week," Francine replied. "Marylee's probably asking me because I'm cheap. I'm not just cheap. I'm free. And it's not a difficult job. If there's a real issue that requires surgery, we'll call an ambulance. I can handle anything else. Don't look so worried. I've been doing this for a couple of years."

She wasn't worried about Francine's skill. Francine had been a registered nurse for twenty years. She'd accepted a job at Storm General after she'd graduated from college, bringing her big city flair out to the country. She was so serious about her job. When they'd struck up a friendship a few years before, Payton had been surprised someone so fun and energetic had never gotten married.

Maybe Francine had known something Payton didn't.

"I wasn't worried about that. I was just surprised. My mother-in-law never likes change. She used the same bakery until Mrs. Mitchell died. Only then did she switch to Marisol's place for her cupcakes, and she required a three-hour meeting to go over what she needed." Marylee's contacts ran deep, but she did not suffer change well.

"So I'm in for a long lecture."

"Very likely. It's okay, though. She'll end whatever meeting you have with a list of the key points she's just gone over. She's big on lists." Payton had practically been handed a guidebook to the care and feeding of Sebastian Rush when she'd married the man. Unfortunately, her mother-in-law had left out key information. She'd given Payton a list of all of Sebastian's favorite foods and the clothing brands he preferred, but no one had informed her that the man needed to cheat at least twice a day.

Not that she cared. It wasn't as though she was a sensual creature. It was better Sebastian found that elsewhere.

"Well, that's good to know. Are you going to be there?" Francine asked. "The whole thing will be infinitely more enjoyable if you're there."

An odd warmth took up inside her. "Of course. I'm afraid my mother-in-law often informs me of my schedule at the last minute."

Marylee expected Payton to be available at the drop of a hat. It had been her place throughout her marriage. She was available to Sebastian, available to the campaign, to the children, to everyone.

Francine's soft voice cut through her thoughts. "On another topic, did I thank you for the teddy bears?"

Payton blushed again. She'd wondered if Francine had known about her little errand. She hadn't said anything, had tried to make the donation anonymous. She'd bought the hospital five hundred little teddy bears for the kids who came through. "I was more than happy to do it."

"Everyone puts money into research and that's wonderful, but sometimes the little things are important, too. Kids are scared when they come in. Having something to hold on to can be very soothing."

"It was your idea. You talked about it at breakfast one day and I looked into it. I just helped it along. I got a very good deal on those bears."

Francine reached across the table, putting her hand over Payton's. "Stop. You don't give yourself enough credit. I want you to say it. 'I did a good thing and I'm very proud.'"

There was that blush again. She needed to stop that. "Fine. I did a good thing and I'm very proud. And thank you for pointing out the need. If you have anything else the hospital needs, please let me know. Storm is my home. I want it to be the best place it can possibly be. I love these people."

She'd spent her life here, watched the children grow, mourned when there was loss. Storm was home no matter how far she managed to roam.

Francine sat back and Payton felt the loss of warm skin over her own. "You're very good to this town. On another note, don't hesitate to call me if Celeste needs someone to calm her down. I'm more than happy to take a look at Ginny. But you should know she's a strong girl. She's healthy and so is the baby. Everything is going to be fine, but you won't convince Celeste of that."

"No. She just lost her son. Somewhere deep inside she's sure there's another tragedy around the corner." It was still hard for her to believe her nephew was gone. His loss was an ache in her soul and probably always would be. She'd stopped her own son when he came home the night before. Jeffry was almost grown, but she'd wrapped her arms around him and he suffered through. He'd even kissed her cheek before he'd gone up to bed. It was good to remember that every moment she had with him and Brittany was precious.

"So when she's upset, I will come out here and I will check Ginny's blood pressure and take her temperature and give Celeste the smallest amount of peace. You call me day or night and I'll be here. We'll get her through this, Payton."

The sweetest tears threatened to pierce her eyes. She held it in, but it was so good to have someone to count on. Travis was lost in his own grief. It was obvious they weren't connecting. She didn't blame him, but knowing her sister's well-being was left entirely to her was a frightening thing. Sebastian wouldn't care. He barely spoke to her family anyway. Marylee was wrapped up in Sebastian's reelection bid. Jeffry was too young and Brittany had to worry about Ginny. She was alone in caring for Celeste. Except maybe she wasn't. Maybe she had Francine.

"Thank you. You can't know what that means to me."

"Anything for you, my friend. Like I said, day or night. You need me and I'm here." Francine grabbed her hand and squeezed, the physical connection so sweet it almost made Payton tear up again. No one touched her anymore. She and Sebastian hadn't been intimate for years, not that she'd ever enjoyed it.

What would it have been like if Sebastian had been softer, gentler, more tender?

She forced her mind away from that dangerous territory and regretfully let go of her friend's hand. She had responsibilities and they didn't include indulging her odd fantasies. She was a grown woman, not a kid experimenting. She'd made her choice years before when she'd opted to please her parents and marry Sebastian. She knew her path. "Now I think Celeste has a coffee cake around here somewhere. What do you say?"

Francine put a hand over her heart. "You're speaking my language, Payton Rush."

With a much lighter heart, she got up and went in search of that coffee cake.

* * * *

Dakota woke up to the sound of chattering.

"Do you think she'll get grounded?"

"Dude, she's like twenty. She has her own place. I doubt Mrs. Alvarez can ground her."

"I'm just surprised the sheriff didn't put her in the drunk tank. That's where she belongs."

"Nah, my sister gets away with everything. That's the way life is." She knew exactly whose voice that was. Her sister. This had to be a nightmare.

Damn it. The night before rushed in. Jacob's funeral, the wake, finding out her dad was gone. The bar, the liquor, him.

She sat straight up and realized she was in her old room at her parents' house. Her home. That stupid apartment wasn't home. It was lonely and bland. Of course, now this place was lonely, too. No one here loved her since Marcus and her dad had left. Her lack of welcome was emphasized by her sister's current discussion.

"I don't know what she was thinking, Lacey. Dakota rarely thinks about anyone but herself." Mallory's voice was accompanied by the clanging of pots and pans. She was likely making breakfast.

Dakota glanced at the clock. Nope. It was lunchtime. She ran a hand over her head, brushing back her hair. She was surprised her head wasn't aching. Her stomach was fine, too.

Because Sebastian wouldn't let you get sick. Because unlike the sheriff, he was actually looking out for you.

Was she really thinking about it? Was she thinking about having an affair with a married man?

"Well, I guess it shouldn't really surprise anyone," her sister's best friend, Lacey Salt, said. "I know when my mom heard about it she just shook her head."

How had everyone heard about it? She shouldn't be surprised. Any one of the neighbors here could have seen the sheriff hauling her out of his car and dumping her on her mom's doorstep. Her mom had probably talked about it over morning coffee. Within seconds the phone lines would have been buzzing with the news that poor Dakota Alvarez was in trouble again.

"She's got a bad reputation," came another voice. She was fairly certain that was Luis Moreno, her sister's boyfriend. Oh, he was one to talk. His sister was pregnant and unmarried. At least Dakota had the sense to protect herself.

And how did she have a bad reputation?

"You know there was a rumor a couple of years back that she did the entire front line after they won regionals," cracked another male voice.

Her stomach turned but not from a hangover. That was Jeffry Rush. Sebastian's son. Again with the hypocrisy.

"Don't bring that up. It's not true," Mallory said with a hard tone.

At least one person believed her. She'd been dating the quarterback and he'd been a complete jerk. She'd broken up with him that night and the next day he'd spread that horrible rumor about her. People still believed it. One more reason to get out of this damn town.

Daddy, where did you go? Why did you leave me?

"Sorry. We're all mad at her right now," Jeffry said. "We're your friends. Maybe we'll be less mad once we can't see her handprint on your cheek."

Dakota got up and searched for her purse. It was lying on the dresser and next to it sat her phone. She caught sight of herself in the mirror. She looked rough, mascara and eyeliner having smudged during the night. She looked older and harder than she thought of herself, but maybe that was a good thing. Maybe if she got harder then no one could hurt her.

She looked down at her phone and there was a text from an unknown number. She flipped through the screens to read it.

Thanks for the save last night, White Lightning. I call you that because you're the brightest thing in the sky. Maybe you'll come by my office sometime. I would love to talk...policy with you.

She wasn't sure how Sebastian had gotten her number but she was so glad he'd communicated. She supposed it wasn't hard for a senator to find someone's cell phone number. He probably had staff to look those things up.

He was still interested. Was she?

The door opened and the one person she didn't want to see walked in.

"Are you feeling all right?" her mother asked. Unlike Dakota, she was clean and pressed, though there were dark circles under her eyes.

"I'm fine. I didn't need the cavalry to ride to my rescue. Did you set him on me?" She wished she'd had the chance to clean up. After the sheriff had shoved her into the back of his squad car, the effects of the emotions and liquor had worked their magic on her. She didn't even remember him hauling her inside. She certainly would have pointed out that she didn't live here anymore.

"I just asked Dillon to send you home if he happened to find you. He said you weren't in a position to drive. He had a friend drive your car here. The keys are back in your purse. Why did you go to that bar?" Her mother stood in the doorway, likely guarding it against her inevitable exit.

As she'd so recently injured a family member, she chose not to barrel through her mom. "I was looking for a good time."

A long sigh came from her mom. "No, you weren't. Were you looking for your father?"

Stupid tears. She really hated them. She tried to call them back but had to settle for simply nodding.

"I thought so. I hadn't thought about looking there. I called all his friends and his coworkers. They all said the same thing. I wish I knew what to tell you. There's not a thing I can say that's going to make you feel better. At least when my father disowned me I could comfort myself that I thought I was doing the right thing. There's no logic to this. All I can tell you is I believe no matter what the reason your father had for walking out, he still loves you."

"Do you think so?"

Her mother stepped up and put a hand on her cheek. "I know so. And I know you don't believe it, but I love you, too."

"Is he coming home?"

Tears streaked down her mom's face. "I don't know."

"What are we going to do?" She didn't know how to face a world without her father.

Her mother put her arms around her. "I don't know that either."

Dakota wanted to shove her away, to be strong and independent. Instead she was a lost little girl and for the first time in a long time, she found comfort from her mother. She cried and cried and wondered if she would ever stop.

Joanne slipped out of Dakota's old room, closing it as quietly as she could. Her heart was so heavy, and if Hector had been standing in front of her she might have found the strength to take a baseball bat to him.

Somehow it was easier to get angry when it was her children and not herself at risk. She could understand how Hector could get angry with her, but these were his babies. How could he hurt them?

Mallory stepped out of the kitchen as Joanne made her way to the living room. She was quiet for a moment, not wanting to talk about Dakota's situation in front of others. Dakota had caused enough scandals. This one Joanne couldn't muster up the strength to blame her for. She was just a girl looking for her father. She was young and she made plenty of mistakes. The last thing she needed was gossip to compound them. She wished Dillon had been a little more discreet. She'd seen the neighbor's lights come on when Dillon pulled up. No doubt the gossip had already begun.

She turned to talk to her other daughter. "You should be with your friends. Dakota's fine."

Mallory shook her head. "They're eating grilled cheese sandwiches. We thought about going into town, but I wanted to stay close to home. I told the rest of them to go ahead and go, but Luis wouldn't hear of it and Lacey and Jeffry agreed. We're just going to hang out here today."

Joanne could understand. They didn't want to be separated. They'd seen how devastated their older siblings were by the loss of one of their own and sought comfort in each other.

"Well, you're certainly welcome to stay. I've got a big batch of stew in the Crock-Pot. I'll make some cornbread for dinner, if your friends want to hang out here tonight." She wouldn't mind the company. She liked listening to them laugh and support each other. Luis Moreno seemed to be a fine young man who took Mallory's feelings seriously. They'd been closer since they'd gone to the spring dance together. Mallory was young, but she had a good head on her shoulders.

Unlike her sister.

"Hey, is she really all right? Despite everything, she's my sister. Even though the girl does know how to slap." Mallory ran her fingers along the red spot. It was easing. Joanne had held an ice pack to it. By tomorrow, it would likely be gone.

God, how had she become such an expert at hiding wounds? Just thinking about it made her weary. She wanted to go to bed and stay there, but she had to be strong for her girls. "She's devastated and there's nothing I can do. She cried herself to sleep again. I wish I could say she's going to stay for a while. I think being back here would do her some good, but I doubt it. I caught her in a moment of weakness. When she wakes up again, she'll likely run."

"Was she really in that skanky bar?" Mallory asked.

The rumor mill in Storm was far too accurate for Joanne. "She went there looking for your father."

"But she stayed for the moonshine? I heard the sheriff caught her drinking moonshine."

What had Dillon been doing? Had he broadcast the incident to everyone? "She was doing what a lot of people do when they're hurting. She made a mistake. I'm just glad she didn't drive home."

"That wasn't her choice," Mallory replied.

She held up a hand. The last thing she needed was to argue with Mallory. "It's over now. We need to move on."

Mallory held her hands up in submission. "I'm sorry. I know she's upset. I'm not trying to make this harder on you."

Joanne reached out and grabbed her daughter's hand. "What about you, sweetheart? Are you all right? He's your father, too."

"I'm fine. I know you won't believe this, but I think this is a good thing."

"How can you say that?"

Mallory squeezed her hand. "Momma, I don't have to tip toe around him anymore. I don't have to worry that he's going to hurt you."

Oh, God. Please don't let her have seen that. She'd been so careful. "He doesn't hurt me. I'm just clumsy. You know that."

Mallory sighed and after one more squeeze, let Joanne's hand go. Her eyes were far too wise for her age. "You can fool yourself, but you can't fool me. I love you, but I'm not that blind."

The doorbell rang and Joanne was happy for the distraction.

Mallory started back for the kitchen. "Saved by the bell. I'll be around if you need me."

Her stomach ached at the thought of Mallory knowing some of the things that went on between her and Hector. She couldn't understand. Mallory was far too young to understand men and the way they dealt with life. She knew she was a disappointment to Hector. She was always getting things wrong. She was the reason he'd left.

She opened the door and Dillon was standing there. Big, gorgeous Dillon Murphy. His shoulders were almost too broad for her doorframe. He'd been so kind to find Dakota, but now she couldn't help but be the slightest bit irritated with him. "Sheriff."

He smiled, showing off that movie star smile of his. When that man smiled, the world seemed to light up. It was another thing she found somewhat annoying about him today. He took off his hat and his hair curled just perfectly. He looked young, though she knew he was close to her age. "I wanted to come by and make sure our patient is resting comfortably."

Out of the corner of her eye she saw a shade moving on the window of the house next door. Why did people have to be so nosy? "Come in."

At least this way they wouldn't know exactly what was being said. She wouldn't put it past the neighbors to be able to lip read.

He stepped inside and looked incongruous in her tiny living room. Such a big presence for a small space.

She moved to her couch and indicated the space across from her.

"Now you can explain how everyone in town seems to know what Dakota was up to last night." She wanted to know how the man who always seemed so protective had turned into such a gossip.

He went a nice shade of red. "Damn, I'm sorry. I didn't even think about it. I had my deputy go back with me to get her car. I think I saw him on his cell. His girlfriend is one of the biggest gossips on the planet. I'll have a long talk with him. He's not supposed to talk about what happens on the job."

At least it hadn't been Dillon. She felt better knowing that. "See that you do. It's not good to have public servants telling tales."

"Is she all right? She was drinking that mix of Cooder's, Joanne. She's lucky she didn't go blind," Dillon complained.

Joanne had to smile. He sounded so irritated. It must be difficult for the sheriff to admit he'd never been able to find Cooder's still. He wasn't the first sheriff to find himself defeated by that ninety-year-old man. That moonshine was a legend across three counties. Every teenager in the area at one point or another ended up trying it and paying the price the next morning. Including herself. "Now, you know no one's gone blind since the seventies. Cooder's got that recipe down to an art."

"I'm surprised you're not more upset."

"It's to be expected. Dakota acts out. She's not ever going to be the kind of girl who takes things sitting down. She's not going to cry and wring her hands and hope for the best. She's going to go out and do something, and when she figures out how helpless she is, she'll burn everything down around her."

"That doesn't sound so good."

She shrugged. "I know my daughter. She's got a good heart under all that sass, but she's been indulged too much. She's too entitled. Unfortunately, she'll have to learn the hard way now that Hector isn't here to make things easy on her."

"Are you going to be all right if he's gone for a while?"

She hadn't even thought about the realities of being on her own. She'd been so worried about Dakota and what the kids would think that she hadn't seen the big picture. If Hector was gone, so was his paycheck. If he was gone, she didn't have access to money. She'd always handed her checks over to him and he gave her a household allowance. Could she even afford to make the house payment? "I don't know. Maybe I can take more hours on at the shop."

She wouldn't be able to keep the house up the way she should. Perhaps Mallory could chip in. Maybe since it would just be the two of them, it wouldn't be so hard to keep things tidy.

She couldn't lose the house. She had to keep everything running properly. She had to make this work.

"Don't worry about money," he said. "I'm sure something will come up. You won't lose the house."

That was easy for him to say. He had a huge family behind him. She could count on her mom for little things, but there was no way she could borrow money from her. The last thing she wanted to do was get her mother in trouble with her father. She'd risked so much already. "Has there been any word on Hector?"

She was only now realizing how much trouble she was in.

Everything was in Hector's name. He took care of all the money. She wasn't even sure she knew where he put the bills and how to pay them. If she could pay them...

Dillon's jaw tightened. "I'm sorry. I don't have any new information on his whereabouts. I can't put a BOLO out on him. He technically hasn't done anything wrong. Leaving town isn't exactly against the law."

She treaded carefully, not wanting to go into what Hector had done that was against the law. "I can file a missing persons report in forty-eight hours, right?"

Dillon was silent for a moment. "Are you sure you want to do that?"

His question sat there between them like a land mine waiting to go off. Did she want him back? Of course. She needed him. He was her husband. She loved him. He was the right man for her. Everything he did, he did because he loved her and wanted her to be the best wife and mother possible.

She could hear her daughter's voice. *I think this is a good thing.*

But her other daughter was lying in the guestroom, having exhausted herself through tears. "Of course. He's my husband."

Dillon sat down on the couch beside her. He took up so much space that their knees were practically touching. She'd always wondered what it would feel like to have that big hand holding her own. Not just in friendship, but with their fingers tangled together like vines woven in a lovely pattern.

God, if she wasn't enough woman for Hector, she was an idiot to even daydream about Dillon Murphy.

"I'm just saying that sending cops out to find a man who doesn't want to be found might be a good way to make him angry."

She hadn't thought of that. Forcing Hector to do something he didn't want to do was a very good way to get hurt. She would find herself "falling down the stairs" or "tripping" over something. How many excuses could she come up with? "I just don't understand."

"I know. I can't imagine how hard this is for you. Do you need anything?"

She shook her head. "No. Now that Dakota's home safe, I can rest a little more easily. I'll think about what you said. Maybe I just need to give him time."

Dillon nodded. "I think that might be for the best. Joanne, we can't pretend it didn't happen. I saw him hurt you, Joanne."

She turned away from him. The shame she felt was like an ice bath. She'd gotten so good at doing just that. She'd pretended he hadn't seen Hector slap her. She'd prayed he never brought it up. "It was nothing."

"Jo, it's everything." He was leaning toward her. She could feel the heat of his big body. "He can't treat you like that. You can't let him do that to you. I can help you. I can protect you."

She sniffled and told herself it was wrong to want to lean against him. She'd wanted nothing more that day than to bury her head against Dillon's strong chest and let him handle everything, but that would be a failure on her part. She'd made her choice and she'd had children and she owed them everything. She couldn't let them know their father wasn't the man he seemed.

She shook her head and forced herself to get off the couch. "No. I made myself plain that day, Sheriff. I don't want you coming between me and my husband. It isn't right."

Dillon stood and suddenly his hat was back on his head and all the intimacy was gone between them. He was polite, but cold. A lawman. "Of course, Mrs. Alvarez. You call me if there's anything I can do to help you out and I'll let you know if any news turns up on your husband." He strode to the door, his boots thudding against the floor. When he got to the front, he swung the door open and turned around. "It looks like your daughter is none the worse for the wear."

She hurried to the door just in time to see Dakota getting into her car. Apparently she'd snuck out the guestroom window. Well, she'd had plenty of practice doing that in high school, though she'd always managed to convince her father she'd been trying to rescue some stray cat or dog, even when Joanne had been able to smell beer on her breath. Maybe Hector had just gone nose blind to the smell.

She couldn't think like that. When had she started having such unpleasant thoughts about the man she'd married?

Dakota's car peeled out of the driveway and Joanne realized their little truce was very likely over.

Dillon frowned. "You tell Dakota to stay out of bars until she's twenty-one. Next time I'll take her in."

Joanne watched as the sheriff drove away. It was a long time before she closed the door.

* * * *

Sebastian looked over the schedule his mother had given him and winced. It kept him in Storm for weeks at a time this summer. Couldn't there be a special session? Anything to get him out of this godforsaken town?

A vision of Dakota played through his brain. She'd been perfectly luscious. Blonde and gorgeous, with firm tits and legs that would wrap around his waist or his neck. He would bet she was a flexible girl. He could prop her ankles on his shoulders and drive into her. She'd be so tight, so hot that way.

He glanced down at his cell phone. Not the official one. Oh, no. He always kept a burner so he could call his ladies without getting in trouble. The number changed as frequently as the women. He paid in cash and tossed them when he was done. Other politicians might be interested in flashing their dicks across the tabloids, but that wouldn't be him. He wasn't about to give any of his hookups leverage to blackmail him.

It happened from time to time that a girl would decide to get a little something extra from their time together. He would simply shrug and tell the girl to try. They would find themselves with absolutely nothing to back up their claims but their "word." He was always quick to explain that their word and reputation, and likely whole future, would be shredded by the press and he would still get reelected.

Of course, the Moreno girl did have proof. Possibly. DNA didn't lie, though apparently Ginny Moreno did. It seemed she'd told everyone that Jacob was her only lover. Lucky for him.

Nothing on his cell. He thought Dakota might text back by now. She'd seemed fairly eager the night before. Eager and sad and more than a little naïve. Poor girl had lost her daddy.

He was more than happy to fill in, in a completely perverted fashion, of course.

He'd known within three minutes of meeting her how to handle her this time around. The first time he'd met her she'd had far too much confidence and youthful arrogance. She'd thought being the prettiest girl in Storm meant she was the queen of the world. Apparently life had taken some of the pluck out of her and that left her ripe and ready for him.

She wanted to feel like she was being taken care of. He'd stopped her from drinking too much mostly because his shoes were very expensive and getting vomit off them would cause questions. He'd just gotten them worn in. He wasn't about to toss them because his date couldn't handle her liquor. That had been the moment he'd snagged her. Funny how things worked. She'd mistaken his desire to keep his shoes clean for an act of kindness and caring and he'd turned it into just that.

He was smart enough to know that appearances were important. As long as Dakota viewed him as a man who wanted to help her, to guide her, she would likely allow him free and easy access to that stunning body of hers.

Hell, he would bet the girl had never really come before. She'd likely dated a bunch of small-town boys with tiny dicks who had no notion what to do with a woman. She'd probably never been adored properly, never had an experienced mouth or cock making love to her. Once he made her howl, she'd let him do all manner of nasty things to her.

But first she had to text him back.

There was a knock on the door. "Come in."

The door opened and a brunette walked in. Tall and lovely, he recognized her from Austin. She'd been around his offices in the capitol building. "Hello. To what do I owe this pleasure?"

She smiled, carrying in an old-fashioned briefcase. It looked like it locked. One of those coded cases. He was more used to seeing computer cases these days, but he had to admire her retro flair. "My boss asked me to deliver this to you in person. It's the highway appropriations bill she's hoping you'll cosponsor."

Ah, Senator Hawkins. She was a smart lady. Quite the up-and-comer. She was from some tiny district in West Texas where the cows likely outnumbered the people. "Yes, I remember that now. I believe I turned her down. I'm not sure that's the right bill for my constituency."

He didn't stand to make any money off the damn thing so he certainly wasn't about to sponsor it. A Texas state senator made $72,000 a year plus a very sadly lacking *per diem*. He didn't work on a bill unless it made financial sense. For him, obviously.

She set the briefcase on his desk and he noticed that, while she was dressed for business, her skirt was just a bit too short to be proper. He let his eyes roam her body. He put her at twenty-nine, maybe as old as thirty-two. A bit long in the tooth for his tastes, but she took care of herself. Her breasts looked well done. Oh, there was no way those babies were anything but silicone. They were too high, too perfectly rounded for her age.

Nothing like Dakota's. All he'd felt the night before was firm, real flesh, the kind no woman over the age of twenty-five really managed to keep. He would bet her nipples were tight little pink buds just begging the attention of a man's mouth.

"Senator?"

He shook off the images, though they'd done something serious to his dick. "I'm sorry. You were saying?"

She leaned in just a little. She'd left one too many buttons undone. He could see the swell of her cleavage. "Senator Hawkins hopes you'll find that the new draft of the bill addresses all of your comments. She really wants this bill to go through and is willing to work very hard to make sure you're happy with it."

He was sure she did. If the state decided to repave most of the highways, her husband's construction firm stood to gain some lucrative contracts.

"There's also another legal document she'd like you to see. If you're amenable to reviewing the new material and giving it a fresh eye, I've been advised to leave the entire package with you." She efficiently unlocked the case and turned it around.

Well, now he was interested. The briefcase contained the newly revised bill that he likely wouldn't read to save his own life and what looked like about fifty thousand dollars in cash. He liked cash. Cash was easy to spend and no one asked a bunch of questions, if it was handled in the proper way.

He closed the briefcase. "Please tell your boss I'm impressed with the changes." There likely were none. He didn't need any now that he was being properly compensated. "Though I will likely need another addendum to the bill before it goes through."

She nodded. "Yes, she understands. Once you've agreed to sponsorship and the bill passes, she's willing to offer you another fifty. She understands the value of having your name connected to hers."

He had powerful friends. He liked to think of it as a consultation fee. "Excellent. Thank your boss for me."

He looked back at his cell. What was taking the girl so long? He was beginning to get nervous. Perhaps he shouldn't have texted her at all. She'd been carried out by the sheriff, and Sebastian didn't need that kind of trouble.

Still, the girl hadn't given him away. She'd pulled a hissy fit that got her out of the door and quick. He rather thought that had been staged for his benefit. Smart girl.

"Senator?"

He looked and Brunette Big Tits was still standing in front of his desk. "Yes? There was something else?"

She leaned against the desk. "My employer might have mentioned that I should make sure you were very satisfied with the deal."

Ah, so the good senator from cow pattieville knew what he liked. He'd have to tell her next time to send one a little younger, but his afternoon seemed to be free. "And just how do you propose to ensure my satisfaction, young lady?"

"I thought I would secure our oral agreement," she said with sexy smile.

He moved his chair back and the woman sank to her knees in front of him, easing his slacks down with a practiced hand.

When her lips closed around him, he shut his eyes and pretended it was Dakota.

Chapter Five

Three days later the Bluebonnet Cafe was humming with activity. Marylee Rush stepped inside and was immediately greeted by the cafe owner, Rita Mae Prager. Her daughter-in-law, Payton, walked quietly behind her. She gave the cafe owner her best lady-of-the-manor smile. It was very important to use local businesses for meeting places. It helped the economy and put a shine on the family name. "Good morning, Rita Mae. I see you've done a fine job as usual. Hasn't she, Payton, dear?"

Payton nodded her approval. "She always does. And they make the finest waffles for fifty miles."

Marylee would have to take her word for it. She would never actually consume carbs, but she'd heard the ones here were delicious. Of course Payton didn't eat, either. No true lady did, but her daughter-in-law had impeccable manners. It was one of the reasons Marylee had chosen her for Sebastian.

If only Layla wasn't so headstrong, Marylee would have found the perfect mate for her as well. But no. Layla had to find her own mate, and everyone had seen how that had gone. Divorce. She didn't blame Layla for her headstrongness. It came with being smart. This time around she would choose better. Her daughter deserved every bit of happiness that Sebastian and Payton had found.

The cafe owner smiled and clasped her hand.

A firm shake was always needed. Even for a woman. It was a sign of strength, and Marylee believed in strength.

"It's a blessing to have you here, Marylee and Payton. How are your children?" Rita asked.

She so loved Southern politeness. It allowed a woman to speak of her true pride and joy long after they left the home. Here in Texas, a properly bred lady always asked after family. "Layla is doing wonderfully. She's got that hospital a-hopping. And, of course, Sebastian is doing fine work in Austin. I can't tell you how proud I am."

She allowed Payton to speak of her children. Payton had been a saint of a daughter-in-law and she'd given Marylee two perfect grandchildren. Brittany was a model student and Jeffry was so handsome and charming, she was sure he would follow in his father's footsteps and go straight to the White House.

It would happen. Marylee would make it so. She'd learned the power of positive thinking.

And careful planning. Between the two there wasn't a thing a woman couldn't accomplish.

She made small talk, asking after Rita Mae's relatives. Her mind was a steel trap of social knowledge. She never missed an opportunity to glean information. Even the smallest detail could prove important.

"Is everyone here?"

Rita Mae nodded. "Yes, I set up a big table in the back."

She gave Rita Mae a little wink. "Give us fifteen minutes to visit and get settled and then send someone back to take orders. Thank you so much. And can I count on you for some of those delicious sandwiches at this year's festival?"

"You know you can, Marylee. We'll have our booth set up and we've already picked our charity. We're supporting the local animal shelter this year."

Marylee approved. Lost dogs and babies played well everywhere. She might even have Sebastian make an appearance. He would look so regal with a retriever by his side. It would be a wonderful photo opportunity.

She nodded to Payton. "We're going to need to replace Celeste. I understand she's going through a very hard time and wants to concentrate on her family. I need you to read the room and give me some good suggestions. Celeste was such a hard worker and the two of you made a great team. Since you're the one who has to work with her, I'd like you to pick."

It would actually be good to get some fresh blood in. She hated to say it, but she didn't actually care for Payton's relatives. Payton herself was a good girl, a model wife and mother. Celeste did her best, but she'd started to hear rumblings about Travis. He worked hard. He worked hard even when the pharmacy wasn't open. Not that anyone was saying anything, but she found it odd that a man like that would work such odd hours.

How hard was it to run a pharmacy after all? It wasn't like what Sebastian had to do. Now there was a job.

And now the Salts had the added problem of a bastard grandchild. Marylee didn't want to hear the argument that the Moreno girl couldn't marry because the father of her child was dead. The damage was done. She'd gotten pregnant out of wedlock and if the good Lord wanted her married, he wouldn't have taken her bridegroom in the first place. She was sullied and that still meant something in Marylee's mind.

"I'll have to think about it," Payton said, showing sound good sense.

They walked through the diner, waving and saying hello. It wouldn't do to leave anyone out. Every single person here was a voter and deserved her attention. She grasped hands and ticked through the facts she knew about each person. The brunette and her husband sitting by the window were rumored to be thinking about changing churches. She'd give a heads-up to the Baptist minister. He was always looking for converts. The elderly couple two tables later had a grandson at Baylor University. They'd sent him there hoping that not being able to dance for four whole years would turn him straight. Marylee didn't have a lot of hope that a lack of a dance floor would make that child appreciate a wholesome vagina, but she smiled and agreed anyway. And there was that poor Joanne Grossman. Oh, such a pretty girl and such potential wasted. She'd married far beneath her and now, if the rumors were true, she'd been left behind by the man who beat her.

She felt an immense sympathy for the girl, but she should have known it would all go bad. She'd married a blue-collar worker. Men who worked with their hands tended to use them in other places, too.

She paused before heading to the back. "Is Aiden Murphy joining us?"

Payton shook her head. "No. He sent Dillon in his place."

That was disappointing. Aiden and his wife were so quick with a good story or a joke to break the ice. She truly enjoyed their company. Their son was a bit quick to write a ticket, if you asked her. Still, she plastered a smile on her face and joined the committee. Dillon Murphy was the only man there and he would look utterly out of place until Sebastian joined them.

She'd had to poke and prod her son. He was a silly boy who never thought his presence was necessary. It was a sure sign of his lack of an ego. Sebastian didn't understand how important he was. It was just proof of his true goodness.

"The sheriff is a good man," Payton said. "And everyone loves him. He also knows his father's business. All the Murphy boys grew up learning to run that place."

Marylee just wished this particular Murphy boy wasn't serious about stop signs. She'd paused for the appropriate amount of time, no matter what that boy said. "Of course."

They reached the back of the room where the committee was already milling about, talking. She was greeted with all the pomp of a reigning queen, which, of course, she was. She smiled and handled it all with grace and dignity. She'd been bred to the role, after all.

She even managed a smile for the sheriff, who needed glasses because she also hadn't changed lanes without signaling. "Sheriff, what a pleasure to have you here with us today. How are your parents?"

The sheriff, for all his flaws, was a very attractive man, and if she'd been years younger he would still have been too rough for her, but a girl could dream. "Mrs. Rush, the pleasure is all mine. My folks are doing well and send their regrets. They'll surely attend the next meeting, but they're waiting on a phone call from my brother, Logan. He only gets to call every once in a while."

She needed to make sure Sebastian was on hand to greet Logan Murphy when he returned home from war. "Of course. Family always comes first."

"I heard a rumor that you lost your assistant."

She sighed. "Yes, the poor girl. She got a job in New York City. I'm sure she's been mugged by now. Or she looks like that Miley Cyrus and thinks balloons make a proper foundation garment. That's what happens when you let your daughters run wild."

"Uhm, well, I was just wondering if you were looking for a replacement?" the sheriff asked. "It's a paid position, right?"

"Yes. I was thinking of asking my granddaughter to do it since she's out of school for the summer."

"Ah," Dillon said, and she could see the disappointment in his eyes.

People should really let her finish her thoughts before they became disappointed. It was truly their fault. Impatience led to bad feelings. "But Brittany seems all wound up in her friend's illegitimate unborn child, so I was going to ask if anyone knew someone with organizational skills. I'm not sure what Brittany thinks she can do. She's a business major, not a midwife. I don't even believe the girl requires one at this stage, but that's my grandbaby for you. She's going to do everything she can for her friend even though her friend makes very questionable choices. I have every hope that Brittany will be a good influence on that girl."

Dillon held up a hand. "I know who you should hire."

"Really?" Opportunity rose quick and fast sometimes, and it took a smart woman to see it. She had three outstanding parking tickets because the city didn't recognize tardiness as a disability. It certainly was when it came to her being on time, and being on time was important, which was the only reason she'd parked in those spots in the first place.

"Yes," he said quickly, betraying the fact that this was important to him. She'd learned how to read people and Dillon Murphy wanted whatever he was about to suggest to be accepted. It was important to him.

And that was very interesting to her. "Who is this paragon of organization? You know I'm only paying minimum wage, right?"

"That's all right. You're very good at helping people to the next level. Working for you opens doors for people that wouldn't have been previously opened."

Well, the young man did know how to charm a lady. "I suppose I do know a few powerful people." All of her instincts were sharpening up. She watched Dillon with the deep gaze of a predator who had just figured out she might not have to pay those tickets she'd racked up. "I'm going to need a name, though."

"Joanne Grossman." He winced. "Alvarez. I meant Joanne Alvarez."

The same sad but pretty woman whose husband supposedly took discipline a little too far? She quickly assessed the facts about the situation in front of her. Dillon Murphy was roughly the same age as the lady in question. They'd likely gone to school together, grown up in the same circles. And the circles in Storm were small. If she remembered correctly, Dillon had been a bit of a late bloomer. He'd grown into his big body later than most boys. He'd been a lanky, sad looking thing for most of his teen years.

And Joanne Grossman had been the beauty queen who ran away with the boy from the wrong side of the tracks.

Had little Dillon never gotten over his crush on Joanne?

Now that the rather brutal Mr. Alvarez had gone missing, was the handsome sheriff hoping to take his place?

She sighed and looked back toward the main dining room, where she'd seen Joanne sitting and eating a breakfast that consisted of oatmeal and coffee. Marylee would have skipped the oatmeal herself, but she was sure Joanne thought it was a proper breakfast. "You mean that girl from the flower shop?"

Dillon nodded. "Yes, she takes the orders and helps run the shop. She's quite good at organizing things. She helped with all the arrangements for Jacob Salt's funeral. They were very fast and managed to get everything in that Celeste wanted."

He wanted this girl in very badly. She was interested in knowing why. Men only worked this hard for one of two reasons: they wanted or they were guilty. What was Dillon Murphy's reason? She wouldn't ever know if she didn't get close to the problem. However, a lady never gave in too easily.

"I'm sure she's an excellent candidate, but I have to think about it. I can get back to you in a few weeks."

He flushed again, a sure sign that wasn't the answer he wanted.

"Of course I might move faster if I wasn't so worried about all those tickets I seem to have." She dangled the lure.

Dillon chuckled. "All right, Mrs. Rush. Consider them taken care of, but you have to come to a full stop when you reach a stop sign."

She smiled. A true lady found a way to solve all her problems. One simply had to be patient. "Of course. Now why don't you go and invite her to join us? If she wants the job, she can start now."

He rushed off and she knew she had a new bargaining chip.

Yes, it was good to get to work.

* * * *

Payton took a look around and wondered how the world kept spinning. It seemed like it should stop sometimes. The funeral for her nephew had only been last week and here she was talking about and planning some future event while her sister was still in mourning. All around her the people laughed and talked like it hadn't happened. Like Jacob hadn't mattered. Like she wasn't going to lose her mind.

Sebastian was going through his days as though he didn't even think about him. He'd even told Jeffry that the best way to get over something like this was to go out and party. She'd overheard them talking when Jeffry had come in late the night before. Sebastian had chided him for being so morose.

This morning her mother-in-law had been up and ready to plan this party like it was the only thing that mattered. Payton wasn't a fool. She knew this Founders' Day celebration wasn't about honoring Jacob. It was about Sebastian's campaign.

She'd been a good wife, a stalwart soldier in political wars, a true daughter-in-law. What did a lifetime of service really mean if the people she served didn't care about her when she needed it the most?

"Having a theme is so important, don't you think?" Alice Johnson, the mayor's wife, was saying.

"Oh, I agree," said her daughter, Tara Douglas. "What are you thinking? I like the idea of Beach Blanket Bingo. Wouldn't that be fun? We could make all the games beach themed."

Payton didn't care about themes. She didn't give a damn about beaches or bingo or shallow women and their shallow lives.

Her life.

Then two sets of eyes were on her. She went on autopilot. Gracious smile. Soft words that offered encouragement but absolutely no commitment.

"Ladies, can I steal Payton for a moment? I have something I need to talk to her about," a familiar voice said.

She glanced to her right and there was Francine. She usually dressed in scrubs. She'd confided once that while it looked like she was the consummate professional, always ready to go to work, she really just liked how comfortable they were. She claimed they were her version of yoga pants. Payton had always wanted to try yoga pants, but ladies in her family neither did yoga as an activity or a fashion statement. Today, Francine was wearing a yellow sundress and a perfect white cardigan, her feet encased in pretty sandals with butterflies on them. They were lovely and whimsical, and Payton was struck by the fact that Francine had sky-blue toenails.

She always used the same sedate polish on her own pedicure. Not too red, but not maroon either. She wouldn't want to offend a Longhorn fan by wearing Aggie colors on her toes.

The other women wandered off, chattering about other themes they could use.

"What did you need to talk with me about?" Payton asked politely.

Francine threaded her arm through Payton's and started to lead her toward the big window. "That was a little lie. I was trying to save you."

"Save me? From what?"

"From all the people talking about stupid things when your heart is aching so badly."

Tears immediately sprang to her eyes. "Where did you get that idea?"

"Because you, Payton Rush, have a good heart and you lost someone you loved and another person you love is still hurting. You ache with it, but you won't let anyone else see. Here you go." She handed Payton a tissue.

They faced away from the committee behind them, looking out over Pecan Street and the Lutheran church where they'd held Jacob's funeral.

"Why are you here, hon? You should be at home with your kids and Celeste."

Payton delicately dried her tears. "I can't. I have to help with the festival. The world moves on, as my mother-in-law would say."

"But you shouldn't have to. You should be able to close off the world and grieve properly."

"I don't know why. No one else is."

"Oh, sweetie, no one else loved him the way your family did. I watch it all the time. It's human nature to shove a tragedy aside at the first available moment. Dwelling on Jacob's death will do nothing but cause these people to have to face their own mortality and honestly, that's not good for anyone. The world does have to move on. You just don't have to join in until you're ready for it. You should be sitting in a room watching old movies and crying your eyes out while your husband brings you gallon after gallon of ice cream. At least that's what I'd do if I were in your position. Except I don't have a husband and I doubt my neighbor's cat is going to supply me with Chunky Monkey."

Sebastian wasn't the indulgent type. He'd never gone to get her a treat because she was down or rushed into the night because she had pregnancy cravings. He'd barely slowed down after Jacob's death. Would he care if it had been Brittany or Jeffry? Or would he have just used it as a campaign platform? She'd heard him talking this morning about some new bill he was planning on cosponsoring to make Texas roads safer.

She knew she was being unkind. Sebastian had an important job, but she wanted to do what Francine had suggested. She wanted to shut the world out just for a little while, to give Jacob's death the honor it should have.

"They're not going to let you slow down, are they?" Francine whispered the question.

If there had been a hint of judgment in the question, she would have been able to walk away with her head held high. But there wasn't. There was kindness in Francine's voice and the slightest hint of conspiracy. As though her friend was already trying to think of ways around the problem. Francine was thinking of her.

"I'm afraid my mother-in-law isn't the 'sit and cry and eat ice cream' kind. I don't think she's had sugar in decades, much less sat down long enough to process an actual emotion." She put a hand over her mouth. Had she just said that out loud? What was wrong with her?

Francine grinned. "There's the spark I always knew you had. There's a firecracker under all that polish."

She wasn't sure about a firecracker. "That was unkind of me to say."

"No, that was truth and you have a place where you can say the truth. We're friends, right?"

Francine was more than a friend, but she couldn't even allow the thought to process. She buried it deep. "Oh, yes. Sometimes I think you're the best friend I've ever had."

Vulnerable. She'd just made herself wickedly vulnerable and she didn't like the feeling. What if Francine didn't feel the same way? That particular question might have been a casual one and Payton had just made a fool of herself. Or she'd made Francine uncomfortable. She would hate that.

Francine gave her one of those sunshine smiles that seemed to bring out the good in Payton. "I'm glad you feel the same. We connect, you and I. And that means that you can say anything to me. I'm a safe place. It's not good for you to bury all the bad stuff. It needs to come out. I know you're a lady, but you're a woman, too. So when you want to say something slightly mean about Saint Marylee, you can say it to me and we'll laugh and then you won't feel so bad about it. Everyone has a secret life, Payton. It's only bad if you don't share it."

The very idea of sharing her inner feelings was foreign to her. She was sure her mother-in-law would tell her not to have any. Marylee would also tell her that having friends outside of the family whom one told one's secrets to was a risk she shouldn't be willing to take.

"Would you mind taking Celeste's place on the committee this year?" The question came out abruptly, and she hurried to explain herself. "Celeste is my partner, but obviously she needs to concentrate on her family this year. You would have to work closely with me. Oh, what am I thinking? You couldn't possibly have time for that. You have the hospital and…"

Francine cut her off by taking her hand. Once more Payton was surprised by the warmth the other woman had. It was like when Francine touched her she imparted some of that lovely heat and for a moment, Payton's skin felt alive.

"I can make the time for you. Of course, I'll take Celeste's place. I would love to."

For the first time in a long time Payton felt a kernel of happiness nestle inside her. "I'm so glad. And maybe you can take me to whoever does your mani pedis. I think I need a change of color."

She was thinking about purple. It would make a nice change.

Chapter Six

Dillon approached Joanne's table with the caution of a man who knew he'd done wrong. He'd handled the situation a few days ago with all the grace of a ham-handed idiot. He'd backed her into a corner and she'd pushed him back like a wounded animal.

That was what he had to remember. She was hurt and aching. He often thought of her as a lovely doe, graceful and fragile, but even a soft animal fought for its life. Joanne was fighting for hers. He just had to find a way to let her know she didn't need to fight alone.

"Good morning, Joanne." He looked down at her sad little breakfast. Oatmeal and water. The cheapest thing on the menu.

She looked up and he could see the fine lines around her eyes that told him she hadn't slept in days. A wary smile crossed her face. "Morning, Sheriff. How are you today?"

"I'm all right."

"Any news?" She gestured to the seat across from her.

At least she wasn't kicking him out again. He sank into the seat and wanted so badly to reach out and grab her hand. "No, I'm sorry. I haven't heard anything new."

Her lips formed a grim line, as though she'd already begun to accept the inevitable. "All right. Well, I've thought about what you said to me the other day."

He shook his head. "I was too harsh with you."

She waved that away. "No, you were being realistic. From everything I can tell, he's walked away on his own. He meant to walk away. I don't know if he's been planning it for a while or if this is some sort of spontaneous moment of insanity, but I have to come to terms with the fact that Hector left me."

Not of his own free will, baby. If he had his way, he'd be right here still slapping you and beating you down. He couldn't tell her that. She wasn't ready to hear anything like that. Yet. One day she would be. One day she would heal enough to see the truth. He intended to be standing beside her when she did. "So you don't want me to file a missing persons report? I'll do whatever you want me to."

She shook her head and he breathed a sigh of relief. "No. He left of his own volition. I even talked to a friend of his. He called him yesterday and asked for his last paycheck to be sent to a new address. I won't even get that. He also cleared out our bank account, according to my daughter."

Dakota worked at the savings and loan. She could likely see that her father had been a selfish son of a bitch. It shouldn't surprise him at all.

"You need to open a new account."

"Yes, Dakota set that up, though she did laugh when I gave her a hundred dollars to put in. One hundred two dollars and fifty-nine cents." She stared down at her hands for a moment. "There's so much debt right now," she said glumly. "I can't think he's going to be making payments on the electricity bill. I assume they'll come after me for his credit card debt as well. I need to find a way to sell the house. I suppose I would need his signature. I can't afford it on my own. I would rather get something out of it than let it go into foreclosure. Mallory and I will move into an apartment. With Marcus and Dakota out of the house, it's just the two of us. We can rent something small. I'm going to think about perhaps cleaning houses in my spare time. I can make money that way."

By being some rich woman's maid? Not if he had anything to say about it. He would make her mortgage payments himself if he had to. He would let her think the money came from Hector. Anything but let her lose her home and be forced to work like a dog. It was his fault she was in the economic situation she was in. He had to be the one to help her out of it. He couldn't live with himself if he didn't.

"I found a job for you."

Her eyes widened. "Really? Why?"

He had to play this subtly. If she thought for a second it was a handout, her pride would take over. For some reason she had an excessive amount of it when it came to him. Luckily, he could tell her the truth this time. Mostly. He didn't need to mention that he'd heard Marylee was looking for someone and he'd managed to write her three tickets in the past two days so he would have leverage to move Joanne into the spot. Marylee hated tickets. He suspected they made her feel like she wasn't the queen of the town. She'd gone for it just like he'd known she would. "I was just talking to Marylee. The Founders' Day celebration committee is meeting in the back."

Skeptical eyes peered at him. "You're on the committee? Are you the resident expert on picnic blankets?"

Oh, he wouldn't have heard that saucy mouth a week ago. He loved it. "No. I'm filling in for my parents, but I do know a surprising amount about picnic blankets."

He knew he'd love to get her on one. He'd love to lay her out and make love to her under a brilliant blue sky.

"All right, I fully believe that your parents have something to do with the celebration."

It was good she believed something about him. "She mentioned that her assistant coordinator quit. She needs someone who can help her organize the businesses and I thought of you."

She flushed, her skin turning the sweetest pink. "I don't know. I've never done anything like it before."

"Sure you have. You've run a family for twenty years. You've managed to handle work and housekeeping and getting the kids where they needed to go, and now you're handling it on your own."

"I suppose I do know how to manage a schedule," she allowed.

"And you know many of the business owners." He knew she coordinated with other businesses for weddings and funerals and parties. She might not realize it, but she was very competent.

She nodded. "But Dillon, I've never spent much time with anyone outside of work."

He knew why. She'd had every second of her time sucked away by Hector. He'd guarded her jealously because he'd likely known if she had friends, she would have people she could turn to instead of him. One of his tactics for keeping her had been isolating her from the town and her friends. "Maybe it's time you did. This is a job you can do when you're not at the florist shop. You don't have to quit. The hours are flexible and more importantly, if Marylee likes you she'll introduce you to everyone. She'll take you under her wing, and it's a formidable wing."

"What if she doesn't like me?"

"There isn't a chance of that happening. You're the most likable person I know. Come on. She invited you to come back. She's eager to put you to work." He held his hand out.

She accepted. "There are a lot of people back there. You really think I'll fit in?"

At least he could give her this. He'd taken a lot from her in the last few days, but he could give her back something Hector had stolen from her. He could give her back a community to depend on. "I think you'll fit in just fine. It's time for you to realize how much people love you, Joanne. And you can get a proper breakfast. Marylee's paying."

She grinned, looking younger than he'd seen her in years. There was the hint of the high school girl in that impish smile. "Thank God. I hate oatmeal. I'm ordering a double waffle."

He walked to the back with her, feeling better than he had in days.

* * * *

Dakota stepped into the Bluebonnet Cafe with her head held high. She wasn't hiding anymore. The last few days had been an exercise in making herself as small as possible so no one would look at her. After she'd heard Mallory and her friends talking about her, she'd realized that maybe she didn't have such a great reputation. It made her do something she didn't like. Think.

She hadn't texted the senator back even though she'd wanted to. She was trying to be a good girl.

She'd only snickered a few times when she'd set up her mother's checking account with a whole hundred bucks. Whoopee. Her mom was a high roller.

And her dad had drained his account. It was sitting at a big, fat zero.

"Hey, Dakota. What are you doing here?" Mary Louise Prager was standing at the hostess station. She was a relatively attractive woman with red hair that could really use a flat iron. She was the niece of the owner of the cafe.

Dakota stared at her like she'd lost her damn mind. What was she doing here? Uhm, that should be obvious. "I was hoping to get some breakfast."

And to show the town that she wasn't the same girl they thought they knew. She was starting something new. She was revamping her image.

Mary Louise frowned. "Oh, I don't think I've ever seen you in here for breakfast."

She smiled. "Yes, I try to stay skinny. So I won't have any of your fatty stuff." That probably came off wrong. She had to watch that. "What I meant was I would love to have a very nutritious meal at your fine establishment."

"Okay." Mary Louise looked down at her seating chart. "We're full right now. Sorry. The committee for the Founders' Day celebration is meeting in the back. They're taking up a good portion of the tables, but I should be able to find you something in ten minutes or so."

"No problem. I'll just find a friend to sit with." She wasn't about to wait around like some pathetic loser. "It looks like half the town is here this morning anyway."

She stepped into the dining room just in time to watch her mother take the sheriff's hand as he helped her up.

What was going on there? There was a look on her mother's face she'd never seen before. Her mom had been smiling, and not in that tight-assed way she usually smiled. She'd actually looked quite lovely. Her mother didn't notice her standing there. She was far too busy staring up into the eyes of the sheriff. He led her toward the back of the cafe, where apparently all the important people in town were meeting.

And now her mom was, too?

The sheriff's hand moved to the small of her mom's back as he ushered her through the door to the back room.

Dakota was left standing in the middle of the cafe. She could hear the whispers of people all around her. They only thought they were being quiet. She could hear them, and every word seemed to cut like a knife.

Her father walked out. Yes, he did. Is it any wonder after all the trouble that girl's caused?

Poor thing. I wonder how her momma's handling it.

I heard they found her at that bar on the edge of town and she didn't have her clothes on.

Gossip. It was going on all around her. She would never get away from it. Not as long as she stayed in this town.

Well, hell, if she was going to gain a bad reputation, the least she could do was earn it.

Her father wasn't going to watch after her anymore. Maybe it was time to find a man who would.

She turned and walked back out of the cafe, passing Mary Louise on her way. "I changed my mind. This isn't my type of place after all."

She pulled out her phone and made her decision.

Her momma didn't care. She was too busy finding another man to take care of her. It looked like it was the sheriff's turn this time. Her sister had her own set of friends, and Dakota knew exactly what they thought of her. Marcus had left a long time ago and now her father wouldn't even return her calls.

She was on her own. She was a smart girl in a dumb town and she had two ways out. One involved stripping at that place on the highway that couldn't even spell cabaret correctly. Vince's Cabarat. Yeah, she wasn't even sure what that meant, but the girls who worked their smelled like smoke and chicken wings and she wasn't doing it.

Or she could take door number two.

I'm sorry to be so late in replying. I'm glad I could play your savior. Wouldn't want the big bad sheriff to sneak into our little fairy tale, would we? Maybe you can pay me back in the future? And I would love to talk...policy with you.

She stopped and realized she didn't have anywhere to go but back to her crappy apartment. She had the day off and no one to spend it with. Her stupid "revamp her reputation" plot had been her whole plan for the weekend and beyond. How foolish she'd been to think she could do it. These people would never see her as anything but trash. Maybe this was why her father had run. He'd gotten tired of all the uppity people looking down at him for not having as much money or not being the church elder or popular among the PTA.

She just wished he'd thought to take her, too.

She prepared for a lonely walk back to her apartment.

A Mercedes Benz pulled up in front of the cafe and the window rolled down. Was that who she thought it was?

She leaned over and sure enough, there was Sebastian Rush. He was dressed in slacks and a dress shirt. The sleeves were rolled up, showing off strong forearms. The dress shirt was open at the collar, hinting at a well-made chest. The senator clearly spent time in the gym. She even liked his salt and pepper hair. It gave him a distinguished air.

"You wouldn't happen to need a rescue, would you?" The sexiest smile crossed his face. He unlocked the door with a flick of his hand.

That had been quick. "You got my text? What were you doing? Driving around town?"

He shook his head. "Yes, I got it. I've been waiting on it. And no. I was on my way here. I'm supposed to join that hen party in there, but I think I'd much rather spend the afternoon with the prettiest chick in town."

It was a bad joke, but she giggled anyway and slid into the front seat. He took off.

"Keep your head down, sweetheart. Until I come up with a reasonable excuse for us to be together, I'd like to protect your reputation."

She slid down in the seat. He wanted to protect her. Oh, she knew somewhere in the back of her head that this was as much for him as her, but he'd said all the right things.

The Bluetooth device came on and she heard the sound of a phone ringing. She kept silent as Payton Rush picked up the other end.

"Hello?" Her boss's voice came on the line. The Rushes owned the savings and loan she worked at.

"Payton, please tell Mother that I hate to bail on her but something important has come up. I'll make the next meeting. This bill I'm writing on highway safety has hit a little snag."

"No problem. We'll handle things here, dear." His wife sounded almost distracted, as though him not showing up was of no real consequence at all.

"You always do." He touched the screen and hung up the call. "What do you say we do some fishing?"

Twenty minutes later she found herself on the edge of Monarch Lake. It was a small body of water but known for its great fishing. Her father had caught many a largemouth bass in this lake. The senator pulled up to a quaint cabin that looked neat and well taken care of.

The senator seemed like a man who valued his possessions.

"My grandfather had it built. I know it's not far from town, but I think it was a world away for him. I like to come out here when I need to be...alone. Come on inside."

He stepped out of the car and she couldn't help but notice how solid he was. Tall and broad.

No one in town would ever think a man like him would look at her. She was just that trampy Alvarez girl whose daddy couldn't even love her.

She scrambled out of the car and right up against him. She had to tilt her head back to look up at him.

"Dakota, do you know what I want from you?" His voice was a low rumble.

"I suppose you want sex."

His hands found her cheeks, framing her face. He looked down at her like she was the loveliest thing in the world. "I want so much more. I want to know you. I want to know everything about you. But, sweetheart, I don't think I'm going to be able to wait to kiss you. Don't make me wait. I want you so badly. I don't know how I'm going to breathe unless I can kiss you."

"I wouldn't want you to pass out." God, that was stupid, but she was the breathless one now. His head lowered to hers and her heart started pounding.

His kiss was light at first, a mere brushing of lips that made her shiver, sent sizzling heat through her limbs. And then he became more demanding, his tongue surging in to slide against hers in a silky dance. His hands moved down her body, cupping her breasts and rubbing against her nipples until she couldn't help the little gasp that escaped from her lips. He pressed his pelvis to hers and she could feel the evidence of his desire. The senator wasn't built on small lines. He rubbed against her, his body showing her what he wanted.

His free hand tangled in her hair, drawing her head back so she was looking into his eyes. "I've wanted you for a long time."

"I wasn't ready." She'd turned him down flat and she hoped he didn't punish her for that. Some men would.

He just smiled and kissed her nose in an oddly tender gesture. "I'm glad you waited. I like this Dakota. This Dakota is mature and knows what she's doing."

He might be the only person in the world who thought that. "I like you, too, Sebastian."

"Do you want me?" The question came out a little gruff, like he wasn't absolutely sure of the answer. Could he have doubts, too?

"Oh, I do. I want you so much. I want you to teach me. I want you to show me your world. I'm so tired of this one." She was weary and he was offering her something new.

"I'll teach you. I'll teach you everything." He kissed her again, a sure sign of his possessiveness. She'd never been kissed with such a slow, hard passion. "Say you're going to be mine, Dakota."

His. She wanted to belong to someone. She'd never imagined it would be him. "Yes."

He leaned over and slid an arm under her knees, picking her up and cradling her to his chest. She felt light and delicate and cared for as he strode inside with her.

He walked through the cabin with ease, like she weighed nothing at all. When he came to the bedroom, he laid her down and stripped off his shirt. Yes, this was a man and not a boy.

A man who could take care of her.

As she surrendered, Dakota vowed that when he left this town, she would be the one at his side.

No matter what.

Crosswinds

By Elisabeth Naughton

About Elisabeth Naughton

Before topping multiple bestseller lists—including those of the *New York Times*, *USA Today*, and the *Wall Street Journal*—Elisabeth Naughton taught middle school science. A voracious reader, she soon discovered she had a knack for creating stories with a chemistry of their own. The spark turned into a flame, and Naughton now writes full-time. Besides topping bestseller lists, her books have been nominated for some of the industry's most prestigious awards, such as the RITA® and Golden Heart Awards from Romance Writers of America, the Australian Romance Reader Awards, and the Golden Leaf Award. When not dreaming up new stories, Naughton can be found spending time with her husband and three children in their western Oregon home. Learn more at www.ElisabethNaughton.com.

Also From Elisabeth Naughton

Eternal Guardians
MARKED
ENTWINED
TEMPTED
ENRAPTURED
ENSLAVED
BOUND
TWISTED
RAVAGED

Aegis Series
EXTREME MEASURES
LETHAL CONSEQUENCES
FATAL PURSUIT

Anthologies
BODYGUARDS IN BED
WICKED FIRSTS
SINFUL SECONDS
ALL HE WANTS FOR CHRISTMAS

Against All Odds Series
WAIT FOR ME
HOLD ON TO ME

Stolen Series
STOLEN FURY
STOLEN HEAT
STOLEN SEDUCTION
STOLEN CHANCES

Firebrand Series
(paranormal romance)
BOUND TO SEDUCTION
SLAVE TO PASSION
POSSESSED BY DESIRE

Acknowledgments from the Author

For every reader, like me, who scheduled his/her classes around their favorite soap opera.

Chapter One

Lacey Salt leaned back against her chaise lounge in the shimmering afternoon light and tipped her sunglasses down to get a better look at the lifeguard on the pool deck of the Cedar Hills Country Club.

The cool water reflected off Luis Moreno's muscular arms, highlighting a body that had transformed nicely from boy to man over the last year. He might be a year younger than Lacey, but Luis could easily pass for nineteen or twenty instead of simply sixteen. Probably a good thing he was taken.

Her gaze shifted to the boy beside him, talking to Luis as if they were best friends while Luis fixed the strap on the boy's goggles. A scowl pulled at Lacey's lips. The boy had splashed water all over her trendy new Victoria's Secret bikini, but more than that, he'd almost ruined the new iPhone her father had given her just this morning. Part of her hoped Luis would shove the little brat into the water and make him scream, but she knew he wouldn't do that. Luis Moreno was way too nice for that kind of thing. Not like her.

Lacey had no use for kids. They whined and screamed and caused all kinds of problems, and she really wished the country club would ban them altogether. Just the thought that she was going to have one in her house soon made her stomach turn.

She looked back at the phone in her hand and swept a finger over the screen. But instead of J. Lo's latest outfit, all she saw was a blur of colors that shifted to familiar faces she'd already spent way too much time thinking about since her brother's funeral.

She still couldn't think about the night Jacob had been driving home from college and was killed on that rain-slicked highway without breaking into tears, but she knew for a fact that having Ginny Moreno move into the Salt family home was a bad idea. So what if Ginny was pregnant with Jacob's kid? She wasn't a Salt and never would be. If Jacob had loved Ginny as much as Ginny claimed, why hadn't anyone known? Why had their relationship been such a secret?

Lacey did not believe that Ginny hadn't known she was pregnant until after the accident. Nine weeks? How could she have not known? So why hadn't they gotten married as soon as they found out she was pregnant?

Those were the hard questions no one in her family wanted to ask. Lacey knew her brother. Jacob had been the most honorable person in town. If he'd gotten a girl pregnant—especially a girl he supposedly loved—he would have married her. He wouldn't have let gossip spread. He'd have done the right thing.

Sara Jane, Lacey's older sister who'd just finished her first year teaching at the local elementary school, didn't want to talk about that, though. Whenever she stopped by the house to check on Mom, and Lacey tried to broach the topic with her, Sara Jane told Lacey it wasn't their business and to stay out of it. But if it wasn't their business, then whose business was it? Her dad was working even longer hours at the pharmacy these days, which meant he wasn't around when Lacey wanted to talk. And whenever Lacey even mentioned the baby to her mom, Celeste Salt would break down into tears and rush for the bathroom. Oh, her mom put on a happy face whenever Ginny emerged from her room—correction, whenever Ginny emerged from *Jacob's* room—but Lacey knew the truth.

Her family was falling apart. Her brother was dead. Her sister didn't care what was going on at home. And her parents barely even talked anymore. Lacey's mom was holding on to the fact that Ginny's baby would save them all, but Lacey was starting to think that baby was the reason everything was turning to shit. If it weren't for Ginny Moreno and her unplanned brat, Lacey's brother would never have been in that car the night it sailed off the road.

"Since when do you follow Ludacris?"

The deep male voice jolted Lacey out of her thoughts. She looked to her left where Luis sat on the edge of the empty chaise beside her in his sexy red lifeguard shorts.

"You into rap now?" he asked, leaning forward to rest tan, muscular arms on his knees.

She blinked against the blinding sun. Or maybe it was Luis's thousand-watt smile. He'd always been a good-looking guy, but his face had changed over the last year until it was now chiseled and just plain hot. "Huh?"

He pointed toward her phone, and his dark, curly hair, longer than he'd worn it before, brushed his jaw in a way that reminded her of Kit Harington, that super hot hunk from *Game of Thrones*. "Ludacris."

Slowly, her gaze shifted to her phone, and she realized she'd jumped to another celeb's social media page. But all she could see in her mind was Luis's carved abs, those strong shoulders, and the way his swim trunks hovered dangerously low, accentuating the carved V of his hip bones.

He's your best friend's boyfriend. What the hell are you thinking?

Frustrated with everyone, including herself, Lacey huffed and sat up straighter. "Not on purpose. I must have switched pages when I was plotting ways to throw that brat into the deep end."

Luis chuckled, and the sound sent butterflies fluttering in Lacey's belly. Butterflies that threw her completely off balance. "I couldn't let you do that. Gotta guard the lives and all that. That's why they pay me the big bucks."

Geez. What the heck was wrong with her? She'd been friends with Luis for years. Had heard him laugh a hundred times. And she'd never responded to him this way. Maybe she had heat stroke.

"I thought you were working," she said, trying to get him to leave her alone so she didn't have to look at his dark eyes that were way too cute. She reached for the sunscreen she'd set on the end of her chaise.

"My shift's over. So you're coming tonight, right?"

She squirted a dollop of sunscreen onto her palm. "Coming where?"

"My place. We planned this like a week ago, remember? *The Grudge* comes on at nine so don't be late. Marisol said she'd clear out so we could watch without her constant chatter."

"Ugh." Marisol was Luis's older sister and guardian. She'd been taking care of Luis ever since his parents had died when he was in grade school. Lacey liked Marisol, but still. She frowned at Luis as she rubbed lotion all over her legs. "You know I hate those kind of movies."

"This one's good. Trust me. And if you get scared, I'll protect you."

Her hand paused on her calf, and another flock of butterflies flittered through her belly.

"Or Jeffry can," he added.

Those wings came to a stuttering stop. Jeffry Rush had been running with Luis for years, and Lacey liked him, but she'd never thought of him as anything more than a friend. Sure, he was a good-looking guy too—dark blond hair, lean athletic body, and rich brown eyes like his father the senator—but he didn't make her heart beat faster.

Like Luis does?

Unease spread through her belly as she rubbed her legs a little harder. "I don't know."

"Come on, Lace. Don't say no. Mallory needs this. Things are tough at home for her right now. She needs a night where we all hang out like old times. No pressure, no stress, just us."

Us... Images rippled through Lacey's mind, but they had nothing to do with the four of them. No, the images she saw were filled only with her and the guy beside her. Alone. Together.

"Lace?"

"I-I don't know." Mortification burned through Lacey. Mallory was her best friend, and she was struggling with the fact her dad had just walked out on her family. But besides that, she and Luis were an item, and Lacey was sitting here having fantasies about Mallory's boyfriend? God, she was sick. The need to run pushed her out of the chaise. She shoved the sunscreen into the bag at her feet, then grabbed the towel from the back of her chair. "We'll see. I gotta go."

She made it three steps across the pool deck before Luis caught her by the arm. "Hey, wait."

Oh, man. His hand on her bare skin felt good. Really good. She'd seriously had too much sun. "What now?"

"Listen." He turned her to face him, but he didn't let go of her arm. And she didn't pull away when she knew she should because his touch sent little tingles over her skin that she liked way too much. "I'm a jerk, okay? I didn't mean to imply that things aren't rough for you right now. I know they are. I know you miss Jacob and that it can't be easy having my sister living in your house. God, I just..." He sighed and looked out over the pool, pain etching lines into his face no sixteen-year-old boy should have. "It's rough for all of us. The whole thing just sucks."

It did. He was right. But she knew he wasn't just talking about what had happened to Jacob. He was remembering back. To the day his parents had died in that wreck. He'd just been a kid then, but Jacob's death, in such a similar way, had to be bringing it all back up for him.

Did Mallory see that? Probably not. Lacey loved Mallory like a sister, but Mallory took Luis for granted. They'd only started dating a few months ago when Mallory had asked Luis to the spring dance, and Mallory never fawned over him the way most new girlfriends did. Lacey wasn't even sure Mallory really liked Luis the way a girlfriend should. In fact, if it weren't for Lacey, the two wouldn't even be together. Lacey was the one who'd pointed out how good-looking Luis was getting. Mallory hadn't even been interested in him until then.

"Look," Luis said, meeting her gaze, his dark eyes filled with so much compassion those butterflies took off all over again. "I just want you to be there tonight, okay? I think it would be good for all of us."

Man, he had great eyes. Dark brown irises and crazy long lashes. Those were the kind of eyes a girl could get lost in forever. And his lips were full and, she bet, super soft. What would he do if she rose to her toes and kissed him right here?

"Say you'll come, okay, Lace?"

Luis squeezed her arm, and the pressure was like a jolt back to reality. Looking quickly away, Lacey realized what she'd just been about to do. Heat swept up her cheeks, and the need to flee overwhelmed her.

"I... I'll see." She tugged her arm from his grip before he could stop her, tossed her bag over her shoulder, and rushed for the building.

Alone in her car, Lacey gripped the steering wheel in both hands and drew in a shaky breath. Holy crap. She'd almost put the moves on her best friend's boyfriend. She was losing it. Seriously losing it.

She shoved the car into drive and headed home. The sun set behind the old stone courthouse as she passed the square. Several people milled about on the streets of downtown Storm, but she braced her elbow on the windowsill, pushed her fingers against her forehead, and angled her face downward so she didn't make eye contact with anyone on the sidewalk. She wasn't in the mood to be friendly, but more than that, she hated how everyone she ran into these days looked at her with pity. And when they started asking questions—how her mom was doing, how Ginny was feeling, and if there was anything they could do to help with the baby—Lacey wanted to scream.

No one asked how *she* was doing. No one seemed to care that she'd lost her only brother. Not even her own parents. They hadn't even once asked how she felt about Ginny Moreno moving into their house.

By the time Lacey made it home and pulled into her drive, she was more keyed up than she'd been before. She turned off the ignition and sat in her car for several minutes just trying to pull herself together, but as soon as her gaze landed on the house, her mood took a nose dive. The Salt home had always been a showplace. Her mom had always been meticulous about the flower beds and the yard and making sure the whole town knew how great the Salts were. Now it was a wreck. The front yard was overgrown and in desperate need of mowing. The flowerbeds were filled with weeds, the plants spindly from lack of deadheading. The garbage can was even sitting out front. No one had bothered to pull it in after garbage pickup two days ago.

She knew she should get out there and help. Her mom was still a mess from Jacob's funeral and her dad was a virtual no-show these days. But she didn't want to do anything to help them. Not when they were treating her as if she didn't even exist. And especially not when Ginny Moreno was their new favorite daughter.

Scowling, Lacey climbed out, grabbed her stuff, then slammed the car door and headed for the porch. The house was quiet when she walked in. She dropped her beach bag and towel on the entry table, not even caring that the wet towel might leave a mark on the old wood. "Mom?"

Silence.

Moving through the first floor, she checked rooms for her mom, but they were all empty. Celeste hadn't been out of the house in days, but if she was gone, Lacey figured that was a good thing for her. For once she wouldn't have to tiptoe around her own stupid house.

She grabbed a soda from the fridge, then jogged up the steps to her room. After flipping on the radio, she flopped onto the bed and opened her reading app. Right now she didn't want to think about real life. She just wanted to get lost in a book. But her phone buzzed before she could do that, and she frowned as Mallory's name flashed on the screen.

Her best friend was the last person she wanted to talk to. Not after all Lacey's crazy thoughts about Luis. She couldn't ignore Mallory though. If she did, Mallory would just show up at her house to see what was up.

"Hey, Mal," she said as nonchalantly as she could, pressing the phone to her ear and rolling to her back on the pink comforter.

"Luis said you're not coming tonight. What's that about?"

Lacey pressed a hand to her forehead. *Stupid Luis.* "Um... I'm not really feeling it tonight. I'm just tired. It's no biggie."

"Lace."

Lacey could hear the exasperation in Mallory's voice, and she knew what her friend was thinking. How could she be tired when she didn't do anything all day? Technically, Lacey worked part time at Cuppa Joe, but Marisol Moreno, who ran the bakery, had told her to take as much time off as she needed to get her head on straight, and so far Lacey didn't feel like she was there. Marisol, being Luis's older sister, knew all about grief and loss. So the fact that Lacey hadn't gone back to work yet had absolutely nothing to do with being lazy, as Mallory thought, and everything to do with simply listening to her boss.

"Come on," Mallory said. "It'll be fun."

Lacey wasn't so sure.

"Besides, if you don't go I won't be responsible for my actions."

Lacey snorted a laugh. "What's that supposed to mean?"

"It means a lot," Mallory muttered. She drew a deep breath. "Luis and I have been talking about... doing it."

"Doing what?"

"You know." Mallory's voice took on an edge of nervousness. "*It.*"

Lacey sat straight up. "*What?*"

"I don't know," Mallory said. "I mean, we've been together for three months already, and he's got girls hitting on him all the time. Luis is Mister Popular even if he isn't from one of the old families in town. I just... I don't want to lose him, you know?"

Lacey's stomach swirled with the force of a tornado. "*That's* why you're going to screw him? To keep other girls away?"

"Ugh. I hate that word. Can't you find another way to say it?"

"If you don't like screw you're not going to like the other ways I say it. Answer the question, Mal."

Mallory sighed. "No, that's not why. Not really. I mean, I care about him. A lot. And we haven't totally decided yet. We're just...

thinking about it."

Lacey couldn't believe it. Didn't want to believe it. Dating Luis was one thing, but sleeping with him... that took their relationship to a whole other level.

"What does Luis think about it?" she asked quickly.

"He's interested. I mean, he's a guy. They're *all* interested."

"Was it his idea or yours?"

Mallory was quiet for a second. Then said, "Mine."

Which didn't surprise Lacey. Mallory's older sister, Dakota, had a reputation for getting around, and Mallory was definitely more of a wild child than Lacey had ever been. But she wasn't like Dakota. She was smart and, because of those brains of hers, one day Mallory was going to do something important with her life.

"I don't know." Mallory groaned. "Tell me what to do, Lace. I don't know what to do."

Lacey knew this was her moment to be the supportive best friend. To talk about the pros and cons. To remind Mallory that she was only sixteen. But she suddenly didn't want to be supportive. She wanted exactly what she'd wanted today at the pool. She wanted Luis. And she knew if Mallory slept with him, her chance to have him for herself was gone.

"I think"— She glanced toward her closet, already choosing her outfit for the evening—"I'm going to come tonight after all."

"You are?" Excitement lifted Mallory's voice.

"Yeah." A voice in the back of Lacey's head whispered she was playing with fire, but Lacey was way past listening. "We'll talk about it all then. Just don't do anything stupid."

"I won't," Mallory answered. "This is going to be fun."

It would be. Lacey would make sure of that. Because she was tired of sitting around feeling sorry for herself. It was time she forgot about everyone else and had her own fun.

* * * *

Luis Moreno dumped his gym bag on the kitchen table and grabbed a cookie from the jar on the counter before heading into the living room. Marisol, his older sister, always brought home a fresh batch of chocolate chip cookies from work, just for him. She was up and gone before the sun, owning and operating Storm's local bakery, and he hated that she had to work so hard, especially because she did it to take care of him, but he definitely enjoyed the perks.

He munched on his cookie as he dropped onto the old couch, kicked off his slides, and propped his bare feet on the dinged-up coffee table. He was still wearing his red lifeguarding shorts, but after work he'd pulled on his favorite black Hollister T-shirt, the one Mallory said made his eyes look dark and sexy. Reaching for the remote, he flipped the channel to ESPN and settled in to check the day's baseball scores. Drawers opened and closed somewhere in the back of the house, and he knew Marisol was back there putting away laundry, but he had a bet with Jeffry on the Ranger game, and right now he needed to know if he'd won before his buddy showed up in an hour.

"Luis?" Marisol called from the bedrooms. "Is that you?"

"Yeah," he yelled, eyes glued to the TV. "I'll come help you in a second."

"I made lasagna. It's on the stove."

He mumbled a thanks and watched the scores roll across the bottom of the screen. A clip from the Ranger game flashed, and Luis lifted the remote to turn up the volume.

"*What a game,*" the announcer said. "*I haven't seen a matchup this explosive since Robin Ventura went after Nolan Ryan back in 1993 and—*"

Marisol stepped in front of the TV and flipped it off.

"Hey." Luis dropped his feet from the coffee table and sat upright. "I was watching that."

Marisol turned to face him. "What the heck is this?"

A rattling sounded, and Luis's gaze shifted to the orange box in her hand. *Trojan* was written in big white letters all across the front.

"Oh, shit."

Marisol's big brown eyes grew wide. "Are you and Mallory having sex?"

Luis cringed. Just the way she said that word—sex—made the hairs on his nape stand and quiver. This was so not a conversation he wanted to have with his sister. She might be thirty-one, but some things should be private from a sibling, even one who was your guardian.

"Answer me," she demanded.

Luis sighed and dropped the remote on the couch beside him. He knew when Marisol meant business. He also knew when he couldn't blow her off. "No. We're not."

"Not yet." Marisol lifted an eyebrow in displeasure.

Crossing his arms, he perched his foot on the edge of the coffee table and pursed his lips.

"I thought you said you were going to wait until college. That you didn't want to do anything to mess up your chance for a scholarship. I can't pay for college, Luis. You know that. College is your way out. If Mallory gets pregnant, you're going to be stuck in Storm forever."

Like her. She didn't say it. She never said it, but Luis knew Marisol had sacrificed her dreams to take care of him and Ginny. She'd stayed in Storm, opened the bakery with a little help from the Rush family, and most days she seemed happy, but he knew what-ifs were always somewhere on her mind.

"We're not having sex, okay?"

"Then what are these?" She shook the box, her long, dark hair falling over her shoulder with the movement.

He sighed. "They're a precaution."

Her shoulders dropped. "Luis—"

"No, listen." He sat forward. "Nothing's happened and nothing's gonna happen. Mallory and I talked about it, and I bought 'em just in case, but I knew as soon as I got the box home that I'm not ready. College is still important to me. And I'm not stupid enough to mess that up."

Relief trickled over Marisol's face, followed by a whisper of guilt. She moved around the coffee table to sit on the edge of the couch next to him. "I'm sorry. I know I should be the cool older sister about all this but—"

"But you can't." He took the box and set it on the floor because just looking at it in her hand wigged him out. "I get it."

"I just... I want you to have everything, Luis. You could really go places. You're smart and funny and so mature for your age—everyone says so. And I just don't want to see you throw it all away for some... girl."

He understood she wanted him to have all the things she hadn't. But he didn't like what she was implying. "Mallory isn't just *some girl*."

She tipped her head and frowned. "Four months ago you had the hots for Lacey Salt, not Mallory Alvarez. You've had a crush on Lacey since you were in the second grade."

Warmth spread up Luis's face, and he crossed his arms over his chest, then leaned back away from her. "Lacey and I are just friends."

"Which is why you're going out with Mallory."

Was it? No. He really liked Mallory. Sure, he hadn't thought much about her as girlfriend material until she'd asked him to the spring dance, but now he was glad she had. Besides which, Lacey had never—and would never—be interested in him, so it was a moot point anyway.

"Look," Marisol said. "I'm not trying to diss on Mallory. I like her. A lot. She's a great kid. She comes from a rough family, but she's managed to get through it better than most. I just want you to be sure she's the one before you take a big step like"—she gestured toward the box of condoms at his feet—"this."

"We're not having sex," he said louder. "I already told you that."

"I know. I heard you. It's just... I love you, you know? And I want you to be happy. I want both you and Ginny to be happy. And Ginny's not happy right now, and I don't know what to do to make her happy. And I have no idea what she's going to do with a baby. She's going to be stuck in this town forever now, with no chance to get out. And I know everyone's excited about this baby and that I should be too, but..."

Oh crap. Marisol's eyes filled with tears, and Luis sensed she was about to completely break down. She hadn't done that yet. Not since Ginny's accident. Not since Ginny left to live with the Salts. Not once in all that time. She'd been the family rock, like always. But apparently even those rocks had cracks.

"Hey." He wrapped his arms around her and pulled her in to his chest. "It's okay. We're all okay."

She grabbed onto his T-shirt as the tears slid down her cheeks. "It's not. Not really. It's like our family's being ripped apart all over again."

He held her as she cried, thinking a little of the same thing. But she saw things differently because she was older. Life hadn't been fair to Marisol. He knew that. She'd been in her third year of college when their parents had died. And instead of going to frat parties and bonfires and football games, she'd suddenly had to drive carpool and attend PTA meetings and help with homework. He missed his parents every day, but he'd only been six when they'd died. Marisol was more a parent to him than he could remember them being. It wasn't the same for her. She had a lifetime of memories with their parents. And her life was the one that had been forever changed when they died.

"We're not being ripped apart, you hear me?" Luis gripped her shoulders and pushed her back so he could see her face. Marisol sniffled and swiped at her tears. "We're fine. Ginny's fine. You've done an amazing job with us, Marisol. You raised us right, and I know Mom and Dad would be proud of what you've done."

Tears filled her eyes again, but she swiped the back of her hand over her face before they could fall. "I just want to protect you both."

"I know you do. But you can't. Not forever. At some point we have to make our own choices. And you have to trust us enough to let us do that."

Marisol rubbed both hands over her face, then dropped them in her lap and glared at him. "I don't like it when you're smarter than me."

He smiled because that was the feisty older sister he knew and loved. "I'll try not to be. At least when you're around."

She punched him in the shoulder. "Fine. Whatever." Then, pushing to her feet, she added, "What time are your friends coming over?"

"Eight."

"Okay. I'm gonna take a shower, then I'm going to take some cranberry scones left over from work to the Salts' and see how Ginny's doing."

"You don't have to leave. My friends like you."

"I know." She moved around the couch. "But you're right. I have to start trusting you to make your own choices. Even if I don't like them."

He rolled his eyes and reached for the remote again, happy this conversation was over. A few tears he could handle, but if it had turned into a waterfall he'd have been in serious trouble. "I told you, I'm not sleeping with Mallory, and even if I were, I wouldn't be doing it tonight."

"Good." Marisol headed for the hall. "At least now I don't have to worry about washing all the sheets."

"Ew!" He picked up his slide from the floor and chucked it toward her.

The slide hit the wall and dropped to the floor. Marisol laughed and disappeared toward her bedroom.

Luis was smiling when he sank back into the cushions. Unfortunately, though, the sportscasters were no longer talking about the Rangers. He watched the ticker, waiting for the score while the shower flipped on at the back of the house, but the longer he sat there, the more his mind drifted to what Marisol had said about Lacey. Images of her curvy body in the lime-green bikini she'd been wearing at the pool today flashed in his brain.

Marisol was right, though he'd never admit it out loud, even to her. He was still into Lacey Salt. More than he should be for a guy who had a girlfriend. For a guy who had a *great* girlfriend. One who liked him so much, *she* was initiating the whole sex discussion instead of it being the other way around. He really cared about Mallory and didn't want to do anything to mess up their relationship, but those feelings he'd had for Lacey for years were still there, lingering beneath the surface. And no matter what he did, he couldn't seem to get rid of them completely.

He frowned and crossed his arms over his chest as he stared at the TV. He hadn't lied when he told Marisol he wasn't interested in sex yet because he wasn't ready. He *wasn't* ready. But something in the back of his mind couldn't help but wonder whether he'd feel the same if Lacey Salt were the one doing the initiating.

Chapter Two

Mallory Alvarez's nerves were a jangled mess as she pulled her mom's ancient Oldsmobile to a stop in front of Luis's small one-story house. She still hadn't decided what she wanted to do or if she was ready to take their relationship to the next level, but she needed to know how he felt about it all before she made up her mind.

She shoved the car into park and killed the ignition. The old vehicle gave a rumbling shudder then went silent. After checking her hair in the rearview mirror, she told herself to stop being a baby. She'd started this whole discussion, hadn't she? She had to be mature about it. Heck, her older sister Dakota was never mature about boys, and all sorts of rumors had sprung up about her as a result.

Her mind skipped to the day Dakota had discovered their father had split on the family without warning. Dakota had flipped out and blamed their mom for not doing enough to keep her husband happy. Mallory, on the other hand, considered Hector Alvarez's disappearance a blessing. He wasn't the perfect father Dakota thought him to be. He treated their mom like shit, and Mallory was tired of the bruises her mom tried to pass off as her being clumsy. Dakota chose not to see the truth because, Mallory knew, her sister was just as screwed up as their father.

Not exactly the person you want to aspire to be, a little voice whispered in the back of Mallory's head.

Shaking off the voice—and thoughts of her sister that would just make her depressed all over again—Mallory climbed out of her car and headed across the walk toward the Moreno's house. The days were long now, and even at 8 p.m., the sky was only just starting to show signs of darkening. She climbed the three porch steps and knocked. Shuffling sounded from inside, and she recognized Jeffry Rush's voice just before the door opened.

"Hey, Mal." Jeffry's rich brown eyes were warm and inviting as he held the door open for her.

"Hi, Jeffry." She handed him the bag of chips and six-pack of root beer she'd brought. "Is Lacey here?"

"Not yet." He closed the door. "Luis is in the kitchen."

"Thanks."

Those nerves kicked up all over again as Mallory headed for the kitchen and Jeffry set the snacks on the coffee table then dropped onto the couch. When she stepped into the room with its U-shaped counter and small round table, she found Luis setting out a batch of Marisol's cookies on a plate.

"Hey," he said, looking up and smiling.

Her insides warmed. God, he was cute. Lacey thought she was the one who'd made Mallory realize how hot Luis was, but the truth was that Mallory had noticed a long time ago. She'd had a crush on Luis Moreno since freshman year. She'd just been too shy to do anything about it until Lacey had nudged her into action.

"Hey." She rounded the table and stepped next to him, wondering if she should kiss him or hug him or...what. She still wasn't totally comfortable with their greetings and they'd been going out for months.

Finally deciding kissing him was a smart idea—especially considering the chat they needed to have—she rose up on her toes and pressed her lips to his cheek.

He looked down at her and smiled wider, and a few of those nerves settled. No matter what they decided, she knew they were in a good place.

"Are those chocolate chip?" she asked.

"Yep." He added the last of the cookies and set the Tupperware container on the kitchen counter behind him. "How was work today?"

Mallory worked part time at the bed and breakfast in town—mostly cleaning rooms and doing laundry. It wasn't a glamorous job by any means, but it was a paycheck. And with things tight at home now that her dad was gone, she was glad for it. "Good. Slow. That reporter who was doing a story on Senator Rush left today. Those reporters are always trying to dig up dirt on the guy."

"Jeffry would probably give them plenty of dirt if they asked."

In their circle it was widely known that Jeffry didn't think too highly of his dear old dad. They got along okay, but Senator Rush was always back and forth between Storm and Austin, and he'd missed a lot of Jeffry's life growing up. Jeffry could never count on him to make the big game or even be there when he needed to talk, and because of that, he'd just stopped expecting anything other than a "Well done, son" pat on the back now and then.

"Yeah." Mallory smirked. "Probably. Goes to show they're asking the wrong people. Though now that he's working at *The Storm Team Weekly News* for the summer, he could write his own story if he wanted."

Luis shook his head and smiled. "So very true."

He moved around the room, gathering napkins and a few snacks from the panty, and as Mallory watched, those nerves jingled all over again.

When he came back to the table and set out a bag of Doritos, she told herself to quit beating around the bush and grasped his hand. "Um. I was wondering if we could talk for a minute."

"Okay." A nervous look crossed his features, then he took a breath and turned to face her. "I was thinking that too."

He was? Oh, man. Her stomach rolled with both fear and excitement.

"Luis, I—"

"I think we should wait."

Mallory eyes widened as she looked up at him, unsure she'd heard him right. "What?"

He grasped her other hand. "I like you. A lot. And I'm not saying I don't want to. I do. I just..." He glanced toward the refrigerator, then refocused on her. "I think it'd be better if we waited until we're both a little older."

Older... It was exactly what she'd been thinking and was too afraid to say. But for some reason, dread filled her stomach just the same.

Her hands grew sweaty, and she gently pulled them from his, not wanting him to notice. "Older like...end of the summer older or—"

"Mal." He reached for her hands again. "Don't read anything into it. I just want the first time to be special, and I don't want to rush it. Okay?"

Relief that he wasn't breaking up with her filled her chest, but then she realized he'd said "*the* first time," not "*our* first time."

The front door opened and closed. "I heard there was a party happening in here." Lacey's voice echoed from the front room. "This doesn't look like a party yet."

Luis leaned down and kissed Mallory's cheek. "Let's have fun tonight. We all need it. We'll talk more later."

Before Mallory could respond, he let go of her and headed into the front room. His voice echoed back to her when he said, "Hey, Lacey. I knew you couldn't say no."

"Well," Lacey answered. "You wore me down. How could a girl say no to this face?"

Alone, Mallory leaned back against the counter and drew in a steadying breath. Talk later. What did that mean? He'd said not to read anything into it, but if there was more to talk about, it meant there was something else on his mind, right?

From the front room, Luis said, "What the heck is that?"

"Something to make sure we all have a little fun," Lacey answered. "Come on. Don't be a stick in the mud. Live a little."

"Does your mom know you took that?" Jeffry asked.

"No. But trust me, she'll never find out. She barely even knows I'm alive anymore."

All Mallory wanted to do was sit in the kitchen until she pulled herself together, but curiosity got the best of her. She moved into the living room, then drew to a stop when she caught sight of Lacey, popping the top off a beer and leaning back against the cushions on Luis's couch. "There's my very best friend in the world."

Shock rippled through Mallory. Lacey never drank. But more than that...her hair was curled all around her face, her makeup dramatic to play up her eyes. And she was wearing heels—something else she never did. Heels, skinny jeans, and a low-cut sleeveless blouse that accentuated her cleavage so much, Luis and Jeffry were practically drooling.

"What are you doing?" Mallory demanded.

"Unwinding." Lacey held up a beer. "Looks like you could use some unwinding too."

Mallory's gaze shot to Luis, standing behind Lacey with a deer in the headlights look, then to Jeffry, trying hard to look anywhere but at Lacey's tits.

Neither boy was going to do anything, Mallory realized. Which meant it was all up to her.

She crossed the room and grabbed both beers from Lacey's hands.

"Hey." Lacey sat forward and reached out for the open bottle, but Mallory twisted it behind her back. "I was drinking that."

"Now you're not."

Mallory slid the unopened beer back into the carton, then grabbed the six-pack and headed for the kitchen.

"Oh my God." Lacey lurched to her feet and followed. "Who made you the party police? What's wrong with you?"

"*What's wrong with me?*" Mallory dumped the open beer down the sink, slammed the bottle on the counter, and turned on her friend. "What's wrong with *you?* We're all under age. Do you not even care that you're in your boss's house?"

Lacey rolled her eyes. "What does my boss have to do with anything?"

"Marisol could get in big trouble if anyone found out we were drinking."

"No one's going to get into trouble," Lacey said in an *it's no big deal* voice as Luis and Jeffry stepped into the room quietly behind her. "And Marisol will never know. She's at my house. I saw her before I left."

"It doesn't matter." Mallory's eyes widened. "She could go to jail."

Lacey shook her head as if Mallory was an idiot, then turned to grab Luis's arm. "God, she's such a party pooper. I don't know how you put up with her. I want to jump on your old trampoline for a while. Come outside with me."

Luis looked over Lacey's head toward Mallory, and Mallory tensed, waiting to see what he would do. They were all friends, but lately, the way Lacey touched Luis whenever he was close was grating on Mallory's nerves. Most days, she told herself Lacey was just a touchy-feely person and that her flirting was harmless and unintended. But right now, watching Lacey hang on his arm and bat her eyelashes up at him as if he were the man of her dreams didn't look innocent. Or harmless. It looked dangerous.

Luis shrugged toward Mallory, then looked down at Lacey, and didn't—Mallory noticed—pull his arm away. "Okay. But only for a few minutes. That thing's so rusty I'm afraid if one of us falls we might get gangrene."

Lacey laughed, slid her hand down to his, and pulled him toward the sliding glass door. "You'll catch me if I fall. I'm sure of it."

They disappeared into the backyard, and though she told herself not to look, Mallory turned to watch them through the kitchen window.

A sharp pain lanced her chest, as if someone had pierced her with a knife. Luis had said no to sleeping with her, but she'd never once heard him say no to Lacey. Though this wasn't the same and he and Lacey weren't having sex, Mallory wasn't stupid. She'd gone to school with Luis all her life, and she'd always known he had a crush on Lacey. Knew because she used to watch him the way he watched Lacey. She thought he'd gotten over that crush when he'd started dating her. Now, the knowledge that Lacey would always be his "first love" was all Mallory could think about.

"He's just being nice, you know," Jeffry said softly at her back. "That's what Luis does. Tries to make everyone feel better. He's the peacemaker in the Moreno family. Always has been. Luis and Lacey...it doesn't mean anything."

Tears filled Mallory eyes. Tears she fought because she didn't want anyone to see her greatest fear. "I know it doesn't. They're just friends."

But something in the back of her mind didn't believe that.

Remembering the alcohol, she looked away from the window, reached for a beer from the carton, popped the top, and dumped it down the drain.

Jeffry leaned back against the counter next to her and crossed his arms over his chest. "It's okay to be mad at her, you know. Just because she's your best friend doesn't mean she can do whatever she wants."

"I don't know what you mean." She reached for the second beer.

Jeffry sighed. "Yes, you do. You don't have to act like it doesn't bother you, because I can see that it does. It pisses me off too."

Mallory's hand shook against the bottle, and she looked up at Jeffry, relieved and even more scared that someone saw the same thing. "What can I possibly do about it? He's had a crush on her since the second grade."

"He's with you, not her."

Mallory closed her eyes against the sting of tears. "For how long? Lacey's always gotten what she wanted. Always." She opened her eyes. "Did you see her new cell phone? She told her dad she wanted it and he gave it to her this morning. She made the drill team without even trying out. She gets straight A's without studying. She only works at the bakery because it'll look good on her college applications. If she wants Luis, all she has to do is tell him."

Jeffry pinned her with a hard look. "Then stop her."

"How? I'm just...me."

"Yeah, you're you. Which is the exact opposite from Lacey. She's been given everything because she's a Salt, and you've been given nothing because you're an Alvarez. And yet, even though you come from the wrong family on the wrong side of town, you've made honor roll every semester for the past two years. You work a part-time job, and everyone who steps foot in the Flower Hill Bed and Breakfast loves you. And you volunteer at the hospital, where Dr. Rush tells everyone who will listen that you're going to be an incredible doctor one day. Everyone in Storm knows that you're not like the rest of the Alvarezes. You work hard for what you have, and you earn it. So work for Luis if he's what you really want. If you don't let Lacey take him away, she won't be able to. But if you sit back and do nothing, I guarantee she will."

The sliding glass door opened while Mallory stared at Jeffry and his words swirled in her head. Lacey's laughter filled the kitchen, followed by Luis's chuckle.

"You guys ready for the movie?" Luis asked.

"Yeah." Jeffry glanced toward the others. "We're more than ready. Right, Mallory?"

Mallory swallowed hard, unsure if she was ready for anything.

"Cool." Luis headed for the front room, and Lacey quickly followed. "Let's get it going."

Jeffry sent Mallory one more pointed look, then followed the others into the next room. Alone, Mallory drew in a deep breath as she thought through Jeffry's advice.

She did want Luis. She cared about him deeply. And she wasn't about to let Lacey come between them.

The opening credits were already rolling when she stepped into the room. Someone had turned the lights down so an eerie blue light from the television shone over the furniture and each face. Jeffry was seated in a chair near the window. Lacey had already claimed a spot next to Luis on the couch, not too close, but close enough to tick Mallory off.

Luis looked toward the doorway and smiled. Patting the cushions on his other side, he said, "Come here. You're going to like this."

Oh, Mallory knew she was going to like this. She crossed toward the couch, but she didn't sit next to him. Instead, she sidled onto his lap, glanced once toward Lacey to make sure she was watching, then brushed her hand along Luis's jaw and kissed him. Passionately.

By the time she was done, she was breathless. Luis looked confused and a little light-headed. Lacey, to Mallory's delight, was pissed.

"Um...what was that for?" Luis asked.

Mallory leaned in. "Just because."

Before she could kiss him again, he drew back, then quickly scooted her off his lap so she dropped onto the cushions beside him. Reaching for her hand so she couldn't climb back on top of him, he nodded toward the screen. "Oh, it's starting. You don't want to miss this."

But Mallory didn't care about the movie. All she saw was the fact Luis was more interested in the TV than he was in her. And that Lacey was watching them from his other side with a very self-satisfied smirk.

* * * *

Luis hit the power on the remote when the movie ended and glanced toward Mallory at his side. "Awesome, huh?"

Mallory shrugged and pushed to her feet as Jeffry flipped on the lamp, illuminating the room in a warm, golden glow. "It was fine, I guess. Not very realistic." She looked around the living room. "Where are my keys?"

A whisper of disappointment rushed through him. "Do you have to leave already?"

"Yeah. I have to be at the B&B by seven tomorrow morning, and if I don't head home soon my mom will call wondering where I am."

Luis frowned up at her. "I wish you could stay."

She didn't answer as she moved away, searching for her keys, but he hoped she knew he truly meant it. Tonight had been odd. Not just because they'd had that conversation in the kitchen but because of Lacey. She'd fallen asleep during the movie, leaning against his shoulder. But more than that, she'd been acting strange the whole evening, flirting with him, touching him, drinking—which was so unlike the good Salt girl the town knew her to be. He just hoped Mallory didn't get the wrong idea because there was no idea to get.

Carefully, he shifted Lacey so she was lying on the couch, then moved toward Mallory. Thankfully, Jeffry disappeared into the kitchen with the empty root beer bottles so they could have a moment alone. Capturing Mallory's hands, he turned her toward him and laced his fingers with hers. "Sorry this wasn't the great night I had hoped for."

Mallory darted a look toward the couch where Lacey slept softly snoring. "I know she's going through a rough patch right now with Jacob's death and all, and I know I'm her best friend and that I'm supposed to be supportive, but I don't like the way she was acting tonight."

"I know." He wrapped his arms around her and pulled her into his chest. "Let's just cut her a break on this one, okay? It was probably alcohol. I bet she drank some before she came over."

Mallory muttered "Maybe" and slid her arms around his waist. Then she pressed her cheek to Luis's chest and relaxed into him, and all the worry he'd had about the night slipped away. She felt good against him. Warm and sweet. Exactly what he loved most about her.

He drew back and looked down. "Let me walk you out."

"I'll do it." Lacey popped up from the couch and stretched. "I have to go home too."

Mallory tensed against him as Luis glanced Lacey's way, and a little of that worry came rippling back. "Why don't I get Jeffry to drive you home, Lace?"

Lacey rolled her eyes and grabbed her purse from the floor beside the couch. "Why? I'm perfectly fine." She hooked her arm in Mallory's and tugged Mallory away from him. "Come on, Mal. I'll protect you from the scary, possessed children of the night." She winked Luis's way. "Catch ya later, handsome."

Luis wanted to reach for Mallory and tug her back, but Lacey had already pulled her to the door. And though it was clear in Mallory's eyes she didn't want to be alone with Lacey right now, Luis knew she'd never say no to her bestie.

Damn, this night had not gone at all as he'd wanted. He'd have to make it up to Mallory. Soon.

"Call me tomorrow," he said to her.

Mallory nodded. "Okay. Bye."

The girls disappeared out the door. He watched through the front window as they crossed the path, then stood next to Mallory's car, but he couldn't hear what they were discussing. Was Mallory laying into

Lacey for her erratic behavior tonight? Or was she letting it all go for the good of their friendship?

Luis bet the latter. Mallory was a true friend. The kind who supported a person through anything and was there when you needed her most. As he watched her talking to Lacey under the streetlight, he told himself that was what he wanted. Stability and strength. Not someone like Lacey Salt, who changed her mind about what she wanted every ten minutes.

He turned away from the window and reached for the bowl of chips and dip. Water ran in the kitchen where Jeffry was cleaning up. He made it halfway to the arched doorway when the front door opened.

Excitement leapt inside him, and he turned toward the door, happy Mallory had decided to come back. But instead of his girlfriend, Lacey walked into the house with a Cheshire grin on her pretty face.

His brow dropped. "Did you forget something?"

"Yep." Something dark sparkled in her eyes. Something hot. "One thing."

Before he could ask what, she crossed to him, rested her hands on his chest, then rose to her toes and pressed her lips against his.

Time seemed to stop. The room spun around him. Still holding the chips and dip, he froze, unable to move, unable to think, unable to react.

Because Lacey Salt was kissing him. Kissing *him*.

She broke the kiss way too soon, then lowered to her feet. Her top teeth sank into her bottom lip in the sexiest way, and she batted her long eyelashes up at him until all the blood rushed right out of his head. "Thanks for the great night, Luis. I'll catch you at the pool."

She turned and sauntered toward the door, waggling her behind in the tight jeans in a way she had to know drew attention straight to her ass. Then she pushed the door open and was gone, disappearing into the night to leave him shocked and completely dumbfounded in her wake.

"Dude," Jeffry said from the doorway. "That is seriously fucked up. Tell me you are not about to fall for that."

Luis turned and stared at his best friend. But he couldn't come up with an answer. Because his head was spinning like a top and, suddenly, he didn't know what he wanted.

Or who.

Chapter Three

Lacey Salt stretched her leg out of the bath water and watched the bubbles slide down her calf. Last night had been fun. More fun that she'd had in forever. And though she knew it was wrong, she couldn't wait to do it again.

Part of her felt guilty for flirting so blatantly with Luis, especially in front of Mallory. But if Luis was so into Mallory, he would have told Lacey to stop, right? And if he hadn't been the least bit interested, he'd have pushed Lacey away when she kissed him. But he hadn't. Instead he'd looked down at Lacey as if he wanted to kiss her again.

Lacey had expected Mallory to say something about her flirting when they walked out to their cars, but Mallory hadn't. Which meant either she didn't care or she just hadn't noticed. Lacey's money was on the fact Mallory hadn't noticed. She could be so clueless sometimes. So really, Lacey was doing her best friend a favor by tempting Luis. No girl wanted a boyfriend who cheated. If Luis was so easily swayed away from Mallory, it meant she wasn't the girl for him, right?

Feeling better about herself, she smiled and ran her hands through the bubbles. Luis was working at the pool again today. Maybe she'd put on her strapless white bikini and go over and watch him again. He was so hot in those lifeguarding shorts. He made her skin burn.

She climbed out of the bath, wrapped a towel around herself, and opened her bathroom door. Her mom had set out a bunch of clothes on her bed that she was supposed to put away, but Lacey didn't feel like doing anything except getting dressed and going to the pool. She wandered into her walk-in closet, slid on her white bikini, then grabbed a pale-yellow sundress that dipped low at her cleavage and pulled it on. She headed back for the bathroom, but the second she stepped out of her closet, she realized she wasn't alone and jumped.

"Hey." Ginny Moreno sat on Lacey's bed and tucked a lock of curly dark hair behind her ear. "I didn't mean to scare you."

Lacey pressed a hand against her chest and drew in a deep breath. "Knock or something next time, would you? You about gave me a heart attack."

Ginny winced. "Sorry."

Shaking her head, Lacey moved into her bathroom, unclipped her hair, and reached for a hairbrush. "What do you want?"

"Marisol said you were at my house last night. I was just wondering how Luis is doing."

Lacey's brush paused halfway down her long hair. It always gave her a little jolt when she remembered that Ginny, the bane of her existence right now, was Luis's sister. She ran the brush through her mahogany curls again, thankful she hadn't washed her hair this time. Too much washing made her hair totally frizz out, especially in the summer humidity. "Fine. Why don't you ask him if you're so worried?"

Ginny sighed from the bedroom. "Because he doesn't talk to me about anything heavy these days. It's like he doesn't think I can handle it, and he's afraid I'm going to freak out or something."

Lacey frowned. Of course Luis was afraid to talk to Ginny about anything serious. Everyone walked on eggshells around Ginny Moreno because of that stupid baby. The slightest mention of Jacob or the accident or what she was going to do with her life *besides* mooch off the Salts sent her into a fit of tears. And tears, as Lacey's mom had pointed out, put stress on Ginny's body, which could cause her to miscarry, so it was best just to avoid them altogether.

That frown deepened on Lacey's face. She almost wished Ginny would just miscarry and be done with the whole baby thing. Lacey's life would definitely be simpler if that happened. Ginny wouldn't have to live in their house, and Lacey might actually get her mom and dad back.

She twisted her hair into a knot, then slapped on some lipstick and mascara. Since she was heading to the pool, she didn't want too much makeup, but she definitely wanted Luis to notice her.

Lacey stepped back into her bedroom and scowled when she realized Ginny was still sitting on her bed. Moving for her desk, she opened her beach bag, desperate to get out of this house as quickly as possible. "Did you want something else?"

"I just..." Ginny twisted her hands in her lap.

She'd lost weight since Jacob's funeral. Even Lacey could see that Ginny's face was a little gaunt. If it weren't for Lacey's mom forcing food in Ginny constantly, Ginny would probably look like a skeleton. Ginny was taller than Lacey by quite a bit—always had been—but right now, with the way she was sitting hunched over on the bed, Lacey felt like a giant next to the girl, which only made her that much more uncomfortable.

"I just..." Tears filled Ginny's dark eyes. "I miss him, that's all. And I know you two were close. I was just wondering how you're able to act like everything's normal when...when it's not."

She was talking about Jacob. Lacey's heart lurched with a hard shot of pain, but instead of letting it consume her, she focused on the anger that whooshed in on its heels. Things were not normal. They were never going to *be* normal again, and nothing she did could change that fact. But more than that, listening to Ginny Moreno, who was the reason things were so screwed up, sitting there asking this question only enflamed her more.

"What normal?" Lacey turned to face Ginny and knew she shouldn't respond, but just couldn't help herself. "You took normal from this family."

"Lacey..." Ginny's shoulders sank even more, and a tear streamed down her cheek. But Lacey wasn't about to be deterred. Not now. Not when Ginny had opened this can of worms.

"If it weren't for you, Jacob would still be here."

Ginny shook her head, tears flowing freely now. "It was an accident."

"An accident that *you* caused. Why were you so distracted that night, Ginny? Were you and Jacob arguing the night you flipped that car and killed my brother?"

Ginny pressed her fingers against her temples. "It wasn't like that."

"Then tell me what it was like." Lacey's blood pumped hot and wild, and she knew she should stop but she just couldn't. The anger had been building inside her for a long time, and she couldn't hold it back anymore. "Because no one seems to know, and everyone's afraid to ask in case it pushes you over the edge. But I'm not afraid. What were you arguing about, Ginny? Were you arguing about this baby?" She glanced at Ginny's belly. "Were you arguing over the fact it's not even Jacob's kid?"

Ginny's head shot up, and her damp, red-rimmed eyes held on Lacey's. "W-why would you even ask that?"

"Because Jacob's not here to tell us the truth. All we have is your version. And I don't believe your version. You were best friends and then you suddenly just fell in love and into bed? Give me a break. If that's true, why didn't he tell us?"

Ginny didn't answer. Just stared at Lacey with wide, fear-filled eyes. But before Lacey could push Ginny harder, Celeste Salt stepped into the open doorway of her room with a basket of laundry in her hands. "Lacey, I have more clothes for you to put aw——"

She glanced between the girls, her expression shifting to concern. "Is everything okay in here?"

Ginny looked down and swiped at the tears on her cheeks. "Fine." She pushed to her feet. "I'm really tired. I think I'm going to lie down for a bit."

She pushed past Lacey's mom and disappeared down the hall. And the minute she was gone, Lacey's stomach dropped from all the horrible things she'd said.

Her mother lowered the basket in her arms. "What on earth was going on in here? Ginny looked like she was crying. She's fragile right now, Lacey. What on earth did you say to upset her?"

Of course her mother would take Ginny's side. That sick feeling in Lacey's stomach turned to absolute heartache. Not for Ginny, but for herself.

With shaky fingers, Lacey grabbed her phone from the desk and shoved it in her beach bag. Just once she wanted her mother to ask what Ginny had done to upset *her*. Just once she wanted someone to care how *she* felt. But Celeste Salt would never do that. Because all she cared about these days was that stupid brat in Ginny's tummy.

"I have to go." The need to flee overwhelmed her, pushing Lacey past her mother and out into the hall.

Celeste turned. "Hold on. You have chores, young lady."

She had chores, but Ginny didn't. Ginny just got to live here for free and make everyone miserable. Heartache turned to a blistering anger that made Lacey's eyes burn. "I'll do them later."

Lacey hit the stairs and headed for the front door. From the railing, her mother called, "Lacey Ann Salt. Come back here."

But Lacey didn't listen. She slammed the door behind her and rushed for her yellow Volkswagen Bug as she swiped at the hot tears streaming down her cheeks. She hated this house and she hated this family. No one understood her. No one even cared. There was only one person who gave a shit and knew what it was like to lose someone you loved most in the world. Only one person she wanted right now.

And he was at the country club wearing hot red shorts.

* * * *

Ginny Moreno didn't even think about where she was going. All she knew was that she needed her best friend.

Hot tears burned her eyes, but she fought them back as she climbed the back steps of Brittany Rush's mammoth house like she'd done a million times as a kid. She knew Brittany was home because Brittany had texted at lunchtime. They'd made plans to get together for coffee at three at Cuppa Joe, but after Ginny's confrontation with Lacey, Ginny couldn't wait that long.

The things Lacey had said...

Ginny stopped on the second step and pressed a hand against her belly to keep the nausea at bay. If Lacey was thinking them, others had to be thinking them too. She'd convinced herself it was such a simple lie—telling everyone that she and Jacob had planned to share the news they were a couple when they came home—but now she wasn't so sure. What if Lacey was right? What if others suspected she'd lied? How was she going to fix this?

She needed Brittany to tell her what to do. Needed to tell Brittany the truth. But even as the thought hit, she knew she couldn't. If Brittany knew the truth, she'd never speak to Ginny again, and right now Brittany was the only friend Ginny had left.

Ginny rushed up the last few steps and pulled the kitchen door open. She was halfway into the house when the man at the counter turned to face her.

The breath caught in her throat, and she froze. Senator Sebastian Rush held a sandwich in his hand and pinned her with a hard look, one that sent fear skipping through Ginny's veins and made every nerve in her body twitch.

Oh God. He was just as handsome as he'd been the last time she'd seen him at Jacob's funeral. Salt and pepper hair, strong athletic body, wide shoulders, and narrow hips. And dressed in slacks and a pale-blue dress shirt rolled up to his elbows, he was as commanding as ever, even in his kitchen. Images of all the nights Ginny had spent with him in Austin whipped through her mind, followed by a wave of terror that made her hands break out in a cold sweat.

What was he doing here? She'd thought he'd gone back to Austin. He'd once told her he didn't even like this town, so why was he still hanging around? What if he was here to tell everyone that she was a liar?

"I..." Words stumbled over her lips. "I didn't know you'd be here. I'm looking for Brittany."

He didn't answer, but his brown-eyed gaze drifted to her belly, and she had another memory flash. Of the nights she'd gotten so caught up in the forbidden passion of being with him that she'd forgotten all about her diaphragm.

Oh God. Oh please. Panic condensed beneath Ginny's ribs, robbing her of all ability to speak. She placed a hand over her belly in a protective move. *Please, please, please don't let this baby be his.*

"Ginny." Brittany stepped into the kitchen with wide, light-blue eyes. "I thought I heard your voice. Weren't we meeting at Cuppa Joe's?"

Relief swept through Ginny. She tore her gaze from the senator, dropped her hand, and looked to her best friend. "I..." *Quick, think of an excuse.* "I saw your text and thought maybe we could go now instead of later."

"Sure. Now's fine." Brittany's brow lowered. "Are you okay? What happened?"

Nerves rattled Ginny's body, and she glanced toward the senator, but he was no longer there. He'd slipped out without her even noticing.

Breathing easier, Ginny swallowed hard and nodded. "I'm fine. Can we just go, though? I'm feeling boxed in today, and I just want to get some air."

"Sure." Brittany grabbed her purse from a hook near the back door. "Come on. Dad's working from home today so I totally know about being boxed in. I always feel like I have to tiptoe around the house whenever he's here."

Fresh air filled Ginny's lungs as they stepped outside, settling her frayed nerves and easing the sickness brewing in her stomach. When they reached the side of the Rush mansion, Brittany stopped and stared at the empty drive. "Wait. You walked all the way over here?"

"I told you I was feeling boxed in."

Brittany turned suspicious eyes Ginny's way.

A tingle ran down Ginny's spine, and she hated that she had to lie to her best friend. The truth was that Ginny couldn't even fathom driving right now. Not after the things Lacey had said. The girl was right. She'd killed Jacob. Killed him by being distracted the night she'd been driving home with him in the seat beside her. But not because of the baby. She hadn't even known about the baby then. She'd been distracted because she'd been in love with Jacob Salt all her life, and she desperately wanted him to love her back.

She couldn't tell Brittany any of that, though, so instead she stepped past her friend and headed toward the street. "I'm fine. Exercise is good for me. Dr. Rush even said so."

Ginny could tell from Brittany's silence that her friend didn't exactly agree. Dr. Layla Rush was her aunt, though, and everyone in Storm knew Layla was the smartest person in town. How could Brittany argue with that?

They settled into a comfortable quiet as they walked down the tree-lined street toward the park downtown. Just being with her friend—even in silence—boosted Ginny's mood and made her feel a hundred times better than she had only an hour ago.

They cut through the park that sat between Brittany's neighborhood and the downtown shops. Feeling more tired than she'd expected, Ginny said, "Do you mind if we stop for a bit?"

"I don't mind," Brittany said. "You sure you're okay?"

"I told you I'm fine." Ginny sat on a park bench under several trees. "You don't have to worry about me so much."

"Sorry." Brittany sat beside her friend. "You have no say in that. My worry is my own."

A whisper of a smile pulled at Ginny's lips, and she leaned her head against her friend's shoulder, wishing life could be as simple as it had been when they were kids and the biggest problem in either of their worlds was which bratty boy had stolen their bikes when they stopped here to climb trees.

Oak and cedar swayed above in the warm summer breeze, and Ginny closed her eyes as she listened, thinking back to a day not long ago when she and Jacob had chased each other under these very trees.

God, she missed him. So much she physically ached. Would that pain ever go away? She didn't know how it could. She felt as if she'd lost part of herself the day Jacob died, and every day living without him seemed harder, not easier. At some point the ache would lessen, wouldn't it? She was desperate for that to happen, but at the same time scared to death. Because the day she stopped grieving for Jacob Salt was the day she was afraid she'd truly lose him forever.

"Okay, I let you have your quiet time," Brittany said. "Start talking or I'm going to scream."

Ginny should have known she couldn't snow Brittany Rush. Her friend was the most perceptive person she'd ever met.

She sighed, sat up, and gripped the bench seat near her legs. "Lacey hates me."

"Lacey does not hate you." Brittany gave Ginny one of her famous *I know what I'm talking about* looks. "You're just the closest outlet for her anger."

"I'm her freaking punching bag, that's what I am. I tried to talk to her today. Just...talk. We live under the same roof but she basically ignores me. It was clear, though, that she couldn't be bothered with me. And the things she said..."

Ginny's stomach hurt all over again just thinking about Lacey's words.

"What did she say?" Brittany asked quietly.

That pain came back, hard and sharp, right beneath Ginny's breastbone, and she closed her eyes. "She said I killed Jacob." Tears burned behind her eyelids. "And she's right. I did."

"Okay, stop. Right now." Brittany gripped Ginny's hand, and when Ginny opened her eyes, Brittany had turned sideways on the bench and was looking right at her. "It was an accident. What happened to Jacob was an accident. You didn't plan it, did you?"

Ginny shook her head and fought back the tears that were threatening all over again. "No."

"You didn't want it, did you?"

"God, no."

"Then it wasn't your fault. It was just a horrible, horrible accident.

And I guarantee Lacey doesn't believe what she's saying. She's just blaming you because she doesn't have anyone else to blame. And because you're there."

Ginny searched her friend's light-blue eyes that were so much like her mother's. Brittany saw things in black and white. There was no gray area for her. Which was the biggest reason Ginny could never tell her the truth about her relationship with Jacob.

She pulled her hands from Brittany's and stood, restless to move. "How can I stay at the Salts' house when Lacey clearly doesn't want me there?"

"Who are you staying for?" Brittany asked. "You or the baby?"

Ginny wanted to say both, but she knew that would sound selfish. But the fact was that Celeste Salt took care of her. She didn't make Ginny do chores like Marisol would do if Ginny were home. She didn't pester Ginny to get a job or help out with family expenses. And she wasn't constantly asking what Ginny was going to do when the baby was born. Marisol had hit Ginny with that one last night when she'd shown up with cranberry scones and a forced smile. Ginny loved her older sister and was grateful for everything Marisol had given up to raise her, but she couldn't think about the future yet when she was still grappling with the past.

"I'm staying with the Salts for the baby," Ginny answered. It wasn't just the right answer. It was true. What did she know about pregnancy and babies? What did Marisol know? The answer to both was nothing. Celeste Salt had given birth to three children and was always helping with her niece and nephew, too. She was an all-around great mom. The kind of mom Ginny wished she'd had; the kind of mom she'd lost in another tragic car accident.

Yes, her baby would be lucky to have Celeste Salt as its grandmother.

No, her baby *was* lucky to have Celeste Salt as its grandmother. Ginny had already decided this baby was Jacob's, and nobody was going to change her mind about that. Not even Lacey Salt and her need to lash out.

"Then you have your answer," Brittany said, again making this easy—right or wrong. There was no maybe. "And you don't let Lacey make you feel bad about doing what's best for your baby."

Ginny faced her friend and again wished she could tell Brittany the entire truth. But Brittany was right. The only thing that mattered was making things right for the baby inside her. Even if that meant changing what she considered as truth.

"Thanks." Ginny forced a smile she didn't really feel. "I think I knew that all along. It just helps to hear it from an impartial voice now and then."

Brittany grinned and pushed to her feet. She had her mother's graceful build and her father's strong chin. And right now she was the only truly good thing Ginny had in her life. Someone she desperately needed to hold on to.

Brittany's gaze skipped past Ginny and narrowed. "Whoa. Hot military man at one o'clock. We don't get many of those in Storm. I wonder if he got off the wrong bus."

Ginny turned to look toward the man dressed in camouflage setting a duffel on a picnic table fifty yards away. He lowered to the bench, pulled off his cap, and scrubbed a hand through his dark hair. And the minute he did, Ginny knew who he was.

"It's Logan Murphy."

"I thought Logan Murphy was still in Afghanistan. He's not supposed to be home for another week, right?"

"I don't know." But wondering gave Ginny something to think about besides her miserable life, and right now she'd take whatever she could get.

She crossed the grass toward the man and stopped several feet away. He was staring off at something to his right—a bird or a squirrel, Ginny wasn't sure which—and he didn't seem to notice them.

Ginny heard Brittany move up behind her and cleared her throat. The man slowly turned his head toward her, and Ginny's stomach gave a little lurch when she caught sight of the piercing blue eyes she used to daydream about when she was fourteen, sitting in the high school stands, watching him play baseball.

"Logan? Logan Murphy? I can't believe it's you." Ginny hadn't seen him in nearly six years, but she always remembered him as being larger than life and wildly handsome. She'd had a brief crush on him in middle school. The kind of crush a girl that age doesn't know what to do with. And just seeing him again made her blood warm in a way it hadn't done since she was a preteen.

He didn't answer. Just slipped his cap back on and stared at her as if he didn't know who she was. And as her gaze skipped over him, she realized something was different about the man before her. Yes, he was more gorgeous than ever—strong jaw, straight nose, perfect lips—and he was bigger, stronger, more muscular than the boy who'd left Storm all those years ago, but this was something else. Something vacant in his pretty eyes that hadn't been there before.

"We probably look different," Brittany said at Ginny's back. "Logan, I'm Brittany Rush, and this is—"

"Ginny Moreno." The blank look quickly fled, and warmth flashed in Logan's eyes as he pushed to his feet and reached for Ginny's hand. "I remember you." The ghost of a smile pulled at the corner of his mouth. "I definitely remember you."

His palm was calloused and rough, and when his fingers closed around hers, she realized the pinky on his right hand was skewed at an odd angle, as if it had been broken and hadn't healed properly. But she was too distracted to look because the sound of his voice—deep and rugged—sent a flush of heat all across Ginny's cheeks. And his skin pressed against hers where he held her shot tingles straight up her arm in a way she didn't expect.

"Um..." Words caught in her throat as those tingles spread all through her body. "I..."

"What are you doing in the park?" Brittany asked. "Do your parents know you're home? Your dad said you weren't due back until next week."

"Ah. Yeah." Logan let go of Ginny's hand, and she tried not to be disappointed at the lack of contact as he tugged off his cap and scrubbed his hand through his hair again. "That's because my dad doesn't know. I caught an early flight. Didn't want to make a big deal out of it."

A nervous expression crossed his features, distracting Ginny from the odd tingles still trickling through her body. Something was up with Logan Murphy, but she didn't want to be pushy and ask. Just the fact he was here in the park instead of at Murphy's Pub reconnecting with his family, though, told her it was something big.

Brittany's phone buzzed in her pocket, and she jumped at the sound, then winced as she pulled it out and looked down at the screen. "Shit. Sorry. I have to take this." She pressed her phone to her ear. "Grams? Yeah. I'm here. I—oh damn. No, no. It's okay. I'm on my way. Give me ten minutes."

She quickly hit *End* and shoved the phone back in her pocket. "Gin, I'm so sorry to bail on you but I totally forgot I was supposed to help Grams with the booth layout for the Founder's Day Picnic."

"It's okay." Ginny turned toward her friend. "We can get coffee another day."

"Are you sure?"

"Totally. Go. I don't want to wind up on Marylee Rush's bad side because I monopolized your attention, so don't you dare tell her you're late because of me."

Brittany gave her a quick hug. "You're the best. I'll make this up to you." She let go of Ginny and looked toward Logan. "Welcome home. I know I won't be the only one to tell you that."

Brittany took off at a run back across the park before Logan could answer, and when she was gone, Ginny looked his way and noticed he'd sat down again and was now leaning his elbows on his knees and running his hand through his hair once more.

Stress and worry radiated off his muscular body in waves, and as Ginny took in his wrinkled uniform and matted hair in need of a washing, she couldn't help but notice that the man looked wrecked.

She'd been wrecked for weeks. She knew how it felt. Whatever had brought him home early was definitely not good.

Slowly, she sank onto the bench next to him, but was careful not to touch him, just in case. For whatever reason—probably because she knew what it was like to suffer alone—she didn't want to leave him.

"So, um, I don't think you can hide out in the park much longer. Sorry."

He huffed a sound that was half chuckle, half snort and dropped his arm. "No, I guess not. Once Marylee Rush finds out I'm home the entire town will know."

"Word does spread fast in this place." She bit her lip, then said, "Is there a reason you don't want to go home?"

He leaned back against the picnic table and stared out at the leaves blowing in the trees. And she couldn't help but notice the lines etched into his face that aged him way beyond his twenty-four years. "I spent all of my childhood trying to come up with a way to get out of this damn town. I told my father I never planned to come back, even on leave. Can you imagine hearing that from your son? That the place you called home wasn't good enough?"

"Yes, actually, I can. I said the same to Marisol several times when I was in high school. When you're a kid stuck in a small town, life seems to pass you by. Everything that happens is happening out there, and you're trapped in one place watching it from the sidelines. It's only when you *get* out of that town that you realize the things that really matter are the things that happen back in the place you were so desperate to escape."

"Yeah. That exactly." Logan shook his head. "They say you can't ever go home. I guess I'm almost afraid they're right."

"You can always go home," Ginny whispered. "If you really want to. That's why they call it home."

Logan turned sad blue eyes her way, but they warmed all over again when he looked at her. And as his gaze held hers, Ginny felt a spark flicker inside her chest. There was something broken in him, something she didn't understand, but it called out to her in a way no one had been able to do since the accident. And though she didn't know what it meant, for the first time in weeks she felt something other than grief.

She felt alive.

Chapter Four

Mallory let the screen door close behind her and dropped her purse on the kitchen table, more tired than she'd been in weeks.

She'd tossed and turned most of the night, too stressed over what had happened at Luis's house to get much sleep. Then she'd been up early at the bed and breakfast and they'd been so busy with tourists flocking to Storm on a sunny Saturday that she'd stayed later than she was scheduled.

"Mallory?" her mother called from the living room. "Is that you?"

"Yeah," Mallory said in a weary tone. "I'm home."

Joanne Alvarez walked into the kitchen wearing a pale-green cotton dress Mallory's dad had once said made her look frumpy and unattractive and eyed her daughter with concerned green eyes. "Honey, what's wrong? Did something happen at the bed and breakfast? You look upset."

Mallory shook her head and quickly turned away so her mom didn't see too much. Pulling open the fridge, she reached for a soda and quickly popped the top. "Nothing happened. I'm just tired. Long day."

She could tell from her mom's silence that Joanne didn't buy it, and just as she expected, when she turned back, her mom tipped her head and softened her expression. "Sit down, Mallory. We haven't had a talk in quite a while. I think it's time."

Mallory only just bit back a groan. A heart-to-heart with her mother wasn't something she was much in the mood for right now, especially when she was still so raw over what had happened with Luis. But she knew not to brush her mom off. Her father had been doing that to her mom for years and Mallory hated it. She'd vowed long ago not to be like Hector Alvarez.

She pulled out a chair and sat on the cracked seat. The table was dinged and battered from years of use, and as Mallory's gaze skipped over the small kitchen with its brown Formica and aged appliances, she realized just how little her father had truly cared about this house and the people in it. No, the only thing Hector Alvarez ever cared about was himself, which was why it'd been so easy for him to walk away.

Mallory's mom set a bowl in front of Mallory then sat in the seat beside her. Her hair was twisted up into a knot and she was wearing more makeup than normal. Makeup that made her look ten years younger. But before Mallory could tell her mom that, she noticed the candy in the bowl.

She eyed the M&Ms like they might just jump up and bite her, then looked at her mom. "When did you get these?"

"I've had them."

"Hidden?" Hector hadn't approved of Joanne or their kids eating sweets. At least not the kind that cost money.

A sly smile spread across her mom's face. "Some situations call for candy, and something tells me this is one of those situations." Joanne propped her elbow on the table and rested her chin on her hand. "What's going on, baby? You didn't look happy when you came in last night and you look less happy now. Did something happen with Luis?"

Just the mention of Luis's name sent all those thoughts and fears rushing through Mallory all over again. She pushed the candy away.

She couldn't exactly tell her mom that she and Luis had discussed sex, or that he'd turned her down. Her mom would flip out if she knew *all that*. And she definitely didn't want to get in to the whole Lacey thing and how that made her feel. So she decided the safest thing was just to hedge. "Things are just...complicated right now."

Joanne sighed and leaned back in her chair. "I know you really like this boy."

"Mom. Don't start." Mallory rubbed her suddenly throbbing temple.

"What? You already know what I'm going to say?" Her mother's voice carried a sharp tone. "Believe me, you don't. What I was going to say was that I know you really like this boy, and if he's the one, then it shouldn't be complicated. Figure out what's so complicated and fix it."

Surprise rippled through Mallory. Joanne had never approved of Mallory dating Luis long term. Not because he wasn't a good kid, but because she didn't think a high school romance should be serious. Joanne had met Hector Alvarez in high school and ran off with him as soon as they graduated, and their life had been far from perfect. In fact, now it was nothing but ruins.

She looked at her mother and blinked several times. "Just...fix it?"

A soft smile spread across Joanne's face, and she rested her hand over Mallory's on the table and squeezed. "Do you want to fix it?"

Tears burned Mallory's eyes, and she nodded.

"Then fix it. There's nothing so bad in this world that it can't be fixed with communication. If he treats you well and respects you—"

"He does."

Joanne's smile spread to encompass her whole face. "—then talk to him about whatever's bothering you. Relationships take work, honey. They're not easy."

Mallory couldn't help but think about her parents' relationship and how hard her mom had worked over the years to fix what was broken between them. But how could you fix something when the other person didn't respect you? That was the key in every relationship, and Mallory knew Luis did truly respect her. If he didn't he would have said yes to sleeping with her even when she wasn't totally sure that was what she wanted. Instead he was protecting her by making the tough decision she couldn't.

Warmth filled her chest. Luis Moreno wasn't at all like her father. He was worth fighting for. So long as he wanted to fight for her.

She needed to see him. To talk to him about last night and make sure everything between them was still solid. Because she loved him. It had hit her in the night when she hadn't been able to sleep. She loved him, and she didn't want to lose him to Lacey or anyone else.

Mallory pushed out of her chair and grabbed her purse. "I need to run to the country club. Can I borrow the car?"

Joanne smiled and rose, then moved toward her purse on the kitchen counter. She fished out her keys and held them toward Mallory. "Say hello to Luis for me."

Mallory grabbed the keys and made it halfway to the door, then stopped and rushed back to kiss her mom's cheek. "Thank you. And that dress doesn't make you look frumpy at all. It makes you look totally curvy and hot and brings out the green in your eyes."

Joanne laughed as Mallory sailed back for the door. "Well, then I'll be sure to wear it more often."

Mallory backed the ancient Olds out of the driveway and prayed it didn't die before she got to the country club. The engine coughed when she pulled into the parking lot, but for the first time in a long time she didn't wish she drove a Bug or a Beemer or a convertible like some of the other cars in the lot. She was too anxious to talk to Luis to notice anything around her.

She shoved the car into park, jumped out, and rushed for the country club's main entrance. Everyone in this town knew everyone else, and even though her family didn't have a membership, she waved at Adam Glenn, a boy a year ahead of her in school who was seated behind the counter. "Hey, Adam. I just need to talk to Luis for a few minutes. I'm not staying."

Adam rolled his eyes and went back to whatever he was doing on his phone. "He's working, Mallory. Don't distract him too long."

Mallory smiled and headed for the locker rooms that opened to the pool deck. "I won't."

Her nerves buzzed as she wove her way through the women's locker room, but this time it was a good buzz, not a bad one. She'd decided on the way over that she was going to tell Luis she loved him. It was totally spur of the moment and crazy, but she felt it was time he knew, especially with all the weird stuff happening with Lacey and the way they'd left things last night.

She pushed the door to the pool open and looked toward the lifeguard chair, but Luis wasn't there. Her gaze scanned the water, then the pool deck, and finally she spotted him. And when she did, her heart dropped straight into her shoes.

He sat on a chaise lounge in nothing but his red lifeguarding swim trunks, facing Lacey, who was wearing the skimpiest white bikini Mallory had ever seen and was laid out before him like an offering. They were both laughing and talking, and neither had any idea she was there. But when Lacey reached out and grabbed Luis's arm, pulling him toward her, every fighting instinct Mallory had roared right to the surface.

She crossed the pool deck and stopped next to them. Luis was the first to see her, and he quickly sat up, his smile transforming to shock and then guilt. "Mal." He pushed to his feet. "I didn't know you were coming by."

Mallory looked down at Lacey. Lacey grinned up at Mallory with that same self-satisfied smirk she'd had last night when Luis had pushed Mallory off his lap. "Hey, Mal. How did you get in? You don't have a membership here."

Mallory's temper bubbled just beneath the surface. Lacey had never blatantly pointed out the differences in their socioeconomic status, but right now she was making it clear to everyone around them that Mallory was poor and not welcome.

She'd deal with her so-called best friend later. Right now, she needed to deal with Luis.

Mallory looked up at him. "Are you on break?"

"Yeah."

"Good. We need to talk."

A worried look passed over his features. "Right now?"

"Yes, now."

She turned for the gate that led from the pool deck to the grass beyond. Waited as Luis caught up with her. He pushed the gate open and held it for Mallory. From her chaise, Lacey called, "Don't yell too loud, Mal. Sound travels over water."

Mallory ignored Lacey's snarky comment and marched far enough away from the pool and into the trees so no one could hear them. She told herself to stay calm, that she hadn't come over here to even talk about Lacey, but the minute she turned and saw Luis's guilty expression, everything she'd been bottling up for two days came spilling out.

"What the heck is going on between you and Lacey Salt?" she demanded.

Luis reached for her hand. "It's not what you think."

"I don't know what I think." Mallory drew back. She was fired up and didn't want to be touched right now. Not if she wasn't the one he really wanted to touch. "Lacey was all over you last night, and you didn't once push her away."

"That's not true. I—"

"It is true. I was there. And I was willing to let it go because, okay, maybe she was drinking last night and she didn't know what she was doing. But she clearly knows what she's doing now."

He sighed and stepped toward her. "Mal—"

She moved back again and swatted at his hand. "No. Don't 'Mal' me. She wants you. I don't know why she's suddenly so interested in you when she never even looked twice your way before, but I honestly don't care. I just care about the truth. Is that what you still want? Her? Because if it is I'll back right out of the picture."

His face paled. "What do you mean by 'still'?"

She tipped her head. "Come on, Luis. I'm not an idiot. I know you've had a crush on Lacey for years. But I thought you were over it. If I thought you still had a thing for her, do you think I would have asked you to that dance?"

He rested his hands on his hips and stared down at the ground. And she waited for him to deny it, but he didn't. He only pursed his lips and kicked a rock with the toe of his bare foot.

Reality settled in hard to steal her breath. "Oh my God." Sickness swirled in Mallory's belly, and all that excitement she'd felt on the way here shattered like glass against the ground. "You do want her."

"Mal." He looked up at her and reached for her hand, and this time she let him because she was too stunned to move. "I'm with you."

I'm with you. Not *I want you*, or *I'm in love with you*. Just *I'm with you*. As if he had no choice. As if he was stuck with her.

Her mother had been stuck with her father, and look how that had turned out. Twenty plus years of misery. She never wanted to settle for something she didn't truly want. And she wasn't about to let someone settle for her either.

The urge to run consumed her. She pulled her hands from Luis's and rushed past the brush toward the front of the country club.

"Mallory," he called at her back. "Wait, please? That didn't come out right. I didn't mean it that way..."

Hot tears were already burning her eyes, and there was no way in hell Mallory was going back so he could see just how much he'd hurt her. She ran for the parking lot as quickly as she could, but when she got there, she spotted Lacey's yellow Bug, and her feet drew to an abrupt stop.

She shouldn't say anything. This wasn't really about Lacey. It was about Luis and what he wanted. But it if weren't for Lacey Salt and the little game she'd decided she was bored enough to play, none of this would be happening.

Mallory swiped the tears from her cheeks, whirled around and headed back for the main entrance to the country club with a new fire burning inside her.

Best friend or not, it was time to draw the line.

* * * *

Lacey dropped her bikini in her beach bag and ran her fingers through her hair. Since she'd only gotten in the pool to cool off, then gotten right back out so Luis noticed the water running down her body, she didn't need to dry her hair. Today had been fun; sun bathing and flirting with Luis on the lifeguard's chair was exactly what she'd needed. She'd known he wouldn't be able to stay away. It was refreshing to have someone want to talk to her. Someone who wasn't bitching and crying and talking about things that only made Lacey want to scream. Really, was it too much to enjoy a hot guy's attention? There was nothing wrong with that.

She smirked when she remembered the pissed look on Mallory's face. Oh, Mallory obviously thought there was something wrong with her and Luis's friendship, but Lacey really didn't care. It wasn't her fault Mallory had shown up unexpectedly. How was she to know Mallory would pop by to talk to Luis? Mallory never came to the club unless she went as Lacey's guest.

Grabbing her bag, she turned to head for the lobby but drew to an abrupt stop when Mallory stepped in her way with hard, narrowed eyes.

"I don't know what's going on with you," Mallory said in a low voice, "but I'm way past trying to figure it out."

Shock rippled through Lacey, but she masked it quickly so Mallory wouldn't see. As nonchalantly as she could, she slipped the strap of her bag over her elbow and reached for her sunglasses from the front pocket. "I really don't know what you mean."

She tried to step past Mallory, but Mallory moved in her way once more. "You know exactly what I mean. You don't even like Luis."

"I do too. He's a very nice guy."

"And he's dating me."

Lacey rolled her eyes. She was keenly aware several elderly eyes were watching their exchange, but that actually worked in her favor. The old biddies loved to gossip. Nothing would convince Luis more that he was with the wrong girl than hearing how Mallory had accosted Lacey in the locker room. "Of course he's dating you. I already know that. I helped set you up, remember?"

She stepped around Mallory, but Mallory shoved a hand against Lacey's shoulder, stopping her. "I'm not kidding here. I don't care if you're bored or lonely or not getting enough attention in that big house of yours. Luis isn't the answer. He's mine. Stay away from him."

Anger pulsed in Lacey's veins. No one told her what to do. No one shoved her. She narrowed her eyes on her *ex*-best friend. "Is that what this is about? You're jealous of me? I can't help it if your boyfriend finds me more interesting than you. Maybe instead of threatening me, you should talk to him about your insecurities."

She moved around Mallory quickly so the girl couldn't stop her. Slipping on her sunglasses, she lifted her chin and headed for the lobby, but inside she was fuming.

How dare Mallory tell Lacey what she could or couldn't do? And how dare she threaten her? Didn't Mallory know who she was? She was a Salt. Everyone loved her parents. They were the perfect family. No one could take that away from her, even with all the tragedy of the last month.

Word of this would spread. Oh, word would spread and Luis would be horrified that Mallory had attacked Lacey when Lacey was already going through such emotional turmoil. Then he'd break up with her.

Lacey reached her car and opened the door to toss her bag across to the front seat. A victorious smile spread across her lips.

And if he didn't break up with her, Lacey would do whatever it took to make sure they still split.

Chapter Five

"Take this up to editorial," Milton Waters said, handing Jeffry a file, "and find out which photographer they're planning to send to cover the Little League tournament next weekend."

Jeffry took the folder from Milton's wrinkled hands and nodded. "Sure thing, Milt."

Milton Waters had been reporting the news in Storm for forty-five years. He was the epitome of a small-town journalist, with his white hair and glasses and his ever-present notebook and pen. But more than that, he was someone who knew what the people of Storm wanted to read and gave them that and more.

The Storm Team Weekly News, the small paper Milt and a handful of others had been publishing for the last forty-five years, never changed. It covered news such as the local youth sports teams, the Founders' Day celebration, the annual pie eating contest, and occasionally included heart-pounding moments such as the time Zeke Johnson's cattle broke through the fences on the Double J Ranch and caused congestion all over downtown Storm. Every now and then, Milton tried to report on Senator Rush's political happenings, but the big papers always seemed to know when the senator was planning a pivotal announcement and swooped in to steal the glory. That, Jeffry knew, was part of the reason Milt had been so eager to hire him on for the summer. Because he hoped having a Rush on staff meant he was finally going to scoop the big city papers.

Jeffry headed up the stairs to the second level of the small brick building that housed *The Storm Team Weekly* in the heart of Storm and shook his head. He wasn't convinced having him on staff was going to do anything to help Milt scoop the city papers, but he'd been thrilled for the opportunity. Sure, some of the subject matter they covered was less than exhilarating, but he loved being around the news. Loved the excitement of chasing a story, even if that story was a cow lost on Main Street. And he couldn't wait to learn more.

He reached the second floor and headed for the open door at the end of the short hall. The "editorial" department was made up of Milt's wife Suellen and their thirty-something daughter, Annabelle, who'd come home a year or so ago from somewhere in the South to help her parents around the paper.

Annabelle was seated at the first desk when he walked into the room. She had dark hair and an easy smile, and Jeffry always felt relaxed in her presence. Small red-rimmed glasses were perched on her nose as she looked up from the copy she was editing. "Hey there, Jeffry. Come to rescue me from this boring job?"

Jeffry smiled. To him the job wasn't boring at all. After only a couple weeks as a part-time employee for *The Storm Team Weekly*, he couldn't believe he'd almost said no to the job because of his dad. Senator Sebastian Rush had been livid when Jeffry had told him he was going to work for, as he put it, a "news rag," because reporters were nothing but slime. But Jeffry hadn't cared what his dad thought. This was for him, and he felt alive when he was at the paper. Energized in a way nothing else seemed able to do for him lately.

"Sorry. No such luck." He handed her the folder. "Milt wants to know who you're sending to photograph the Little League tournament."

Annabelle huffed and rolled her chair over to a file cabinet adjacent to her desk. "Bobbie Joe. The only photographer we have." She slid the folder he'd brought up into the cabinet, then wheeled back to her desk. "Pop knows that. I swear he's getting senile in his old age."

Jeffry chuckled. The Waters family had a warm, comfortable way about them that he found refreshing. They were always hugging each other, laughing, making jokes, even when they were working, which was something he longed for from his family but knew he would never have.

Annabelle jotted a note on a piece of paper and handed it back to Jeffry. "Take this down to him. You know, life would be a hell of a lot easier if he'd use that damn smart phone I gave him. He wouldn't have to send you up and down these stairs ten times a day."

"I don't mind," Jeffry said. "It's good exercise, plus it gives me a chance to learn all the different departments and how they work."

Annabelle huffed again. "All four departments and the five of us who work them? You stick around here, Jeffry Rush, and you're going to wind up running this newspaper one day. Run. Run away fast. I'm warning you right now. If you don't, you'll get sucked in and you'll never escape."

Jeffry smiled. The teasing tone in Annabelle's voice told him she wasn't serious, though he wondered why she'd really come back last year. Yeah, her parents were older, but they hadn't slowed down at all, and the paper definitely didn't need her—yet.

"Annabelle Tallulah Waters," Suellen called from a door at the back of the small room that opened to her office. "Are you talking smack about your daddy again?"

Annabelle rolled her eyes. "No, Mama. I'm talking smack about the whole damn family!"

"Ungrateful daughter," Suellen muttered. But still there was no bite in any of their words, and when Jeffry looked down, Annabelle was grinning.

What would it be like to have a family that close? Where you could joke around without everyone getting all uptight and offended?

"Hiya, Mallory," Annabelle said, leaning to her left to look around Jeffry. "You come in to give us a scoop on the upcoming pie eating contest for the Founders' Day celebration? I heard Anna Mae's giving her sister a hard time about this year's pie selection. Rita Mae's still baking pies for the event, isn't she?"

Jeffry turned with surprise and looked Mallory's way. Her face was drawn, her eyes a little bit wild, and he knew with one look that something bad had happened.

"Hi, Annabelle." Mallory lifted a hand in a half-hearted wave from the doorway where she stood. "No scoop. Sorry. But yeah, as far as I know, Rita Mae's still doing the pies. Um..." She bit her lip. "I was wondering if I could talk to Jeffry for a few minutes?"

"Sure thing." Annabelle pushed to her feet and snatched the paper she'd just given Jeffry from his fingertips. When he turned, she said,

"Go. Take your time. I'll make sure Dad gets this."

"Okay." He looked back at Mallory, not particularly wanting to talk about whatever was bothering her here at the paper. "Wanna take a walk?"

She nodded. "That sounds good."

The park was in the center of town, so they headed that way. Mallory was silent as they walked, but Jeffry could tell from the way her shoulders hung that something heavy was weighing on her.

Stupid Luis. He'd known as soon as he'd seen Lacey kiss him last night that he should have stepped in and slapped Luis upside the head until he came to his damn senses.

They finally reached the park and found a bench beneath an old oak tree. As Mallory sat and twisted her hands together in her lap and still didn't say anything, Jeffry realized he was going to have to pull it out of her.

"I'm guessing you didn't come all the way down to the paper because you can't live without me."

Mallory laughed, but the sound quickly turned to a sob, and she dropped her face in her hands and shook.

"Stupid fucking Luis," Jeffry muttered. He scooted close and wrapped a hand around Mallory's shoulders, then awkwardly pulled her in so she was leaning against his chest. "It's okay. Whatever happened it's going to be okay."

"No it's not," Mallory muttered. "I messed things up."

Jeffry squeezed her arm. "No you didn't." Luis had messed them up by being a total jackass, but Jeffry didn't say so. "Tell me what happened."

Mallory sniffled and swiped her forearm over her eyes as she sat up. "I went over to the pool to talk to him because last night was so weird, you know? I wasn't even going to say anything about Lacey. But then when I got there, he wasn't working. He was sitting on a chair next to her and she was wearing this super-small bikini, and she was flirting and touching him, and he was flirting back. They both stopped talking when I walked up, like I'd totally interrupted their important conversation. And I was just... I was mad, you know?"

Jeffry's heart ached for her. Mallory was a sweet girl who came from a crappy family. Luis was the only positive things she had going right now, and he was fucking it all up because of a stupid childhood crush on Lacey Salt. "What happened then?"

She sniffled again. "Then I told him I wanted to talk to him, and we went out on the grass, and I asked him what he wanted. If he wanted Lacey or not. And, Jeffry..." Her shoulders sank, and her eyes slid closed. "He said he was with me."

He didn't see the problem. "*With you* is a good thing."

"No, it's not." She opened her eyes and shook her head vigorously. "He could have said he wanted me. He could have said he loved me. He could have said a hundred other things, but instead he made it sound like he was stuck with me."

"Mal, Luis is a guy. Guys don't always say the right thing at the right time. That doesn't mean he meant it the way you're taking it."

"Maybe." She shook her head and pushed to her feet. "I don't know. But here's what really pisses me off." She turned to face him, but instead of heartache, fire flared in her eyes now. "Lacey is supposed to be my best friend. She's not supposed to steal my boyfriend. She's trying to take Luis away from me because...because I don't know why. It's the same shit my sister does when she sees something she wants. She goes after it and doesn't care about anyone else's feelings. She broke up, like, three couples in high school that way, and I'm sure she's still doing it now. I never thought Lacey was like her but I'm starting to think she is. God, I just..." She looked up at the branches above, lifted her hands and dropped them in defeat. "I'm surrounded by people who just don't give a shit."

Jeffry chuckled and reached for her hand, pulling her back to sit next to him again on the bench. "You and me both. Have you seen my father? He and your sister are more similar than you think. He rolls over anyone who gets in his way politically and never much cares for the consequences."

Mallory bit her lip, and a nervous expression crossed her face.

His brow dropped. "What?"

She slanted a look his way. "He hit on Dakota last year. Did you know that?"

"*What?*"

Mallory winced. "I didn't say anything because, well, he's your dad and all, and I know things have been strained between you. But..."

She looked out at the park, and as she hesitated, clearly not wanting to go on, a sizzle of heat spread between Jeffry's ribs. But it wasn't the good kind of heat. It was the kind that made you see red. "But? Keep going."

Mallory sighed. "I only know because Dakota came by the house one night after Mom and Dad had gone to bed, all fired up because your dad had propositioned her and how dare he think he could get someone as young and hot as her. I don't know the details. Just that Dakota turned him down, which for her I guess was a big step toward doing the right thing. Not that she hasn't backtracked—a lot lately—but, whatever."

She turned to look at him and winced again. "I'm sorry. I shouldn't have said anything. It happened a long time ago, and I didn't come down here to tell you all that. I don't even know why I did. I guess just because I'm so upset about what Lacey's doing, and because I've seen Dakota do the same damn thing to other people. I just..." She shook her head as tears filled her eyes once more. "I never knew what it felt like."

Fury rumbled inside Jeffry, making his nerves hum and his vision narrow, but he forced the anger back for the moment and wrapped an arm around Mallory again. "It's okay. I get it and I'm not upset. My dad's an asshole. He always has been. If this is true, then it just takes that assholeness to a whole new level."

Mallory chuckled, but again it turned to a sob, and Jeffry held her as she fought through her emotions. He rubbed a hand up and down her arm and cursed Luis and Lacey and what they were doing to this poor girl. But mostly he cursed his own father.

Mallory sniffled. "It hurts even more to know I'm not only losing my boyfriend, I'm losing my best friend too, you know?"

"If she doesn't care about your feelings, she's not a true friend."

"I know that." Mallory wrapped an arm around Jeffry's waist, settling in even closer. "I feel like you're the only person I can talk to about this." Her crying slowly subsided, and she rubbed her thumb along his ribs. "I don't know what I'd do without you right now, Jeffry."

Her words echoed in the air around him as tingles spread across his ribs where she touched him. But instead of stimulating something warm inside, confusion and a need to escape rolled through his belly.

He grasped Mallory's shoulders and gently pushed her away, then quickly rose from the bench so she couldn't touch him again.

Startled, she looked up with damp brown eyes. "What's wrong?"

"Nothing." He stepped back from her, unsure what was happening. What was that feeling putting pressure on his chest, making it hard to draw breath? He took another step away and forced himself to stay calm when all he really wanted to do was turn and run.

"Jeffry?"

"I...I gotta go, Mal." He turned before she could stop him and walked quickly away from her. "We'll talk later."

He couldn't draw a full breath until he was back on the sidewalk in front of the newspaper. But when he did, he realized he'd just bailed on Mallory when she needed him most. He didn't understand why he'd run from her. Mallory was his friend, not any kind of threat. But he'd just rejected her, exactly like Luis.

"Shit," he muttered, closing his eyes. He'd told himself he'd never be like his father, but today he'd treated someone the same calloused way his father always treated him. And that meant before long—if he wasn't careful—he'd be grade-A asshole, exactly like Sebastian Rush.

* * * *

Luis felt like shit. He needed to talk to Mallory but as he'd taken his last break when Mallory had shown up at the pool, he'd worked nonstop until closing. And since it was a Saturday night and good weather, the pool had stayed open until eight.

He'd texted her several times, but she wasn't answering. He thought about going over to her house, but he was afraid Mrs. Alvarez would get mad at his stopping by so late. And what if Mallory had told her mom about the whole Lacey thing? Technically he hadn't done anything wrong. Yeah, Lacey had kissed him last night, but it had been a chaste kiss, and he hadn't kissed her back. Mallory didn't even know about that, so, really, she was upset over nothing, right?

He rubbed a hand against his forehead as he crossed the parking lot toward his car and tried to convince himself that Mallory was making a bigger deal out of all of this than it was worth. Dusk was just settling over Storm, the summer days warm and long. He tugged open the rear door of the old Jeep Cherokee he'd saved several summers' worth of money to buy and tossed his duffel into the back while his mind spun around the events of the last two days.

Lacey was just having fun. Blowing off steam because of the crap going on at her house. She was the only one from their group who wasn't working. Yeah, she had a part-time job at Cuppa Joe, but she hadn't been back since Jacob's funeral. She had to be bored at home, right? She wasn't really interested in him. If she was, he'd know, wouldn't he?

A car rumbled to a stop in front of his Jeep before he could come up with an answer, and he looked toward the familiar yellow Bug with a whisper of both excitement and dread.

Lacey lowered the passenger window and grinned. Her curly chestnut hair hung around her face, and her wide brown eyes sparkled with both mischief and intrigue. "Just get off work?"

Relax. Talking to a friend is not cheating. You're only being nice.

"Yeah." He stepped up to her window and bent so he could look across the passenger seat at her. "What are you doing here?"

She shrugged. "Had to get out of the house for a while. Have you eaten?"

Say yes, a voice whispered in the back of his head. *Tell her to leave before you make things worse, jackass.*

"No," he heard himself say.

"Sweet." Lacey held up a white paper bag. *Bluebonnet Cafe* was printed in big blue letters across the front. "I have plenty to share. Hop in."

Luis hesitated. His conscience urged him to say no, but he didn't really want to say no. What was he going to do with his night? Drive over to Mallory's and beg her to forgive him... when he hadn't done anything wrong in the first place?

"I don't bite," Lacey said, her grin widening until it encompassed her pretty face and made heat rush all through Luis's belly. "Much, anyway."

Before he could stop himself, he pulled the passenger door of the Bug open and slid in next to Lacey. As soon as he closed the door, she shoved the car into drive and whipped the little Bug out of the country club's parking lot.

"Where are we headed?" he asked when he realized they were on the main road moving west out of town.

"The lake. I need some fresh air, and I bet the sunset over the lake is awesome right now."

That voice in the back of Luis's head screamed that being alone with Lacey at the lake was a bad idea, but he shoved it aside. They were just eating. And talking. There was no harm in either of those things.

"You look like shit, you know," Lacey said as she drove. "Things with Mal not go so well?"

Luis huffed and rested his elbow on the windowsill so he could rub his aching forehead. "Not great, no."

She glanced sideways at him. "You two didn't break up, did you?"

He frowned and stared straight ahead. But something pinched in the center of his chest. "I'm not sure. She's pissed at me."

"Huh," was all Lacey said.

Monarch Lake was only a few miles out of town, in a small valley between rolling hills and surrounded by trees. All the locals knew the best swimming spots, and most summer days, the lake was packed. But at eight thirty in the evening, the majority of people who'd ventured out for the day had packed up and disappeared. Lacey pulled onto a gravel road then drew to a stop near the water's edge, but Luis was too lost in his thoughts about Mallory and what had happened between them to notice the beauty of the lake.

Lacey popped the driver's door and climbed out. "Man, that's gorgeous."

He turned to look her way. She stood next to the car in a pale-yellow sundress. Fading rays of sunlight shimmered over her in ribbons of gold and orange and purple. And as he studied her, he couldn't deny that she was a total looker, especially with all that soft brown hair falling in gentle curls down her back and a broad smile across her pretty face. Was it any wonder he'd been crushing on her for years? Lacey Salt was every guy's fantasy.

His mind instantly shifted to Mallory, and he looked away from Lacey, focusing on the dashboard as a strange feeling rolled through his belly. Being with Lacey up here at the lake wasn't a good idea at all. He had a girlfriend. Mallory was his girlfriend, not Lacey. *Mallory.*

"Um, Lace. I don't think—"

She grabbed the bag of food, reached for something from the backseat, then slammed the driver's door and walked around the front of the car. "Get out, handsome. I'm not eating in the car."

Handsome. The word spun in his head as he watched Lacey carry a blanket down to the grassy area near the water. He needed to go back to Storm. Needed to forget all about Lacey Salt and whatever games she was playing. But as soon as she turned and waved for him to join her, his willpower crumbled and he reached for the door handle.

Lacey laid out the blue-checked blanket, then knelt and pulled out a burger and handed it to him. Nerves vibrated through Luis's fingers as he took the burger and sat on the blanket beside her. They were just having dinner, right? A man had to eat.

Lacey ate half her burger in silence, and they watched the sunset over the lake, the fading light creating a multicolor glow all across the wide Texas sky. After wrapping up her burger, Lacey tossed it back in the bag and sighed. "I love this place. I always feel better when I'm here."

Luis finished his own burger and wadded the wrapper up before placing it in the bag. Unfortunately, the food hadn't done anything to settle his stomach. "Me too."

"Remember when we were in middle school and we used to come out here and spy on the high schoolers making out on the beach?"

Luis drew his legs up and rested his elbows on his knees. He was still wearing his lifeguarding shorts, but he'd thrown on a white Nickelback T-shirt before leaving work. They were just talking. Reminiscing. There was nothing wrong with that. "I remember Marisol used to bust my ass for sneaking out."

"And I remember Ginny was always up here with a different boy."

Luis smiled, relaxing as the conversation drifted. They were just friends. It was okay to have a girl friend without her being your girlfriend. "Yeah. She was a bit of a wild child. I'm pretty sure she was just doing whatever she could to get your brother to notice her, though."

Lacey's smile slipped, and Luis instantly realized he'd said the wrong thing.

"Shit. Sorry." Mentioning Jacob was so stupid. "I didn't mean to make you sad."

"You didn't." Lacey looked down at her hands, resting on her knees. "Everything makes me sad these days, so don't worry. Mallory doesn't get that. My parents don't get it. No one does. You can't imagine what it's like to lose someone you love."

"Yeah, I can," he said softly, his mind turning to thoughts of his parents.

Lacey looked his way with weary brown eyes. "You're probably the only one who does."

"Is that what's been going on with you the last few days?"

Her brow dropped. The sun had set, and darkness was slowly creeping in, but the temperature was still warm, and the way her eyes shimmered in the fading light made him even warmer. "I don't know what you mean."

"Come on, Lace. You know you do." He looked back at the lake, and even though a tiny part of him was sad he was finally facing reality, he knew this was all for the best. He couldn't keep fantasizing about Lacey Salt. It wasn't fair to him and it definitely wasn't fair to Mallory. "I get it. I mean, you're in a crazy place. Nothing makes sense. No one seems to understand you, even you. And you just want life to be normal again so you're reaching out for anything you can to make you feel normal. But this isn't you, and it sure as heck isn't me."

Her hand landed against his shoulder, and before he realized what she was doing, she'd straddled his hips and settled herself onto his lap. "What if I told you you're what I want?"

Blood rushed straight to his groin, and his stomach flopped around like a fish out of water. He lowered his legs to the blanket and froze, unable to think or move or speak.

She brushed her fingers over the stubble on his jaw, and tingles spread all across his skin, wherever she touched. Leaning toward his mouth, she whispered, "I know you've had a crush on me forever, Luis. I can't believe you never said anything. I never would have turned you down. I've wanted you for months now."

Her lips pressed against his, soft and sweet and all that he remembered from her kiss last night. But this time they were insistent, and when her tongue swept along the edge of his mouth, he didn't even think. He opened in reflex and let her in.

She tasted faintly of the burger she'd just eaten, but he didn't care. Her mouth was warm and wet and so damn erotic, blood pumped through his veins making him hard and hot and achy.

Her slick tongue slid along his, and she tipped her head the other way, kissed him deeper and moaned. And the sound supercharged his libido, making him slide his hands around her shoulders so he could hold her close while he kissed her back. While she made him crazy with her mouth.

A little voice in the back of his head whispered, *This isn't real. Lacey Salt is messing with you,* but he ignored it. Because all he could think about was how soft and wet her mouth was. How smooth and silky her skin was. And how long he'd daydreamed about a moment just like this.

She let go of his face and reached behind her head. Luis kept kissing her, wanting only a little bit more. Fabric fell against his hands at her waist, then her fingers closed over his and she drew his hand up.

Something warm and soft and full filled his palm, and he broke away from her mouth long enough to look down to see what it was.

His eyes grew wide. She'd untied the halter of her dress. That warm, full object in his hand was her breast. Her very naked, very plump breast. Shades lighter than the skin of his hand. Shades lighter than Mallory's breast, which he'd held and touched like this just a few nights ago when they'd made out in the backseat of his car.

Mallory's voice suddenly echoed in his head from earlier in the day. *"I don't know why she's suddenly interested in you when she never even looked twice your way before..."* And a chill spread down his spine.

Lacey gripped Luis's shoulders, dropped her head back, then rocked her hips against his and groaned. "Oh God. That feels so good. Don't stop touching me."

Panic condensed beneath Luis's ribs. Panic and a sea of guilt that pushed him into action.

He let go of Lacey and quickly pushed her off his lap. Sweat streaked down his spine as he stumbled to his feet and tried not to fall over.

"What the hell, Luis?" Lacey's irritated voice echoed up at him. "What's wrong with you all a sudden?"

"I..." Shit. This was wrong. He'd just made out with Lacey Salt. *With Lacey Salt.* A girl who hadn't shown any interest in him romantically until two days ago. He didn't want Lacey. He knew that now. What he'd felt for her was nothing more than a stupid crush. He wanted Mallory. Mallory didn't play games with him. Mallory didn't try to mess with his head. Mallory cared about him—really cared about him—in a way Lacey never could. "I have to go."

He took a step toward the car, but Lacey lurched to her feet and grabbed his hand. "You're not going anywhere."

Luis turned to face her, startled by the cold bite in her voice. She was holding the dress together at her chest, but her eyes were on fire in the fading light.

He'd upset her. She had every right to be mad. He'd let things go too far and now she was hurt that he'd rejected her. But this wasn't right. And as much as he didn't want to hurt her more, he needed her to get it. "I'm sorry, Lace. I didn't mean—"

"Get back on the blanket, Luis."

The calm tone of her voice was in direct contrast with the fire swirling in her dark eyes. His stomach tightened. "Lacey, I'm sorry, but

I'm in love with Mallory. This was a giant mistake. I didn't mean to—"

"I don't care what you meant to do. You've wanted me forever. We both know it. So get back on this blanket and fuck me like we both know you want to do."

He recoiled at her words and stepped back. Something wild flashed in her eyes. Something he hadn't seen before. "No." He shook his head. "I'm not going to."

He turned for the road, desperate to get away from Lacey and this entire night as fast as he could.

"Come back here, Luis. Come back right now." Lacey's voice echoed in the night at his back. "If you walk away from me, you'll regret it. I swear you'll regret it forever!"

Luis pushed his legs into a jog as a new sense of panic rushed all through his chest. The only thing he regretted was being a stupid, idiotic asshole to the one person he cared most about in the world.

He just prayed she let him make it all up to her before it was too late.

Chapter Six

A tapping sound roused Mallory from the restless sleep she'd finally fallen into.

Rubbing her eyes, she sat up and looked around her dark bedroom. Another tap echoed from the direction of her window. "What the...?"

She threw back the covers, crossed to the window, and pulled the curtain back at the corner. Then jumped when she saw Luis standing in the bushes outside her house. Letting go of the curtains as if they'd burned her, she lurched back.

Her heart rate shot up, and her hands grew sweaty. What was he doing here? She didn't want him here. Not when she'd already been rejected twice in one day. Was he here to make her feel worse?

"Mal?" he said in a low voice. "Mal, I know you're in there. I saw the curtain move. Come outside for just a minute, please? I need to talk to you."

Mallory's pulse turned to a roar in her ears, and indecision pushed at her from every angle. Her foolish heart wanted her to rush right out there, but her wounded pride was still licking its wounds.

He'd hurt her today. Hurt her more than she'd thought he could. It wasn't just that he hadn't fought for their relationship like she wanted him to; it was that the longer this dragged out, the more she saw her mother in her actions. She loved her mom, but Joanne Alvarez had turned a blind eye to everything Hector had done for way too many years. Mallory had vowed long ago not to be like that, and standing up for herself and the things she wanted was the only way she knew not to become her mother.

"Mal." His voice grew weary. "At least come to the window. Please?"

Mallory's hands itched to pull the curtain back, so she twisted them behind her back and held completely still.

"Shit," he muttered. Then closer, as if he'd moved right up to the glass, "I'm sorry. I'm sorry about everything. I've been a jerk, and you have every right to be mad at me, I just..." He hesitated. "I want you, Mal. Not Lacey. Just you. And I should have told you that earlier only I was...stupid. Please, please give me another chance and I promise I'll make it up to you."

Tears filled Mallory's eyes. Tears and hope. Something she'd lost sometime during the day. She was just too afraid to reach for it.

"Mal?" he said again, his voice strained and sad. "Please?"

Her stomach tightened with a thousand different doubts. But the biggest was whether or not she could trust him. She wanted to trust him, but in the back of her mind all she could think about was how awful she'd felt after she'd left the country club today. She never wanted to feel like that again, and she didn't know what he could say to reassure her that would never happen.

She wanted to ask if he'd told Lacey he wasn't interested in her advances. Wanted to ask if he'd told her to back off and quit flirting with him. Wanted to ask what had happened to make him come here so late at night to tell her these things. But she couldn't. Because she was too afraid of the answers. And because she didn't want to be like her mother.

Several minutes of silence passed, and then softly from outside, Luis said, "I'm not giving up on you. I'm not. I'm just...not, okay? This is the real deal. Somehow, I'll prove that to you."

Warmth gathered around her heart where it pounded against her ribs. Her hands grew sweaty. And that hope—the hope she'd tried like crazy to keep at bay—came rushing back.

Oh God, she wanted him. Wanted *them*. And though she knew it made her weak, all she could think about was telling him that before he left.

She bolted for her bedroom door and peeked out into the hallway, excitement and fear pushing her forward. Her mother was sound asleep. Tiptoeing toward the kitchen, she carefully unlocked the door with fingers that shook, then stepped out into the warm night and rushed around the side of the house.

Her feet drew to a stop as she searched the empty yard, then she whipped around to look down the dimly lit street, but it too was empty.

That racing heart slowed. He'd already left. She'd wasted too much time. For a moment, she thought about going after him, but then remembered she was wearing nothing but short cotton sleep shorts and a tank with no bra. She could go back inside and change, but she didn't know which way he'd gone, and he lived clear across town. She wasn't stupid enough to walk alone at night—even in Storm—which meant her only other option was her mother's Oldsmobile.

Her gaze drifted to the drive, where the beast of a vehicle sat parked. No way she could start that without waking her mother, and if that happened she'd have to explain why she was sneaking out in the middle of the night.

She looked back down the empty street and knew she'd have to wait until tomorrow, after her shift at the B&B, which started way before Luis even rolled out of bed.

"*I want you, Mal. Not Lacey. Just you.*" Warmth filled her chest as she remembered his words, and that hope lifted her mouth into a wobbly smile. She could wait until tomorrow. She could wait forever for Luis if she had to. Because he'd just proved he was nothing like her father. He was a guy worth waiting for.

* * * *

Jeffry Rush downed the rest of his energy drink as he looked at the rundown old house on the outskirts of town, the crumbling stucco and missing paint not surprising him. It had been converted into four apartments, five if you counted the garage apartment that was his destination.

He crumpled the can and tossed it into the garbage can that blocked part of the driveway. Nobody else had bothered, and empty beer cans littered the street.

Once, this section of Live Oak Street had been nice. Now it was a dump. There'd been a flood back in the seventies, and most of the houses had never been fixed up. White trash tended to congregate in places like this, and though he'd never considered himself elitist in any way, right now he knew he was a thousand times better than the person inside that apartment.

He checked the time on his cell phone. It was ten o'clock in the morning. Early enough for her to be up on a Sunday. Knowing her, though, she'd probably been out partying last night and was currently passed out on her couch. All the better for him. She didn't know he was coming, so she wouldn't be that snarky, uppity girl everyone knew and hated. She'd be vulnerable and weak. And she was about to get the shock of a lifetime.

He climbed the metal stairs and headed for her door. Stopping in front of her apartment, he remembered everything Mallory had told him, and the way his dad had flat-out denied it when he'd asked about it last night at home.

"She's a tramp, son. She threw herself at me. Do you honestly think I would be interested in someone like her? I'm a Rush. She's...nothing. Besides which, I love your mother. I would never do anything to hurt her."

His dad might be an asshole, but he wasn't a cheater. His mom wouldn't stay with someone who cheated on her. His grandmother would never allow it.

Anger rushed back through Jeffry's veins, and he closed his hand into a fist and banged on the door.

A groan echoed from the other side. She was in there, dammit. He pounded louder.

"Okay, okay," she muttered from inside. "Stop the fucking pounding." The door flew open, and Dakota Alvarez stood in the dark apartment wearing nothing but a black lace bra and a silky short pink bathrobe open to her navel. "Yeah? What the hell do you want?"

Oh yeah. A total tramp. No way his dad would even look at someone like this.

She lifted a hand to block the sun, her glossy dark eyes finally focusing on his face. "Jeffry? Wh-what are you doing here?"

"I know what you are, and I know what you're after, and you're not going to get it so back the fuck off."

The blood drained from her face, and her eyes grew wide. "I don't—"

"That's right. You don't have a fucking clue who you're messing with. You think it's harmless to flirt with and proposition a married man? A senator even? It's not. He's not interested in slutty girls like you and he never will be. You won't get any money out of him. You'll get nothing. And if you ever do anything to mess with him or my family, if you even think about going near him again, I'll make your life a living hell. Guaranteed."

"I...but...he..."

Jeffry turned for the stairs, feeling better with every step. No one messed with his family. The Rushes might be fucked up and dysfunctional in a variety of different ways, but they were his, and he'd protect them with his last breath.

He made it to the landing on the chipped metal stairs before Dakota's voice rang out from the railing above. "How did you know?"

He glared up at her. "From your own lips."

Her face went ashen. "But I—"

He shook his head at her utter stupidity. "You were dumb enough to tell your sister."

* * * *

Mallory put away the last of the breakfast dishes in the kitchen at the Flower Hill Bed & Breakfast, anxious to finish her shift so she could go see Luis.

"That's the last of it, Anna Mae," she said to the white-haired woman seated at the kitchen table, making a list of items they needed to restock in the kitchen. "Is there anything else you need me to do?"

"No, no," Anna Mae said. "I think that's all. Oh, but could you be a dear and get me that cookbook from the top shelf there before you go? I want to make those pecan rolls again and I can never remember how much yeast to use."

"Sure." Mallory pushed to her toes and reached for the handwritten book on the top shelf. Some of the oldest families in the town had donated recipes for a charity cookbook a few years back to help Allison Kenney, a six-year-old at the local school suffering from leukemia. Sadly, Allison had passed, but the cookbook lived on, in her name.

The front door to the old Victorian echoed from the parlor, followed by Marisol's voice. "Anna Mae? Are you here?"

Butterflies churned in Mallory's stomach as she looked toward the archway that led to the front of the house. Marisol would know if Luis was still at home. Mallory could find out where he was without having to call him.

"In here, sweetie," Anna Mae called.

Marisol swept into the room with a smile and a pan covered in foil that smelled of cinnamon and sugar. "Oh, good morning, Mallory. I didn't realize you worked Sundays."

"I don't always," Mallory said.

"The rooms are all full," Anna Mae muttered. "I need as many extra hands as I can get." Her brow wrinkled and she pushed to her feet. "What's in that pan?"

Marisol shifted one hand under the pan, then peeled back the foil. The scent of warm, homemade cinnamon rolls filled the kitchen.

"Ooh," Anna Mae said with a grin. "Girl, you just made my Sunday."

Marisol smiled. "This batch is free. So long as you sit and enjoy one with me."

Anna Mae moved toward the cupboard and pulled down three plates. "Don't have to break my arm to get me to agree. Mallory?"

"Um." Mallory glanced toward Marisol. She didn't really want to stay; she wanted to find Luis—was anxious to find Luis—but she didn't want to be rude. Especially to the sister of the guy she was in love with. "Okay."

"Wonderful." Anna Mae handed Mallory the plates, forks, and a serving utensil. "You give these to Marisol and I'll get us three coffees."

Mallory brought the plates to the table while Marisol removed the foil and scooped a gooey hot cinnamon roll onto each plate. "So Luis was still asleep when I left. You two must have been out late last night."

Heat rushed to Mallory's cheeks. Yes, Luis had been out late last night, but she didn't really want to share the things he'd confessed at her window near midnight. Those she wanted to keep all for herself.

"I guess so," Mallory said, sinking into the chair on the far side of the table. "I didn't look at the clock. So Luis is still at home?"

Marisol slid a plate across to Mallory. "Sleeping like a bear."

A smile spread across Mallory's face. After this, she was going right over to his house and waking him up. With her lips if she could.

Anna Mae brought three steaming coffee cups to the table. "It's so nice to have a moment like this while the guests are off checking out the sights. Lord knows, soon enough I'll be inundated with requests for tea and sweets all over again. I swear I can't keep enough of your white chocolate macadamia nut cookies on hand, Marisol."

"Oh, the cookies!" Marisol wiped her hands on her jeans and rushed for the archway toward the dining room. "I left them in the car. I'll be right back."

Anna Mae chuckled as she sank back into her chair with a groan. "I don't know how that girl does it. Up early every day with her bakery, taking care of that brother of hers, and now with her younger sister pregnant..." She shook her head and sipped her coffee. "God clearly knows only young people can deal with children. Why, if the good Lord thought to give me a child at my age, I'd probably forget where I left the little bugger."

Mallory smiled and reached for her coffee. The back screen door burst open just as she lifted it to her lips, and Dakota rushed into the room with wild blonde hair she obviously hadn't combed yet this morning, dark circles under her eyes as if she'd forgotten to wash her face, rumpled shorts, a frayed blue T-shirt, and two different color flip-flops on her feet.

"Dakota?" Worry skittered Mallory's nerves, and she quickly set down her coffee and pushed to her feet. "What's wrong?"

"What's wrong? *What's wrong?*" Fire flared in Dakota's eyes. "What's wrong is that my sister is a backstabbing, lying, two-faced little bitch."

Mallory's mouth fell open in absolute shock.

"Whoa, missy," Anna Mae said from her seat. "You're in my house right now. You watch that mouth of yours. I'm not about to look away like your mama."

Dakota's fiery gaze shot to Anna Mae but darted right back to Mallory. "You promised you wouldn't say anything. You promised and you lied."

Mallory had no idea what Dakota was talking about, but she could tell that something was seriously wrong. She skirted the table and reached for Dakota, but her sister swatted her hand away before she could touch her.

Mallory lifted her hands in surrender. "Okay, calm down. Tell me what happened."

"I'll tell you what happened," Dakota growled. "Jeffry Rush accosted me at my apartment this morning."

"He *what?*"

"He said you told him about me and the senator."

Mallory's mind spun. She had no idea what Dakota was talking about. Her and the senator? Senator Rush?

Before Mallory could ask what that meant, Dakota said, "No one knows about that but you. I never told anyone that he hit on me last year except for you. And you went and told Jeffry fucking Rush? He thinks I'm a hussy trying to bleed money out of his family. You've ruined my reputation!"

"Oh shit." Mallory's conversation with Jeffry yesterday in the park whipped through her mind. "I...I didn't say anything bad about you, Dakota. I didn't think he would take it that way. I told him that the senator hit on you, but that you turned him down. You did the right thing there. No one would ever think you were a hussy for that." She was going to have a serious talk with Jeffry. How could he have misread what she'd told him?

"You are so incredibly naïve," Dakota sneered. "You don't know the first thing about how the world works."

Mallory stared at her sister, confused about what was happening. Anger radiated off Dakota in waves. This was about more than what Mallory had told Jeffry. There was something else going on here. "I don't—"

"Understand?" Dakota's brow lifted. "Of course you don't. How could you? You don't know the first thing about men. You can't even hang on to your own man and he's only a high school boy."

A whisper of fear rushed down Mallory's spine. Luis. She was talking about Luis. She swallowed hard, almost afraid to ask. "What about Luis?"

"Oh, you haven't heard?" Smug victory spread across Dakota's face. "Your boyfriend fucked your best friend up at the lake last night. Everyone in town is talking about it."

A gasp echoed from the doorway, and Mallory knew Marisol was standing there listening, but she couldn't turn to look. "N-no. That's not true."

"Oh, it's true," Dakota said, twisting the knife. "Adam Glenn saw them together on a blanket by the lake getting all hot and heavy, and I heard when he asked Lacey after church today if that was them, she didn't deny it."

"I..." Mallory's legs grew weak, and she reached out for the table.

"I don't believe it."

But even as she said the words, she knew they were a lie. Something *had* happened last night. She'd felt it when Luis had stood outside her bedroom window and confessed his feelings. She just never in a million years thought it would be this.

Dakota laughed, but the sound held no humor. "Still so naïve. Your boyfriend is a lying, cheating son of a bitch, Mallory. Just like you. I hope you're both extremely happy together."

The screen door slammed shut with a crack, but Mallory barely heard it. Because her legs gave out before she even knew what was happening.

Dance in the Wind

By Jennifer Probst

About Jennifer Probst

Jennifer Probst wrote her first book at twelve years old. She bound it in a folder, read it to her classmates, and hasn't stopped writing since. She took a short hiatus to get married, get pregnant, buy a house, get pregnant again, pursue a master's in English Literature, and rescue two shelter dogs. Now she is writing again.

She makes her home in Upstate New York with the whole crew. Her sons keep her active, stressed, joyous, and sad her house will never be truly clean.

She is the *New York Times*, *USA Today*, and *Wall Street Journal* bestselling author of sexy and erotic contemporary romance. She was thrilled her book, The Marriage Bargain, was ranked #6 on Amazon's Best Books for 2012, and spent 26 weeks on the New York Times. Her work has been translated in over a dozen countries, sold over a million copies, and was dubbed a "romance phenom" by Kirkus Reviews.

She loves hearing from readers. Visit her website for updates on new releases and her street team at www.jenniferprobst.com.

Sign up for her newsletter at
http://www.jenniferprobst.com/newsletter
for a chance to win a gift card each month and receive exclusive material and giveaways.

Twitter: jenniferprobst

Facebook: https://www.facebook.com/jenniferprobst.authorpage

Also From Jennifer Probst

Marriage to a Billionaire Series:
The Marriage Bargain
The Marriage Trap
The Marriage Mistake
The Marriage Merger
The Book of Spells

Searching for Series:
Searching for Someday
Searching for Perfect
Searching for Beautiful
Searching for Always
Coming Soon: Searching for Mine

Other Sexy Contemporaries
Executive Seduction
All the Way

The Sex on the Beach Series:
Beyond Me
Chasing Me
Summer Sins

Dark Blessings Series:
Dante's Fire

Stories for the Whole Family:
A Life Worth Living

Acknowledgments from the Author

A huge thank you to the amazing, creative, talented team behind the brilliance of the Rising Storm series. I'm so honored to be able to participate in such a ground-breaking series. Big smooches and hugs go out to Julie Kenner and Dee Davis for the creation of this monstrous masterpiece, Liz Berry and MJ Rose from Evil Eye Concepts for gorgeous covers, packaging and marketing, all of my fellow authors who inspired me and kept me glued to the page, Inkwell Management and my publicist Jessica Estep for always providing me support and great PR, and of course, the readers. I hope you enjoyed this episode as much as I did writing it!

Chapter One

Logan Murphy paused in the doorway of Murphy's Pub. Already the sounds of Irish music, loud revelry, and laughter drifted to his ears. In his mind, the sounds echoing were different. Gunfire. Screams. The roar of the engines. His team's orders yelled above screeching noise and smoke.

He fought the sudden shakes that gripped his body and squeezed his eyes shut, dragging in a lungful of air. Dammit. Not now. Not here. He needed to get himself together because he was about to walk into his own welcome home party. How would it look to his family and the town if he lost it before he even entered? Everyone needed him to play his part so they could feel safe and proud of his accomplishments in a war that was supposed to be over and barely got news time unless a certain amount of people were killed. They needed him to smile, tell them everything was okay, and fall into inane conversation about the upcoming Founders' Day celebration. They needed him to look at pictures of graduations and newborn babies, and humbly acknowledge their pats on the back and hearty thank yous for serving his country.

They did not need to know the truth.

Guilt assaulted him but he was used to beating it back into the closet. Slowly, his muscles eased and he was able to wrap a blanket of calm around him. Better to be numb. It worked best for everyone involved. Pretend he was fine and eventually, maybe, he would be.

Finally, his fingers closed on the door and he pushed his way into the pub.

A loud shout greeted his ears, and he was enfolded in a mass of people raising their glasses and greetings of "Welcome home." The pub enclosed him in familiarity, from the sweeping mahogany bar to the battered chairs and booths and the scarred plank floor. Endless bottles of Irish whiskey lined the shelves, and draft taps of Guinness stood proudly, ready to be poured. The dartboard and pool table still held the place of honor in the back, and the air filled with the scents of coffee, burgers, and the same pine cleaner his father always used.

He stumbled only once when he caught sight of his picture mounted in a place of honor over the bar. He was in his uniform, looking out of the frame, his gaze reflecting the seriousness of his job and the excitement of youth.

Logan quickly looked away and tried to concentrate on the crowd swarming around him. He swallowed back the edge of a slight panic attack and breathed through his nose nice and slow, like he'd been taught.

He could do this.

His mother was the first to pull him into a squeezing bear hug. He laughed, because Sonya Murphy hadn't stopped hugging and kissing him since he came back a few days ago. Her curly russet hair tickled his nose but he allowed her free reign, knowing she was trying to make up for the years he'd been away. "Mom, I can't breathe," he said teasingly.

Her blue eyes shimmered with tears and happiness when she finally pulled away. "I can't believe you're finally home," she sniffed. "And don't tell me what I can and can't do. Mothers have a right."

"That's right, son. Your mama's been dying to spoil someone for a long time." Aiden Murphy stepped over and pulled Sonya close. His parents had always had an affectionate, easy relationship, and some of the tightness in his gut eased in their presence. "Patrick's cut her off from surprising him at his place with beef stew. Seems he's afraid she'll walk in on some intimate time with Marisol Moreno."

"Knock it off, Dad," Patrick grumbled. A faint hint of red flushed his cheekbones. Hmm, interesting. Patrick had been chasing Marisol for a while now. Maybe he'd finally managed to get her to commit to an actual relationship other than a maybe-there-was-more friendship. Logan raised a brow at his older brother. Patrick always had a competitive streak with Dillon and him, seemingly needing to beat them and shine on his own. With Dillon being a cop and Logan joining the military, Patrick had the classic middle brother syndrome. He always believed he had to work harder for his parents' attention, since Dillon got the older brother privileges and Logan was considered the adored "baby" of the family. Deciding to train as an EMT was a good choice, and Logan was proud of his brother's goals.

"I'll be glad to step in and receive Mom's cooking," he stated, keeping the heat off Patrick for now. Maybe they'd share a beer later so he could catch up on what was really going on in his life. Things had been chaotic since his return and they hadn't had any quality time yet.

"Hey, what about me?" His older brother Dillon pushed himself into the circle, pressing a kiss on Mom's cheek. "I'm always grateful for your handouts, Mom, especially the Irish soda bread."

Sonya laughed with delight, surrounded by her boys. "You're all welcome to my cooking, and you know it. Finally, I'll get to go to church this Sunday and have my boys at a proper family dinner."

Dillon rustled his hair in typical older brother fashion and handed him a Guinness. "Here you go. Let's see if you grew up a bit overseas and can finally hold your liquor."

Patrick snorted. "I can drink both of you under the table and you know it."

Logan gave a fake sneer. "When I'm done with you and you're drooling like fools, I'll put your mugs up on Instagram. A little Storm entertainment."

"No bar fights," a gruff voice sounded. Michael Murphy, his grandfather and patriarch of the family, stepped into the circle. Logan had heard he mostly kept to the back of the bar now, letting his son lead, but he'd always be the bedrock of the Murphy clan. With his black hair gone silver and those piercing blue eyes, his presence brought a sense of stability and leadership that eked down to each member. People always told him he was his grandfather born again, with the same type of muscled build and Black Irish good looks. They'd always been the closest, and even now, his grandfather seemed to sense there was much more going on beneath the surface than he was letting on to his family. Michael Murphy locked gazes with him, studying him hard, then slowly nodded. The gesture spoke volumes of understanding, as if he knew this homecoming party was painful to get through.

Yeah. Life was a bitch. He got a party for surviving.

His friend got a funeral.

Logan cleared his throat and tried to distract himself. "You keeping my brothers in line while I was gone, Grandpa?" he asked.

"I try, but they're an unruly lot. My grandson seems to think he can ticket me for speeding. Seems power has gotten to his head."

"You were going twenty miles over the limit! I have to do my job, and nepotism isn't part of it."

Logan grinned. "Don't worry, Grandpa. I bet I have a few people I can call and pull some strings for you."

"Now, that's what I'm talking about."

Dillon groaned. "You were always his favorite, Logan. Some things never change."

Everyone laughed. Logan clicked his glass to Dillon's and Patrick's. In that moment, surrounded by the tight-knit circle of his family, his past faded away and there was only comfort and security. He tried to hold on to the feeling, savoring the rare seconds of peace, but as always, it was over too quickly.

His name boomed from the right and he was thrown into the fray of people he hadn't seen in years. People who'd stayed in Storm, made lives here, got married, had kids, and lived a full life. People who cared about him and his family, and had been there to take care of them while he was away. He shook hands with his Uncle Zeke and hugged his Aunt Alice. Then nodded to others who crowded in and thanked him for his service, and he tried to be the polite, upbeat hero they desperately needed him to be.

It was only when he faced the Salts that his composure left.

Jacob was gone.

The hole in his gut opened up, filling with darkness and a pained grief that whipped through his body. He'd been in gunfire, driven near roadside bombs, and watched his friend explode in pieces in front of him. Yet Logan had survived.

Jacob had been driving home from college with his whole life ahead of him when it was stolen in moments. What random Fate or God decided on who got to stay or who got to go? The questions spun endlessly—like a twisty mess in his head threatening to take him over, body and soul.

Ginny could've died, too. The thought of her being hurt terrified him. After seeing her in the park the other day, he hadn't been able to stop thinking about her. It was as if they'd forged a strong connection after only a brief time. Logan kept going over the encounter. He'd been seriously losing his shit, suddenly thrust back into the so-called normal world where you grocery shopped, took your dog for a walk, and didn't think a loud noise was a roadside bomb. He'd finally arrived home, and instead of heading to his family's house, he ended up wandering the park like a homeless person.

So fucking humiliating.

But when he'd spoken to Ginny, an odd hum of understanding passed between them. She got it. She'd gone through her own hell with losing Jacob, and that moment he looked into her troubled brown eyes, he was a goner.

She'd still been young—a few months shy of fifteen—when he enlisted, but even then he remembered how much he liked her. She made him laugh with her mischievous antics and joy for life, even after losing her parents so young.

Of course, she was pregnant with Jacob's baby. And living with the Salts. And probably not interested in a fucked-up, useless, twenty-four-year-old war veteran.

Still, his instincts screamed there was something special between them.

He needed to find out.

He shoved his taunting thoughts aside and faced the Salts head on. Celeste looked fragile, standing next to her husband. Her gray eyes were haunted, and fine lines bracketed her face that told him she rarely slept. He knew the signs well. She smiled tentatively and reached out to touch his arm. "Welcome home, Logan. Everyone's missed you."

Her husband, Travis, held her elbow as if without his support, she'd collapse. "Thank you for serving our country, son."

The words hit him hard and he gritted his teeth. "I'm so sorry to hear about Jacob. I tried to get my release early to attend the funeral but I wasn't able to."

Celeste nodded. "Of course, we completely understand." She took a deep breath as if looking for strength. "Jacob would've understood. We're all so proud of you."

"I can't imagine what a rough time this is for you. If I can do anything—anything at all, please let me know."

"We appreciate it," Travis said. Even though he held his wife, when he looked down at her face there was a faint distance there. So different from when his father and mother shared a glance. As if the Salts went through the motions but the intimacy was gone. Of course, losing a child could do that to a marriage.

He didn't have time to mull it over though, because Ginny suddenly stepped forward, a tentative smile on her face. Travis immediately let go of Celeste's elbow and reached for Ginny, his expression paternal. Celeste's face lit up a bit too as she stood by, as if some of her troubles were eased just by being in Ginny's presence.

Logan knew what that felt like.

The sucker punch happened low in his gut. A pleasant, warm feeling trickled through his veins. Damn, he felt like he was in some chick flick movie, but he'd never experienced such a chemistry with any other woman, not like this.

Not like her.

"Welcome home, Logan," she said softly, her words echoing their talk in the park. He stared at her beautiful face, glowing with her pregnancy. Smooth, golden skin. Those wide dark eyes, so full of mysteries and secrets he wished he could delve into. Curly black hair tumbling over her shoulders. Tonight, she wore black pants and a simple black lacy top that stretched over her small breasts. Her lips were a deep red. Logan tried not to stare at that mouth, which looked lush and ripe like a Red Delicious apple he wanted to bite into. Her belly only showed a tiny bump, confirming Jacob's baby was growing inside her body.

What was wrong with him? He'd imagined being a bit disgusted by himself for being attracted to a pregnant woman, but in his heart, he only recognized Ginny. The girl he'd grown up with. The girl with the hearty laugh and sparkling eyes, and impish trouble she'd get into with her friends. In the years he'd been away, she'd changed. Ripened. There were regrets and secrets in her eyes that called to him, because he had his own.

It was almost as if they were soul mates, finally reunited.

Of course, that was crazy.

Right?

He must've been staring at her for a while because Celeste frowned. He forced himself to speak. "It's good to be home. How are you feeling, Ginny?" Logan craved a more intimate conversation, but Celeste seemed to keep a protective eye on her houseguest.

Ginny shifted her feet. Her hands automatically came to rest on her stomach. "Okay. Morning sickness has been hard. I'm taking it a day at a time. Like everyone, I guess." She glanced at Celeste. "I'm being well taken care of, though."

Celeste smiled and patted her arm. "We take care of each other now. And once the baby comes, maybe we'll be able to see past some of the pain and savor some joy. We'll have a permanent part of Jacob with us."

Ginny winced. Was she embarrassed to be carrying Jacob's son? Or was it just hard to hear his name spoken aloud? Logan wondered how deep her grief went. He ached to hold her gently in his arms and take care of her. He was sure the Salts gave her what she needed, but he also knew about the downfalls of a small town, especially Storm. The town loved their gossip, and judgment. Sure, they gathered to support their own—families were tight here. But like any place, there were things beneath the surface, and he bet a few people hated the idea of Ginny bringing Jacob's illegitimate child into the world.

If Logan was by her side, he wouldn't let anyone hurt her.

Travis seemed distracted. "Sweetheart, can I get you a drink?"

"Yes, a white wine would be nice." Her husband disappeared with what seemed to be relief, and Celeste gave a deep sigh. Her gaze was a bit off focus, as if she had trouble concentrating. "Everyone is so happy to have you back safe, Logan. What are you going to do now? Help your father with the bar? Or do you have other plans?"

He tried not to jerk. The words hit him like ice water flung in his face. What was he going to do? He had no plans; he'd been active military for so long now. Did he even know how to do anything else but handle a gun, hunt terrorists, and take orders? Was the rest of his life about polishing the bar and serving drinks? No, if he thought about that now he'd go nuts.

"I'm sure Logan needs some time to settle," Ginny cut in. She smiled at him in a show of support. "One step at a time." She paused. "For all of us."

Celeste nodded. "Of course, of course. I hope we'll see more of each other soon, Logan. And congratulations."

He wondered what she was congratulating him for. Surviving? Coming home? Serving his country? He noted the firm clasp of her fingers on Ginny's arm while Celeste tugged her away, like a protective mother hen. Interesting. He wondered how Marisol felt about having her little sister at the Salts. It was almost as if she'd been replaced, and he remembered how close the sisters were. Marisol had stepped in to be a parent to Ginny and Luis. Did she feel like she wasn't enough? Or was it easier to allow the Salts to offer a secure home when there was a baby on the way?

Ginny glanced back once. Their gazes met, and the quiet crackle of awareness lit up between them. She felt it, too; he was sure of it. He needed more time with her, but he doubted he'd get two seconds tonight. Already, the crowd pressed in, lining up to shake his hand and welcome him home. He shook off the faint panic that nipped at his nerve endings, dug deep, and re-settled himself.

Show time.

* * * *

Kristin sat with her brother, Bryce, his wife Tara, and her friend Joanne at the end of the long bar that served as the town's most popular watering hole. She'd always enjoyed coming to Murphy's. It was a nice place to get a quick drink, chat a bit, and never feel like you were doing something tawdry. A true family establishment, always spotless, and the pub food was delicious.

She smiled, watching Logan surround himself with family, obviously bantering with his brothers. They were a close-knit group, and she'd always appreciated that about the Murphys. Even though she had her brother and they had a great relationship, she'd always wished for a sister. Someone who shared the same type of emotions, hormones, and a lust for shoe shopping. As much as he tried, Bryce just never got it.

He'd never understand about Travis.

As if she'd conjured him up with her thoughts, Travis appeared through a gap in the crowd. Logan was disentangling himself from his family and was immediately stopped by Celeste. Travis held himself stiff at his wife's side, his hand holding her elbow like a true beloved husband would. Kristin's stomach immediately lurched, and her skin broke out in a fine sweat. What was she doing? She had to stop. They had to stop. He'd lost his only son and needed to be with his wife, yet Kristin still longed to be the one to comfort him at night, to hold him through his tears, to be the one with the right to stand by his side.

It would never happen.

"I have to go."

She tore her gaze away at the sound of Joanne's voice. Her friend wrung her hands around the cup of tea she held, her gaze nervously scanning the crowd as if she expected her husband Hector to come barreling at her, fists swinging. Kristin shook her head. "You just got here. Relax for a bit. You've been so stressed lately. You need some downtime."

Joanne chewed at her lower lip. "Some part of me thought Hector would show up. The whole town's here, and he rarely missed a big event."

Kristin's thoughts flashed in neon. *Especially if there was free alcohol.*

Joanne's husband had been an abusive, mean drunk who used his fists to get what he wanted. Recently, he had just disappeared in a cloud of smoke, and no one knew why he'd left or where he'd gone. Personally, Kristin thought it was the best thing to ever happen to her friend. She needed to blossom on her own without fear of violence and consistently being worried about her children.

Of course, Kristin said nothing out loud. She'd confronted her friend once before with disastrous results. They might each know the other's secrets, but neither wanted to face them. As the thought processed, Kristin glanced over once more. Then froze.

Travis weaved his way through the laughing crowds with a determined look on his face.

And he headed right toward her.

Heart hammering in her chest, she jumped up from the stool in a combination of terror and joy. "Don't leave yet. I-I'll be right there. Bathroom."

Before Joanne could respond, she bolted toward the long hallway that led to the restrooms. Keeping her head down so she wouldn't be engaged in conversation, she reached the swinging door of the ladies' room.

A hand grasped her upper arm. She stilled.

They breathed hard in the silence, both of them acknowledging what they wanted. The sounds of the party drifted down the hall. Slowly, she turned.

She had to blink away tears when she gazed at his face. The strain of tension around his kind brown eyes. The familiar curve of his lip. The sharp slash of his cheekbones, and hard jaw, and the delicious smell of his musky cologne.

His voice broke. "I can't do this anymore. I can't stop thinking about you. Wanting to be with you. I hate myself but I need you, Kristin."

She flinched. How badly she wished their love for each other could be clean and pure and good. He hated himself for his feelings, which made her feel dirty, but she couldn't fight their connection either. She lay in bed every night and yearned for him. When they were together, she felt complete for the first time in her life. He was hurting from the loss of his son, and Celeste couldn't give him what he needed.

But she could.

Without a word, she tugged him around the corner, opening the janitor's closet in the corner of the musty hallway. She stepped in, shut the door, and went into his arms.

The kiss was full of desperation, and anger, and frustration. She opened her mouth and let his tongue take what he needed while she clung to his shoulders, burying her fingers in his hair and giving herself over to the moment. He held her tight against him so each hard muscle pressed against her. Her soul soared, and Kristin knew as long as he was in her life she'd take any crumb she could. She was meant to love this man, no matter how wrong it was, and she realized in that moment she'd do anything for him.

Anything.

"I tried to stay away," he muttered, nuzzling her neck. "I want to be the husband she needs now that Jacob is gone. I need to be there for my children. But I'm existing in a fog. I'm constantly numb, and the only time I'm alive is when I'm with you."

"I know," she whispered. "It's going to be okay. I'm here when you need me. I'll always be here."

"Don't leave me. Please—"

His plea came from his heart, and she kissed him long and deep, showing him she belonged to him whenever he wanted her. "I won't."

She didn't know what was going to happen. Her gut warned her disaster loomed in the future, but for now, she was with Travis, and nothing else mattered. "Come to me after the party."

"Yes. Celeste takes sleeping pills now. I'll come to you tonight."

They broke apart slowly. He let her go out first, and she checked to make sure the hallway was clear before rejoining the party. When she got back to the bar, she noticed Joanne had fled, and Tara was talking in the corner with Marisol Moreno. Kristin's brother was staring at her with a questioning look. She slid onto the stool. "Why did you let Joanne go?"

"Dakota came in so she went to go see her. Where were you?"

"I told you. Bathroom."

"You have lipstick smeared all over your lips."

She turned red, reached into her purse for a tissue, and scrubbed at her mouth. "Bad lighting. Guess my touch-up failed," she joked.

"What's going on, Kristin? I've been worried about you lately. You seem...distracted."

Oh, God, she hated lying to her brother, who was a pastor to boot. But she wouldn't allow him to get trapped by her deceit. It was her choice, and she'd protect her secret to the grave. She forced a smile. "Work's been extra busy lately, and I'm still rattled by Jacob's death. I think about it all the time."

Her brother's face softened in understanding. "Yes, I think we've all been affected. I've been trying to meet with some people. I'm going to see Celeste and Travis this week and see if they'd agree to grief counseling. Ginny, too."

She kept the smile pasted on her face and tried not to react. "I think that's a good idea."

He kept staring at her thoughtfully. "Marriage becomes even more difficult after the loss of a child. They both need time to heal and grow back into their relationship."

Nausea hit her. "Yes, I'd imagine it must be difficult for them now."

"Hmmm." His one word spoke volumes but she didn't say anything else. He might suspect something, but she refused to vocalize the truth. "You know I'm here if you ever want to talk, right?" he asked.

She reached over and squeezed her brother's hand. "Yes. Thanks, Bryce. I appreciate it."

Kristin took another sip of her wine and said a quick prayer for forgiveness. Bryce always preached that anything could be forgiven, as long as one was truly sorry and intended to never repeat the sin.

Kristin was sorry for the lies. But not for her other sins.

Because she didn't intend to give up Travis Salt.

Chapter Two

Dakota Alvarez walked into Murphy's Pub and was immediately overwhelmed.

The whole town was here, laughing and partying, and welcoming home Logan Murphy. She'd always liked Logan, and had once thought he'd be a good boyfriend for her. After all, he wanted out of Storm as badly as she did, but besides quickly joining the military, he'd never really seemed interested and now it looked like he was sweet on Ginny.

Resentment built inside. Jacob. Then Logan. Seemed the bitch stole everything good and possible in her life. But none of that mattered anymore. She was the one who would come out on top because she'd finally found someone who understood her. A real man. One with power and status and a touch that could pleasure her more than she'd ever been before.

Senator Sebastian Rush.

It was the only reason she was here tonight. She'd heard he was attending, and Dakota thought it would be a good opportunity to see him since everyone was here and no one would get suspicious. Since their first encounter, she'd been careful, just like he needed her to be. Yes, she lost her shit when she'd discovered Mallory ratted her out by telling Jeffry about her first encounter with the senator. She'd been so dismissive of his advances, believing she was way too hot and young for him. Dakota had confessed the whole thing to Mallory, laughing at the pathetic old man who came on to her and her blistering rebuff.

If only she'd kept her mouth shut. But maybe this was a good thing. It was publicly on record she'd rejected him and was worried about her reputation. No one would ever think they'd now be involved in an affair. As angry as she was at Mallory for betraying her, things might be better this way. She wasn't a silly, stupid girl who didn't know how to play the game. There were rules for powerful men in politics, and she needed him to trust her completely before he'd do what she needed.

Take her away from here. Protect her. Care for her.

Like her father had.

The thought of her precious father drove a painful ache in her heart. God, she missed him so much. He'd been the only one to understand her. She headed toward the buffet to get some food and passed her sister, Mallory. Dakota glanced over, but her sister never even acknowledged her. Fine. She was still upset because she couldn't handle the truth. It wasn't Dakota's fault Mallory had chosen a big fat cheater for her boyfriend. She'd been doing her sister a favor by telling her about Luis screwing Lacey Salt. Dakota had tried to save her from further humiliation. But of course, once again, she'd become the bad guy, and the whole situation was twisted around to blame her for speaking the truth.

Dakota was so much better than her. More grown up and mature. She'd be the one out of here, probably famous and rich, and she'd never come back to her sister or her lame mother again.

Dakota filled her plate and got a soda, sharing a few words with some of the townsfolk, who looked at her with a twinge of pity. Since her father disappeared without warning, she was somewhat of a tragic figure now. She hated them all for pitying her, but most of all, she hated her mother for being so weak. Joanne had been the one to drive her father away, with her whining and incompetent ways. She could never get dinner on the table on time, or do the chores needed to take care of the family. Her father had to work so hard and rarely got back anything. And her mom was so clumsy! Always falling down stairs or burning her hand on an iron. Her father always told her in secret he'd pitied her mother, but had fallen in love and decided to help her be better. He'd tried so hard, but Joanne just refused to listen. Dakota pitied her, but couldn't help the faint tinge of distaste for her failures. Her dad deserved someone better and had been driven away by her mom's constant complaining.

Dakota scanned the room, looking for Sebastian, and frowned when she saw her mom.

She sat at the bar with Pastor Douglas. She held a drink in her hands and was chatting away like nothing was wrong. Anger and frustration simmered. Why wasn't her mom more upset? Why wasn't she looking as hard for her dad as Dakota was?

As if she sensed her gaze, her mom finally spotted her and jerked. Saying a few words to the pastor, she set down her drink and began making her way over. Dakota gritted her teeth, ready to tell her mother exactly what she thought of her.

"Dakota, honey, what are you doing here? And why are you dressed like that?"

Hurt lanced through her. Oh, Mallory got to do anything she wanted because she was the perfect child. Why was she always treated so badly? "There's nothing wrong with my outfit! And why wouldn't I be here?" she challenged. "Mallory's here. So is the whole town. The question is why are you here, Mom? Dad's only been gone two weeks, and already you're out here partying, happy he's gone. Why are you betraying him like this?"

Her voice was getting higher, and her mother got that suffering look on her face that Dakota despised. Like she was reaching for patience and channeling some type of martyr. Her soft voice grated on Dakota's nerves. "I texted you twice to ask if you'd come with us, and you never responded. As for Dad, that's the reason I came tonight. I was hoping maybe he'd show up."

Tears stung her eyes. Her deepest, most horrible fear was her father would never come back. That he didn't love her as much as she believed, which would mean her whole life was a big fat lie. She channeled her hurt into anger. It felt so much better to be mad than sad. "You made him go away! I'm the one who's been looking everywhere, trying to track down where he is. Why don't you hire a private investigator or something? Why do you have to be so useless all the time?"

"I know you're upset, Dakota. I'm doing everything I can, but I can't afford a PI right now. I'm trying to save our house and pay the bills on one salary now."

"You wanted him gone! You wished this would happen and you're not sorry!"

"Dakota—"

"Leave me alone," she hissed. Since her mother had started a new job for Marylee Rush in addition to working at the florist, she'd actually started looking more attractive. Healthy. She didn't seem to have any more accidents. Her skin glowed. And now Dakota was falling apart because the only man in her life who gave a crap left her. "I can't stand your lies anymore!"

"Dakota, cut it out." A cold voice snapped to her left. Mallory glared at her, laying a protective arm on their mother's arm. "Mom did nothing wrong. Maybe it's time you grew up and realized the truth. We're all better off without Dad." She paused, and the next words hit her like a slap in the face. "You're just like him. You enjoy hurting people. Don't you?"

Dakota gasped. She saw the truth in her sister's eyes. The confusion in her mother's. She saw the united front of her family, of which she was now a permanent outsider. Something broke inside her and oozed out in a mess of emotion.

"You're just pissed I told you your stupid boyfriend is a loser!" she hissed.

"It was the way you told me, Dakota. I'm not going to let you hurt me anymore. I'm done."

"Girls—what is this about?" her mother asked, glancing back and forth between them.

In that moment, she felt her sister slipping away, leaving a cold stranger behind. Another person who didn't care if she lived or died. Emotion choked her throat, and silly tears threatened her vision. She wouldn't let them see her cry.

A hush fell around them, and she felt the crowd's eyes on her. Judging. Pitying.

"I hate you both!" she shrieked. "Stay away from me—both of you!"

Her mother called her name but she stumbled across the room in her red stilettos, out into the humid summer air that wrapped around her in a big bear hug and squeezed tight. She raced around to the side of the building, pressing her back against the stone wall so no one could find her. Choking back sobs, she looked at the night sky streaked with stars and wished her dad was here. He'd hug her, call her princess, and make everything all right.

She was so afraid nothing would be all right ever again.

Dakota stayed there a few minutes, making sure she wasn't followed, when she heard voices. Knowing she recognized the husky, sexy tone, she peeked around the building and saw the senator with his wife, Payton, and his mother, Marylee, stepping out of his Mercedes as their driver held the door open.

"I told you we'd be late, Sebastian. We should have been the first ones here to welcome Logan home. This doesn't look good."

Sebastian sighed and faced his mother. "I'll make a proper speech. Politicians are always late to these events. It won't be a problem."

"It better not be."

Suddenly, the senator's gaze fell upon her face. He lifted a brow in surprise, and Dakota ducked back behind the building. "Mother, Payton, I'll meet you in there. I have to make a very quick call and I'll join you shortly."

"Make sure it's quick," his mother admonished. The two women were ushered into Murphy's and the Mercedes pulled away, leaving them alone. She heard heels crunch on gravel and then he was beside her.

"Now, this is a nice surprise," he growled. His gaze raked over her figure and she shifted on her high heels, suddenly feeling sexy and confident. She'd dressed with him in mind, with a body-hugging red Lycra dress, stopping mid-thigh and dipping low in the front for a nice peek at her cleavage. She'd put on bold red lipstick and curled her hair so it was loose and wild. Dakota shivered at the male lust that lit his eyes, and excitement curled in her belly. When she was near him, thoughts of her broken family faded away, leaving only the demands of her body and the promise of a bright future.

Even though he was married.

"I wanted to show you my new dress," she said with a flirty smile. She tossed her hair and let him look at her. "Do you like it?"

"I'd like it better off."

Her smile widened. She leaned in and whispered in his ear. "Then why don't you do something about it?"

He wrapped his hands around her waist and dragged her close. Nibbled on her ear, bit her neck, and then she was moaning until he kissed her, making her want him right there. He was so much older than her, but with his hard body, customized suits, and addictive scent, she'd begun to fall hard. Dakota adored the way he treated her like a real woman, in bed and out. He finally broke the kiss, and they were both breathing hard.

"I intend to," he growled. "Later. I'll come to you."

The first time, it had been at his cabin at the lake. Since then, they gone there or he had come to her apartment. Dakota liked the way he filled the small, cramped space with his presence. He'd bring over gourmet takeout dinners and fancy bottles of wine, and eat with her before he took her to bed. Then he adored her body and took her to crazy places where he wrung out endless orgasms, leaving her in a satisfied, naked heap.

"Are you coming in?" he asked.

She shook her head. "No. My mom's in there and she gave me hell. I can't believe the way she's acting with my dad gone. I knew she never loved him. I hate her."

He tipped up her chin, looking sympathetic. "It'll be okay, baby. I have something for you that may cheer you up."

Dakota brightened. "What is it?"

He laughed, his hand running down her body. "You keep being a good girl and I'll give it to you later. Are you a good girl?"

Heat sizzled through her. She lowered her eyes. "I thought you wanted me to be bad?"

He squeezed her breast. "As long as you're in private with me, you can be a very bad girl. When we're out in public, you're a good girl. Right?"

She pouted. "I'm not stupid," she said. The memory of Jeffry Rush calling her a slut at her own home shuddered through her. "The only problem we may have is your son," she said. "He found out about us. He said nasty things about me."

Sebastian grunted in dismissal. "Sorry, baby. Jeffry came to me and asked if I had ever come on to you, and of course, I had to deny it. I had no idea he'd come to your house and confronted you. You understand, right? I had to say those things to throw him off track. But I'm not worried about Jeffry. We're covered now, and he won't be bothering you anymore."

She nibbled at her lip. "I don't know. Maybe you shouldn't come over tonight."

Dakota held her breath, waiting for his reaction. Would he get mad at her? Walk away? Or let her sass him?

He watched her for a while, then slowly reached inside his suit jacket. Pulling out a small velvet box, he handed it over to her. "Maybe this will show you how important you are to me."

Her fingers trembled as she took the box. Snapped the lid open. And gazed at the most gorgeous diamond earrings she'd ever seen.

"Oh! Oh, Sebastian, they're beautiful!"

He grinned, looking pleased by her reaction. "Good, I'm glad you like them. I told you, baby, you keep being a good girl and the sky's the limit."

She looked up, overcome with the rush of power this man held. Diamond earrings? The closest she'd ever gotten to nice jewelry was a gold bracelet her father had given her years ago for her birthday. Her mother had frowned, upset he hadn't used the money on her stupid bills she always bitched about. But her father knew his daughter was worth it.

Just like Senator Rush.

Dakota threw her arms around his neck. "I promise to show you how much I love them later," she said in his ear.

He kissed her once more, then stepped back. He pulled a neat white handkerchief from his pocket and wiped his mouth of any trace of lipstick. "I'll look forward to it. Now, let me do my duty and I'll see you later."

He walked away, leaving her alone. But the moon was full over her, the stars sparkled, and her diamond earrings outshone them both.

Dakota knew it would all work out. Sebastian was crazy about her. He just needed enough time to realize she was the one he was meant to be with and not his boring wife, Payton.

Chapter Three

Senator Sebastian Rush couldn't wait to get the hell out of this party and into Dakota's bed.

He tamped down his impatience and concentrated on his job. God, some of these small town parties were just painful. The same boring people, the same conversations over and over again. He was meant for bigger and better things, but for now, his job was to make the town happy and remind them why he was the only one worth voting for.

Sebastian smiled and made small talk while he thought of Dakota naked. Of her lean, long legs wrapped around his pumping hips. Of that delicious, firm, young flesh that women lose as they age. Pity. Thank goodness Payton was classically beautiful to still look at, held impeccable manners, and never wanted to be touched.

They made the perfect team.

His wife stuck by his side as they worked the room. His mother, Marylee, held court on the opposite side. She enjoyed approaching a political opportunity like a general. Flank the crowd and work their way in, so no one was missed and everyone felt important. It was a brilliant approach that always worked.

He spent some time with the hometown hero, making sure to take a bunch of pictures that would be leaked to the media by an unknown source. Being hooked up with anyone in the military was a win/win and he bet Logan Murphy could be a big help with this next run. He'd mention it to his mother so she could come up with a good advertising campaign, using Logan to his advantage.

When Payton guided him over to her sister, he kept a big grin on his face and refused to flinch. Ginny Moreno was at Celeste's side, her hand resting on her stomach in an almost unconscious declaration as he made his way closer. His skin prickled with fear, but she averted her gaze like they had never slept together.

Good. Exactly how he needed it to be.

"Celeste, how are you holding up?" Payton gave her an airy kiss a few inches from her cheek. Though the sisters were close, Payton never showed affection in public, even with family. Sebastian had always found Celeste as dull as dishwater, and he suspected Travis was banging someone else, but it wasn't his business.

Celeste took in a ragged breath. "Some days are good, and some I can barely get out of bed." She tried to force a smile and glanced down at Ginny. "But we're all concentrating on the baby and keeping ourselves busy. Right, Ginny?"

Ginny nodded, completely ignoring him. Better that way. Every time he slept with Dakota he made sure she took her birth control pill. He was now a bit obsessed about it. But who would've thought the little bitch would get knocked up?

Sebastian stiffened. He needed to make sure that their affair never got out. Best to consistently drive the point home that Ginny was carrying Jacob's baby, and keep the focus on the tragic love story that ended in a cycle of death and rebirth. He'd seen something like that on TV and thought it was a great analogy he intended to use in one of his future speeches.

Payton focused on Ginny. "We're planning a memorial in the park for Jacob. Something to keep his memory alive. We were thinking of a bench, but I hope you'll be a part of the decision."

Celeste nodded. "Yes, Ginny is family now. She's a part of everything we do."

"Of course. Why, Brittany thinks of you as a sister," Payton said. "You know we're both here for you, Ginny. No matter what you need."

Ginny shifted her feet, looking a little sick. Sebastian knew he had to wrap it up and get the hell out of here. Spending too much time with Ginny was too dangerous. He spoke up. "I see my mother making her way over. Will you excuse me a moment?"

"Of course," Celeste said.

Payton nodded her approval and he took off. For God's sake, why did his past have to always catch up with him? Why did he have to sleep with her? Sure, she was hot, and young, and forbidden fruit, but Dakota was way more exciting in bed. He glanced at his watch and wondered how quickly he could leave and get to her place.

When Jeffry had confronted him, he'd had to rely on his sense of self-preservation to act shocked and affronted. In those two seconds, looking into his son's face, he knew lying was his only recourse. So, he'd gone on the attack, calling Dakota a slut, and swearing on his family he would never, ever be attracted to someone of such a low level.

Jeffry had bought it.

Now, he just needed to keep up appearances and make sure he stayed away from Dakota in public.

His mother appeared beside him and motioned him to lean over. Her face was arranged in a pleasant smile, but her voice was cold and demanding. "Sebastian, you need to do a speech. You do have one prepared, right?"

Kind of. He'd scribbled some notes but had gotten distracted doing other things. Not that his mother needed to know. "Of course."

"Good. I'm already coming up with a plan to include Logan and his military background. Before everyone gets too drunk and sloppy, I think this is a good time."

He didn't argue. He'd learned early in his youth arguing with his mother was pointless, and life was much more pleasant if he agreed earlier on rather than later. Marylee knew how to keep her children in line and get what she wanted. She could hold a grudge longer than anyone in Storm, and put her focus on ruining anyone who displeased her or got in her way. She also thought her children walked on water and were the brightest stars in the galaxy. Sebastian was proud to be her son.

Straightening his suit and tie, he squared his shoulders and walked up to the small podium Murphy's held for the occasional Irish karaoke. As he stood up there, looking over the crowd, he cleared his mind, thought over his brief notes, and slipped into professional politician mode.

"Excuse me, ladies and gentlemen."

The room quieted. He smiled, overlooking the many townspeople of Storm, Texas, and knew great things were ahead. As he launched into his speech, which would be quoted and referred to as "heartfelt" and "moving" in the *Austin American-Statesman, San Antonio Express-News*, and *The Storm Team Weekly News*, he thought about Dakota waiting for him, naked.

Chapter Four

"Ginny, let's go out. How about the Bluebonnet for lunch?"

Ginny looked at her best friend, Brittany. She sat cross-legged on the bed, frowning with concern. Ginny couldn't blame her. She wasn't fun anymore. She was young, unmarried, and pregnant, living in a house with Jacob's family, stuck in a lie. A lie that could never be told.

She'd been numb for so long, Ginny wondered if maybe she'd just go through the rest of her life like a shadow of her former self. But when she saw Logan again at Murphy's, the deadness inside her faded and heat flamed back. Suddenly, she ached to be near him, feel him touch her, bask in the warmth of his smile.

At the same time, guilt sank into her bones and tortured her. It wasn't right to feel this way about Logan, especially in such a short time. She loved Jacob. She'd loved Jacob for years, and knew him as well as herself. Jacob ate Lucky Charms cereal from the box and picked out all the marshmallows. He was tone deaf, but a great dancer, and his hair used to flop in his face in that sexy manner that made her fingers itch to brush it back. He was always late but he was so charming everyone forgave him. Jacob loved helping people, was a great friend, and a tender lover, even if it was just for that one drunken night.

How could she be suddenly fixated on Logan Murphy?

She'd been so young when he left. Ginny remembered he was easy going, and liked to tease her about the trouble she got into. He used to tug at her hair and shake his head with laughter, and his gaze was always open and warm.

But Logan had changed. He seemed harder, more haunted. She

wasn't surprised. Ginny doubted anyone came back from war the same person. There was a new directness when he looked at her now. Almost as if he'd made up his mind about something and nothing would stop him.

A shiver raced through her. Of course, she had no right to think about Logan in that way. She was pregnant with Jacob's baby, living with the Salts. She allowed herself to be smothered and pampered by Celeste, and felt her own sister slipping away. When was the last time she'd spoken to Marisol? Too long. It was uncomfortable for her sister to come here to visit, and Ginny didn't like to go out much anymore. Too much gossip and staring. As much as the majority of the town seemed to support her, especially since the Salts were behind her, there were still plenty who thought she was the worst kind of woman ever.

A slut.

And the person who had killed Jacob.

"Why don't we just stay here for lunch?" she suggested. "Celeste said she'd do grilled chicken and salad. She just brewed some sun tea—decaf."

Brittany sighed. "Sweetie, other than the party at Murphy's, all you do is sit in this room all day. It's not healthy. You need social interaction. We can have lunch, then go visit Marisol and Luis."

Ginny nibbled on her bottom lip, torn. It would be nice to go out and see her family. She was conscious of her growing belly, but she could wear her extra baggy T-shirt and the white shorts that had been too big for her last summer. Now, they were just the right fit.

"I don't know, Brit."

Her friend leaned over and gave her a hug. "I know you're sad, but I won't let you stay in this room for the rest of the pregnancy. It will be good for both of us. Please?"

The idea of venturing out scared her, but she was getting tired of the same four walls. Tired of the same thoughts spinning over and over in her brain. Brittany must have sensed her waffling, because she jumped up from the bed. "Yes! We're going out! We'll put the radio real loud and sing country songs and eat pie!"

Ginny laughed. Guilt flared for lying to her best friend, but she squashed it. She couldn't think about the truth. Senator Rush didn't even look at her when he stopped by the party, and she couldn't bear to see a look of disgust or accusation from him. No, she'd keep out of his way and concentrate on doing everything to make sure this baby knew from the beginning Jacob was the father.

Anyway, the baby *could* be Jacob's. It was possible.

"Come on, let's go!"

Ginny followed Brittany out the door, peeking her head in the kitchen. Celeste was staring blankly at the wall, a spoon in her hand. "Umm, Celeste?"

She spun around and pasted a smile on her face. "Hi, girls. I'm whipping up a nice healthy lunch. We can eat outside on the deck today."

"I'm sorry, but Brittany and I are going out. Is that okay?"

Brittany shot her a weird look, but Ginny had learned Celeste needed to know where she was or she panicked. "Are you sure? I bet I can do better than Rita Mae."

Brittany cleared her throat. "Aunt Celeste, I think Ginny and I need to get out a bit. Take a drive. Maybe stop by and see Luis."

"You're going to see Luis?"

The high-pitched voice made Ginny turn. Lacey stood framed in the doorway. Dressed in tiny denim shorts and a low-cut halter top, her usual sweet expression was replaced by anger. Ginny couldn't figure it out. Lacey used to be so sweet, but over the past few weeks, she'd changed. She was sharp, sarcastic, and downright mean. Ginny and Brittany tried reaching out to her several times, but Lacey pushed them away. Even now, she didn't understand the venom in her gaze when she stared at Ginny. "Yes, I haven't seen my family in a while. Want to come with us?" She'd seen Luis and Lacey together a few times, and though she thought he was dating Mallory, Ginny wondered if Luis and Lacey had hooked up instead. The sound of her brother's name seemed to jolt Lacey. Almost as if she was jealous.

Lacey practically sneered. "I already saw him at the club. Maybe you should check with me instead of Mallory if you want to know his schedule. We've been...hanging out." The smirk on her face spoke volumes, and Lacey's words brimmed with an undercurrent of meaning. Were they sleeping together now? Ginny's head spun. She absolutely had to talk with her brother. She'd been drowning in her own troubles for so long, it was time to reach out to her family. Even when she'd been away at college, she enjoyed talking to Luis and getting updates on what he was up to. She felt completely disconnected since Jacob's death.

Celeste didn't seem to acknowledge Lacey's strange behavior. "I'm making lunch, Lacey. Want to join me?"

"You were making lunch for Ginny, not me. No, thanks."

With a final glare, Lacey stomped upstairs. Celeste shook her head. "She's still upset over Jacob," Celeste explained. "But she's a good girl. Very dependable. We just need to be patient with her."

Ginny didn't know if that was the greatest form of therapy with grief, but she stayed out of it. "Yes, I know she's going through a hard time."

"Will you text me when you're heading home? Just so I know you're okay."

Ginny quickly agreed, and Brittany dragged her outside. She slid into Brittany's car and tilted her head up to the sun. The burning heat baked her skin, but she ached to thaw some of the numbness inside her. The car hit the paved road with a screech of tires, and then they were off, driving fast, with the radio blaring Blake Shelton, and for a little bit of time, she thought maybe things would be okay.

"I see Lacey is still giving you attitude. Something's up with her," Brittany said. "More than just with you, I mean. She's been so moody lately. I've tried talking to her but she refuses to tell me anything."

"Jacob and Lacey were close. So I can understand why she's angry with me. She's just trying to cope like we all are."

"Well, I love her because she's my cousin, but her attitude has been off the charts. Plus, I've heard some wicked stories about her and Luis. We definitely need to get the dirt."

Ginny sighed. Guilt nipped at her. "I know. It's just been easier to stay in my room. All I want is to have a healthy baby."

Her friend glanced at her with a soft expression. "You will. Aunt Celeste has Francine check on you regularly, and you're doing everything right. But hiding isn't going to change anything, sweets. Jacob wouldn't want this for either of us. We'll get through it together."

Ginny's throat tightened. Brittany always stuck by her, no matter what, and her friendship meant everything. "Girls over bros, right?" she quipped. It had been their motto over the years and through their dating experiences.

Brittany giggled. "Yes! Except when they're very handsome, heroic bros. Like Logan Murphy."

Ginny's heart tripped at the sound of his name. "It's nice to have Logan home safe."

"Nice, huh?" Brittany shot her a look. "I saw the way he looked at you. It was kind of hot. Like he wanted to gobble you up and protect you at the same time. You used to have a crush on him, remember?"

Yes. Instead, she'd hooked up with Jacob and the very married senator. Ginny wished she could go back and do it all over again. She would've never slept with Sebastian Rush and Jacob would still be alive.

And she wouldn't be pregnant.

Her hand rested again on the slight curve to her belly. "Like you had a crush on Marcus?"

Brittany waved her manicured hand in the air. "Yes, but Marcus isn't here now." Her friend paused, seemingly lost in her thoughts. "Would you go out with Logan if he asked you?"

Ginny shook her head. "No! I just lost Jacob, and I'm pregnant with his baby. I can't even think of being with someone else. Anyway, I'm sure Logan wants nothing to do with me. He's being nice, that's all."

"I don't think so. What do you feel about him? And no lying. I'm your best friend. Lying is a crime."

She opened her mouth to deny her feelings, but instead told the truth. She owed Brittany that much. "I—I like him. When I'm around him, he makes me feel safe, yet there's this connection between us, too. I don't know. It doesn't matter."

Brittany sighed. "It might. Listen, I know you loved Jacob. But you're young, and you still deserve happiness. Logan seems like a good guy, and he knows your situation."

"I can't betray Jacob. Or the Salts. It would be wrong."

"Aww, Ginny, you'll always love Jacob, and you'll have his baby. But he's gone, sweetie. Life goes on, and you shouldn't be miserable for the rest of your days. I'm asking you to be open to the opportunity to spend more time with Logan if that's what you both want. That's all."

Ginny pondered her friend's words as they pulled into the Bluebonnet Cafe. The lot was jammed with cars since it was the prime lunchtime. Her tummy flip-flopped with nervousness, but she followed Brittany into the cafe, trying to look like she belonged. They waited at the front for a table, and her gaze scanned the room. She hoped they snagged the back booth so she could relax and hide from any probing eyes.

Rita Mae caught sight of them and gave them a cheerful smile. "Well, hello ladies, isn't this a surprise! Anyone joining you?"

Brittany grinned. "Just us. And make sure you don't run out of the coconut cream pie. It's Ginny's fave."

Ginny smiled back and relaxed when she caught no judgment in the owner's eyes. "Not a problem. I just whipped up a few fresh ones. Hmm, a little busy, wanna sit at the stools?"

Ginny opened her mouth to say no, but her friend already agreed. Rita Mae handed them two menus and guided them over to the high countertop that held plenty of comfortable space. Swallowing hard, she slid onto the red stool and began to study the menu. Brittany was chattering nonstop, and she kept one ear on the conversation and the other on the patrons. She was beginning to relax and getting excited over a meal out. She'd been nauseous on and off for a while, and it seemed her stomach was just beginning to settle. Then she heard it.

Whispers. "I can't believe she's flaunting herself in public."

Another voice. "Used to be God-fearing church people around here. Now it seems we encourage free sex and illegitimate babies in this town."

"Those poor Salts. Taking her in and trying to give her a home."

"Well, I'm not surprised. The whole Moreno family has been trouble. The sister just couldn't keep them in line."

Ginny clutched the menu. Frozen, afraid to look up, shame filled her. This was what she'd wanted to avoid. Her neck tingled from the heat of the stares until even Brittany realized they were being sought out. She stopped chattering and craned her neck around.

Ginny dared to look up.

Four older women gathered in the small booth, sipping tea and staring at them. The coldness in their eyes was withering in their judgment. Brittany turned back and gripped Ginny's hand. "Don't you dare let them chase us out of here," she said. "Ignore them."

Ginny tried, but the words were already spilling through her brain. She craved her safe room again, where no one could get to her. "I have to go," she whispered frantically. She stood up, swaying slightly on her feet, and realized she was about to topple over. Horror washed over her. Her foot twisted, her balance tilted, and she braced herself for an embarrassing, humiliating fall in front of her accusers.

Hard arms caught her halfway down. The musky scent of man hit her nostrils, and suddenly she looked up into a pair of gentle blue eyes.

She gripped his broad shoulders, and something deep inside shifted and sighed in pure pleasure.

"You okay?"

She managed a nod. Slowly Logan righted her, keeping a supportive hold under her elbow. The sudden intake of breath from the booth of onlookers made her cheeks turn red. Oh, God, she had to get out of here.

"I was just leaving."

His face hardened as he focused on the group of ladies, now clucking their tongues. "I hope not. I haven't had Rita Mae's pie in years, and I shouldn't indulge alone. I was lucky to score a booth. Come join me."

The whispers grew louder. "Absolutely distasteful."

"Well, I never!"

"If only the Salts knew about her behavior."

Brittany slid off the stool. "Hi, Logan. Seems you're just in time. Will you join us for lunch?"

Ginny sent her a pleading look, but Brittany ignored her.

"A great plan. Follow me." He gently guided them past the booth and stopped right in front of the gossiping women. "Good morning, ladies." The silver-haired, perfectly coiffed and perfumed group stared. Logan was quite handsome, and as the returning hometown hero, a local celebrity in Storm. They offered him polite greetings, their stares resting on Ginny while she turned twenty shades of purple and wished she could disappear. Logan spoke in a pleasant tone. "It's nice to know you can count on townsfolk for support, isn't it? Why, I remember my father telling me some stories that would turn your hair white. Boys sneaking into rooms. Drinking underage. Real sinful stuff."

The ladies stared.

"Good thing we don't judge in Storm. Would be awful if my dad decided to spill some classic gossip and secrets. But there'd be no reason for that. Right?"

One of the women cleared her throat. "Right."

Logan nodded. "Exactly what I thought. We're all good Christians here. Well, good day, ladies. Have a nice lunch."

Ginny tried not to gape as he calmly took her hand and walked to his booth. She dropped in the seat, shaking, while Brittany howled with laughter.

"Oh, goodness, that was the best! Did you see their faces? You learned some hard-core fighting tactics, Logan!"

He smiled, but it was strained. Ginny wondered what had happened in Afghanistan. Was he haunted by memories? She woke up almost every night, sweating, a scream trapped in her throat as she relived the accident and waking up without Jacob.

"In Storm, the best fights are with words. They're just bored out of their minds and looking for some mean fun. Don't pay attention to them, Ginny."

He really was a hero.

Ginny wondered guiltily what it would be like if he was *her* hero.

They ordered their food and chatted about light topics, catching Logan up on some of the news in town. Ginny engaged in the conversation and tried not to stare. Today, he wore jeans, a simple black T-shirt, and some kind of braided bracelet on his wrist. Ginny also noticed he radiated a deadly quiet as he ate and listened, almost as if he was consistently aware of every person who entered and exited the diner. He was so sexy, and seemed so much older than his twenty-four years.

"Where you girls headed next?" he asked. He reached over for the ketchup and his fingers brushed hers. Her skin tingled.

"Visiting Luis. Wanna come?" Brittany asked.

"Have to head back to Murphy's. Told my dad I'd help him out with a few shifts so he could take some time off." His gaze swung to hers. Blue eyes pierced right through to her soul. "Wanted to know if you'd have dinner with me tonight, Ginny."

She blinked. Rubbed her belly self-consciously. "Oh. Umm, I can't."

"I'll be right back, guys. Restroom," Brittany announced. Sending Ginny a warning glance from across the table, she disappeared in a flurry, leaving Ginny and Logan alone in the booth. On the same side. Next to each other.

"You don't want to go to dinner with me?"

Ginny fiddled with her napkin. She did. Right now, she couldn't think of another thing she'd rather do, but there was no way she could open the door to a relationship. Did he feel sorry for her? She tilted her jaw and met his gaze. "Why? Feel sorry for the poor, lonely pregnant girl?"

He reached out and pushed the hair out of her face. Gentle, but commanding. She fought a shiver. "No. Because I like your company."

"Logan." Her voice broke. "What do you want?"

"To spend some time with you. Is that so bad?"

"Yes. People will talk."

A smile touched his lips. "People always talk in Storm. They like gossip. It always dies down because there's always a new story to take its place."

"Jacob's death isn't just some local gossip. Neither is a baby."

He took her hand, entwined his fingers with hers, and squeezed. "I'm sorry. I didn't mean to make light of losing Jacob. I think about him all the time. The loss of life. How you almost died with him. I can't even imagine what you're going through, Ginny. Thing is, I want to be there and help you get through it."

She sucked in her breath at the raw honesty and need carved in the lines of his face. Her secret dream had always been for a man to take care of her. A man who was gentle and exciting, and who cared about her feelings. Sebastian had been a thrilling distraction. Having a secret, illicit affair with an older man called to her sense of adventure and wild soul. But she'd quickly grown tired of feeling like a dirty little secret. Ginny had always truly known the man she wanted was Jacob. Her feelings for Jacob had been real, built on friendship and a slow, steady burn toward love. They'd never had a chance to see what would happen between them, and she'd regret that for the rest of her life.

But this connection to Logan felt so...different. Was it because she'd changed? Or was she so lonely in her grief for Jacob, she was transferring emotions to Logan that really weren't there?

Confusion swamped her. Logan remained steady beside her, his gaze never faltering as he waited for her to speak. Those blue eyes gleamed with understanding, as if he knew all her hidden thoughts. In that moment, her churning insides calmed, and her body hummed pleasantly as the energy between them surged. No, these feelings must be real. Oh, God, what was happening to her?

Guilt exploded. She was living a lie. How could she drag Logan into her world when he thought the baby was Jacob's? She squeezed her eyes shut and fought her feelings. She had to protect him. From herself.

"I can't," she said again. "I have to go see my brother."

He didn't fight her. Logan released her hand, stepped out of the booth and allowed her retreat. When she tried to reach for money to pay for the lunch, he cut her a stern glare. "My treat."

"Thank you."

"Welcome. I'll see you later, Ginny."

The words held a promise she didn't have the strength to decipher now, so she just nodded, motioned to Brittany, who was coming back from the bathroom, and hurried out.

Chapter Five

Hannah Grossman turned onto the long dirt road that led to the Double J. Ranch. The familiar sprawling house over acres of ranchland always made her catch her breath. There was something so rustic and uncivilized about the spill of land, sky, and animals roaming within the fence limits. The sun dappled over the trees as she pulled up to the oversized white wraparound porch.

She climbed out, flipping her braid over her shoulder in a habitual gesture, and blinked up at the male figure coming over to greet her. He was dressed in his usual suit and tie, his black dress shoes kicking up gravel as he walked over.

"Morning, darlin'."

Tate Johnson leaned down and pressed a kiss to her lips. His gray eyes sparkled with his usual good-natured humor, and she smiled back at him. "Morning. How come you're not at the office?"

Tate's family owned the ranch, which had been passed down through generations. As the oldest, he'd been the one slated to take over, but Tate had always been the bookish one in the family. Instead of cattle and pasture, he craved books and legal jargon like food and water. He used to tell Hannah stories of how he felt as if he was an outsider, since his entire family's genes ran with the blood of ranching in their veins. Except him.

His brother Tucker backed him up, and together they convinced their father to let Tate pursue his own dreams. He left the ranch to go to law school, and came back to set up a practice in Storm. He helped by handling the Double J's legal matters, and Tucker never made him feel out of place. The brothers had always had a strong bond, though they were very different. But Hannah knew sometimes, deep inside, Tate still felt displaced around the ranch.

"Have to be in court late today. Figured I'd stay and steal a kiss."

"Steal two."

He grinned and did exactly that. His embrace was comforting and secure, just like the man himself. They'd been dating almost a year now and had settled into a routine. He was dependable, kind, and steadfast. He was the type of man she'd always dreamed of marrying, and things were easy between them. There were never any surprises with Tate, and she liked it that way.

"How's Bella?"

Tate jerked his head toward the stable. "Holding her own. Tucker's worried, though. This foal is important to him, so he spent the night in the barn."

Hannah shook her head. "He should've called me earlier."

"My brother is stubborn. He likes doing things his own way."

Hannah let out a breath and grabbed her black vet bag out of the back seat. "He's still not a vet. I'll go take a look."

"Good luck. I'll call you later to check in."

"Have fun in court."

He kissed her one last time and headed toward his luxury black sedan, which looked completely out of sorts on the ranch. Hannah waved and waited until he disappeared down the road.

Then she stared at the barn.

Her heart was beating way too fast, which both confused and pissed her off. Ridiculous. She was here in the capacity of a vet. She was Tate's girlfriend, maybe future wife. There was no reason to get nervous around Tucker Johnson.

Squaring her shoulders, she marched through the doors.

The scent of hay and manure hit her nostrils. The beautiful black horse lay on her side, breathing labored, as she tried to gather strength to push her foal into the world. The peace of the stable wrapped around her, and she quieted on the inside, the way she always did around animals and their environments.

"I told you not to check in until sometime this afternoon."

Her head turned in the direction of his voice. He was lying on the floor of the stall, hidden in the shadows. Long, jean-clad legs stretched in front of him. His Stetson was cocked low on his head as if he'd just been caught lazing around on his work time. Strands of dark hair stuck out and lay haphazardly on his forehead. Her gaze met and locked with steady hazel eyes that pulled her in and refused to let go.

A shiver raced down her spine. The blast of heat between them struck her breathless, but she'd prepared for it this time. Hannah managed to keep the emotions off her face, even though she was worried. It was growing stronger. Each time they were in each other's presence, that flicker of tension was beginning to spark to an all-consuming fire.

No. She wouldn't let it.

She couldn't let it.

"Tate said you've been with her all night."

He rolled to his feet in one graceful motion, a small smile on his face. "Bella's my responsibility."

"And mine," she said heatedly. "She's my patient. I was here at her birth, remember?"

His lips kicked up higher. "Yes, ma'am. I knew her labor wouldn't be a problem until today. Wanted to save you the trouble of pulling an all-nighter with me. You were more needed at the clinic." He paused, his next words pulsing with meaning. "Or with my brother."

This time, she jerked and averted her gaze. "Next time don't think. Just let me do my job."

She approached Bella, murmuring softly, kneeling in the hay while she quietly examined her. Gently probing, stroking her flanks, she donned her gloves and felt where the foal lay. After checking her heart and lungs, she finally stood. "Almost time. She's holding her own."

Bella had difficulty giving birth before. Tucker clenched his jaw and nodded, but she glimpsed the worry in his eyes, the stiffness in his muscles. He had good reason. Unlike Bella's previous stillborn births, this foal was alive. But Hannah wasn't sure if Bella would be sacrificed for the birth. The mother wasn't strong, and her health had declined sharply over the last few months.

"Then we wait," he declared.

"Yes," she said. "We wait."

Tucker watched while she settled herself near Bella on a bale of hay. He handed her a bottle of water and sank back down to the ground. Pulling off his hat, he dragged back the thick strands of hair from his forehead before resettling it on his head.

"See Tate?"

She took a sip of water. "Yeah, he was heading to court."

"Off to save the world, one client at a time, huh?"

Her voice softened. "Yeah. That's what he does best."

They lapsed into silence. Hannah glanced away. How had Tucker become more to her than just Tate's younger brother? Was it the quiet depth of the man who held a thousand emotions brimming in his hazel eyes? Was it the way he handled the animals, with a strong gentleness and husky voice that promised everything would be okay? Was it the deep laugh that vibrated from his chest and pumped the world full of joy?

He was like his brother, but so different. The love of land and animals beat in his blood. He was a wild spirit, somewhat untamed, but each time they talked, something between them began to shift and grow. An understanding and a connection.

Over the past few months, Hannah had realized a terrible, terrible truth.

She was in love with one brother, but wanted the other.

"How's your sister?" Tucker finally asked.

Hannah tried to drag her thoughts to practical matters. "She got another job working with Marylee, but she's having a hard time without Hector. Dakota has been a handful. I think Mallory is doing better, though. I don't know. I hate to admit it, but I'm glad he's gone. I think she'll do better without him."

"Never liked Hector much. He drank all the time and talked too loud. A scary combination for a man."

She'd never told anyone she suspected Hector abused Joanne. Her sister had many secrets, and since their parents ostracized Joanne for marrying Hector, Hannah bet it made it even more important for things to work out for her marriage. She needed to show her parents she'd made the right choice. Hannah didn't agree with her father cutting her sister off, but no matter how many times she broached the subject, he'd remained firm. Knowing Hector was hitting her sister didn't help her cause either, but Joanne steadfastly denied it. Hannah probably should have fought harder to help Joanne, but though they loved each other, there was a slight distance between them. Almost as if they couldn't understand one another, no matter how they tried.

Secrets. So many secrets to keep.

"So, Doc, how's the new rescue?"

Hannah smiled. One of the hazards of her job was getting too attached to the animals that came in and out of her door, especially the homeless. She worked closely with the animal shelter, but once in a while, a dog or cat would steal her heart, so she'd add them to her growing menagerie. Tate was patient and accepting, but constantly warned her to try and be professional. He believed being a vet was similar to a lawyer. Treat the animals like patients. Do your best but be reminded you couldn't save them all.

Still, her soul screamed "Just one." If she could save one more, the world would be better.

She was such a sucker.

"I named him Fred."

"That's so undignified," Tucker grumbled. "For God's sakes, why?"

She laughed. The terrier mix had been left tied to a tree when found. His body had scars, one ear had been chewed almost off, but his eyes still held the steadiness of a dog who refused to give up on people. "I don't know. He just looks like a Fred. He's an old soul. Tough. Kind of ugly in a really good way. Nobody messes with a Fred."

"He getting along with the others? How many do you have now?"

She wrinkled her nose. "Six. Three dogs, three cats. Tate keeps telling me to be more professional. Says I can't save them all."

"Tate is right. Then again, you can save at least one."

Startled, her gaze swung to his. Her breath strangled in her chest, and her palms grew damp. The air charged with sexual tension, and then Bella struggled to move and the spell was broken.

It ended up being another two hours before the foal was safely born. Two hours of safe conversation. Two hours of trying not to look each other straight in the eye again. Two hours of denial.

When the foal stood on shaky, reed-like legs and Bella was stable, they both stood close and stared at the mini miracle before them. As in any birth, it seemed the other animals sensed the end, and the soft mutters of whinnies and screech of roosters and groans of cows mingled together in a symphony. They were dirty and sweaty and smelly. Sweat poured off both of them in rivers.

Hannah had never been happier.

They grinned. "Hell of a sight," Tucker said. "Makes everything just a bit better."

She sighed in pure pleasure. "Yeah."

This time, when they glanced at each other, they didn't look away.

They spoke words within those few moments; they spoke questions they'd been too afraid to utter; they spoke a plea that mingled bodies and souls and her very, very fragile heart.

God, she wanted him. Ached to reach out and touch him. Run her hands over the sharp angles of his face, trace the full curve of his lower lip, caress the small scar that hooked over his right brow from a rock fight gone terribly wrong.

"Hannah."

She shuddered. Very slowly, she took a step forward. A few inches separated them. They stood, together, in the dim of the barn, and wished for something they couldn't have.

Because if she touched him, she'd destroy everything.

Hannah shook her head and stumbled back. His face closed up.

"I have to go. I'll come back and check on her later."

She grabbed her bag with shaky hands and raced out of the barn, hoping she could forget.

Hoping she wouldn't.

Chapter Six

Payton Rush gripped the coffee cake and weaved her way down the corridors of the hospital. Her day had been filled with endless tasks for the upcoming Founders' Day celebration, specific phone calls to the wives of her husband's political supporters, and stopping by to check on Celeste. Her poor sister seemed run down, but when she talked about Ginny and the baby, her eyes lit up. It seemed to be the only thing holding her fragile body and soul together. Payton ached for her and wished she could do more.

Francine had been making regular visits to help ease Celeste's mind, and constantly reassured her Ginny's baby was healthy and strong. When Payton had visited her sister today, Celeste said she planned to drop off a coffee cake to Francine as a thank you, but Payton swept in and told her she'd make the trip for her.

Francine seemed to be a light in her world she selfishly guarded. The two women had formed a strong friendship in the weeks since Jacob's death. Payton liked how the woman was so different than the usual crowd who surrounded her. Francine loved to laugh and enjoyed a good joke or teasing remark. She was also extremely astute and always seemed to know when something bothered Payton. Lately, her very controlled and sterile life had a bit of spark in it, and she didn't want to question the feelings behind it.

Her heels clicked smartly on the floor and she paused in front of the break room. The front nurse said Francine was on a short lunch break and to go right in. Being the wife of a senator had many perks. One was the easy entrance and exit in most public buildings at her discretion.

Payton smoothed her hair and, noticing the door wide open, stepped in. Francine was sitting at one of the tables, flipping through the pages of a magazine while she ate her sandwich. She glanced over and her face lit up. "Payton! What a surprise. How are you? Are you okay?"

Payton smiled. "Yes, everything's fine. Celeste made her special coffee cake you love so much, and I wanted to drop it by."

"Well, aren't you the sweetest thing ever! You know well this is my secret weakness. Problem is, my uniform is getting a bit tight from all my indulgences."

Payton's tummy fluttered a bit as she took in Francine's spotless green scrubs. She was small, but curvy in a very nice way. Not like her own skinny, almost bony body that never seemed able to hold an hourglass shape. "You look beautiful," she burst out. Shocked at her candor, she walked over to the table and put the cake down. "I mean, you certainly don't need to lose any weight."

Francine's brown eyes sparkled with merriment. "Coffee cake and compliments! This really is a perfect day." They smiled at each other. "Now, there's no way I'm eating alone. I'm cutting both of us a piece and you have to stay and talk to me a bit."

Warmth suffused Payton. She helped cut two pieces and nibbled at the moist cake. Most of the time, she was too nervous to eat in front of people, but Francine made her comfortable. They ate in silence for a bit, enjoying the delicious cake, enjoying each other's company. Payton's lingering tension drifted away. "Do you usually eat your lunch here?"

Francine popped the last morsel in her mouth. "Unfortunately, yes. My shifts tend to be busy, and I don't like to take time away from my patients. I'm a bit of a workaholic, I confess."

"Your career saves lives. You're needed here." Payton admired Francine. She did something important with her life. Sometimes Payton wondered if she looked back on her life one day, she'd discover nothing of value. Oh, sure, she adored her children and took pride in being the best wife and mother imaginable, but she gave nothing of true value to the world. She kept her gaze averted, wondering if Francine ever found her lacking.

"Payton." She looked up. Francine's eyes were like warm chocolate, comforting and rich. "The kind of work you do every day is just as important. Raising children. Giving back to the community.

Trying to instill values and defending your beliefs to the town. You're a very special woman. I just hope you know that."

Payton flushed with pleasure, her lips curving up in an answering smile. "Well, now you made my day perfect." A rush of energy hummed between them. She wiped her mouth with the napkin and tried not to wonder at her trembling fingers. "Honestly, we so appreciate you checking in on Ginny."

"It's not a problem. I enjoy it. How is Celeste?" Francine's brows drew into a frown. "She seems a bit run down herself."

Payton sighed. "She's going through such a difficult time. I wish I could help her, but losing a child is such a painful experience, I'm afraid I can only be there for her when she needs me."

"Yes. I suggested grief counseling, as did Pastor Douglas, but I don't think she's ready. She seems extremely focused on the baby." Francine paused, as if trying to decide to say her next words. "*Jacob's* baby."

Payton shifted in the chair. "Yes. She's clinging to Ginny and the baby like it's her last link to sanity. It terrifies me to think of how she would be without this hope. This...miracle."

The moment Celeste had announced Ginny was carrying Jacob's baby, her first reaction was the knowledge it was impossible. Only a handful of people knew about Jacob's childhood accident, but how could she have possibly challenged her sister at the time? When she was steeped in such grief? Payton hadn't said a word to her husband or her sister, but now with Francine, she had the opportunity to confess her concerns.

Francine tapped her lip in thoughtful silence. "I never discuss patients' information. But Celeste told me you knew about the results of Jacob's accident and the high improbability that he'd ever father children."

Payton nodded. "I was at the hospital after his fall. It was heartbreaking. Celeste and Travis had decided to tell him the truth when he was older and more able to handle it."

Payton would never forget that day. Her sister had called her from the hospital when Jacob was around ten. He'd slipped from a high tree branch, crushing both testicles in a horrific fall. He'd gone through tests, and the doctors had sadly informed Celeste he would have a very high percentage of sterility. The inability to father children had devastated her sister and Travis, but they'd decided to keep the truth from him, afraid Jacob wouldn't be able to handle it until he was older.

Only a few people knew about the accident. Celeste and Travis. Francine. The doctors. And Payton.

Francine seemed to choose her words carefully. "Ginny is a beautiful young girl. Do you think there's any possibility she was with another man besides Jacob?"

The possibility of such a thing terrified her. Yes, the doubts had crossed her mind when she'd heard about the baby. But Celeste had told her emphatically that Ginny confirmed Jacob was the only man she'd been sleeping with. She had to believe her sister was right. Besides, Jacob and Ginny had been best friends for so long, the entire town suspected love would blossom between them. Even Celeste had wondered if such a close friendship would lead to more. Ginny wouldn't lie about a baby—it was beyond comprehension.

"I haven't discouraged my sister on the belief that this baby is a gift from God," Payton said. "Ginny truly loved Jacob and swears there has been no one else. I believe her. And Celeste needs to believe in her, too. This baby is the only thing she has left. After all, it is possible." Celeste leaned over the table. "You believe it, don't you, Francine? That it was a miracle and meant to be? That Ginny is carrying Jacob's baby?"

Somehow, Payton needed to hear Francine say the words.

Francine waited a while before answering. A mix of emotions brewed in her eyes, and she seemed hesitant when she spoke. "I've seen amazing things in my career as a nurse. Actual miracles. Doctors say a person will never walk again, and a year later, I see this patient walking on his own. Jacob's death was such a terrible tragedy. Is it possible? Yes, anything is possible."

Payton noticed Francine refused to say she believed it was Jacob's baby, but it was enough reassurance to cling to. It was possible. Ginny was a good girl and her daughter's best friend. Somehow, Payton also believed Brittany would tell her the truth about the baby if Ginny confessed anything, since Ginny told Brit everything.

No, Jacob and Ginny's baby was a miracle. It would heal her sister's family and bring hope that everyone desperately needed.

"Thank you, Francine. I can't tell you how much better I feel."

"I always feel better after I see you," Francine said softly.

A blush heated Payton's cheeks. Her belly tumbled in a delightful roller coaster. Afraid of the burgeoning odd feelings, she jumped from the table and began cleaning up, keeping herself busy. "Well, I've taken up enough of your time. I'm off to meet with Marylee about the upcoming election."

Francine also stood. "If you need any help, please let me know. I worry about you working too hard."

"Same for you," Payton said back, teasingly.

"If you ever want to take a break, please call me. We can get a cup of coffee and pie at Bluebonnets."

The idea was so wonderful, Payton found herself nodding. "I'd like that."

"Good."

The silence spoke volumes, but then a voice came over the loudspeaker paging a doctor, and the spell was broken.

Payton walked out of the hospital with a full belly and an even fuller heart.

* * * *

Luis Moreno froze at the door to the hospital break room.

His head spun. He cradled his stitched-up hand and wondered if the painkillers had already taken hold and he'd hallucinated the whole conversation.

But no, he'd literally just swallowed them with water and made his way up to the main floor to give a quick thanks to Francine for helping out his sister. No way was he drugged up yet. And he wasn't dreaming. Unfortunately.

Holy shit. Ginny might not be carrying Jacob's baby.

He leaned against the wall, numb with shock. He'd heard Jacob's name as he reached the door, and a quick peek showed Payton and Francine engaged in conversation. He hadn't planned to eavesdrop. He'd ducked back automatically, curious as to what they were saying about his sister's friend, and bam, the truth had exploded at him like a fucking array of bullets.

He heard the rustle of paper and carefully stepped back until he was hidden in another hallway. What should he do? He didn't think he could pull off going in there to thank Francine now. He'd probably question her, and half of him didn't know if he could handle more truth.

Was it a miracle and truly Jacob's baby?

Or was Ginny lying to herself and the whole town?

Damn, he felt as if he was caught up in the crazy soap opera Ginny loved as her guilty pleasure. This whole day had been a clusterfuck of mega proportions. He'd tried to go see Mallory this morning with a bunch of roses he'd bought from Pushing Up Daisies and beg her to talk to him. He was sick over the incident with Lacey and just wanted his girlfriend back. Luis hoped a heartfelt apology with a damn good explanation might help right things.

The flowers thrown in his face told him it was a big fat no.

So, he'd slunk back to work at the club, and on his way back out he found one of the members trying to change a tire. The guy had looked like he'd never gotten his hands dirty, so Luis offered to help. The jack was one of those cheap ones only to be used on occasion, and combined with his distraction over Mallory, the damn thing had collapsed and sliced his hand open.

Luis had scared the poor guy shitless. With blood everywhere, he'd wrapped it up, told the guy to call management to help him with the tire, and took off for the hospital. Thank God his hand wasn't crushed, but he definitely needed stitches. He was supposed to be meeting Ginny at the house in a few minutes, but the damn accident had thrown him off schedule.

After the ER, he planned on stopping in quick to thank Francine, then heading home to hang with his sisters, and mooching a big sympathy dinner from Marisol. Instead, he had this stuff in his head he couldn't un-know, and Luis had a feeling it was gonna be bad. Especially if anyone talked or found out about Jacob.

Ditching his plan to thank Francine, he turned and headed back out of the hospital and to his car. He needed a few minutes to clear his head and make a plan. Should he confront Ginny? She was so vulnerable now. Losing Jacob in the accident had given her survivor's guilt—he'd heard about that on some *Dateline* episode or something—and her entire life now spun out of control. Now that she was living with the Salts, they hadn't seen each other as much, and they'd always been extremely close. He missed her, especially with the shit going on with Mallory and Lacey. Sure, she was a girl, and his sister, but Ginny got him. She didn't judge or try to push him in one direction by being a mom. He could tell her things he told no one else.

Hurt sliced through him. She should've told him the truth. He could've handled it and helped her, no matter how she decided to proceed. Now, he had to make a decision to confront her about what he learned or go along with the lie. If it was a lie.

Maybe it was a miracle.

He drove off and settled into a comfortable speed on the highway. The thing that really bugged him was the way Ginny had acted when she called or visited from college. She'd changed. He'd caught her secretly giggling on the phone at times, and then she'd get pissy when he asked who she was talking to. And she didn't hang out with Jacob specifically when she came home for break. Wouldn't she have told him if they were seeing each other?

Jacob had been a good guy, and pretty down to earth. He wouldn't have caused Ginny to begin wearing different clothes that made her look older, or appreciated tons of make-up. When she talked to Luis from college, her stories were filled with undertones of a secret life she didn't talk about but seemed bursting to confess. Suddenly, she was conversing about current events? Or her sudden passion for wine? Nothing made sense. Luis had suspected she was involved with some older guy, but didn't push for details. He also felt guilty for questioning her. Ginny never lied, especially to him. There was no reason.

But things didn't add up.

Suddenly, she comes home after the car crash, announces the secret affair had been with Jacob, and she's pregnant with his baby.

Luis suspected a bigger truth, but he wasn't sure if he wanted to know. He was worried about Ginny. Maybe he'd talk to her. He'd been selfish lately with all the crap with Lacey and hadn't been a good brother.

When he pulled into his house, Brit's car was there along with Marisol's. He relaxed at the idea of some quiet time with his family. There had been too much drama lately with the girls in his life, and he craved some normalcy. As close to normalcy, of course, that the Morenos could obtain with no parents and little money.

The delicious smells of dinner hit his nostrils. Meatloaf. Potatoes. His fave. The house was spotless but threadbare, from the odd assortment of old furniture pieced together, along with a few personal knick-knacks from their parents scattered around the house. The fake Oriental rug was worn. The paint on the walls was dull and needed a fresh coat. But it was the only home they knew, and even if it didn't have the luxury that Jeffry's home had, Luis loved its comfort.

"Oh, my God, Luis!" Ginny came running over, hugging him

hard. "Francine called and said you had to get stitches. Why didn't you answer my text? We were going to head over there!"

Marisol joined them, a serious frown marking her dark brows. "Luis Moreno, I can't believe you didn't even tell me you got hurt! Are you okay? Let me see it!"

He laughed at his sisters' overprotectiveness and held up his hand. "Just a cut, nothing serious. And I was driving. You always tell me not to text and drive, remember?"

Brit laughed in the background, perched on the floral couch. "I told them you were tough, Luis, but they didn't believe me. You're still the baby in the family, you know."

"Screw you, Brit."

She laughed again. Brit was like an additional sister, since she was close to Ginny. At least, Brit was visiting Ginny at the Salt's all the time now. The idea that Ginny lived with the Salts made his gut lurch. He didn't like it but had to accept she was probably getting a cushier ride over there. The Salts and Rushes weren't like them. They were rich and belonged in Storm like it was their royal right. The Moreno family existed on the surface, just barely accepted due to the tragic loss of their parents.

He pushed the thoughts aside. "Is that why I'm getting meatloaf?"

Marisol rolled her eyes. "Yes, you spoiled brat. We haven't seen Ginny and Brit in a while, so I thought it would be nice to have dinner with just us."

"I like it. Let me shower and change."

"Typical. Then you can show up and everything will be done, right?"

Luis gave a pained expression. "Oh, my hand, it hurts bad. But if you want me to wash dishes, I'll do it. For you."

She swatted him with the dishtowel, and Ginny laughed. Luis was smiling when he headed for his room to clean up.

They feasted on dinner, laughing and catching up, and trying not to go over things that made them sad. Marisol and Luis kept the conversation light and gave Ginny a bit of a break from the drama.

They ended up in the living room, drinking iced tea while Ginny curled her feet under a bright yellow crotchet blanket their mom had knit years ago. Marisol finally ventured into heavier topics. "How are you doing over at the Salts, Ginny? Are you okay?"

Luis read more into his sister's question. She was asking if she'd failed to provide what Ginny needed. Luis was always trying to reassure Marisol she'd done the best job she could. Acting as a sister and substitute mom was hard for anyone. They'd both acted out at various times. Luis couldn't help being a dick once in a while, but he always tried to make it up to her.

"Things are good," Ginny said. "Celeste kind of hovers, but in a good way. She's just really worried about the baby. And of course, Brit keeps me company."

Brit sighed. "I've been telling her she needs to get out more."

"You can come here anytime," Marisol chimed in. "Seriously. I'll cook you dinner or if you have a craving, you can stop by the bakery. I—I don't want you to think we're not here for you, even though you live with them now."

Ginny blinked back tears. "No, it's not like that! I miss you both so much. I'm just overwhelmed sometimes, thinking about the pregnancy and what I'm going to do afterward, and missing Jacob. I'm a big mess. Soon, I'll be a big, fat mess."

Luis groaned. Girls and their weight. He just didn't get it.

"We'll help you," Marisol promised. "We're in this together. I know the Salts will help a lot, but this is your baby, too, Ginny. When you figure out what you want, we'll back you up."

"Thanks. Oh, God, here I go again. I cry all the time. What I really need is the updates. What's going on with both of you?"

Luis remained silent. So did Marisol. He knew she dated Patrick Murphy casually but liked to keep it quiet. Patrick rarely came by the house, and Luis didn't know what type of relationship they had. Maybe they were friends with benefits? Marisol was always so tight lipped about her personal life. Not like Ginny. Ginny shared things—or she used to—but his oldest sister always seemed as if she made every move knowing she'd be judged.

Brit broke the standoff. "Luis, what's going on with you and Lacey? My cousin's been acting so strange lately. Not her usual sweet self."

He fought the urge to groan and squeeze his eyes shut. Ugh. He so didn't want to talk about this. But Ginny looked eager for him to confide in her and he felt bad. He decided on the short version. "I made a mistake with Lacey. I got mixed up, and Mallory thinks I cheated on her, which I didn't. Course she didn't believe me. Lacey is also pissed at me now, so they're not talking and it's been a big mess."

"Wow," Ginny said. "Lacey and Mallory are best friends. No wonder Lacey is acting different. That also explains the comment she made about you this morning. You're not sleeping together?"

Ah, shit, this was awkward. "No! We didn't sleep together. We, uh, were figuring things out."

"Want me to talk to her?"

"No! Really, guys, it's better if we work this out ourselves. Don't talk to Lacey." He sensed a bigger lie coming down the pipe, and he didn't want Ginny and Brit making things worse. Luis knew losing Jacob was making Lacey crazy. He'd been an ass choosing Lacey over Mallory. His real heart lay with Mallory. He just had to find a way to make it up to her. If flowers and apologies wouldn't work, how could he convince her he truly loved her? The whole thing made his head hurt, but he tried to concentrate on Ginny.

"I won't say anything if you don't want me to," Ginny said. "Swear."

"Thanks." He probed her gaze. If Ginny swore there was no one else, how could he not believe her? His sister could never keep such a huge secret. Maybe he was wrong about her strange behavior in college. Maybe it really was Jacob's baby.

He couldn't imagine the outcome if it wasn't.

Ginny stretched her legs out. "How about you, Marisol?"

"Working a lot and trying to put in some extra hours."

"Seeing anyone?"

Marisol sipped her tea and lowered her eyes. "Not much time for dating, Ginny."

"Not even for Patrick Murphy?" Brit teased. It was known in the town they were good friends, and some had speculated how serious things really were between them. Some said they dated, some people insisted it was only friendship. But both Marisol and Patrick kept their mouths shut.

"Occasionally," Marisol offered. "He's my friend. Nothing exciting going on though."

They chatted a bit more, catching up, until Ginny yawned and decided to head back. While Brit took a moment to head to the bathroom, Luis walked Ginny to the door and pulled her aside. He didn't have as much time alone with his sister anymore. Maybe if he gave her an opportunity to talk, she would.

"Hey, Gin. I know things have been hard since the crash and

Jacob." He shifted his feet, uncomfortable with his emotions. "I feel like I haven't been there for you."

She grabbed his hand and squeezed. "No, Luis. With this whole thing with Lacey, and Mallory, I feel like I haven't been there for you. I kind of hid myself away for a while, you know? But I'm trying to reach out more."

He took a deep breath and met her gaze. "Remember when you told me about the night you snuck out with Brit under Marisol's nose, and went to that rock concert out of town?"

She looked surprised at the shift in subject but smiled. "Yeah. Marisol went to check on me, and you covered. Said I was sleeping at a friend's and that I'd called to let her know, but you forgot to tell her. Saved my butt."

"Yeah, I did. Ginny, you can tell me anything. The beauty is, I don't care what it is. I got your back."

She blinked. He caught a flare of guilt in her eyes, but it was gone quickly and then she was ducking her head. One hand lay on her belly as if to protect the baby inside. "I know," she said softly. "I appreciate it."

He waited, trying to sense if there was any type of reveal coming, but she just smiled at him and pressed a kiss to his cheek. Then she headed to Brit's car and got in.

A moment later, Brit came out, and the two girls drove away. Luis stood watching and wondered for a long time if that moment would come back to haunt them both.

Chapter Seven

Logan tamped down his excitement as he waited outside Murphy's for Ginny. He'd worked hard trying to finally score this date, which he pitched as a friendly get-together so she wouldn't freak out. After consistent calls and gentle pressure, she'd agreed to meet him this Friday night. *After* dinner. She was a smart one, deftly avoiding the whole romantic candlelit meal he'd wanted to sneak in. But he agreed. He tried to pick her up, of course, but she didn't want the Salts to think she was going on a date.

Logan hoped by the end of the night he'd change her mind.

He couldn't get her off his mind. Ever since the afternoon in the diner, he lay awake at night, thinking about her. She kept him occupied, since he barely slept anyway, and sometimes he actually drifted off in a somewhat peaceful state with her warm brown eyes and smile as the last image behind his closed lids.

He saw her turn the corner, her smile tentative as she walked over. Dressed in a casual summer dress with white and red roses, flat sandals, and her wavy hair twisted up to reveal the long length of her neck, she looked so good he just wanted to stare at her.

Sometimes, during the hours of suffering in blistering heat, dust in his eyes, his hands cramped around his weapon, he'd dreamed of Storm. Dreamed of iced tea and pretty girls in summer dresses, just like Ginny. The funny thing was, if she was too innocent he didn't think he'd be interested. Her scars were hidden, like his, and one soul recognized another.

"Hi."

"Hi." He grinned like a teenager, cleared his throat, and tried to find his cool again. "You look nice."

She blushed. "Thanks. I'm bigger." Her hands nervously tugged at her dress. "I mean, I gained some weight."

"Hope so. Means the baby's growing." Logan had decided he didn't want to treat her pregnancy like an inconvenience they tried to avoid as a topic of conversation. She was going to be a mother, and he needed her to know he was okay with it. Pretending she was single with no baggage was just stupid, and he didn't play those games. Not anymore.

"How's your morning sickness?" he asked.

"Much better. I have more energy, too."

"I'm glad."

They stared at each other for a bit, until she ducked her head. "So, where are we going?" she asked. "I don't want to go anywhere with big crowds."

He'd already planned for that. "We won't. I think you'll like what I have on the agenda. Hop in."

Logan gestured to his black Chevrolet Camaro, still in perfect shape after the years he'd been gone. His father had kept his brothers' grubby hands off the old classic, knowing Logan had loved to tinker for hours with the car, his first and most precious worldly possession. His best friend, Marcus, had also been into classic cars, and they used to spend endless days tinkering with engines and trying to restore old junk cars.

She climbed in, and he put on the air conditioner with the windows down, his favorite way to drive. With a quick tap of the button, Garth Brooks came blasting out the speakers, and he pulled out of the pub, hitting the open road.

They drove in companionable silence. His finger tapped to the beat, and he caught her humming some of the lines under her breath. The hem of her dress flipped up and revealed her golden brown thighs. Logan enjoyed the view and the company until he finally pulled into the off-road ice cream stand and parked.

He glanced over. The scent of greasy burgers, fries, and shakes drifted around them. People sat gathered around the picnic tables, or in their cars with the windows down, enjoying a sugar rush. Ginny laughed and shook her head.

"Well, this isn't gonna help my weight problem," she grumbled.

Logan grinned. "Gonna help your happiness factor, though," he pointed out. "My momma used to take me and my brothers out here when we had a huge fight. We'd be crammed in the back of our station wagon, refusing to speak or look at each other, and she'd pull into this stand and announce if we wanted ice cream we had to talk to each other. By the time we had our cones or shakes, we were chattering away and forgot what we were mad about."

"Your momma was always smart," Ginny said. "And I could never resist a black and white shake. Let's do it."

"That's my girl."

He ordered her shake, and he got chocolate on a waffle cone with rainbow sprinkles. It was melting faster than he could eat it, so they perched on the hood of the car rather than inside, and she laughed as he tried to lick it like he was in the ice cream Olympics.

"You're going to get a stomach ache!" She was laughing and handing him napkins, and when he finally finished, he was wearing more than he'd eaten.

But Ginny was smiling and happy. And his heart moved a bit in his chest, less hollow than it had been in a long time.

When he was cleaned up, they hopped back in the car and drove. She didn't ask any other questions, and she relaxed into the seat, her face free of worry lines, her full lips curved upward in a hint of a smile. They sang loud, with him off-key, until they came to the outskirts of the town, away from the bustle of Main Street and into the ripe, lush landscape Storm was known for.

He veered off a dirt road that had no signs, driving through underbrush for a while until he finally made a sharp right and cut the engine.

Ginny gasped.

It was a hell of a sight. A gorgeous slice of Texas lay before them in all its heated glory. The sky was a blue-black studded with a million stars, and the sloping lines of the fields sprawled before them. Gray-green scrub dotted with cerulean and purple wildflowers were scattered over the sloping lines of the field sprawled before them. Twisted live oak trees grew high and strong. Off in the distance, she caught the gleam of the barbed wire fence that held the cattle, and the flash of white from the water tanks. The vast quiet almost burned the ears, making an onlooker feel like the only person in the world.

"This is so beautiful," she whispered.

"Let's go."

They got out of the car and he lifted her so she perched on the hood. Ginny sighed, taking in the view, her breathing deepening as if trying to drag in each precious breath of pure oxygen. Logan smiled, enjoying her company, and settled beside her.

"This is my secret place," he explained. "Growing up with my brothers was fun, but chaotic. Sometimes I craved quiet, where I could actually think and be on my own, but it seemed no matter where I tried to go someone found me."

Ginny laughed.

"I kept driving farther out until one day I got to the outskirts and just decided to find some unknown roads for an adventure. I came here a lot when I needed clarity."

"No one ever found out?" she asked.

"Nope. Once Patrick tried to follow me but I lost him miles back and he never discovered where I'd been."

"Did you come here when you decided to enlist in the military?"

He nodded. "I craved big things. Not sure why. Dillon was happy to settle here. Patrick, too. I always dreaded staying and running the pub my whole life. I wanted to see the world."

"And you did. You also saved people."

His gut twisted. Somehow, he couldn't stand the thought of her believing the lie. He was no damn hero. Logan didn't like to explain what had happened in Afghanistan, but at night, he was taunted by his failures. Nightmares. Panic attacks. For the first time, he wanted to talk.

"I didn't save anybody," he said stiffly. "They put a spin on it because everyone needs to believe in something good happening over there."

She tilted her head and studied his face. "Tell me what happened."

No one else knew. So at the top of the hill, in the middle of the darkness, he decided to tell her the truth. "There was nothing heroic about it. Our vehicle went over a road bomb, killing and injuring three of my friends. Me and two other guys crawled out of the vehicle and made it to the rocks. Tommy didn't. His legs got blown off, and he was unconscious on the ground. That's when we heard the gunfire. Adam covered me while I went back to grab Tommy and dragged him to cover. We stayed our ground and waited for backup."

He paused. Sweat broke out on his skin and his lungs had trouble filling up with air. Damn PTSD. Logan gritted his teeth and hung on, knowing the hard part was getting the words out, but needing to do it. "Assholes got closer, and Adam got shot. I tried to help. I couldn't. When backup came, they were both dead. But I was alive."

Alive.

He'd attended mandatory counseling. He knew it was textbook to question why he was the only one saved. The only one to make it out.

Still didn't make it any better.

Shame was a constant companion. He'd failed. Somehow, some way, he'd let his entire unit down, lost his comrades, and had to live with it.

She reached out and squeezed his hand, but he couldn't look at her. Couldn't see the pity and questions in her eyes. Slowly, she lifted his hand, stroking his crooked pinky finger with a gentle touch. "Did you get this from the accident?"

"Yeah. My only real injury. They tried to fix it, but I wouldn't let them. I needed something to remember. Every day, when I look down, I see the evidence of what happened. I'll never let myself forget my friends and what happened to them."

"I understand. But maybe you can get yourself to forgive."

His breath rushed free and clear, bursting from his constricted lungs. A tiny sliver of peace cut through him. How did she do it? How did she make him feel better about things?

"I never sleep," she said quietly. "Every night I dream about the car crash. Of me driving sloppily, being distracted by my own ridiculous emotions. Jacob and I had been arguing over something silly. It happened so fast, and when I woke up, Jacob was dead. But I drove the car, Logan. I should've seen the deer. I'm the one who really killed him, no matter what anyone tells me, and I live with that every day of my life."

This time, he turned, and their gazes locked. Tears glittered in the dark depths of her eyes, and something rose up inside him as one kindred spirit recognized the other. Damaged. Alive when they didn't believe they should be. Together for a reason he couldn't figure out and didn't care to.

His voice was choked. "You get it, then."

"Yeah. I get it."

Their fingers entwined, and then he leaned over and kissed her. His soul sighed in pleasure as much as his body while his lips slid over hers with a gentleness and subtle heat that wrapped around him. He fell into her, kissing her deeply, and she kissed him back, belonging to him for a little while.

They drifted apart slowly, reluctantly. Stared at each other for a long while. "Logan, I don't think I can do this. It's complicated. I think I've loved Jacob my whole life, and I'm still dealing with his loss. I'm also having his baby. I'm on a different course from you, Logan, and you have this whole big life you can live."

Years ago, he would've agreed with her. Today, he realized all he wanted in his whole big life was to spend time with this woman he was falling for and help take care of her. The idea of a baby didn't scare him. Things had been so mixed up for him, there was an odd sense of order to his feelings for Ginny. Crazy? Definitely. But true.

"What if I told you being with you is the big thing in my life? I know you loved Jacob, and I know it seems fast. I'm not going to push. I just want a chance. Am I wrong, Ginny? I feel this connection between us—and it's growing stronger. But if you don't feel it I'll walk away and leave you alone."

She hesitated, but eventually nodded. "Yes. I feel it, too."

"Good." He smiled and tipped her chin up, staring into her face. "Give me a chance, then. I want to be with you when you birth this baby and hold your hand. I want to help you. And it's not because I feel sorry for you, or want to be some type of hero. You don't need me, Ginny. You have a family and the Salts and you're strong."

"Then what do you want?"

"Time. I want to spend time with you, take you out, make you happy. I've never told anyone else except my therapist about Afghanistan. I want a chance to see if you can fall for me, like I'm falling for you."

"This is crazy!" She gave a half laugh, her body trembling, and Logan pressed a kiss to her forehead.

"Maybe. Right now, just sit with me and keep me company. I'll drive you home and hopefully you'll let me see you again. Okay?"

He wanted to kiss her again, but he kept still, enjoying the confused look on her face, the want in her eyes she refused to give in to yet.

"Okay."

They smiled at each other. Then sat in silence, holding hands, looking at the stars.

Chapter Eight

Marisol watched her sister's face light up and wondered what was really going on with her and Logan Murphy.

Since Ginny had come to the house last week, Marisol realized she'd been resentful of her sister's new family, but didn't know how to handle it. She missed her sister. She missed taking care of her, even though it was hard, and craved to be a part of her pregnancy.

So she'd decided to be more active in trying to see her and forge their own relationship, separate from the Salts. It might be Jacob's baby and therefore Celeste was by necessity a part of the equation, but Marisol had been taking care of Ginny since she was young. She might have made mistakes and struggled to keep a roof over their head and food on the table. She might be looked down upon from the town for the occasional trouble Luis got into, or the way she tried to be independent from the do-gooders who only wanted to judge. She knew she sometimes came off as snobby and cold. But dammit, this was her family, and her niece or nephew. She deserved to be part of it.

Marisol took off a precious evening from Cuppa Joe and decided to host an impromptu get-together for Ginny and Luis's friends. She kept it simple, bringing home sandwiches from her cafe, her famous chocolate chip cookies, and turtle brownies, and made large pitchers of sun tea. The result was the perfect combination of casual and intimate, and Marisol loved seeing everyone a bit more relaxed and happy. Since Jacob's death, there had been little to celebrate, except Logan's return, and seeing the group of tight-knit friends dive into casual gossip and laughter warmed her soul.

She felt Patrick move beside her before she even saw him. Her skin tingled in response, but Marisol kept a tight rein on her emotions. Their long-term friendship had slowly evolved into casual dating, but she preferred to keep from crossing over the line to physical. Unfortunately, she had a bad feeling her time was beginning to run out.

"Another successful event," he drawled in her ear. "It's nice to see Ginny smile. Been a long time."

Marisol turned to look at him. Those pale-blue eyes shimmered with a mix of warmth, mischief, and lust. It was the lust that she kept trying to deny and push back into the very neat compartment of friendship. Patrick Murphy had the ability to command her body to full attention, but she'd kept that a secret from him and the rest of the town. With his coal-black hair, piercing eyes, and athletic build, he made the women in town pant for a chance to date him. She'd encouraged him a few times, holding her breath to see the results, but Patrick ignored her matchmaking attempts and kept asking her out. Kept steadily pushing her past her comfort zone and into physical intimacy. He was so damn stubborn.

Marisol was more stubborn. She already saw her future if she let herself really fall for Patrick. Disaster. For one thing, he was a workaholic. But more than that, his family was the heart and soul of Storm, and hers was…not. She'd still be known as the poor little misfit who had to struggle to raise her siblings after her parents' death. She hated the sympathetic clucking and gossiping behind closed doors while they quietly judged her attempts and found her failing.

Marisol had no time for a romantic relationship. She knew love led to one place only: heartbreak. People left. It was so much easier to deal in reality and things she could control. Patrick had been her friend for so long, she'd fallen into a pattern of trusting him more and more, but she couldn't allow them to be lovers. Yet, she couldn't say no to him every time he asked her out. She kept telling herself one last time, and then she'd refuse to see him again. It never happened. The worst part was the instinct that screamed Patrick was beginning to run out of patience.

Marisol re-focused. "Yes, but Ginny seems to be smiling specifically at Logan," she pointed out. "What's going on with them? Did Logan say anything?"

Patrick gave a very male shrug. "Nope. Haven't had a good long heart-to-heart with him yet. If they're hooking up, I think it's great."

She gasped. "Great? My sister is pregnant with Jacob's baby and living with the Salts. What could possibly be great about that?"

Dark brows drew in a frown. "I think Logan knows the deal. If he's ready to accept it, and Ginny's happy, why deny them?" He inched closer. His husky voice spilled past her ear. "Sometimes change is good, Marisol."

His words held buckets of hidden meaning she didn't want to deal with. Her temper spiked. "Don't you think my sister has been put through enough drama without adding a relationship at this point? You know what the town will think?"

His lips tightened. "Who cares? Haven't you learned there's always gossip? Ignore it and they focus on something else."

"That's because you've never been the target of gossip. You're a golden child, remember?"

"I think you have me confused with Dillon or Logan," he retorted. "What are you really upset about, Marisol?"

She drew herself up to her full height. "Nothing. Forget it. I'm going to talk to Ginny later. Jeffry is here. I'll be back."

Marisol dove into the crowd and pushed the confusing thoughts about Patrick to the back of her mind. Why couldn't things have stayed the same between them? Good friends. Buddies. Until that damn kiss that sparked stuff she didn't want to face. After that, things had changed, and every time they saw each other, the casual stuff was gone. What was left was brooding sexual tension and an urge to explore more with him.

No. She had to break it off. Soon.

She reached the chattering group of good friends and tried to relax. "Hi, Jeffry. Glad you could make it."

He grinned at her easily and snatched up a mini taco. "Thanks for having us, Marisol."

"Welcome. Glad the whole crew could come." She scanned the group, noting Luis in one corner and Mallory in the other. Luis looked miserable, staring across the room with a longing look on his face. Mallory seemed determined to ignore him, but Marisol saw the sneaking glances she aimed at Luis. Poor kids. She'd heard about the drama with Lacey, but felt terrible Jacob's little sister wasn't here. Lacey desperately needed support and her friends right now, and Marisol hoped they patched things up. Brit was over by Ginny and Logan. "Where's Dakota?"

Jeffry shook his head. "Mal said she didn't want to come. Had other plans."

Marisol sighed. Dakota was having her own growing pains since her father disappeared. She felt bad for Joanne. It was so hard to keep family together after a loss. Still, maybe it was for the best since many had suspected for a while about hidden abuse. If Hector was beating Joanne, then it was a gift and they shouldn't look too hard to get him back.

"Penny for your thoughts?" Tara Johnson Douglas asked, handing Marisol a glass of wine.

"Not sure they're worth that much." She smiled at her friend. "Just thinking about everything, I guess. Ginny, the baby—"

"My cousin?" Tara's expression held only teasing, but Marisol saw something else flitter across her eyes.

"Like I have time for that," she laughed and walked away, thinking that Tara saw too damn much.

Marisol concentrated on entertaining everyone and managed to keep busy enough so Patrick couldn't try to corner her with a heart-to-heart talk. Frustration carved out his features, but he didn't push. She kept her gaze on Logan and Ginny, noting the almost intimate gestures. His hand resting casually on her shoulder. The way his gaze was completely focused on her when she spoke. The gentle way he pushed back her hair from her face and made sure she always had a water bottle in her hand.

Oh, yeah. This was trouble.

By the time the party was finished, and everyone but Luis and Ginny were gone, she decided it was time for some truths. She pulled Ginny to the couch and clasped her hands. "Did you have fun?" Marisol asked.

Ginny smiled, her eyes bright. "I did. Thanks so much for throwing this party, Marisol. I've missed you." She blinked, staring down at her clasped hands, and her voice came out ragged. "I know I was really hard on you. I was mad you weren't Mom, and kept such a tight hold on me. I couldn't wait to get out of here and do what I wanted. But I never really told you how much I appreciate you and everything you did. Now that I'm having a baby—" She choked on the rest of the words, and Marisol shushed her, giving her a quick, hard hug.

"You didn't have to. And you're going to be okay. This baby is going to be a wonderful thing. A gift."

Ginny nodded, wiping her eyes. "Yes, a gift. Celeste calls him a miracle baby."

"Or her." Marisol laughed. "Anyway, I'm glad to see you happy for a bit. And it's good to have Logan back, isn't it?"

Marisol let the question dangle and got her answer immediately. Raw emotions flickered over Ginny's face. Seconds ticked by as Marisol waited.

Finally, Ginny answered. "I actually wanted to talk to you about Logan. I—I've been seeing him a bit, as friends. But he's interested in more. I don't know how it happened, but I think I have feelings for him, Marisol. How is this possible? I'm still in love with Jacob. Sometimes I feel like my heart is in actual pain when I think about never seeing him again. Am I screwed up? I'm so confused because when I'm with Logan, I'm actually—happy." Ginny teared up. "Is that bad? Do you hate me?"

Marisol's heart broke for her sister. Ginny had always been willing to take a risk and reach for love. Not Marisol. She preferred her safe environment under control and rarely thought about breaking out. But right now, looking into her sister's face, Marisol realized Ginny needed her permission to feel again. Logan Murphy was a man with a good heart, like Patrick. He loved his family, had honor, and had fought for his country. Maybe she couldn't rationalize love, or have it happen in the right time, in a tidy way?

Marisol squeezed her hand. "No, honey, I don't hate you. No one will hate you. We all know how much you loved Jacob, and trying to be happy again isn't betraying his memory. Logan seems like a good man. If you two have real feelings for each other, and realize some of the obstacles you'll have, how can anyone term that bad?"

Ginny gave a jerky nod. "Yeah. I just didn't know how you'd feel about it. He's not like any other man I've met. It's almost as if we're connected in this strange way and understand one another."

Patrick's face flashed in her mind. "Yeah. I know what you mean."

Her sister wiped her face and took a breath. "Okay. I needed to see what you said first. I want to talk to the Salts about this, too. Logan asked me to go to this party with him as his date. I want to go but I said no because I haven't told Celeste or Travis yet. I don't want them to think I'm forgetting about Jacob."

"Loving someone else doesn't mean you forget or replace the ones you've loved before. I think about Mom and Dad every single day. Being happy to be alive and enjoying time with you and Luis isn't a betrayal. It's just a celebration of life." The words startled her, and the image of Patrick burned in her vision. Funny, maybe she should be taking her own advice and not let her past guide her present.

Ginny's eyes softened. "Yeah, maybe you're right."

"Ginny, this is your life. The Salts need to step back and allow you to have your own life. Understood?"

"Understood."

They hugged and Ginny stood up. "Thanks. I have a lot to think about."

"I'm always here. We're family, and nothing will ever replace that."

When her sister left, Marisol felt as if things were shifting, both on the inside and out. She hoped they were all ready for it.

Chapter Nine

Dillon Murphy watched Joanne's car drive past and immediately noticed the taillight. Hector had busted it a while back in some half-drunken accident he'd gotten away with, and it had never gotten fixed.

Anger cut through him when he thought of the abuse Joanne used to suffer. No more. He'd made sure Hector was run out of town, and he had no regrets. No, the only regret he currently had was his inability to spend some quality time with Joanne.

Now seemed like the perfect time.

He hit the lights on the squad car, pulled out of his hot spot to catch speeders, and took off after her. The car eased over to the curb, and Dillon left the lights going as he stepped out and slowly strolled toward her. He leaned over and paused by her open window. Her face was only a few inches away, her breath a delicious rush of mint, her stunning green eyes emphasized even more by her thick lashes.

"Officer Murphy." Her voice held a bit of teasing. "I wasn't speeding."

He grinned slowly. "No, ma'am. But I have to ticket you for a broken taillight."

Her lighthearted manner faded with real concern. "Oh, I keep forgetting to get it fixed. There's so much going on lately, I barely have time to do anything."

Dillon hated the way her natural sensual manner faded under stress. Damn, he didn't mean to remind her of the worries in her life right now. "No problem," he said smoothly. "Follow me to the garage and we'll get it fixed now."

She frowned. "I have to get to work and I need my car."

Even better. "I'll drive you to work and pick you up. I'm out on rounds anyway so it's no inconvenience." Dillon watched her hesitate. Nibbling at her bottom lip was a task he very much wanted to do himself. He gave her a needed push. "You need to fix it, Joanne. This way it'll be done. Let me help."

She smiled, and Dillon's damn heart stuttered. This woman had always been the one he'd never forgotten and always wanted. To have a chance to make her happy and show her how good life could be away from her asshole husband was something he couldn't turn away from. "Okay, thanks."

"Great. I'll pull out and just follow me over."

He kept a slow, steady pace until they got to the auto repair place and he personally made sure the car would be done by five p.m. and ready to be picked up. Then he escorted Joanne into his cruiser and began driving her to work.

"A real modern-day type knight, huh?"

He gave her a playful wink. "Least I can do. How's the new job going?"

She lit up. "Great! Besides the pay and benefits, I'm learning a lot. Of course, dinner isn't on the table at the regular time, and I'm behind on laundry but—" She trailed off, realizing what she'd revealed.

Yes. Hector wasn't around any longer to punish her for household tasks that weren't done. Sickness curled in his gut at the idea of how her life had been. How trapped she must've felt, even though she consistently defended Hector.

"Good. I'm glad you're challenged at work, and you learned there's nothing wrong with being off schedule."

A faint blush crept over her cheeks. "Yes. Well, I'm adjusting but it's going well."

"How are the kids?"

Joanne sighed. "Dakota doesn't come around often since Hector left. I'm worried about her, but every time I try to approach her she shuts me down. Mallory is also going through a hard time—something to do with Luis but she won't tell me too much. And Marcus? I spoke with him briefly last week and told him about Hector. He's been angry with Hector for years, and now he's even more angry with the way Hector up and left me and the girls."

"I know it's difficult, Joanne, but I think you'll all come out stronger in the end. You're tougher than you think."

✻   She stared at him, startled. "You think so?" she asked softly.

He wished he could gaze at her face all day. All night. All the time. "Yeah, I do."

She cleared her throat. "Thanks, Dillon." His name sounded like music on her tongue. He opened his mouth to invite her out, but dammit, they pulled up to Marylee's office and the moment passed. She opened the door and climbed out. Dillon caught a glimpse of long, tanned legs and black heels. "I'll see you at five?"

"I'll be here."

The door slammed and he watched her walk down the pavement and disappear.

Dillon drove back to work, counting the hours until five.

* * * *

Ginny sat on the bed, propped against two lace-covered pillows, and waited for Celeste and Travis.

Brit had been gently pushing her to confess her true feelings, and finally she'd confessed. She was falling for Logan. Hard. After only a few times of seeing each other, she couldn't think of anything else but the next time.

He called her every night like clockwork, interested in her day, asking questions about the baby and how she felt. She'd memorized his face, and the way his brow quirked when he grinned, and the power and gentleness of his giant hands when he guided her down the steps, or into the car. They'd hung out at Marisol's party, and she had no desire to talk to anyone else.

He'd hinted that he'd like to ask her on a real date. Dinner and a movie. The small-town theater was always popular on the weekends, and everyone would know they were a couple. But she'd wanted Celeste and Travis to know about it before she said yes. It was crazy, but she felt like she needed their approval. So she'd skirted the issue the best she could, hoping against hope that he'd ask her again.

Not that Logan cared what the Salts thought. Or anyone for that matter. He'd told her over and over the baby didn't concern him, and in fact, made him happy. He'd said a piece of Jacob would be with them always and that it didn't affect his feelings for her.

Her world had crashed around her—literally and figuratively—until she wondered if she'd ever have another shot at happiness. After all, she'd made so many mistakes.

Logan was her shot.

At first, she struggled with balancing the beginning of a relationship with a lie. She kept pushing Logan away, and he kept pursuing until she realized seeing him was becoming more important than anything else.

He could never be told she'd slept with someone other than Jacob. But over the past weeks, each time she thought about the baby, she came to the stronger conclusion the baby *was* Jacob's. There was just no way life could be that cruel to give her a special connection with Logan and have this be Senator Rush's baby.

Maybe, this one last time, she was meant for happiness after all.

A gentle knock sounded at the door, and Celeste and Travis came in. Celeste looked worried as she hurried over to her to sit on the edge of the bed, automatically feeling her forehead and cheeks as if she had a temperature. "Should I call Francine?" she asked nervously. "Are you not feeling well?"

Travis stepped into the room and closed the door behind him. "Ginny, what can we do?"

Her eyes filled at the concern on their faces. She'd become close to the Salts in these past weeks. They'd treated her like their daughter, keeping her safe and protected, and though Celeste was sometimes more overprotective than her sister had ever been, she accepted it. "No, I just wanted to talk to you both about something. The baby's fine. I feel wonderful."

Celeste let out a breath. "That's a relief. Tell us what's bothering you."

Ginny twisted her hands together, not knowing how to start. Brittany had urged her to tell the Salts about Logan to see their reaction. They'd never have a shot at dating or exploring a real relationship until they were able to stop hiding. Or rather, stop herself from denying they were nothing more than friends. But did she have the strength to continue the relationship if the Salts disapproved? Her stomach lurched, but she clung to Brit and Marisol's assurance that being with Logan was a good thing.

"I know you both were happy when Logan Murphy came back into town," she ventured.

Celeste nodded. "Yes, he's our local hero. I can't imagine what the poor man went through over there, but he was always kind to Jacob and Lacey. Is he in trouble, sweetheart? Are you worried about him?"

Ugh, this wasn't going well. She was tripping around the subject. Ginny forced herself to take a deep breath and keep eye contact. "I haven't told you because it felt awkward, but Logan and I began seeing each other. As friends," she said quickly. "He knows about the baby, and Jacob, and...everything. He's been really supportive and in the past few weeks we began, well, we began, well—"

"Falling for each other?" Travis interrupted.

Ginny's voice broke. "Yes. I didn't plan to have feelings for someone other than Jacob. Especially with the baby, and living with you, and how good you've been to me. And I don't want you to think I'm disrespecting Jacob's memory." Emotion swamped her and tears filled her eyes. Pregnancy hormones seemed to make her so moody and weepy. "I don't want to sneak around, but I feel as if I have a shot at exploring a relationship with Logan. But there's already so much gossip and I don't want to disappoint you."

Travis stared at her with a strange type of grief and understanding she'd never seen before. Celeste looked a bit in shock and seemed to be processing the information, but then took her hand. "Oh, sweetheart, I'm sorry you've been upset about this. I'm surprised, of course. I don't know Logan that well, but if he cares about you, I don't think Jacob would want you to be alone. Jacob loved you. You're carrying his baby—a miracle—and I believe he'd want you to be happy. Logan seems like a very good man."

Ginny sniffed. "He is. I wanted to be sure you were both okay with the idea of us going out together before I let it go any further."

"Does he make you happy, Ginny?" Travis asked seriously.

"Yes."

He nodded. "Then this is the right thing. You should go out with him and be happy. Life is too short, and Jacob's death taught us all that."

Travis looked so sad as he spoke the words, Ginny's heart broke. Celeste avoided looking at her husband. "You have our support," she said firmly. "No more getting upset. It's not good for you or the baby."

Ginny gave a half laugh. "Okay. Thank you. For treating me like family."

"You are," Celeste said. "Now get some rest. Can I bring you some water?"

"No, I'm good. Thanks."

They left her room and Ginny collapsed back on the pillows, exhausted. It seemed a path was clearing ahead of her, allowing Logan into her life in all ways. Was it a funny type of fate? Did it even matter? So much had happened to her in the past month, it was too overwhelming to try and figure out.

She just needed to decide if she was going to open herself back up to the possibility of love with Logan Murphy. It involved a baby and a complicated future she couldn't figure out.

Ginny sat on the bed thinking for a long, long time.

Chapter Ten

"Closing time, Pop."

Logan dimmed the lights and began his closing ritual behind the bar at Murphy's. It was odd being back, but strangely comforting. After being overseas and happy to leave the small town behind him, he now felt as if he'd come full circle.

He was finally back home.

And he was happy.

He wiped down the counters and washed the rest of the glasses and thought about Ginny. She'd been letting him in slowly, but was still hesitant about allowing him to be more than a friend. That one kiss they'd shared had been explosive, but he needed to go slow. She was vulnerable, and pregnant with another man's baby.

And he was falling in love with her.

Yep. His family needed to know how important she was to him. They might be concerned, but family stuck together, and he had no doubt they'd back him up.

On cue, the door opened and his brothers came into the pub. Dillon was still in his uniform, and Patrick wore a pair of worn jeans and a beaten-up T-shirt. His hair was a bit messy and looked like he'd just rolled out of bed. Probably pulled an all-nighter by the looks of it. They grunted a greeting, took their respective places on the barstools, and without a word, Logan poured out three Guinnesses. The perfect head on all the beers gave him a flash of pride. Still had the touch.

They each drank in silence, letting the day wash over them. In those few seconds, drinking the beer, all together again, Logan felt almost clean, without the stain of war and death on his soul.

Finally, Patrick spoke. "Dude, you didn't tell me something was going on with you and Ginny. Marisol was asking me questions I couldn't answer. What's up?"

Dillon raised a brow. "Ginny Moreno? She's pregnant with Jacob Salt's baby, right?"

Logan groaned. There went his small moment of peace. He'd been wanting to confide in his brothers for a while, and now was the perfect time. If he pursued this relationship seriously, he needed his family's backing. It would be too hard for both of them to be torn apart by other's opinions, or they'd never even have a chance.

Steps sounded behind him, and his father took his place by his boys, awaiting his answer. Logan propped his elbows on the bar and spilled the truth.

"I'm kind of crazy about her. We've been seeing each other for the past few weeks, but she doesn't want to move out of the friend zone."

Patrick shot him a gloomy look. "Been there. Done that. Wrote the book."

"You and Marisol haven't moved out of the zone?" Dillon asked, surprised.

"Yeah. She's afraid we're gonna ruin the friendship. I know she's attracted to me, I frickin' feel it, but she's so damn stubborn. And, I think, scared to death."

Dillon nodded. "Marisol never had time for a personal life with the cafe and raising Luis and Ginny. She's probably freaked out, especially with you. You're a bit intense, little brother."

"Screw you. At least I'm not panting over a married woman."

Dillon drew back a fist. "Mind your own fucking business. Joanne deserves someone who treats her right."

"She's had you panting since grade school, buddy. Make a move, won't you?" Patrick taunted.

Logan sighed. He'd been through this scene a million times. His brothers' Irish tempers burned hot and bright, but they never held grudges, even after fists flew. Aiden's voice cracked the whip.

"Not now, boys. Logan needs us."

Patrick and Dillon slowly calmed. Logan's lip twitched at the heated look that passed between them, but then they went back to drinking their beers and the tension eased.

"You just got back, man. I know you don't talk about it, but I bet things were tough. I see it in your eyes sometimes," Dillon said. Logan stiffened but didn't respond. Because his brother was right. "I just worry about you getting involved with her at this point. She's gonna be a mom. She's living with the Salts, and when the baby comes, who knows what will happen? And do you even know about her past relationship with Jacob? Did she want to get pregnant? Was she sleeping with anyone else besides Jacob?"

Logan shook his head hard. "No, they'd always been friends and fell into something more. She hasn't been with anyone else. We've talked. A lot. She gets me in a way I've never had before with a woman. And I get her. She's not a liar. She's straight up about the issues and respects the Salts and her family. Ginny Moreno is a hell of a woman, and I want to be with her."

Patrick studied his face, then slowly nodded. "I know you don't need anyone's approval, but I've got your back. If you trust her, I trust her. And if you think you love her, I say go for it."

Relief cut through him. Patrick was right. He didn't need his family's approval, but to know he had it made all the difference. "Dillon?" he asked.

Dillon finished his beer and wiped his mouth. "I agree with Patrick. I'm worried, but I'll back you up and help any way I can."

"Thanks, guys. Pops?"

Aiden Murphy looked more worried than his brothers. "If you pursue this, you are taking on the role of being a father. Are you ready for that, Logan? This is not the type of situation where you can date casually and then break it off without another thought. If you pursue her, make sure you want her for good."

His parents' marriage had taught him many things. Even in Afghanistan, sometimes he'd drum up an image of them in the kitchen, laughing and teasing each other while they fell into their routine of taking care of their three boys. It was a simple life. A hard life. A beautiful life. One he wanted for himself. Here, in Storm, with Ginny.

"I'm ready, Pops. The more time I spend with her, the more sure I am."

"Then you have my blessing."

Logan grinned. "Good. Now I have to find a way for her to agree to go out."

Dillon groaned. "We're all a bit fucked up, aren't we?"

Patrick cupped his beer. "Yeah, but it's the only life we know."

Logan looked at his brothers and they all burst out laughing.

* * * *

Ginny swallowed hard as Brit pulled up to Murphy's Pub. After her talk with the Salts, Brit had insisted she take the first step to show Logan she cared. He was getting off work now, so she decided to talk to him once the pub closed. Brit had insisted on driving, knowing she'd be a wreck.

Brit was right. She was nervous about taking this step from friendship with Logan, but her body also simmered with excitement. She craved his company all the time, and if she wasn't with him she wanted to be on the phone with him. His courtship had been quite sneaky, well planned, and exactly what she needed to begin to fall in love with him.

Now, it was her turn to give back.

His stories about the war tore her heart to pieces. She ached to help him heal as much as he helped her. He understood the horror of the car crash like no other. People looked at her with sympathy but little knowledge of what she really felt. Logan knew. He'd watched his friends die while he raged uselessly beside them. He owned a guilt that would never truly go away. She'd never stop feeling guilty about driving the car and killing Jacob, though she knew technically it wasn't her fault. It haunted her.

But when she was with Logan, the demons quieted and she was happy for the first time.

"Are you ready to go get your man?" Brit asked.

Ginny laughed. "Yeah, like a bad country song."

"A good one," she corrected. "Want me to wait here for you?"

"Would you? I'll let you know if he's in there. He may be able to drive me home."

"Okay. Good luck, girlfriend. Remember, you deserve happiness, too."

"Right."

Ginny slid out of the car and pushed the door open to Murphy's.

And came face to face with his whole family.

Her face burned as Dillon, Patrick, and Aiden Murphy stared back at her. Logan was behind the bar, and they were all drinking beers, bonding. Embarrassment hit hard, and she stumbled to try to look cool and make a hasty retreat.

"Oh, my goodness, I'm so sorry! I—I didn't realize you were having a family get-together. I'll come back later."

She turned, but Logan's call stopped her.

"Ginny! Don't go. I was going to come over later to talk to you."

She slowly turned. His brothers were smiling at her, their faces open and friendly. She relaxed slightly. "Do you want to stop by when you're done?"

Logan narrowed his gaze at her. Intensity beat from his frame, and shivers coursed down her spine. He was so sexy and commanding. "No. We're done here. Come in the back with me."

She followed him obediently, noting the quiet amusement in his brothers' faces and the kindness in his dad's eyes. He led her into the supply room and closed the door. Various boxes and bottles sat upon shelves that crammed the small space, but Ginny only felt his intense body heat and the delicious smell of his musky cologne. His jaw was rough, and his blue eyes burned bright as he stared at her.

What if he was coming over to break things off? What if he'd decided she was too complicated to get involved with and he realized he didn't want to get involved? He kept staring at her, and she shifted her feet, getting more nervous.

"What did you want to talk about?" she asked hesitantly.

He took a step closer. Her gaze fell on those lush lips and she remembered the feel of them sliding over hers. Giving such sweet pleasure. Adoring her in a way that shattered her heart because she never believed she'd experience something beautiful again after losing Jacob. Oh, God, focus.

"I know you're worried about letting me be more than your friend. But I'm not going to stop, Ginny. Not until you let me put my arms around you, and kiss you, and let me take care of you. You wormed your way into my heart, and I can't go back. So, this time, formally, I'm asking you to go out with me. In public. As more than my friend. As your boyfriend."

"Logan—"

"I'll talk to the Salts personally. I'll talk to Marisol and Luis and make sure they know my intentions. My family knows how I feel about you, and they back us both up one hundred percent."

"Logan—"

He cupped her cheeks with tenderness and stared down at her, all the rough and naked emotion in his eyes. "I can't let you say no anymore. Let me in. I won't ever hurt you, I swear. Just let me be part of your life and give us a chance."

"Logan!"

"What?"

"Yes." She breathed the word out softly, watching his eyes widen slightly and a delicious flare of desire light up his face. "Yes, I don't want to fight it anymore either. I want to be with you. I think about you all the time, and I told the Salts and my family about my feelings, and I'm ready. I'm ready to take a chance."

And then she wasn't talking anymore, because his mouth covered hers and he was kissing her. She clung to him, opening to him, her body shivering with pleasure as he thrust his tongue into her mouth and stroked her cheeks and made her feel like the most beautiful human being in the world.

And Ginny swore in that moment to protect the baby's secret with her life. Logan and the baby were her future. There was a bright light she'd cling to and fight for to her last breath, and no one would ruin this for her.

Not even the truth.

Chapter Eleven

Marcus Alvarez drove into Storm in his battered baby blue 1971 Chevrolet Impala and fought the immediate clutch of claustrophobia.

He was home.

The wind whipped through the windows and he passed the familiar businesses he hadn't seen in years. He slowed his speed and crawled down Pecan Street, passing the Lutheran church where his mom used to force them to attend Sunday services, and the Bluebonnet Cafe, which still held the record of baking the best pies in the world.

There was Prost Pharmacy and the wine shop, the exact place he'd gotten into a fistfight with Ivan Reid and came home with a bloody nose. His father had called him a pussy and told him not to embarrass the family if he couldn't win over a skinny bully.

His head pounded, but he kept driving, making a right onto Main Street and heading toward Murphy's Pub, hoping he'd get there before closing. He'd heard Logan was back in town from overseas, and he was looking forward to seeing him. He kept in touch with no one else from the town, other than his mother and sisters, and always kept his distance. In fact, he'd never really believed he would ever return, not as long as his father was there.

Of course, the son of a bitch had done another number on them with his disappearing act. Besides putting his mother into a financial tailspin, Dakota was acting out more than usual, and he was really afraid Mallory wouldn't be able to hold them all together.

The guilt flared again, but he beat it back down. He'd left them all with a violent son of a bitch to defend themselves. He wasn't proud of his actions, but at the time, it was either lose his soul or leave town.

He'd chosen to leave.

Marcus passed Pushing Up Daisies, and parked near Murphy's. Hopefully a good beer and conversation with his friend would help settle him. Then he might be able to head home with his head clear and strong for what awaited him.

Grabbing his keys, he slammed the door and walked around the car. His legs ached after the long hours driving, and he stretched, shaking out his muscles.

"Nice car."

He jerked his head around and stared at the guy in front of him. The smell of booze drifted from him in waves, and his mouth curled slightly upward, giving him a glimpse of yellowed teeth. Definitely drunk. Swayed a bit on his feet. Probably mid-thirties, with a shaved head and a muscle shirt. Definitely an asshole.

"Thanks."

He turned to walk away but the guy staggered over and had the balls to lay his grubby hands on his baby. There was little he loved in his life. His mother. His sisters. Logan. And his beloved Chevy that he'd restored piece by piece with his own hands while his father insulted him on his lack of mechanical ability.

"Don't touch."

The guy swirled around. Uh, oh. Marcus figured he was too drunk to be a real problem, but he held the dangerous edge of a man who had nothing to lose and held the fake courage of a drunkard who could take on the world and win. He really didn't need this shit now.

"You got a problem with me?" he jeered. "Whatsa matter? I'm not good enough to touch your precious car? Why don't you come over and show me, tough guy?"

Marcus let out an impatient breath. "Look, buddy, just walk away. I don't want any trouble. I'm heading to Murphy's for a drink. Okay?"

The guy grinned. "Yeah, sure, sure. Have a good time. I'll just wait here for ya."

And then he sprawled himself over the hood of his car.

Marcus winced. This didn't bode well. No one sat on his damn car, especially a smelly, mean drunk.

"I'm gonna give you one more chance, dude. Walk away. Please get off my car."

"Sure, sure. Oh, wait, I gotta take a piss. You don't mind, do you?" Marcus watched in horror as the guy got off the car and began to pull down his zipper, swaying slightly on his feet.

He was so not gonna piss on his car.

Marcus grabbed the guy by the arm, dragging him away. He meant to get him at a safe distance and try to talk him down, but it was too late. The drunkard got a flash of adrenaline, and he went for it. He was sloppy but fast, his fists flying in a tangle, trying to beat on Marcus's face.

Marcus cursed, ducked, and instinctually did the only thing left.

He gave him the left hook.

With a howl, the guy went down, screaming and flailing on the pavement like Marcus had ripped his guts off. Yep, a real coward underneath the bullying exterior. Marcus tried not to sneer.

"Hey, break it up! Police!"

In a flash, Marcus caught a uniform coming at him, and suddenly he was pushed against the side of the building, his palms flat on either side of his head. Ah, shit. This was so not happening.

"Hands on the wall. Don't move!"

He tried to remain calm as the cop checked on the drunk guy, who was still crying like a pussy and telling the cop Marcus had jumped him out of nowhere. Footsteps pounded on the pavement and a crowd of new voices hit his ears, but he knew better than to turn around.

"What happened? Are you all right, Dillon?"

Dillon? Dillon Murphy?

"Yeah, just an assault and a couple of drunks."

Now a female voice, oddly familiar and sweetly sensual, drifted to his ears. "Oh, my God! I saw something from the rearview mirror but I didn't have time to come get you, it happened so fast. Where are Ginny and Logan?"

Logan? And who was talking? He knew her. Knew that voice like she'd come to him in a dream. Odd.

"They're still inside. They were just getting ready to leave. Step back, I'm gonna have to bring these two into the station."

Marcus raised his voice. "Excuse me, officer? I think there's been a misunderstanding. Can I turn around and explain?"

"Slowly, please. And keep your hands up."

Hands in the air, he swiveled around and came face to face with Dillon Murphy.

And Brittany Rush.

God, she was all grown up and she'd gotten more beautiful. Thick blonde hair. Wide blue eyes. A perfect round face, with pink lips and a slamming body. His spit dried up as he looked at her for a long time, noting the shock and something else in her eyes. Something he might have to explore later.

"Marcus?" she gasped.

Dillon frowned. "Marcus Alvarez?"

The party wasn't full yet. He caught sight of Logan and Ginny joining them, taking in the drunk blabbering on the ground, and Marcus's hands in the air. Everyone stared at him in shock until finally, a deep roaring laugh from his best friend, who he now wanted to clobber, filled the air.

Logan shook his head, pure mirth in his eyes. "Son of a bitch. You sure know how to make an entrance. Welcome home, buddy."

Marcus groaned.

Yeah.

He was really fucking home.

Sign up for the Rising Storm/1001 Dark Nights Newsletter
and be entered to win an exclusive lightning bolt necklace
specially designed for Rising Storm by
Janet Cadsawan of Cadsawan.com.

Go to http://risingstormbooks.com to subscribe.

As a bonus, all subscribers will receive a free
Rising Storm story
Storm Season: Ginny & Jacob – the Prequel
by Dee Davis

Discover More Rising Storm

Storm, Texas.

Where passion runs hot, desire runs deep, and secrets have the power to destroy...

Nestled among rolling hills and painted with vibrant wildflowers, the bucolic town of Storm, Texas, seems like nothing short of perfection.

But there are secrets beneath the facade. Dark secrets. Powerful secrets. The kind that can destroy lives and tear families apart. The kind that can cut through a town like a tempest, leaving jealousy and destruction in its wake, along with shattered hopes and broken dreams. All it takes is one little thing to shatter that polish.

Rising Storm is a series conceived by Julie Kenner and Dee Davis to read like an on-going drama. Set in a small Texas town, *Rising Storm* is full of scandal, deceit, romance, passion, and secrets. Lots of secrets.

Look for these Rising Storm midseason episodes coming soon!

After the Storm by Lexi Blake
In the wake of Dakota's revelations, the whole town is reeling. Ginny Moreno has lost everything. Logan Murphy is devastated by her lies. Brittany Rush sees her family in a horrifying new light. And nothing will ever be the same...

Distant Thunder by Larissa Ione
As Sebastian and Marylee plot to cover up Sebastian's sexual escapade, Ginny and Dakota continue to reel from the fallout of Dakota's announcement. But it is the Rush family that's left to pick up the pieces as Payton, Brittany and Jeffry each cope with Sebastian's betrayal in their own way...

... Season 2 coming September 27, 2016. Sign up for the newsletter so you don't miss a thing. http://risingstormbooks.com

After the Storm

By Lexi Blake
Rising Storm Midseason Episode 1
Coming March 29, 2016

Secrets, Sex and Scandals…

Welcome to Storm, Texas, where passion runs hot, desire runs deep, and secrets have the power to destroy… Get ready. The storm is coming.

In the wake of Dakota's revelations, the whole town is reeling. Ginny Moreno has lost everything. Logan Murphy is devastated by her lies. Brittany Rush sees her family in a horrifying new light. And nothing will ever be the same…

* * * *

Ginny came to wake slowly, the sounds from the rest of the house bringing her out of the sweetest dream. She'd been with Logan. He'd walked in and there had been a bundle in his arms. Little Bit. Their baby. In the dream there hadn't been anything between them. Not even Jacob. In her dream, she'd known Jacob was alive and happy. Everyone was happy, but she'd been the happiest of all because she'd made all the right choices and they'd brought her to this incredible man and their amazing family.

"Hush. She needs her sleep, Luis. I won't have you waking her up because you're angry with your girlfriend." Marisol's voice was faint as though she was standing outside Ginny's door trying hard to keep quiet.

Luis was not. "I'm not angry with Mallory. I'm pretty pissed at Ginny though."

"Watch your language."

Yes, she really wished she could have stayed in that perfect dream. Ginny sat up. It was getting more and more difficult as her belly curved.

She might as well paint a scarlet letter on her maternity clothes. There was no hiding this particular sin. It was out there for all to see.

How was it possible that mere months before she'd had

everything? She'd gotten out of town. She'd had a future. She'd had her best friend at her side.

What would Brittany think of her now?

Ginny's heart threatened to seize. How selfish was she? All she could think about was herself and not the people she loved. Brittany had heard devastating news. She'd found out her father was a liar. She'd learned her parents' marriage was based on deception. Her family was crumbling around her and all Ginny could wonder was "does she still like me?"

Ginny Moreno stood and looked at herself in the mirror, not quite recognizing the girl who stared back. Oh, she had all the same features of the girl who'd grown up in this room, but there was something not right. It was a little like those "find the difference in the picture" games she'd seen in magazines. Subtle little shifts had changed her. One lie here, a little subterfuge there, and she was a different person altogether. She was a person who hurt the people around her.

Her stomach rumbled and a fine trembling shook her hands. She might want to stay in this room for the rest of her life, but she couldn't because she wasn't alone. She had a baby growing inside her. A baby who was proof of all she'd done wrong in her life.

It's a child, Ginny. Not a burden.

That moment from the day before was so clear in her mind. Logan had looked so horrified when he'd said it. He'd rejected her utterly, but he'd defended her baby.

Her baby. This child was hers. It might not be Jacob's. No, she had to stop thinking like that. More likely it wasn't Jacob's. She'd been fooling herself all along. She'd done everything she could so she didn't have to admit the mistakes she'd made.

But this baby couldn't be a mistake. This baby couldn't start his or her life as a mistake. This baby had been a choice. The one good choice she'd made in all of this mess. She put a hand on her belly as though she could feel her child.

"It's you and me, Little Bit. I'm so sorry I've made a mess of things, but I've got some time to sort it out. I love you. I love you and that's all that matters. Everything else is a problem to be solved, but you and me are going to be fine. We'll get through this."

The town might hate her for what she'd done, but she wouldn't let them take it out on her baby. No way. A fierce protectiveness swept through her body. Everything she'd done so far had been to protect herself. She could see that now. She'd deluded herself into thinking the baby could be Jacob's so she could look at herself in the mirror. She'd let herself lead the Salts on so she would be protected and loved because she'd hated herself. She could give herself a million excuses, but at the end of the day, she'd done it.

She'd found the love of her life and she'd still kept it up because she'd been afraid of losing it all. Well, she'd lost it.

1001 Dark Nights

Welcome to 1001 Dark Nights… a collection of novellas that are breathtakingly sexy and magically romantic. Some are paranormal, some are erotic. Each and every one is compelling and page turning.

Inspired by the exotic tales of The Arabian Nights, 1001 Dark Nights features *New York Times* and *USA Today* bestselling authors.

In the original, Scheherazade desperately attempts to entertain her husband, the King of Persia, with nightly stories so that he will postpone her execution.

In our version, month after month, each of our fabulous authors puts a unique spin on the premise and creates a tale that a new Scheherazade tells long into the dark, dark night.

For more information about 1001 Dark Nights, visit www.1001DarkNights.com.

On behalf of Rising Storm,

Liz Berry, M.J. Rose, Julie Kenner & Dee Davis would like to thank ~

Steve Berry
Doug Scofield
Melissa Rheinlander
Kim Guidroz
Jillian Stein
InkSlinger PR
Asha Hossain
Chris Graham
Pamela Jamison
Kasi Alexander
Jessica Johns
Dylan Stockton
Richard Blake
The Dinner Party Show
and Simon Lipskar

Made in United States
North Haven, CT
10 August 2022